Stacie,

love lyrics

&

Lies

Live your own love
song!

L. M. CARR

Edited by Danielle Bisaillon
Proofread by Elaine Dunn
Cover Design by © Cassy Roop of *Pink Ink Designs*
Interior Design & Formatting by © Juliana Cabrera of *Jersey Girl Design*

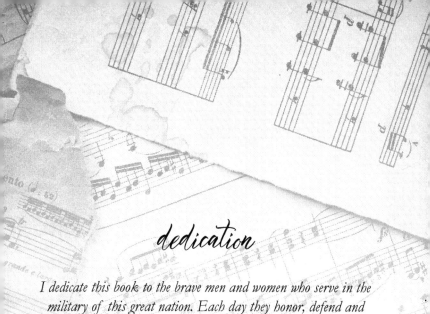

dedication

I dedicate this book to the brave men and women who serve in the
military of this great nation. Each day they honor, defend and
protect my freedoms. Because of them, I have the freedom of speech
to write my heart's desire without the worry of persecution.
For this, I thank you.

Acknowledgments

As always, I need to thank my husband and kids for their continued support. Thank you for listening and offering feedback.

Thank you to Danielle B. for editing and helping to make everything sound right. Elaine D., thank you for proofreading. You ladies are invaluable to me and I am forever grateful to have you.

Thank you to all the author event coordinators who work tirelessly, organizing and hosting such terrific events. Without you, authors and readers may never have the chance to meet in person. So, thank you!

"*I will sing of your love and justice; to you, LORD, I will sing praise.*

Psalm 101:1

Chapter One

"OH, FOR THE LOVE OF ALL THAT IS HOLY!" I YELL, finally kicking off the covers and jumping to my feet. Dragging my weary body to the window, I pull the curtain back and peer outside to see what the ruckus is about at this ungodly hour. Although I've been home for almost two weeks, my internal clock hasn't regulated itself back to time on the western hemisphere. I look over the tall trees and notice the early morning sun casting an orange glow as she ascends over the horizon. A horde of testosterone walks around the flat backyard that some would consider small by their standards while others would consider it to be big enough to house several families.

Like worker ants, each man, strong and well-built, moves quickly, transporting the materials with bulky arms, attending to the task at hand to begin the project of extending my grandmother's home.

"Why must you even insist on this addition, Gram?" I growl quietly, wishing my grandmother would realize this whole thing is entirely unnecessary. Some people live contently in a clay hut; they don't need a remodeled bathroom or their own bedroom. A simple place to rest their head at night is sufficient.

I yawn loudly and grab my head when a throb reaches my temple. Between not sleeping, living on caffeine and working until the bar closes every night this past week, a migraine headache was inevitable. Hoping for some relief, I reach for the Advil and swallow a mouthful of tepid bottled water before I stare at the suitcases in the corner of my room and exhale deeply.

Endless questions fill my mind about the wonderful, beautiful people who'd become my family. I saw betrayal and hurt in their dark chocolate eyes when I told them I was leaving. I wish I had had more time with them, but the news of Gram's health forced me to come home early.

Come back when you can. You are always welcome here.

Wrapping my arms around my body, I comfort myself, hoping they know how much I love them and long to be reunited. The simplistic life I'd become accustomed to is a far cry from this rushed life here back in the states. The quiet rhythm of the djembe drum in my head is soon replaced by an annoying beeping sound.

Feel the music in your soul. Let it speak for you.

I sigh heavily, walk back over to the window and glare at the huge diesel truck as it works tirelessly with its engine roaring, attempting to back up the small mountain that is our driveway while hauling a huge load of lumber. It's enough to build a small mansion, not an addition to a pre-existing home. I stare at the offensive vehicle until the noise ceases, and the engine shuts off. One of the laborers, wearing the same matching T-shirt and carpenter jeans as all the others, begins the duty of directing the large pallets filled with long wooden planks and plywood.

"Gram!" I bellow, my voice screeching wildly, as she slowly walks onto the driveway. Her gait is awkward as she carries several bottles of water in her arms and something tucked in the crook of her elbow. She holds out the drinks for the two men, offering a refreshment along with a bright smile. Flocking to her, another man receives her gift with a quick nod and a word of thanks before returning to work.

I'd always admired my grandmother's giving nature and charitable spirit, but sometimes she doesn't know when to stop. Her benevolent heart may be her downfall.

"Get out of the way, Gram!" I mumble through gritted teeth as my grandmother wanders closer to ground zero. Standing there with a pensive look stretched across her face, my gram loosens her hold on the object wedged beneath her arm. I recognize it immediately. My eyes shoot wide in horror and my hands spring to my head, my fingers clutching the nest of wild, blond curls. "Don't do it! Don't you dare!" I cry in disbelief when she unveils the picture of me in a gold cap and gown from my college graduation two years ago. She kisses the glass encasement and prepares to put it on display for all to see. "No! No! No! Please don't!"

She does.

"Gram." A garbled sigh releases. The exasperation filling me hits an all-time high because my grandmother's quest to marry me off and produce grandchildren before she dies continues to be her daily goal. Even while I was away, she'd ask if I was seeing anyone. I went to Africa to volunteer— not to find love.

"You drive me crazy sometimes!" Annoyed words tumble from my lips.

Most of the men glance at the photograph, smile tightly then side step her, ignoring her words as she undoubtedly rattles off my qualifications and statistics. Gram steps back, allowing the pickup truck to fill the vacant spot.

Although my bedroom window is closed, the vibration coming from the truck rattles the panes. I roll my eyes at the sound of the music as I lift the frame, preparing to ask the driver to have some consideration. Thankfully, when the roaring engine ceases, so does the music. I narrow my eyes, waiting several minutes to catch a glimpse of the offender.

It's *him*. My heart flutters at the thought of seeing him in the flesh once again. After spending nearly eight months half way around the world in a remote African village, my libido shifts into overdrive every time he's near. I am a walking, frustrated ball of estrogen in serious need of release.

My eyes zero in on the mighty man sitting in the truck and the first thing I notice is his long, tatted and beautifully tanned arm, bent at the elbow as he, presumably holds a phone to his ear. I wordlessly encourage him to step into view, giving me an opportunity to ogle and lust after him. Moments later my belly flutters when the truck's driver's side door opens and he slowly steps out with a huge smile on his face as he disconnects the call. His smile transforms into a victorious grin while he slides the phone into the front pocket of his jeans before slamming the door shut. Judging by the victorious expression on his face, whoever was on the other end of the line must have given him some wonderful news.

This man with skin the same color as warm caramel is incredibly beautiful and I'm completely enthralled by his confident stride. Every muscle strains against his jeans as he walks until he stops abruptly, returns to the vehicle and opens the door. My eyes travel the length of his body when he leans in, stretching forward to retrieve something. A bright shirt covers his back and his jeans fit snuggly around his legs and ass. I run my fingers through my hair, wondering what it would be like to dig my nails into his skin as he drove into me.

A chuckle escapes and I cover my face as a wave of embarrassment washes over me. I need to have sex soon.

Strolling over to the mountain of materials, the man in charge, wearing a blue bandana to restrain his dark hair and sunglasses to shield his eyes, calls the men over. With full lips, he speaks to them as they acknowledge his presence. Although some of the men appear to be older, there is no mistaking who is in charge. There's an aura of confidence and stature as the sexy foreman points to a pallet of lumber. The line of muscle along his bicep flexes when he picks up a roofing shingle and inspects it. Flipping the pages attached to a clipboard, the man in my dreams continues to give orders.

For only working here two or three days a week, he seems to have everything under control.

My gawking session is interrupted by Eminen's *Love The Way You Lie*, the ringtone for my best friend and college roommate, Mackenzie. I plop on my bed, roll over and answer the call, catching up on irrelevant and useless things about the latest bar gossip. One would never guess how intelligent she actually is or the 4.0 GPA she maintained while partying through her collegiate career. Too bad her choices in men don't reflect her incredible IQ. I disconnect the call after half-heartedly agreeing to go to a party with her next weekend. Hearing my grandmother's laughter and sensing she's up to something, I return to the window.

Standing there quietly, I watch my grandmother stride right up to the man who is once again on his phone. I notice black earbuds dangle from his neck and thoughts of licking it encourage my tongue to lick my lips. After ending his phone call, the man in charge turns to fully oblige her, leaning down to listen to her ramblings while her fingers trace the flat image of my face. He unscrews the bottle of water and curls those lips, welcoming several quick drinks. I follow the trail as the water slips down his throat, his Adam's apple rolling slightly. Although I can't hear what she's saying, knowing Gram, she's probably giving him my ring size as well as my medical and dating history.

"What are you up to now?" I whisper to myself, watching their interaction.

Smiling at her, he appears to be listening as he nods. I appreciate his warm and friendly smile. His teeth are bright white against his tanned skin. I consider it mildly endearing to watch my gram use her charm until she turns and points in the direction of my bedroom window. Following the line of sight, he lifts his sunglasses and finds my eyes. He licks his lips before he grins crookedly, sliding his glasses back in place.

"Shit!" I yell and then gasp, jumping back to seek refuge behind the curtain as a tidal wave of humiliation crashes over me, leaving my insides a jumbled mess. Eyeing my journal on the floor, I growl beneath my breath, "Tsunami." Until I hear the backdoor squeak open and slam shut, I remain frozen. Gram's familiar whistle confirms she's back in the house, but the tune of Ritchie Valens' "La Bamba" piques my curiosity.

After haphazardly tossing on my bathrobe and jotting down a few more words in my journal, I make my way downstairs, ready to confront my grandmother and demand that she check herself into a psychiatric ward because they would agree she's certifiably insane. I round the corner with a heavy stomp and a scowl on my face.

"Gram! Why would you—"

My step freezes when I realize standing next to her at the kitchen table is the same gorgeous man who has had a starring and recurring role in my dreams for the past two weeks since my return. *Don Delisioso* is what I call him when he's whispering sweet nothings to me in Spanish.

Incredible hazel eyes, a beautiful and alluring combination of light brown and green, snap up and meet mine, piercing me with an intense look. Those same eyes drag slowly over my body, pausing momentarily at my thighs where the lavender silk ends with a soft touch of lace. Continuing their ascent, he falters again at the hint of cleavage peeking out from where the sash is lax. I drop my eyes, denying them the opportunity to stare at him a second longer. As if he stepped out of a Telemundo novella, his face is perfectly shaped with its strong jaw and naturally tanned skin. A blue bandana restrains the obsidian hair that frames his face. I swallow hard and immediately tighten the sash, wishing my bathrobe touched the floor.

Frank Sinatra's smooth voice croons through the radio speaker that sits on top of the refrigerator. I stretch on my tiptoes to lower the volume. Apparently Gram isn't only losing her mind; she's losing her hearing, too.

"That's a great song," a deep voice comments. "I love Dean Martin, too."

"Oh, I love them, but she doesn't," Gram adds, turning to address me with pinched lips. "Good morning, my beautiful girl," she sings sweetly, quickly changing her tone and ignoring how God-awful I look with my tight curls and unwashed face dotted with freckles from my past days in the sun.

"I never said I didn't like Sinatra. He's just a little cliché."

My eyes sweep to meet his when he speaks. "Cliché? Come on now..." Feigned horror is stretched across his gorgeous face. "Sinatra is classic."

I purse my lips and slightly roll my eyes then grin.

Gram waves me over. "I'm going over the blueprints. There's a question about two of the windows. Come have a look." I respond with narrowed eyes and a subtle shake of my head.

"I'm sure you guys can figure it out," I respond flatly, knowing the motive behind her review of the plans we've looked at a million times before.

I walk to the counter and make myself a cup of coffee, trying to ward off the feeling of being watched. Explanations of how the sun filters in from the left side of the house and the need to diminish the glare when she's watching Jeopardy doesn't afford him the opportunity to get a word in edgewise. I drop the spoon into the sink and turn around, leaning casually against the counter with my legs crossed at the ankles. Sipping the hot beverage, I watch his fingers move around the paper design, pointing to various things while his left hand remains flattened. My eyes notice the absence of a ring on his fourth finger.

At least this one's not married, I think to myself. The image of my grandmother telling her new neurologist that I could be his next wife elicits a muffled chuckle, leaving a small smile on my face.

"What do you think?"

I blink furiously, bringing myself back to the here and now.

"I'm sorry. What'd you say?"

The old rotary house phone attached to the wall rings, prompting her to walk over to it.

"Matthew, why don't you explain it? It sounds so much better coming from you." My grandma suggests with a sly smile. She picks up the white receiver. "Hello?"

Matthew? Funny thing...he doesn't look like a *Matthew*.

He smiles in return and beckons me with a tip of his chin, but I remain still.

Huffing quietly, my gram walks over, stretching the coiled phone line to the point it may break and places her hand on my arm, forcing me to take the six steps to stand next to him. My senses awaken, going into overdrive the moment I breathe in. The fresh scent of soap mingled with a hint of cologne infiltrates my nose. I wrack my brain trying to remember the jingle for the soap advertisement on television. Maintaining my posture, I allow my eyes to move slowly, glancing sideways to take in the view of his muscular forearm which is covered in colorful and intricate designs.

"We haven't met *officially* ... although I've seen you often." He extends a hand and smiles. "Mateo."

Moving the coffee cup to my left hand, I hesitantly slide my right hand into his, allowing my fingers to graze the rough surface of his palm as his fingers close in around mine. My gaze drops to the contact of our hands. While it's true that we haven't "officially" met, the subtle nods, the stolen glances and wordless interactions were sufficient for him to consume my thoughts constantly.

"Cat," I offer my nickname rather than my given name. "It's nice to *officially* meet you."

"Cat?" he asks, his eyebrows knitting together.

"It's short for Caterina."

With his brows still displaying confusion, he parts those lush lips to speak while his eyes drop to our linked hands. A charge of electricity shoots through my arm, igniting a fire in my entire body.

He tilts his head and hums. "That's interesting...your grandmother said your name was Beth."

My eyes drift away for a moment and I shake my head, sighing heavily as I clarify that Beth was my mother's name.

He nods with understanding and his face relaxes, allowing a small smile to tug at his mouth.

"The pleasure is all mine, Caterina."

My pulse quickens at his words. Licking my lips, I pull my hand from his hold and tuck a loose strand of hair behind my ears before I turn my attention to the blueprints.

With a sudden shifting of his weight, he brushes his arm against mine.

"I won't bite," he whispers, holding my stare.

While words evade me, my eyes speak volumes.

I startle and look at him again. He simply smiles brilliantly.

It's my turn to drag my eyes over his lean body, bent at the waist as he leans forward over the kitchen table. The sound of his voice is one of the most beautiful things I've ever heard. It's not quite as deep as Barry White; it's more of an Elvis Presley sultry.

"Unless you want me to."

I release a loud laugh along with a snort. "Okay, lobo," I retort. Gone is the image of beautiful Elvis Presley and his blue suede shoes now replaced by a big bad wolf.

A lovely sound escapes as he snickers quietly. "You speak Spanish?"

"Not really. I have an eclectic taste in music. Los Lobos was one of my favorite bands although I never quite understood why they called themselves the wolves."

His hazel eyes light up and dance with delight for some reason. "My abuela loved Ritchie Valens."

"Cool," I respond with a definitive nod.

Feeling slightly uncomfortable with his pensive stare, I take a sip of coffee and change the subject.

"Do you have any idea when you'll be done here?" I ask, wondering how long I can enjoy the view of his fit body under that T-shirt and jeans.

Mateo's lips pull back in a grin. "Trying to get rid of me already?"

A chuckle masks my nerves.

"You're not here that much to begin with," I retort with a dry look.

"Ahh, so you've noticed." His eyes move around my face, taking in my appearance which includes my wild hair.

"Your crew slacks off when you're not here." I offer playfully then quickly clarify that I'm only teasing.

He shrugs his broad shoulders and smirks. "I've got another project going on. Can't exactly be in two places at once, you know?"

He returns his attention to the blueprints.

A strange thought about cloning him enters my mind. He could work on Gram's house and his clone could be locked away in my room.

"Now you listen here. I said no already," Gram says for the third time. "I am not interested. No, I did not call you last week and I certainly didn't give you my credit card number." She slams the receiver down firmly and turns to face us. "Some people are so pushy."

I smile at the irony.

"Relax, Gram. Some people don't know when to leave well enough alone."

"As I was saying," he says with a grin, "if we move this window..."

The purr of Elvis Presley's smooth voice returns.

When appropriate, I nod my head as though he's got my full attention. Little does he know that if he wanted to recite the Gettysburg Address on stage, I would be the audience. I would listen.

"Yeah, that sounds wonderful."

The man and my gram turn to look at me simultaneously. The furrowing of my grandmother's gray eyebrows indicates she's not pleased with my inattentiveness.

"Sorry, Gram. I'm still half asleep." I step back, nod a silent salutation and retreat to the comfort of my room.

I begin my ascent up the stairs then freeze when I hear my gram explain how I just started working a second job since my return from volunteering in Africa and how it's already taking a toll on me. She continues to tell him that I'm going to be a huge star.

I clench my teeth and roll my eyes, annoyed and angry that her condition is worsening on a weekly basis.

Nice, Gram. Real nice.

"I completely understand. I've got a couple of things in the works, too. It gets tiring," he replies.

"I see something in you. You're going to be a star, too."

A tiny sarcastic chuckle emerges quietly. "Sure, Gram. Maybe he'll be a home improvement star on HGTV."

After closing the door, I palm my forehead and shake my head at the insanity of her words. I pick up the journal, reach for a pencil and crawl back into bed. A fevered rush of words scatter onto the blank page as images of him, of his face, of his scent, of his arms flood my mind.

I startle awake from the loud pounding on my bedroom

door. I sit up and with a quick glance at my phone, I notice the time is almost three o'clock in the afternoon. Through gritted teeth, I express my regret at having wasted my entire day off.

Bang. Bang. Bang.

"Coming!"

I pull the door wide open and come face to face with the angry face of my uncle.

"What?" I hiss. "What now?"

"What are you doing *sleeping*? You're not all," he air quotes, "*depressed* again, are you?" He says it as if it's a forbidden act as his eyes flitter around my room, causing the grimace to deepen.

Narrowing my eyes before closing them momentarily, I calm myself down. I swallow hard and speak. "I'm perfectly fine." *As you want everyone to believe you are.* "I worked late last night and then the construction guys woke me up early," I reply, frustrated that I need to explain myself to him. "What's your problem anyway?"

"This." He gestures with his hand, drawing attention to the clothes strewn on the hardwood. "I refuse to let you sit around and waste your education or frolic around in other countries. What do you think? You're going to sit on your ass and let everyone else support you?"

"Who do you think I am? Your ex-w—"

I scowl then roll my eyes, knowing my uncle has never supported me financially and has no say in what I choose to do. I purse my lips, forbidding them from spewing hurtful words I'll later regret.

"Uncle Johnny, I'm tired. I'm trying to get used to being back here and I have laundry to do. And second of all, I took a little time off from school. You can be as mad as you want, but it was my choice to go. And... I won't ever rely on anyone, especially a man, to take care of me. I promise. I'm sorry your ex took advantage of that, but that's not me." I smile, which in turn eases the look of stress on his face. "Trust me when I tell you that I'm not going to waste my education— I worked way too hard to get where I am now. I do have goals *and* I'm still trying to get used to the time change so cut me a little slack, okay?"

"Cat," he begins with an unsettling sigh. "You're so much like your mother. My sister had her head in the clouds about music and fame." He expels a deep sigh, causing the crisp white cotton of his button-down shirt to rise and fall. "Look how that turned out."

I cringe internally at the comparison. My mouth tightens into a hard, angry frown and my eyes drop to the loosened, light blue tie. I bite back a sardonic chuckle as the image of me choking him with it forms in my mind.

"I'm *not* her. I won't make her mistakes," I respond sharply. "I have no intention of following in her footsteps."

He stares at me with blue eyes that match my own then ends the conversation. With one slow nod, I know my words have pacified him...for now.

"You're a good kid, Cat." He smiles weakly and closes the door as he turns to leave.

I call after him. "Are you going to be around this weekend?"

His eyes dance with humor. "Not sure yet. Why?"

"I have to work and I don't want Gram to be alone for too long."

Chuckling lightly, he shakes his head. "She can take care of herself for a few hours if not more."

"So why exactly did you move back in then?" I ask sharply, once again trying to secure his real motive.

My uncle rolls his eyes and smirks, obviously exasperated from the same constant question.

"Are you in some kind of trouble? Did something happen? Are you running from the mob?"

Laughter erupts from the pit of his belly which is flat

and hard from hours at the gym.

"See you later," he responds. I hear his quick footsteps as he jogs down the stairs. The fading purr of his sports car confirms he's left to go somewhere in a hurry.

Chapter Two

"I'M NOT JEALOUS AT ALL," I GROAN PLAYFULLY as Mack makes her way to the main bar.

"Wanna trade places? I'll work the back bar," she teases. "Try to have a *little* fun."

I roll my eyes and feign a smile, knowing how busy it's going to get later. So it's completely understandable that I work the smaller bar while I get back into the rhythm of things—especially tonight. Everyone within driving distance will be here to see the performance.

Standing at my bar at the back corner of the club, I shout over the music and ask two women what they would like to drink as I wipe the counter off with a damp cloth.

"Two Key Lime Martinis," the one in a silver halter top replies.

I nod and set two gold cocktail napkins down, turning my back and reaching for the bottles. I proceed to mix their drinks while more people crowd around them.

"Here you go. That'll be eighteen."

A crisp twenty-dollar bill is left without so much as a simple thank you.

Twenty dollars for two cocktails...that money could feed an entire village for three weeks.

I turn to cash out the order and find a pair of familiar eyes reflected in the mirror. I drop the two dollars in the tip jar, breathe deeply to gain some confidence then turn around, coming face to face with *Don Delisioso's* mesmerizing eyes.

"Hey. What can I get for you?" I lean forward and ask while trying to get a whiff of his intoxicating scent.

Gram wasn't too pleased with me three days ago when her request that I carry the jug of lemonade along with cups of Italian ice out to the hardworking remodelers was rejected. Her eyebrows furrowed as her plea turned into a demand which went unheeded.

I had tossed her a look and said, "Gram, they're grown men. I'm sure they can get their own drinks if they're thirsty."

This is different I think as I look around quickly; it's my job to serve him.

"Do I know you?" he asks with a smile. "You look a lot like this little hottie whose house I'm working on." He tips his head slightly and narrows his eyes as if he's thinking hard. "She's not too happy that I'm there."

I grin, conceding to my amusement. "Funny. What can I get for ya?"

His eyes peruse the bottles of alcohol as his tongue moistens his lips, eventually landing back on me and locking with mine.

"What'll it be?"

Mateo considers my question as his eyes drop to my cleavage.

"What's good?" He grins devilishly.

"Sorry. Milk isn't on the menu."

He laughs.

"I like you. You're funny."

"Oh, yeah. I'm a real barrel of laughs," I retort dryly.

"What have you got for bottled beer?"

"They're all behind me." I motion with my chin to the row of bottled beer before rattling off the list I've committed to memory.

He lifts his arm to reveal the beer he'd been drinking. Keeping his eyes on me, he raises it to his lips and tips it back, emptying the remnants into his mouth before swallowing with a smirk and placing it on the bar.

My core responds with immediate throbbing.

"I'm in the mood for something different. What have you got on tap?"

I huff dramatically, semi annoyed with his flirtation and my stupidity for falling for it. Pursing my lips, I shift my eyes to the levers on my right and raise an eyebrow. He peruses the eight varieties before settling on one.

"Sam Adams Rebel."

I snap my eyes up to meet his eyes and I mumble, "Long or short?"

This beautiful man releases a sexy, confident grin. "Tall and long."

Shaking my head to ward off the inappropriate images, I bite down on my bottom lip to suppress a smile as I fill the glass.

I push the tap back, ending the flow of beer, and set the glass down. "That'll be six."

He reaches into his pocket and slides a ten across the bar. "I didn't know you worked here."

I turn to cash out his beer and get his change, maintaining constant eye contact in the mirror until I turn to face him with four dollars in my hand. Sliding it back to him, I reply, "There's a lot you don't know about me."

"I know you're sexy as hell," he adds with a wink before he slowly turns away. Bobbing his head and moving his shoulders to keep in rhythm with the music coming from the stage near Mackenzie's bar, he glances in that direction. I take the opportunity to admire his profile. My fingers long to trace over the tip of his nose down to his luscious lips and under his structured jaw.

Mateo turns to walk away.

"Hey! You forgot your change!" I call out, causing him to look back over his shoulder.

"Keep the money and buy some earplugs. I know you don't like the sound of screwing early in the morning."

My shoulders shake with quiet laughter, remembering how I stomped outside in my pajamas this morning, and yelled up that they needed to work quieter because the constant sound of the drill was driving me crazy. The banging of hammers and the annoying whir of drills only seemed to get louder so I turned my music up to drown out the noise.

"You like to play games, don't you?" I yell as he continues to walk through the large, bustling crowd.

"Excuse me, can we get some drinks here?" A man shouts while a few people sneer about how slow the service is.

"Sorry!" I smile tightly and take his order.

An hour later, the bar is busier than ever as our state's Golden Girl is back home from a six-month tour. She's doing a one-night only promotional concert; it's a sold-out, standing room only event. While the beautiful singer with long blond hair, wearing black leather pants, a sparkling camisole with matching stilettos, takes the stage, I continue to serve drinks. The crowd goes wild when she sings the song that quickly became a chart-topping single on the radio. I quietly mouth each word as she belts it out on stage, hitting a high note, displaying her incredible range and talent. Everyone's attention is fixated on the performance so I use the time to restock the bar.

Don Delisioso comes over and orders another beer.

"Enjoying the show?" I ask.

A quick shrug displays his casual demeanor.

Refilling another pint, I inquire about who accompanied him because it appears that he came to the bar alone.

"Why? You want to ask me out?" he teases, eyeing me over the bar, allowing his eyes to linger on my black shorts.

"Settle down, Donny D. You're not my type," I say, gesturing with my hands in a "slow down" motion.

"What about my D? How come I'm not your type?" he asks, leaning over the bar to hear my response.

I roll my eyes in exasperation and slide his beer across the mahogany surface.

"You're just not," I reply with a conciliatory smile. "Here you go. This one's on me."

"We'll see about that," he mumbles with a crooked smile. Tipping his chin in thanks, Mateo walks away to enjoy the rest of the show.

Throughout the night, I listen as the petite twenty-six-year-old croons some familiar songs along with some unfamiliar ones from her upcoming album.

"Cat," my manager calls, carrying a bottle of champagne and chilled flutes. "I need you to drop these off in the back room before the show ends."

I grimace, trying to avoid the impending and inevitable conversation.

"Can't you get Lou to do it?" An exaggerated whine slips from my lips. "I'm busy."

"He's *busy*. You've been standing around for the last twenty minutes watching the show and singing along to almost every song."

"Fine," I huff, grabbing the bottle and tray from him before setting off to the room where performing artists get ready.

The hallway leading to the green room is narrow, its walls lined with photographs and scribbled autographs. I pass the ladies' room as muttered grievances about life's injustices fall from my lips. I tuck the bottle of champagne in the crook of my arm and balance the tray on one hand so I can share my complaints with Mack. She'll commiserate with me. I walk forward slowly as I text my best friend until I hear someone ask what I'm doing back here. My eyes snap up and I stand before the manly beast.

"Hi." Mateo smiles as his eyes roam down my bare legs. "Need a hand?"

I slip my phone back into the back pocket of my tiny black shorts and readjust my hold on the contents in my hands. "No. I'm all set, but thanks for the offer," I answer nervously when he stares at me with those eyes.

I glance over his shoulder as another man steps out of the restroom. My eyes travel to the brightly colored flyer with Chloe's picture on it. I notice several of the small tabs have been ripped off; apparently, backup singers are needed. I chuckle, thinking how some people would do anything to have the opportunity to work with her.

"Isn't the bar out *that* way?" He points behind me.

"This is for Chloe." I lift the bottle of champagne and give it a little shake. "I guess they're celebrating her upcoming album."

He nods thoughtfully. "I hear it's good. She's working with new artists."

I tilt my head to the side thoughtfully. "You don't strike me as a Chloe fan."

With a quick shrug, he responds, "A fan? I wouldn't exactly say that, but her voice is..." His eyes dance as he searches for the right word, "Rich. Whether you're a fan or not, you can't deny she's got talent...and she's a great songwriter. No one is crazy enough to miss an opportunity to work with her."

Disbelief spreads across my face as I try to read between the lines.

"Have you got a little crush on Chloe?" I wrinkle my nose for dramatic effect. "Awww, that's cute. I bet you think she's gorgeous. What's the word you used? Hottie?" I tease, trying to get him to admit he's star struck by her and perhaps admit his infatuation with the blond beauty.

Mateo laughs at my comment. "It's hard to tell with all

that shit plastered on her face. She's not natural looking like you."

Natural looking? I'm not sure if there's supposed to be a compliment in his statement or not.

Sensing my unease, Mateo clarifies his words. "You're... naturally beautiful. You don't need all that makeup to look good."

I suck my lips inward, suppressing a smile as his eyes burn into mine. "Thanks."

The door at the end of the hall opens and I notice Chloe's manager step out, complaining about the service and wondering what's taking so long for the champagne. I take a small step to the side, using his body as a shield from her daggers and insults. After a final derogatory shout, she slams the door shut.

My eyes widen and my eyebrows touch my hairline, causing my forehead to wrinkle.

"Great," I sigh, allowing the sarcasm to reign.

"Want me to bring that for you?" he offers, realizing I'd have to face the angry manager.

"No, thanks. I've got it."

Just then the door reopens and the name "Randall" is screamed. I wince at the sound and shiver as does one of the photographs that rattles against the wall.

He tilts his head and singsongs. "Offer still stands."

I mentally consider my options and since my night was going considerably well, I decide I'd rather not take the chance of being on the receiving end of her wrath. Her reputation precedes her.

"Thanks! I owe you. I make a killer chicken salad so don't bring lunch tomorrow."

He takes the bottle and flutes then smiles. "It's a date."

I laugh. "No, it's chicken salad."

When I wake up the next morning, my hair is a wild mane of frizz. With only five hours of sleep, a long nap will surely be on my agenda this afternoon.

"You're up early," my gram comments, offering a quick kiss on my cheek.

I yawn then nod in agreement as I prepare a cup of coffee and inhale the sweet scent that fills the air. "The bar was busy last night... Chloe was in town for a performance."

My gram's hand stills, causing the pot of marinara sauce to boil violently. "Was *he* there?"

I take a sip and shake my head nonchalantly. "I didn't see him."

"Has he called you?"

I inhale quietly. "No. I don't think he knows I'm back."

Round and round the wooden spoon goes as Gram's frustration with the entire situation becomes even more evident. She reaches for the bottle of dish detergent.

I move quickly and replace the soap with extra virgin olive oil. "This will taste much better." I smile when her expression turns somber.

"Sorry. My brain is cuckoo lately."

Gram adds a tablespoon or two of the oil before speaking again. "If I were you, I'd give him a piece of my mind."

"Hey now, you don't have too much of your mind left so let's not give any away, okay Ma?" My uncle, unshaven and dressed casually in board shorts and a T-shirt, teases as he walks into the kitchen before offering a quick kiss to the top of her gray streaked hair. "Mornin'."

Gram turns the knob, lowering the heat on the sauce, and proceeds to prepare his breakfast while he sits at the kitchen table and unfolds the newspaper. He pulls the paper apart, foregoing the sports section for the business section.

Steam rises from the dish of scrambled eggs, bacon and toast that are set before my uncle as if he were the king of the castle.

"Gram, where are you going?" I ask as she piles freshly baked muffins onto a crystal serving tray.

"I thought the boys might be hungry."

"They're men not boys and they can feed themselves."

"And *this* is why she doesn't have a boyfriend," she mumbles quietly as she steps outside into the morning sun.

I open the fridge and the pantry cabinet, making a list of ingredients I need. My phone rings and an unknown number flashes across the screen. "Telemarketers," I mumble and ignore the call.

Minutes later, my uncle growls, "Unbelievable!"

I flinch at his harsh tone. My pencil slides across the Post-It, scrawling a straight line that runs off the small yellow paper.

I look up and find him grimacing while he reads the front page which boasts about Chloe's performance last night. Filling the room with an annoyed voice, my uncle reads the details, snapping his teeth at the idea of a promotional competition, calling for singers to audition for a "once in a lifetime" opportunity to work with the music industry's newest rising star.

He snaps his attention to me. "Did you see this?"

I suck my lips in before responding, "Not in the paper, but I heard about it at work."

He continues to read the article, causing the lines on his forehead to deepen.

"I still think you should have sued. You had every right to and the statute of limitations hasn't passed yet." He stands and walks over to the counter.

"It's not worth it," I exhale.

"Like hell it's not! Do you have any idea how much money you'd be making right now? You wouldn't have to be busting your ass working two jobs." He returns to the chair, leans back and tilts his head, looking up at the ceiling. "Sometimes I wonder about you, kid. It's like you've got your head in the clouds."

"Only when I sit on your shoulders," I offer as a response, trying to smooth out the tension radiating from him.

A chuckle escapes, indicating that he's succumbed to the humorous image of me as a child sitting on his shoulders, chasing the clouds as we ran and played throughout Gram's backyard.

I reach up and touch the now faded scar by my right eye. "I almost lost an eye because of you."

He gives me a frustrated look laced with remorse. "I told you to duck. It's not my fault you didn't listen."

"I was three," I laugh, defending myself.

"Still. You've should've listened."

"Whatever." I smirk. "I'll be fine."

He tosses a hard glare at me at my use of the word "fine."

Walking across the kitchen, he places the dirty dish in the sink, pours another cup of coffee then leaves the room.

"We do have a dishwasher, you know," I call before he rounds the corner to answer a call on his phone.

A mop of light brown hair and a half smile peek around from behind the door. "I know, but she likes to feel needed."

I roll my eyes, thinking that if he weren't so obnoxious at times, I might perhaps like him as much as I used to when we were younger. Gram breezes back into the kitchen, carrying an empty tray.

"Don't forget I have an appointment tomorrow at one," she reminds me. "I want to leave by twelve so we aren't late."

"I didn't forget. We won't be late. After all, we're going to see my future husband." I smile and scrunch my nose. "I can't wait."

She walks over to the table and refolds the newspaper, pausing for a moment when she sees the huge image on the front page. She swallows and sets her shoulders straight then raises her chin indignantly.

"Did your uncle see this?"

I nod. "No need to get upset, Gram. Like I told Uncle Johnny, it's not worth it."

Her penciled in eyebrow rises sharply, matching the harshness of her words. "It *is* worth a lot."

Without another word, she heads over to the sink, turns on the faucet and washes the dishes. I offer a side hug. "I'm running to the store. I'll be back in a bit. Need anything?"

"A bottle of rat poison."

"Gramma! Stop that," I laugh. "Besides, it probably wouldn't kill 'em anyway."

Walking to my car, I look over to where the framers are screwing together the long sheets of plywood, forming the skeleton of a new room. Two men work simultaneously as music blasts from an old radio. My eyes travel around in search of Mateo, the handsome and sexy foreman, but he's nowhere to be found. I look for the third work truck, but that's gone, too.

After downshifting to ease my trek down the hill leading to the main road, I make a mental note to have my brakes checked and switch my tires for the winter. I wrack my brain to remember the name of Gram's old mechanic friend. Without making too much of a spectacle with my old car, I run my errands in record time. My stop at the grocery store is quick and before I realize, delicious chicken salad with mesclun greens is nestled between buttery croissants.

I crank the umbrella, shielding the patio table from the midday sun and set down two placemats. The workers descend from their perches high above the ground where the new construction abounds and pile into the white pickup trucks. I read the name "Cruz and Sons" and think about how nice it must be to be able to work together, building something worthwhile that bears the family name.

Balancing the small tray of sandwiches, two bottles of Sam Adams Rebel, a water bottle and bowl of fresh berries, I place it all down gently then glance over my shoulder, waiting for my guest to arrive.

I open the bottle of water and sip while I wait.

I wait.

And wait.

And wait some more until my uncle walks over, grabs a sandwich and a bottle of beer then leaves without so much as a thank you.

"You're welcome!" I shout sarcastically, adding the word "jerk" under my breath.

Riddled with annoyance, I pack up the uneaten lunch and shove everything into the refrigerator. I run upstairs to change and text Mack on my way back down.

"Gram, I'll be back later," I yell as the screen door slams shut. I toss my bag onto the passenger seat and pull the two latches. I give a final push and watch as the roof folds back on itself, providing an unlimited view of the bright blue sky.

I plug my phone into the auxiliary and crank the music, letting the unjustified and quite unexpected wave of disappointment fade away. I sing along and let the wind have a field day with my hair.

"*What* happened to you?" Mack asks when I park my car behind her Honda coupe.

I laugh at her comment and adjust the rearview mirror to look at myself.

"Wow! I do look crazy!"

I open the glove compartment and grab a headband before securing my wild mane into a low knot at the nape of my neck. I tuck the errant pieces behind my ear, wishing I had a strong jawline like my best friend.

"How do you always look so put together?" I ask, stepping out of my car and tossing a dirty, yet playful, look in her direction.

"Rule number one. Never ride with the windows down." She points to my hair and grins. "Exhibit A."

I sigh dramatically.

"But I like riding with the windows down," I whine playfully as we step into Trina's Treasure Shop and browse the newest shipment.

"You sound like a dog," she laughs.

"Hi, girls," Trina calls from behind the counter. "Cat, we got a few new things in yesterday. I might need you later this week."

"Okay. Thanks!" I offer a smile, ready to make an offer that my part-time employer pay me in clothing rather than minimum wage.

Over the long rack of consigned garments, my best girlfriend and I swipe hangers to the side as we talk about our summer plans before she heads off to do her internship at Columbia in the fall.

"What about this one?" I step out of the dressing room and spin around, hoping this one won't be rejected as all the others have been.

"Cat, you look like a frumpy flower child."

I point to the headband covered in small daisies, stating the obvious. "Exhibit A."

With a quick roll of her eyes, she ignores my comment.

"You have a great body. You need to show it off." Mack holds out a piece of material which some might call a dress. "Try this on."

My lips part in protest.

"Go!"

I strip down to my underwear and shimmy into the red dress. Looking over my shoulder, I see the open back reflected in the mirror and notice it conceals my small tattoo. I free my hair and shake my head around wildly, breathing even more life and bulk into it. Dramatically, I pull the curtain back and step through, sauntering across the room as the rising star did on stage.

"Super Star!" I throw my arms in the air and freeze, striking a ridiculous pose.

"Wow! Just wow!" Mack walks over and lowers my arms, pushes my breasts together to reveal more cleavage. With a tight grip, she corrals my hair as she looks over my shoulder. "You look amazing." She eyes me carefully. "You *could* be a star."

My lips pinch as a grimace emerges. "I was just kidding, Mack."

My face looks the same, but the rest of me doesn't.

"This isn't me. You know I don't need to be the center of attention and this dress screams, 'Hey, everyone! Look at me!'"

Mack's lips tighten into a hard line. "Oh yeah, you're happy letting someone else have all the attention."

"Don't start. I already got an earful from Gram and my uncle."

Mack's lips pull back into a grin. "And how is *Uncle Johnny*?" She waggles her eyebrows and licks her lips.

I gag dramatically. "Eww! That's disgusting! He's my uncle, you creep."

"You don't see him like the rest of us do."

"The rest of you weirdos." I shiver and grimace at her words.

"Call me whatever you want, but he is hot and ridiculously sexy."

My hands cover my ears and I sing Twinkle Twinkle Little Star, trying desperately to eradicate the images she's subjecting my mind to. Mack motions with her fingers that her lips are zipped.

The moment I free my ears, she asks, "Have you ever noticed how women look at him?"

Images once again fill my mind and my stomach rolls. "He's my uncle. He's old. And you're sick in the head." I tap my temple with my index finger.

"He's less than ten years older than you and only eight for me. That hardly qualifies as old."

She yanks the black dressing room curtain with finality, leaving me dumbfounded at the idea that Mack has a major crush on my relative.

Walking to the check-out counter, I purchase a few things. I step aside, making room for Mack to buy her clothes including the red dress I hung back on the rack.

"Did you see Randy last night?" Mack asks as we walk side by side, exiting the small shop. In no time at all, the sky has become overcast, looking ominous with gray clouds.

"No, but I also wasn't looking for him," I lie.

Understanding my desire to change the subject, Mack suggests we grab a quick lunch. The chicken salad sandwich in the fridge doesn't sound so appetizing anymore since I was stood up for lunch by Mateo.

"Who was that guy who kept going to your bar for drinks?"

"What guy?" I ask nonchalantly, wondering how she noticed Mateo's frequent visits when her bar was ten times busier than mine.

"Tall, dark and handsome. Sexy as sin."

I shrug, pretending not to know who she's referring to.

"He practically stared at you all night."

"You do know you're not supposed to drink on the job, right?" I purse my lips and smirk.

"Let's see if he shows up again tonight."

"Why would he? Chloe's not performing and you know as well as I do that everyone there last night was there for one reason." I remember his comment about her talent and a wave of jealousy crashes over me.

I pick at my salad while Mack scrolls through Facebook.

"Did you see this?" She turns her phone in my direction, revealing the announcement that's in the newspaper.

"Yep. I saw the flyers last night."

My best friend tosses me a knowing look.

"Don't you start with me, too."

She sighs. "I think you should—"

"—And I think you should drop it." I set my fork down, push away from the table and walk to the ladies' room.

Locking the stall door, I sit on the toilet and screw my eyes shut, wishing everyone in my circle would mind their own damn business.

Minutes later, I return to the table to find remorse on Mack's face. No words are needed to relay her thoughts. I simply nod, indicating I accept her unspoken apology.

"We should have a party at my apartment!" Her excitement lightens the somber mood as the cute waiter who clears our dishes smiles at her. "You can come, too if you'd like," she offers to him.

He grins deviously at her and leaves our bill.

"How do you do that?" I ask, pulling money from my wallet.

"Do what?" she inquires with a grin as she adds her portion of money. She knows exactly what I'm referring to as she reaches into her bag, pulls out a pen and scribbles her phone number on the back of the check.

"You make it look so easy."

"It is." She tosses the pen in her bag and stands. "Besides, I gave him *your* number not mine."

"Mack!" My eyes widen and I want to reach across the table and slap that stupid grin off her face.

"What? Cat, be honest. You need to have some fun. And he was definitely fun."

"I'm not you. I can't flirt with guys then sleep with them like it's no big deal, you know that."

"Who said anything about sleeping with him? God, you're such a slut!" Mack laughs as we leave the restaurant and walk to our cars, settling on a date for "beverages with boys."

"How did you get in to Columbia again?"

"I slept with the admissions officers."

"There's like eighteen of them!" I squawk playfully,

knowing that behind her flirtatious persona is an incredibly smart woman who graduated magna cum laude.

"I've been a busy girl." She winks and offers a quick hug. "I'll see you later."

Wanting to avoid the business district, I take the long route and walk along the sidewalk back to my car as light rain begins to fall. The words of my family and best friend fill my mind as I wipe away the heavy moisture that now pelts my face as the sky opens up. It reminds me of the countless tears I shed years ago because of him.

My eyes round and my mouth drops open before an endless litany of curses tumble from my lips at the sight of my car filling with water. I didn't think I had to worry about rain when I decided to leave the convertible top down. I drop my bag onto the seat and struggle with the vinyl roof, attempting to secure it shut.

Distracted by my thoughts, my hands continue to work in the rain until I finally relent, scream at the heavens and give up the fight. I plop myself into the driver's seat, bang my palms on the steering wheel, gripping my fingers around until my knuckles turn white. The frustration and disappointment building up from the last few days finally win out and spill from my eyes. Tapping my forehead against my fisted hands, I close my eyes as the rain adds insult to injury.

A voice calls out. "Hey, need a lift?"

I don't have the energy to raise my head.

"Can I help you?" the voice asks again.

Seconds pass by until I realize the person is speaking to me. I lift my head, shield my eyes and peer in the direction of the voice. My heart soars, then plummets at the glimpse of him as he signals and veers the white pickup truck over into the fire lane.

My pulse quickens as he steps out of the truck and strides over to me. Rain drenches his button-down shirt and dress pants.

"Hi," Mateo says. The confusion is clear on his face. "Why are you sitting in the rain? You're getting all wet." His beautiful, sultry timbre is matched by an equally beautiful face framed by dark hair. He opens my door and reaches for my hand. "Let's get you inside." I stare at the extended hand as he offers shelter from the worsening conditions around me.

My eyes travel from his hand, to his rolled-up sleeve to the collar of his light yellow shirt before meeting his hazel eyes.

"You're getting soaked," I squeak, realizing I look and sound like a drowned mouse. After securing my bag, I place my hand in his and relish the feel of his touch when his fingers close around mine while his thumb grazes over my knuckles.

Wordlessly, he guides me to the truck, opens the passenger door and closes it behind me. Instead of opening the driver's side door, he returns to my vehicle and wrestles with the roof until the material is secure, shielding the interior from further damage.

My eyes wander around the cab of the pickup truck, my ears take notice of the soft music filtering in. I spot an empty water bottle in the drink holder, a small tattered notebook, and a manila folder peeking out from its place hidden between the center console and the seat.

The opening of the door startles me, and I look up. Drenched from head to toe, Mateo steps into the cab and exhales loudly, running his hand through his hair, giving me a clear view of his face. Slowly, he turns to face me.

"I think you need a new roof. Or maybe a new car." His quiet laughter prompts a turn of my lips upward into a small smile.

And new brakes and new tires. "I need a lot more than that," I mumble quietly.

He shifts his body to face me and those hazel eyes pierce

me with question and mischief. "And what exactly do you need, Caterina?"

I drink in the man before me. The soft cotton plastered against his skin, the moisture on his forearm, the slow trail of rain rolling down his neck send a shock wave of lust through me. My body responds immediately as my nipples harden against my bra.

I swallow the excitement of my name on his lips.

Glancing down at my chest, Mateo remarks, "The roof is really hard to put up. My guess is the hinges are rusty and might need a little lubrication to make it easier to open and close."

I understand the implication of his words; he isn't talking about my 1995 Volkswagen Cabriolet. I glance in the side mirror at my car with its "classic" license plate and know I should take my savings and purchase a new vehicle.

"It's a little past the expiration date," he adds with a touch of humor.

His word "date" lingers and reminds me of the uneaten lunch I prepared for him. "I need lots of things, but I'll figure it out. No need for you to be concerned." My response is harsh and edgy.

With narrowed eyes and a furrowed brow, he silently questions my tone.

"Sorry I missed our lunch date today."

I smooth back my hair and adjust my headband before turning to him. "It wasn't a date. It was just chicken salad."

"Either way, I'm sorry I missed it. I couldn't get out of a prior commitment."

A sarcastic reply falls silent on my lips. I slide the elastic band off my head, comb my fingers through the long, wet strands, and again secure the headband in place. My face, tainted with a hint of annoyance, is now unobstructed.

"You're mad at me," he states confidently.

I shake my head and mumble, my voice rising. "What?!

Why would I be mad at you?"

"I can tell when women are mad. Admit it, you're mad."

Crossing my arms across my chest, I prepare to defend myself against his accusations.

Mateo nods with his chin. "See, that right there."

"What?" I demand with a scoff.

"You crossed your arms."

Both of our eyes drop to my folded arms, revealing my cleavage.

"I'm..." I stutter, "I'm cold."

"I can see that." He smirks at my failed attempt to hide the arousal of my breasts before continuing, "Can I take you home?"

My eyes snap up in shock as my lips part to respond.

"To *your* home," he stares at me with hazel eyes that could make me forget my own name, "unless you want to go to mine."

Part of my brain tells me to slap him while the other implores me to kiss him.

"My house is fine."

He inquires about my car and suggests that he and his cousin can drop it off later. Not knowing whether my uncle will be home or not, I accept his offer.

"What are you doing down here? Bidding on a new job? Are you doing commercial work?" I ask as we drive along the busy streets until the road transforms into the quiet paths of my neighborhood.

He reaches for the knob on the radio and turns down the music.

I watch as he blinks several times before responding with a hesitant, "I got called in for a meeting about another job earlier than expected. I was going to go after work, but when the boss calls, I go."

"Cool."

"And you?"

I tell him about shopping with Mack and our quick stop for lunch but refrain from mentioning the party we've planned.

He parks the truck in the same spot as he has done several days in a row.

Awkward silence fills the space between us.

I reach for the handle and pull gently, disengaging the door and letting my leg dangle in preparation for the step down.

"Do you want to come in?" The offer slips through.

With a look of inquiry, Mateo keeps his eyes fixed on me. "Do you want me to come in?"

My lips separate, yet no words escape. I know the wanton expression on my face is answer enough.

The feel of Mateo's hand slowly sliding across my skin as he pulls my leg back into the cab releases a yelp of lust. He moves closer and extends his reach to close the door, eventually resting his hand on my upper thigh.

His face, his mouth, his eyes. Everything is millimeters away; I could almost taste the scent of him. My tongue slips through to moisten my lips and savor the flavor.

Moving his hands from my thigh, he ignites a trail of desire as his fingers skim over the denim to the damp cotton of my tanktop. The light touch makes me shiver as my arms fall heavy.

"Cat, I *really* want to kiss you. I've been thinking about it for days."

A whimper of approval escapes.

Cupping my jaw in his hands, Mateo brings my mouth close to his, joining them together with a tender whisper of a kiss. He parts my lips with a slide of his tongue before dipping into my mouth. His soft tongue makes acquaintance with mine and like old lovers meeting after years apart, the embrace in our mouths is familiar and welcoming.

I moan into his mouth.

He angles my head to deepen the kiss and I feel his hard body press against mine. My fingers dance along the material covering his legs. My core clenches and I squeeze my thighs together to quash the feeling. Sensing my desperation for his mouth and more, Mateo pulls my body flush against his and I scramble to follow his lead. I find myself straddled over him, moving back and forth over the strain of his dress pants, trying to relieve the tension building between my legs.

A sex fiend takes ahold of my body and attempts to ride out an orgasm. Mateo's hand slides down to my ass, securing me, encouraging the rhythmic movement against him. My hands grip the back of his head, my lips devour his until I explode with a mangled cry against his neck.

I sag with relief.

"That was incredible." Sweet words and tender nips dot from my clavicle to my ear, sending chills down my spine.

I hide my face in his neck and kiss it softly before I shift my weight to dismount him.

"Stay right where you are," he commands, halting my attempt to right my clothes and locate my dignity. The feel of his length twitching beneath me reminds me of the bell in a boxing match, signaling the start of the next round. My body is ready for round two and more.

"Shit," I squeal when through the truck's back window, I catch a glimpse of my uncle's car pulling into the driveway.

I scramble off Mateo's lap and press my back against the seat, covering my face with my hands to hide the flush of embarrassment now staining my hot cheeks. Slow words of apology tumble from my lips. "I am so sorry. I don't know what just happened, but I am so sorry and completely mortified."

Uncle Johnny's car comes to a quiet lull beside the truck, and I can feel the weight of his stare through the window.

"Who's that?" Mateo asks tensely. I turn to see anger or perhaps a hint of jealousy marring his handsome face.

With a quick tap on the closed window, my uncle waits for me to lower it. I press the lever, but quickly realize that there's no power since the truck is off. Johnny's eyebrows rise, his patience waning quickly. I hear a click as I reach for the door handle, but stop when I feel Mateo's hand on my thigh. The sound of the window rolling down draws my attention back to my uncle.

"What?" I ask flatly, ignoring the look he offers back.

"What's going on?" He asks me before he looks past me at Mateo. His gaze follows the long, extended arm and the large hand on my thigh.

"Nothing. I'll be in in a minute."

Warning me with a stern look, my uncle nods his disapproval and turns away.

"Who's that guy?"

"He's a pain in my ass— that's who he is."

"Ex-boyfriend?"

I hide my disgust in a cough. "Oh, my God! No!"

Raising a curious brow, Mateo continues the inquiry.

"He's my uncle. And before you say it—I know he doesn't look that old."

"Your uncle? He certainly didn't act like one. Are you sure he's your uncle?"

I ignore his last comment, wanting to return my lips to his.

"I'm sorry again about before. I don't know what happened. I don't usual—"

The attack on my lips halts my words.

"No apology necessary," he mumbles against my swollen lips. I feel my pulse quicken as a rush of adrenaline surges through my body.

His phone sitting on the center console rings just as I ask if he's going to be here tomorrow. I hope my anticipation isn't too obvious.

Reaching for it, Mateo eyes the incoming number

hesitantly then says, "I've got to take this."

A feeling of dismissal slides over me, and I mouth, "Okay. See you later."

Pinning me with a hard stare, Mateo clears his throat and answers the phone with an air of professionalism. "Hello?"

The person on the other end of the line speaks while he looks out the driver's side window. The one-sided conversation muffles as my brain tries to understand what just happened a few minutes ago. I reach for the door handle to see myself out, but a firm hand lands on my thigh and holds me in place.

"Sure. Tomorrow at ten sounds good. Thanks."

He disconnects the call and tosses the phone onto the dash. The deep exhale makes me think all is not well.

"Everything okay?" I ask with genuine concern.

He nods, turning his head to face me while the hand on my thigh tugs gently, causing my legs to part.

"Everything is good." The firm hand slips higher on my inner thigh and a current of excitement shoots through me.

Wanting to take what he's offering, but knowing I shouldn't, I slowly bring my legs together, effectively trapping his hand, shutting down his attempt to restore us back to the intensity of moments before.

"I won't be here tomorrow."

"Oh." The single word slips from my tongue, revealing my disappointment.

"Going to make the big bucks working somewhere else?"

He smiles, dropping his eyes to my playful lips. "Something like that."

After giving me a quick final kiss, he insists I owe him a lunch date.

I step out of the truck and laugh before turning around to stand in the door. "It wasn't a date. It was chicken salad."

His eyes narrow into slits as a grin tugs at his lips. "Fine. Then you owe me a real date that doesn't involve chicken salad. Steak and lobster?"

I crinkle my nose at his suggestion.

The sweet sound of laughter emerges from his mouth.

"What's that face for? A date or the food involved?"

With a smug grin, I simply shrug even though my belly somersaults at the idea of going on an actual date with him. I would probably eat anything he wants to feed me.

Stepping back into the cab, I grab his phone only to be met with resistance on the black screen. "Unlock your phone, please." I extend my hand.

He taps a quick five-digit passcode and hands it back to me. I detect humor in his expression.

I begin the process of adding my name and number to his phone.

"What? How do you—" I ask abruptly when I realize my name is already listed as a contact.

As realization hits me, I blink slowly and draw out my words. "Did my gram give you my number?"

A look of guilt washes over his perfect features, and he turns his eyes away.

Unbelievable.

My gram's relentless attempts to meddle in my personal life have reached the point of no return.

A dark chuckle filled with cynicism escapes. "Is she paying you to take me out?"

His eyes snap to mine in disbelief, but his silence speaks volumes.

"Well...she did offer to make lasagna for me every week."

I smack his arm when I realize he's teasing me. I miss the contact when I pull my hand away from his skin.

A bubble of bravery floats from my lips. "So if you had my number already, why haven't you used it?"

"I did," he retorts with a smile. "I actually called you earlier today, but you didn't answer and I don't usually leave voicemail."

"Oh," I utter, suddenly feeling awkward.

Mateo offers a reassuring smile. "I'll call you later."

Excitement soars through me until I realize I'm scheduled to work.

He must notice the hint of wariness etched on my face. "What's wrong?"

"I have to work tonight, but you can text me."

With a quick nod from left to right while his eyes hold mine, he says, "I don't want to text you."

"What?" I screech. "Everyone texts."

"I'd much rather hear your voice and the sounds you make."

My cheeks flush red with embarrassment.

"You're not going to let that go, are you?"

He grins salaciously, reaching for his phone. "Never."

If I've learned one thing from life, it's to not dwell on the past.

Dropping my eyes, I inhale deeply before finally looking back up to meet his.

"I guess I'll talk to you later then," I announce as I close the door and turn away.

I stop when I hear the window roll down.

"I'll be thinking about you."

I swallow hard as I meet his stare.

"Liar," I counter with a smirk. "I'm sure you say that to all the girls."

"Nope" He raises his chin confidently. "I speak the truth. My words don't lie."

A muffled crack of laughter spews from my belly. "Now I *know* you're lying."

"Cat," he calls, halting my stride as I turn to face him. "That kiss and the ...let's just say it was more than I expected and so much better than I'd imagined."

I drop my eyes and smile as my cheeks flush pink. "Me, too."

"See you later, beautiful." He snaps a quick picture of me just before he rolls the window up and backs out of the driveway carefully, avoiding the mountains of lumber piled high.

Feeling giddy, my light footsteps carry me inside the house to where my uncle waits at the kitchen table, his hands clasped around his cell phone.

"What's up with you?" I ask, opening the refrigerator to pour a glass of orange juice.

He raises his empty glass, silently asking for more.

"Who is that guy?"

I scrunch my face at his question before I gulp down the drink and refill his glass.

"He's the guy doing the addition. Why?"

"The other guys left already." He takes a sip. "Why was he still here? And why are you soaking wet?"

Oh, Uncle Johnny, you have no idea how wet I am!

Inhaling quietly to suppress my laughter, I debate my response of answering honestly or initiating an argument. My mother's feisty spirit, quick tongue and spite reside deep in me even if she no longer does.

"He let me ride his lap and gave me a fantastic orgasm."

A spray of orange juice covers the maple wood of the kitchen table.

"Jesus Christ, Cat!"

"Hey! You're the one who asked." I shrug my shoulders and smirk, exiting the kitchen dramatically.

My pace up the stairs quickens into a trot when I hear him holler, "Goddammit!"

Finding solace in the confines of my room, I tap the music app, grab my journal and lie diagonally across my bed. My front teeth nibble on my bottom lip as my fingers work furiously, jotting down multiple lines and chorus that fill the page with the words. My mind is overflowing with thoughts as my hand races to keep up.

Hunger. Need. Touch. Date. Kiss.

"Uncle Johnny?" I call out, searching the house for him with the intention of asking for help to get my car home. I didn't really plan on taking up Mateo's offer to have my car towed home.

Where are you? I need to get my car.

I wait for a response.

Call a tow truck.

A second text comes through as my fingers type a response.

Or better yet, call your new boyfriend.

I growl through gritted teeth.

Fine.

After a quick Google search, I call around looking for someone who is willing to tow my car home at a reasonable rate.

"Three hundred dollars? Are you serious?" I bellow into the phone.

"Take it or leave it, lady."

"Never mind," I say, quickly remembering Gram's friend, Tom, used to own a towing business.

I leave a voice message which is quickly returned.

"Oh, I don't know. I don't think Violet would be too happy to see me. She said some pretty mean things about me. I know they were lies, but it still hurt like hell."

"I know she did and I'm sorry about that, but you have to remember her mind isn't what it used to be. With a softer tone, I plead, "I can give you $200 to get my car home." Please, Tom. I'm begging you."

The older man on the other line finds compassion and agrees to tow my car home.

An hour later, my vintage Volkswagen is parked in the

driveway.

"Here," I hold out a Tupperware container of chicken salad along with a few small bills totaling two hundred dollars.

"Keep your money."

"No, it's okay. I want to pay you. I insist."

"You're stubborn like your grandmother."

I laugh. "I've heard that before. Will you at least take half the money and some chicken salad home?"

"Okay," he says, accepting the square food storage container. "Is this her recipe?" "Of course!" I smile.

"How's she doing? Is she gonna get better?" Genuine concern is evident in his tone.

"Oh, you know Gram..." My words float in the air as I shift my weight awkwardly before I confess. "Probably not. She's actually getting much worse."

I reach into my back pocket when my phone rings. I thank Gram's scorned lover again before I answer the call.

Since I don't recognize the number, I decline the call and let it go to voicemail, then quickly mentally chastising myself when I realize it might've been Mateo. I check my voicemail and sigh at the recording for a local charity event fundraiser. Opening the Uber app, I arrange a ride to Mack's apartment then scroll through Instagram and Twitter while I wait. A wide smile crosses my face when I see the most recent photos on Abimola's page, detailing his work in Africa.

Another swipe brings me to Chloe's page as images of the rising popstar flash across the screen. Pictures of her in the studio. Pictures of her writing song lyrics. Pictures of her with her manager. It's not until the last image appears that my stomach rolls and turns at the sight of her with him.

"Would you mind changing the station?" I ask when a familiar song filters in and fills the small space of the Prius.

Dark eyes meet mine in the rearview mirror. "Sure. No problem. I'm not much of a fan of her music anyway."

I chuckle and continue to peruse the photos on my phone. I know I'm a glutton for punishment, torturing myself, but I can't help it. It's like watching a gruesome car accident in slow motion.

Stepping out of the Uber, I thank the driver for the ride and unlatch the gate leading to the stairs.

"What the hell happened to you?" Mack, wearing only a black bra and a lace thong, asks immediately when I walk through the door of her studio apartment in the building her father owns. "Did someone rain on your parade?"

"Something like that."

I look around her usually tidy apartment and note how messy it is. Perhaps she'd been cured of her OCD. "I think I'm rubbing off on you." I pick up a red nightie and drop it on the bed.

"I had an unexpected guest earlier," she replies nonchalantly, shrugging her shoulders as she tosses her long red hair back.

"Lucky you!"

"I'll be ready in five." Mack leans over and looks into the mirror, covering her lashes with thick mascara to accentuate the beautiful color of her green eyes.

"Hey," I start, "do you mind if I work the front bar tonight? I had to drop a hundred bucks to get my car towed home. My uncle wasn't around to help."

"What happened to your car? Did it finally die?" She laughs.

"I don't see the point in spending all that money on a car. I don't even know what I'm doing or if I'll need a car."

"You should hear back soon, right?"

I nod, hiding the disappointment that no letter arrived again in today's mail. "I think so."

"Are you having second thoughts?" She pulls on a tight black T-shirt and smooths the material over her ample breasts.

I sigh heavily. "I'm worried about Gram. And my uncle—" The words morph into mumbled curses of frustration.

"Cat, your grandmother is going to outlive us all. Physically, she's in great health." She tips her head to the side and smiles. "Besides, I'm sure Johnny can help take care of her."

"Johnny?" I narrow my eyes with curiosity.

"Sorry! *Uncle* Johnny. Better?"

"Please don't say you have a thing for him."

Mack opens an expensive looking tube of lipstick, puckers her lush lips and stains them a deep shade of crimson. She air-kisses several times.

"Why do you spend so much money on that stuff?"

"A girl's got to always look her best. Besides cheap makeup isn't good for your skin."

I roll my eyes, knowing she'd give me a full lecture about the cosmetics I usually buy at Walmart.

Her perfectly arched eyebrows waggle. "Let's go make some money!"

Chapter Three

AROUND HALF PAST NINE, MY EYES FINALLY flutter open and scan Mack's small living room. I call out to her, but I get no response. Agreeing to go out after work was a bad idea. Agreeing to Fireball shots was an even worse idea. Pressing the button and listening to *his* voicemail was the worst idea ever.

"I heard you're back. I miss you."

Liar.

"Please call me."

Liar.

"We need to talk."

Liar.

"I want things to be the way they used to be."

Liar.

"I love you, Cat."

Liar.

At least Mateo's sultry voice telling me he thinks my car was stolen makes me laugh. I realize I never told him I had arranged for a tow truck.

I shower quickly, throw on a pair of Mack's yoga pants and T-shirt then arrange for an Uber to pick me up so I can get Gram to her appointment at one. I send Mack a text, letting her know I've left and send another to my gram, telling her not to worry and that I'm on my way home. Neither responds to my texts.

Overcome with an obligation to thank Mateo and explain what happened, I press the button and call back the number on the screen. After three rings, it goes to voicemail. I hang up and send a quick text instead.

Sorry about my car. I had it towed. Thanks anyway.

Again, I get no response.

I eye my cell phone suspiciously, wondering if the ringer is on or if it's broken.

Waving a friendly hello to the construction crew except for their foreman who isn't here, I walk into the house and set my bags down.

"Gram?"

After several minutes of silence, I stand in the entryway and notice nothing is written on the dry erase board by the door. Then I realize my car is gone.

"Oh, Gram!" I mumble.

My worried thoughts are interrupted by the ringing of the house phone. Thinking it's another telemarketer, I answer with a brusque, "Not interested," and hang up. Immediately, it rings again, but this time I pick up and ask, "What do you want?"

"Hello. Caterina?" a frail voice speaks.

The hair on my arm stands at attention.

"Yes."

"This is Olga Waters down at the hair salon. Your grandmother is here getting her hair done."

Confusion mars my face as I glance at the clock.

"Okay..."

"Has she been feeling well?"

My impatience is growing rapidly. "She's fine. How can I hel—" The words falter and my heart races at the sight of the white pickup truck. Returning my attention to the call, I ask how I can help her.

"Violet drove down here."

"I know."

I close my eyes in exasperation. "Is there something you need to tell me? Is Gram okay?" I'm momentarily distracted by the sound of a door closing.

"Maybe you need to come pick her up and see for yourself."

"Mrs. Waters, with all due respect, thank you for your concern, but I'm sure Gram is fine at the salon," I lie, not wanting to bring my grandmother's worsening health issues up to a virtual stranger.

"Well, okay dear, but don't say I didn't warn you."

"Thank you." I disconnect the call, place the receiver back on its perch and rest my forehead against it.

"Hello? Anyone home?" A man's voice breaks through the chaos running through my brain and prompts me to raise my head. Fully expecting to see Mateo standing there, a wave of disappointment washes over me when I see his cousin, Junior, instead.

"Hi." I force a smile. "What can I do for you?"

"Mateo wanted me to give you the updated blueprints." He holds out a rolled column of paper bound together by large rubber bands. "He made the changes your grandmother asked for."

I nod and thank him.

Lingering for a minute, he asks if everything is okay.

"Yeah, it's fine. My gram is being silly again. No worries though."

Something in his expression causes concern.

"What's going on?" I ask.

"I saw your grandmother leave this morning."

I shrug, wondering what's so odd about that. "Okay..."

"She was wearing her pajamas and slippers."

"She what? She got in the car and drove away like that?"

He nods sheepishly, knowing he probably should've stopped her.

"I thought she was kidding, but she drove off."

Weighing my options quickly, I ask if he can give me a ride across town to the hair salon she's been going to since the late seventies.

He obliges, escorts me out to the truck and even opens the passenger door after offering a hand to help me in. The contrast in the color of our skin reminds me of vanilla ice cream swirled with rich caramel.

"Thanks," I say, slipping my hand from his.

Junior smiles and closes the door.

"Where to?" he asks, maneuvering the truck through the maze in the driveway.

I give him directions to the salon. We ride in comfort, making small talk along the way.

I find out Junior's real name is Emmanuel, named after his father and his father before him. The story that every firstborn son is named Emmanuel elicits laughter and confusion when the entire family gets together for the holidays.

"It takes about twenty-five minutes just to say goodbye to everyone in the family— and that's just all the aunts." He laughs quietly before turning his gaze on me. "Puerto Ricans...we like to kiss."

An uncomfortable shadow falls over me like a thick blanket when his eyes hold mine.

"Where's Mateo today?" I blurt out, an obvious reaction to the situation.

"Teo?" He shrugs, his thin lips pinching as he exhales sharply and turns the dial on the radio. "Who knows. Probably out screwing around like usual or chasing another dream." The sound of lively Spanish music pipes through the speakers.

I want to rush to Mateo's defense, but my efforts would

be in vain. The truth is I don't really know anything about him other than he was willing to let me orgasm on his lap.

"You can pull over here." I point to the fire hydrant across the street from the salon. "Thanks for the ride. I really appreciate it." I look over to where Junior sits, remembering what happened in that very spot not even twenty-four hours earlier. A warm flush of embarrassment creeps across my face and I smile weakly.

"Anytime you need a ride, sweetheart, you give me a call."

My eyes widen into big circles of shock and I separate my lips, ready to spew words of disgust until I realize he's being genuine. He would have no way of knowing what happened between Mateo and me...unless Mateo told him.

"Thanks again. I'll see you around."

I step out and close the heavy door, waving a quick goodbye when he pulls the truck back into the flow of traffic toward the financial district. A familiar figure comes into view even though two blocks separate us. I race across the street, dodging the cars and miss being struck by a town car that eventually stops in front of the tall, sprawling building.

The bell on the door signals my arrival, and all eyes turn on me.

"Where's Violet?" I ask, scanning the empty chairs.

"I'm right here!" Gram lifts the old-fashioned hairdryer and ducks beneath it.

"Gram!" I shriek in horror as my jaw nearly hits the floor. "What did you do?" I quicken my steps to her and run my fingers through her bleached-blond hair until the longer strands of purple that hang over her eyes slip through.

"What? You don't like it?" She smiles brilliantly.

I stutter, thinking of a coherent response. "It's just so... so...wow." My gaze falls to the nightgown she's wearing. "You should've gotten dressed first, Gram."

"I am dressed." She grins, kicking her feet out from under the seat as if she were a six-year-old. "See!"

A frown tightens on my face at the sight of her nightgown and tattered slippers.

"You ready to go?" I ask, helping her to stand and walk to the counter. "I'll come back with her payment later." Shannon, the owner, nods and offers a sympathetic smile.

Guiding my grandmother to my car, I gasp and force down the string of curses when I notice the front quarter panel of my car is heavily dented. "What did you do?" I whisper while helping her into the seat. The squishy sound beneath her produces a goofy grin on her face. "Oh, excuse me," she whispers. "I think I wet myself."

On any other occasion, I would laugh at the absurdity of the situation, but my grandmother's weakening mental state and the fact that my car is smashed is no laughing matter.

"That's the seat, Gram. Not you." I look down to wear a small puddle of water remains on the floor mat. "Here you go." I click her seatbelt into place and walk around to get into the driver's seat. My backside sinks into the soggy material as I reach over my left shoulder for the seatbelt. I suppress the string of profanities from escaping although my blood pressure continues to rise.

I send a quick message to my uncle, informing him of his mother's morning activities then toss my phone in the glove compartment. My agitation compounds when a car approaches slowly and then stops. Those stifled words find release from my lips as I close my eyes, knowing exactly who is staring at me. There's no point in trying to hide or avoid him. I step out of my car and stand beside his shiny luxurious vehicle, looking straight ahead into his face and bracing for the impact he is going to have on my heart.

"Caterina..." I stiffen at the use of my full name as it transports me back to another time in my life. "How are you?" he asks from the rear passenger window as his tanned hand reaches out tenderly. I make no attempt at contact.

His blue eyes, a lighter shade than mine, soften and

display regret and longing. ""I've been trying to reach you. Why haven't you returned my calls?"

I don't try to hide the contempt in my voice. "I was away."

"Away?" After widening his eyes momentarily, he asks, "Where exactly were you?"

A sardonic chuckle emerges through my tight lips. "Africa."

He releases a breath, sighing in relief. "Oh good. I thought you were going to say something else, but seriously where were you?"

"Of course you don't believe me. I don't know why I even said anything to you. According to you, I'm a liar."

A hint of remorse and shame slip through his serious expression. "Don't start that again. That was a long time ago."

"Yes, it was, but I lost almost two years of my life...how could I ever forget?"

"Would it have been too much to call me?"

"I've been busy," I respond flatly despite wanting to tell him that I hate him and I'd rather never speak to him again.

"Sweetheart, surely you can't be too busy for your father." He can't hide the heaviness and anguish in his eyes.

"You're not my f—" I inhale deeply, silencing myself before I spit regretful words about the abandonment of his only daughter when he stood by and allowed injustice and greed to win.

A car horn interrupts his words, causing him to turn and snarl in the driver's direction. The serene countenance morphs into a mask of anger.

Looking back at me, his voice softens. "I want things to be the way they used to be."

The idea of "the way things used to be" makes my stomach wretch.

"Please try for me."

For you? I want to demand.

Again, the hint of remorse slides across his face. "I miss

you very much."

I don't return the sentiment.

"Promise you'll call me sometime. I want to hear all about your trip."

"It's Africa. It's hot and people are starving. What else is there to tell?" I deadpan. His haphazard attempt to determine if I'm telling the truth or lying to him about my trip to Africa is so transparent, my stomach rolls.

A pained look flashes on his face. "Is everything okay? Are you feeling well? Are you taking your medication?"

I snicker contemptuously. "I'm great. Prozac and I are living the American drea—"

A long, single honk immediately followed by three quick successions of an impatient driver's horn interrupts him once again.

"Go around, you goddamned bastard!" A raised fist accompanies his angry words.

"You're holding up traffic," I state the obvious.

"Do you think I give a damn? I don't care about them!"

Caring for others isn't something this man does well... unless you can help advance his name in the industry.

"Well..." I wave apologetically to the driver who veers into the other lane to continue on before I turn deadly eyes on him. "You're causing a scene and I don't like to be the center of attention."

The look on his face indicates my words have struck a nerve. "I remember and I'm sorry about that."

"Whatever," I mumble and look back at my grandmother who is now singing loudly.

"How is she?" My father tips his chin toward Gram.

"She's living the dream, too," I reply sarcastically.

"Cat, call me if there's anything I can do."

I swallow the cynical response that he's already done enough.

"Come to the house for dinner. We can talk."

Don't hold your breath is what I say in my head, but "We'll see" escapes. With two dismissive words, I send him on his way as I lower myself back into the car.

"Who was that?" Gram asks in a jovial manner.

A forced smile tightens my lips and my chest aches, knowing she would have threatened to kill him with her bare hands had she remembered who he was.

"He's no one, Gram. No one at all."

"Where the hell have you been?" I bellow, jumping to my feet, dropping my journal on the couch to race over to confront my uncle when he walks through the door. "It's almost six o'clock. What happened to you? You can't just disappear and leave me here alone!"

Johnny looks weary and disheveled as he lifts the lid to see what's for dinner before scrunching his face in disgust. He quickly covers the pan and sighs. Rubbing his neck with his palm, he closes his eyes and cracks his neck. I notice the distinct stain of lipstick on the collar of his untucked shirt.

"Not now, Cat." He moves to sidestep me.

"What do you mean? I've been trying to reach you since yesterday. I texted and called you probably a hundred times! I had to leave Gram alone last night while I worked."

I match his movements and block his entry into the dining room.

"I'm sure she's fine."

"She missed an appointment yesterday."

"So reschedule it," he barks as if speaking to one of his secretaries.

"It was with her neurologist."

His step freezes and his body stiffens, finally understanding my implication.

"What happened?" His harsh tone softens as he exhales

quietly.

"I can home from Mack's and Gram wasn't here. I got a phone call and—"

As if I had called her name, Gram breezes into the room and smiles brightly.

"What the fu—"

I toss him a look with pursed lips and a raised eyebrow.

"And how's my favorite and most handsome son?"

My uncle leans down and offers his cheek, accepting his mother's kiss and the caress of his five o'clock shadow.

"Ma, I'm your only son." As one arm closes around her thin body, he hugs her close.

"And that's why I love you so much. You take good care of me unlike my daughter over there."

Arguing that I'm her granddaughter will only cause more agitation so I ignore her comment and suggest she show him her new haircut and color.

Running his fingers through her nearly shaved head, he smiles. "It's...different, but it looks good."

I shake my head and screech, "Don't encourage her."

"You're no fun! That's why no man wants you."

"Thanks, Gram," I sigh, forcing the insult down with a hard swallow.

Needing a reprieve from the day from hell, I grab my bag and announce that I'm leaving.

"When will you be back?"

I turn to answer my uncle.

"Who knows? Maybe I'll keep on driving."

"Quit being so dramatic," he mumbles, pulling his cell phone out of his pocket.

Glancing quickly behind me, I spit out, "Her refills need to be picked up at the pharmacy. It's the CVS on Third Street not the other one," before I push the door open and slam into a wall of hard flesh that smells absolutely incredible.

"Whoa!" Mateo's hands reach out to secure my arms.

"Where are you off to in such a rush?"

I look up and meet his gentle gaze filled with kindness and longing. Overwhelmed by the past twenty-four hours, I feel moisture pool in the corner of my eyes and I bury my face in his chest, waiting for the tears to fall.

As if it were the most natural thing in the world, Mateo wraps his arms around me and rubs small circles against my back.

"Wanna take a ride?" he asks, his lips against my hair.

I smile and simply nod because words are lodged deep in my throat.

"Come on," he says, guiding me to the truck. Kindly, Mateo opens the door and closes it once I'm settled in the seat.

"Where do you want to go?"

I glance out the window, wondering where, besides Africa, I would go if given the chance again. My mind drifts, speculating briefly where my mother went when she left.

"Are you hungry? We can grab a bite to eat."

"Actually, food sounds really good," I reply, realizing I haven't eaten anything all day.

Mateo backs out of the steep driveway and takes a left toward the eastbound highway.

I clear my throat. "Why'd you stop over?"

A puzzled look crosses his face.

"I mean...Junior and the rest of the crew worked all day. They just left a few hours ago. They ate the rest of the chicken salad I made for lunch."

His eyes narrow briefly, and he hums in question then cries dramatically, feigning shock. ""What? You gave away my chicken salad?" He laughs. "That is not right!"

I shrug playfully. "Hey, you weren't around again so I let them have it. Somebody had to eat it."

His entire body stiffens at my words before his mouth slowly morphs into a salacious grin. "Don't say things like that to me, Cat."

"Like what? I have no idea what you're talking about," I state casually, biting my inner cheek to force back a smile.

"Somehow I don't believe you."

I freeze. "I'm not lying to you!"

Judging by the expression on Mateo's face, I think I've overreacted so I offer a small smile. "I wouldn't lie to you. They really seemed to enjoy it. This one guy moaned when he finished."

After cursing beneath his breath, Mateo remains quiet for a moment.

"I meant to call you today, but I didn't have a chance. I thought maybe you were still mad at me so I had to come see for myself."

"Mad at you?" I chuckle lightly. "I wasn't mad at you."

"Oh, that's right." He winks. "I wasn't sure if I was forgiven or not after I gave you a ride...home."

My cheeks flush pink, enjoying his *not so* subtle reminder of me pleasuring myself on his lap.

"So what'd you do today aside from feeding my guys?"

"I spent the day picking herbs in the garden with my grandmother, but I think I got a little too much color though. See?" I adjust the material on my shoulder to reveal the line of lighter skin surrounded by red.

"That line looks thin," he remarks after inspecting it closely at a red light.

"Bikini tops usually are," I retort with a smirk.

His nostrils flare subtly and his jaw ticks.

"How'd your appointment go?" I ask, reaching for the knob to change the radio station to something more alternative.

"Good." He nods before continuing, "It went pretty well and I'm really excited about it." A hopeful smile crosses his face. "I should know more in a few days."

"Is it a big job?"

He hums, tipping his head side to side while considering my question. "It could be the biggest thing I've ever done."

"That's great that you've gotten this big job. You do really good work. Do you have a portfolio of the houses you've worked on?"

"I do, actually."

"I'd love to see it someday...if you don't mind." My finger stills when I hear Dashboard Confessional's newest song. "Great song!"

Mateo reaches for the knob and I fear he's going to change it so I cover his hand, preventing his movement. "I'm just raising the volume."

I nod and remove my hand, instantly missing the contact.

"So aside from walking around in your bikini top in front of my guys and picking herbs, what else did you do?"

I smile then slowly inhale a small breath, my chest rising and falling with so many emotions. "It seems my grandmother is getting worse by the day, but I did manage to get some writing done," I answer honestly but don't elaborate. This guy doesn't want to know about my life. "I'm glad you came by. It was a welcomed surprise."

Mateo pulls the truck into an open lot covered in dirt and gravel. Several other vehicles are parked rather haphazardly since there are no lines or parking spaces. A weathered green sign with red letters signifies the restaurant's name. I scrunch my nose then bite my lip to mask my unease.

"What's the matter?"

"What?" I ask, realizing the expression on my face is a dead giveaway.

"Are you a picky eater?"

"No!" I blurt. "Well, sometimes a little. It used to drive my parents crazy."

"What'd you do? Sneak food under the table for the dog?"

I laugh remembering how many times I begged for a dog so I could do that very thing. It was something that always happened in the movies.

"Not quite. I learned to mix the food together so the flavor I liked masked the others."

"How did you survive nearly a year in Asia?"

I squawk, "Asia?"

He replies sheepishly. "Yeah, your grandmother said you were in Asia earlier this year."

I nod with understanding as my lips tighten into a hard line. "I wasn't in Asia."

"You weren't? Where were you then?"

"Africa."

"She was close," he responds playfully. "...it does start with an A."

We share a moment of laughter at my grandmother's expense.

Mateo looks at the cars pulling in to the lot and asks, "Why Africa?"

Looking directly into those beautiful pools of brown and green, I counter, "Why not Africa? It didn't hurt that I know someone who was from Africa. When he asked me to visit, I jumped at the chance and ended up staying to help."

"He?" he inquires with raised brows.

I grin, detecting a speck of jealousy. "Yes, *he* is a sixty-five-year-old man who left his village as a boy, taught at Yale and now, in his retirement, runs a volunteer organization in Guinea."

Mateo starts to laugh. "You said all that with a straight face...I almost believed you. But don't worry, I have my ways of getting the truth out of you."

"It is the truth!" I retort with a grimace, slapping his bicep.

He nods as if placating me. "Ok, Pinocchio." He links his fingers with mine and raises them to his mouth. Keeping his eyes on me, he kisses my knuckles sweetly.

"Back to food. Tell me what you ate there?"

Shaking my head then rolling my eyes, I tell him how

I lost nearly twenty pounds from eating nothing but yams, green bananas and cassava. "I wouldn't eat a lot of the other food. Especially the meat."

"I don't have that problem." Suggestive, hazel eyes turn to meet mine. "I always eat what's in front of me." A pink tongue slips through and moistens his luscious lips.

An unfamiliar feeling, one that I hadn't realized was dormant until recently, awakens and causes my core to throb, the ache shooting straight through me.

"You're—" My cheeks flame as if they were burned by the sun.

"I'm what?" he teases, prompting me to answer as if he's enjoying the torturous game.

"You're bad!"

Shifting his position, he leans forward to whisper in my ear. His proximity drives me wild and I shiver. With his full lips at my lobe, a raspy timbre growls, "You have no idea how bad I can be."

My reaction is not what he expected when laughter from the pit of my belly erupts and slices right through the sexual tension like a hot knife through butter.

"You're good with your words. A real smooth operator."

Mateo pulls back and joins in my amusement then begins singing the words to Smooth Operator by Sade, snapping his fingers to keep rhythm.

"You can sing and you're funny! I'm impressed. I think I like you even more now."

He grins roguishly.

"Seriously...you can really sing." I can't contain the surprise in my tone. "You've got a great voice."

"So I've been told," he states, opening the door. He glances at me curiously. "Wait, did I hear you correctly? I think you said you like me even more now."

I stammer as I get out of the truck. "Uhhh..."

"Don't worry. I already knew."

"Who said I liked you?" I demand with mock annoyance. "My gram?"

He laughs and shakes his head, sliding his pinched fingers across his lips.

"Just so you know you can't believe a word she says. Her mind..." I spin my finger in a circular motion near my temple.

"She's adorable," he comments.

I appreciate the sincerity in his compliment.

"Ready to go?" Mateo asks, extending a hand. My eyes fall to the sweet gesture and I smile then nod as I slide my hand into his.

"Ready."

Upon entering the small restaurant, I feel as though I've been transported to another world. The décor and the vibe scream Little Havana right down to the lively music and beautiful people. An older man stops to greet Mateo with a hearty handshake and a huge smile. A quick conversation in Spanish ensues between them.

"This way," Mateo takes my hand once again, links his fingers with mine and leads me to a square table by the back.

"Don't we have to wait for the hostess to seat us?" I call out after him.

"Hey, Teo!" a voice booms. I look to see the bartender waving from across the restaurant.

A smile is returned as a greeting.

"What is this place?" I ask, taking in the atmosphere as the aroma wafts into my nose.

"A slice of heaven."

A waitress with gorgeous soft skin, hair as dark as midnight and red rosy lips approaches and kisses Mateo's cheek. "Haven't seen you in a while."

"Ahhh, I've been busy," he offers almost apologetically.

She looks at me through the corner of her dark brown eyes and her lips tip down into a frown.

He continues to assuage the hurt look on her face.

"What's up with you? Things good?"

The smile he gives her is laced with intimacy and respect. A shot of jealousy injects directly into my veins, and I move my hands out from underneath his, but his hold tightens and he pins me with a hard look.

"You never answer my texts or calls. I've left you a million messages."

He returns his attention to her, rolling those beautiful eyes and tightening his lips. "You know how I feel about that."

"Iza," the bartender calls in the distance, drawing my attention to the fresh mint being muddled in a tall tumbler. The goddess of curves standing in front of us turns and waves her pen in the air, signaling her impending return.

"What are you guys having to drink?"

Looking up at her, I respond quickly—too quickly. "Mojito?"

"Are you asking or telling?" she snickers with a grin.

I smile tightly, feeling slightly embarrassed, hating the jealousy I feel toward this woman. "Mojito."

"Bucanero," he replies.

"And to eat?"

Mateo's lips part and a symphony of the most romantic and erotic words slips through as he points to various items on the plastic-coated menu.

"Bueno," she agrees before she departs.

With Mateo's gaze still on me, his lips remain in a sexy smirk, his mouth says nothing until the moment of awkwardness, the quiet lull, passes.

"Do you come here often?" I ask, my eyes slipping from his face to the tanned skin of his neck.

"Are you trying to pick me up?" he inquires playfully with the slight tilting of his head.

It's my turn to offer a side grin. "Funny, Donny D."

"Donny D? Who's that?"

I laugh, refusing to reveal my nickname for him. "Nothing. Tell me how long you've been coming here."

"Since it opened a few years ago. They have the best Cuban food around."

I scrunch my nose, a sign of my skepticism until my expression softens. Remembering the way his tongue rolled against his teeth or the way Spanish words floated from his lips when he ordered a variety of food from the menu spreads a lustful glow across my face.

"You're very... expressive," he comments.

I blink furiously and clear my throat. "Um...how so?"

Leaning forward, Mateo closes the space between us and whispers, "I'd give anything to know what you were just thinking about."

I lose all sense of control and close my eyes. Floating away on a cloud of lust, I lick my lips before reopening my eyes. "Food," I mumble almost incoherently. "I was thinking about food."

"Food is good...especially when the taste lingers on your tongue."

I gulp and pull back as Iza sets our drinks down on round coasters made of thick paper. I thank her before taking a quick drink to distract myself from the conversation filled with beautiful Spanish words and coy smiles that flow reciprocally between her and my dinner companion.

I resist the urge to ask who she is or comment on her attractiveness.

"So tell me about you."

I sigh. "There's not much to tell. I live with my gram and my pain in the ass uncle. I graduated from college and spent some time in Africa. End of story."

He nods intently. "Parents? Siblings?"

My eyes round in worry as confusion appears on his face. I rely on a diversion to distract him from inquiring more about my family.

"I had tons of stuffed animals whom I considered my siblings when I was a kid. And I was a nerd. I read everything I could." I laugh at the memories. "There was this one time I read about Mount Kilimanjaro for a class project and everyone was convinced I really went there."

"Sounds like you're a good storyteller."

I shrug nonchalantly.

"How about your parents?"

Anxiety creeps in at the inquisition. "My mom died when I was younger and I don't have much of a relationship with my dad." Sadness mocks me. "At least I don't anymore."

Reaching across the table, Mateo takes my free hand in his and slides his thumb over my skin. "Shit, I'm sorry. I didn't know."

"Thanks. It sucked for a long time, but then you learn to move on."

"Were you close? he asks softly.

Warmth emanates from my heart. "We were two peas in a pod. We had so much in common. We liked the same music, movies and our style in clothing was pretty much the same...until she left."

"So she was a hippie, too?"

My mouth drops open. "I'm not a hippie! I prefer to call it eclectic."

His eyes drop to the V-neck oversized shirt where my cleavage peaks through and several colorful necklaces hang.

"Nice necklaces."

My fingers slide upward and glide over the cheap, cosmetic metal. "I picked these up at work the other day."

"Where do you work?"

I toss him a side-eye, knowing he's already seen me bartend.

"I know you bartend, but your grandmother said you work two jobs. What else do you do?"

"I run an online sex chat room," I deadpan. "I'm good

with words."

A sexy chuckle releases from his lips as he suppresses a full-blown guffaw, knowing I'm teasing.

"Me, too."

I lean forward, eyes bulging. "You do online sex chats?"

Moments slip by as he penetrates me with a dark expression.

"I'm good with words. You said so yourself." He laughs.

I sip the refreshing beverage and shake my head.

"Now tell me where you really work."

My grin widens and my excitement bursts through, imagining myself perusing the aisles of clothing. "I help out at the consignment shop downtown. It doesn't pay much, but Trina is fun to work with and I get first dibs on the clothes. My mom introduced me to second-hand stores."

He chuckles, but I get the feeling he's mocking me.

"What?"

"I've never heard of anyone so excited to wear someone else's hand-me-downs."

"You'd be surprised. Some people in this city wear things once and toss them aside."

He nods as he considers that fact.

The tempo of the music changes and there's an electric charge in the air. I feel Mateo's movements before I actually *see* him when he begins to tap on the edge of the table. His head bobs and his shoulders sway as his fingers move in sync with the percussionist who is sitting on stage, beating the drum into submission.

"I love this song!"

Mesmerized, I keep my eyes on the person in front of me and laugh with excitement and humor when he raises his hands, clapping them above his head before rising to his feet.

"Baila conmigo." He extends a hand and offers a smile that I can't resist. "Come on, dance with me."

"Here?" I squawk.

His fingers beckon me once again. "Here."

"I'm going to embarrass you," I sing with promise, standing and placing my hand in his. "I don't have much rhythm when it comes to dancing."

His lips thin and stretch across his face, revealing a bright smile. Mateo's arms welcome me and pull my breasts flush against his hard body. I can feel the heat emanating from his skin. A smile tickles my lips when my cheek lands on his chest close to his broad shoulder. Slowly, a trail, led by my eyes, travels upward to his neck then his face. I blink lazily and consider his eyes. Eyes filled with mischief. Eyes filled with intrigue. Eyes filled with desire.

"Just hold on," he warns as he moves behind me, pushing his hard front into my back. One hand spreads across my ribcage while the other slides over my arms until he grips my fingertips. I feel the slow rolling of his hips as he guides my body, swaying me left then right. "It's all about your hips." In an instant, I'm spun around and pulled tightly to face him.

Mateo places a firm hand at the small of my back and joins our bodies as if they are one. Never once pulling his eyes from mine, he steps forward then back and rotates his hips, moving with the music, making love to me without shedding a single article of clothing. Under his guidance, I follow effortlessly and match his every step. My body, fueled by sensuality and passion, ignites into a frenzy. I laugh, loving every second. Flying out, my body spins as I twirl beneath Mateo's fingers. I struggle to contain my pleasure as I toss my head back and laugh while he sings along to every word as if he'd written the lyrics himself. I hit Mateo's chest with a hard thump. I look up and see his roguish smile just before he lowers his head, skimming my cheek with his until he reaches my ear.

"You're a good dancer," he murmurs with a sexy rasp.

The proximity of his mouth to my earlobe causes my tongue to peek out and glide across my lips in anticipation as I draw my eyes upward. "You're a good teacher."

"You know what they say about a man who can dance, right?" I ask teasingly as he continues to move us around.

His eyes challenge me humorously.

"That he's probably gay."

Mateo's hand slips lower to grab my ass, cupping flesh and squeezing it before he pushes his erection into my stomach and raises an eyebrow.

"I feel it in my veins." Mateo continues to hold my attention and my body even closer until, as it had mere minutes before, the tempo changes back to its original form. "Music...it's in my blood."

I bite my lip as my eyes drop to his mouth. All this talk about veins and blood conjures up the image of him sliding his rock-solid length into me.

I clear my throat as he holds my gaze. "You would love the African culture. Music is such a big part of who they are."

He narrows his eyes. "I'd love to go there." He pushes against me once again.

I'm no match for Mateo Cruz as my face flushes pink.

I don't want to remove my hands from his arms. I don't want to peel my body away from his. I don't want this moment to ever end.

My fingers itch to slide through his hair, to tug firmly at the base of his neck and angle his face. I long to press my lips against his and to kiss him until the sun breaks through the dark night sky.

Mateo sings softly in my ear as we continue to move together in a slower pattern.

"What's this song about?"

"Lovers." His lips pull back into a sly grin. "He's chasing her, but she keeps running away."

"Sounds cliché." I look away from the intensity of his stare.

"Actually, there's more to the whole story. They were

young lovers, but he wanted to give her more than he could offer so he set off to make something of himself. When he returned, she was engaged to someone else. She didn't wait for him."

"What a bitch!" I quip.

"Well, he did make promises he didn't keep and, in doing so, he broke her heart. In the song, he tells her all the reasons he loves her, reminds her of the flame between them, and tells all that he's going to do to win her back."

"Sounds terribly romantic," I reply dryly, thinking about the tale of broken promises and broken hearts.

"You don't think it's romantic?"

"I don't believe in romance. Eventually people's feelings change and bad things happen. People get married and profess their undying love and then somehow end up falling in love with someone else."

Mateo cocks his head to the side, watching me carefully as if trying to understand my words.

"I take it there's an ex out there who broke your heart."

He moves us effortlessly to the music, hypnotizing me with his scent and proximity to reveal more.

My breath hitches and I shrug, breaking contact with his eyes.

Tucked beneath his chin with one hand clasped with his between our chests, Mateo continues to dance slowly until his name is called.

"Teo," Iza calls, "La comida."

"Food's here," he announces, his voice jarring me from a quiet trance. I draw a glance upward to meet his face and find him staring down at me.

"What?" I ask shyly.

A soft kiss graces my forehead and whispered words are uttered. "Broken hearts can be mended."

He doesn't wait for a response, choosing instead to lead me back to the table by the hand where he pulls the chair out and waits for me to sit. His hands remain on the back of the seat while he lowers his face so his mouth is close to my ear.

"Gracias por el baile."

"Thank you," I return his words of gratitude.

Set before us are several beautifully presented, Caribbean-inspired entrees served on large, colorful square dishes. The aroma and spices infiltrate my nose, yet I manage to keep a straight face to hide my apprehension.

"Close your eyes."

I respond with a wrinkled brow.

"Trust me."

It's a command not a question.

My lids close slowly and my sense of smell and hearing are heightened.

I hear the fork scrape against the porcelain as food is gathered.

"Inhale."

My eyes open and I see the raised utensil hovering before me. A look of warning passes over Mateo's face.

"Close your eyes and inhale."

I oblige, following his directions.

"Now tell me what you smell."

Licking my lips, I swallow hard and make every effort to concentrate, but the lingering memory of his expression distracts me.

"Smells... spicy."

"Try again. Concentrate this time."

Again, I moisten my lips and inhale slowly.

"Garlic."

"Go on," he encourages.

"Peppers and onions ...and..."

I can't seem to figure out the overpowering scent, but it's fresh yet spicy.

"Cilantro," he adds. "Now open."

My eyes open involuntarily.

He shakes his head once and murmurs. "Mouth."

The one word draws my attention to his mouth as he cools the food down with a slow breath of air.

"Keep your eyes closed."

The red and green lights on the makeshift stage and the faces of the other people in the restaurant disappear for a final time when I close my eyes. My mouth opens and every taste bud on my tongue buzzes with anticipation, preparing for the introduction. He moans quietly when my lips close around the fork tines.

I chew slowly, combining the grains of fluffy rice and flavorful, melt-in-your mouth, tender meat together to form an explosive marriage in my mouth.

"Good, right?"

My eyes snap open as I swallow. "Oh, my God!" I screech with exhilaration. "That was incredible! What is it?"

Mateo gathers a second helping and slides it into my mouth before he feeds himself. With a knowing grin, he chews slowly then swallows. The movement of his throat and the idea of the same utensil in both of our mouths are erotic and tantalizing. I feel my body temperature rise.

"*Ropa vieja,*" he utters before providing a full explanation of all the ingredients and preparation needed to create this masterpiece.

"That's a lot of work," I comment on the laborious task.

"But it's worth it." He scoops up a small flattened banana chip, drizzles it with a green sauce then offers it to me. "Try this."

I savor the crispy fried goodness and enjoy the combination of flavors.

"That's good too. Some kind of banana? It's sweet and salty."

He flashes me a wicked grin as he sinks his teeth into the other half as chimichurri sauce coats the side of his mouth.

"*Platano maduro,*" he says once his mouth is empty.

I take a sip then help myself to more stewed meat.

Pointing to the other two entrees, Mateo rolls his tongue, using delicate Spanish words to explain what each dish is. Bravery and courage have joined forces as I taste and venture into the unknown.

Iza stops at our table to check on our food, and I offer a tight smile when I overload my fork and rice falls onto the plate.

Left alone once again, I lean forward. "You realize I have no idea what you're saying, but the words you're using sound so erotic."

"Erotic, huh?"

"I mean exotic." I chuckle, looking away from the mischievous look in his eye.

A symphony of hypnotic and mesmerizing words floats from his perfect mouth and a chorus of rolled sounds, revealing his pink tongue, make me fall even more in love with this foreign language.

"Spanish is a beautiful language."

He counters. "I think any language is beautiful. It's all about the words and the story being told."

I nod in agreement, wishing I had immediate access to my journal so I could capture this experience and all the emotions running rampant through my body.

"That's probably why I love music so much," he breathes.

"Me too—well, I used to." My voice matches the melancholy expression on my face.

He blinks slowly as if trying to gauge my response.

"When I was a kid, I had an uncle who was in a band. He was a meanest son of a bitch, but as soon as the music came on, he became an entirely different person on stage. He came alive."

"Were you close to him?"

"Not really. He only took an interest in me when he realized I could sing. Everyone wanted to see the little kid who could sing like Tito Nieves."

The surprises keep coming. "I didn't know you actually sang in front of people."

"There's a lot you don't know about me."

I raise my glass, offering a *touché* as he uses my own words against me.

"Where'd you grow up?" I ask, beginning a deluge of inquiries.

"I kind of bounced back and forth between New York and Puerto Rico."

"You?"

"I've been here my whole life except for the few years down south."

He cocks a thick dark eyebrow with curiosity.

"I'll save that story for next time."

A crooked grin tugs at his tanned cheek.

"What's that for?" I tip my chin at his expression.

"I'm glad there'll be a *next* time."

"It's just an expression and you *are* working at my gram's for a few weeks so I'm bound to run into you."

I know humor shines in my eyes and the slurping of my beverage adds to the playfulness radiating between us.

"It might take me months if your grandmother keeps changing the plan."

Tightening my lips, I shake my head adamantly, sadness and frustration marring my countenance. "I know she can't help it, but she's driving me crazy."

He rushes to her defense. "She seems like a nice lady... even if she is trying to pawn you off to anyone who'll take you."

I gasp. "*Pawn me off?*"

"Oh, yeah. She told me all about the trouble you caused when you were younger."

Although I know he's teasing me, it wouldn't be the first time my past has been spread around like wildfire.

"Maybe I'll have to fire you and hire someone else to finish the house."

"Who's getting fired?" Iza asks, stepping up to the table, beginning the task of clearing dishes. "Teo doesn't need that job. He's gonna be a st—"

A single utterance in Spanish silences her immediately.

Iza clears the dishes, heaving stern looks in his direction as the tension between them builds.

With a gentle hand placed lightly on the center of my back, Mateo guides me out of the restaurant to where his truck is parked. He hasn't spoken a word aside from asking if I was ready to leave. I want to rewind the minutes back to the light-hearted atmosphere we shared.

"Thanks for dinner," I say with a smile as we exit the parking lot. "I'll grab the check next time. It's only fair."

Mateo tosses me a sideways glance and smirks. "I don't think so."

The ride back to my house is filled with easy laughter. A light banter ricochets between us, each challenging the other with music trivia.

"No way! I don't believe it! That was a Whitney Houston original."

"Wanna bet? Google it," he encourages.

"Yes!" I reach into my bag and pull my phone from the bottom, my fingers searching frantically, desperate to set him straight. I tap the button and speak while my eyes challenge his. "Siri…"

Scanning the site, my hidden suspicion that he knows more about music than I do is confirmed when there in black and white, a long sentence declares Dolly Parton to be the original lyricist of the song *I Will Always Love You.*

"Damn," I growl, closing the app on my phone. My pride takes a hit of defeat. "*How* did you know that?"

"I'm a fan of music. I pay attention to the words and the story they tell."

"I do, too, but that's just weird that you knew that."

He shrugs his broad shoulders before he angles his head to look at me. "You, *mamacita,* lost a bet."

The term of endearment tickles my belly and I suppress the growing throb in my core. "We didn't shake on it." I cross my arm and shield my tightening nipples.

He extends his large hand, turning it palm up and rests it across my thigh. He looks at me with hooded eyes. "No, but you gave me your word. Doesn't that count for something?"

Wordlessly, my hand is invited to join his. I slide my hand along the callused skin of his palm and link my fingers with his.

"My word is good." I confirm with an awkward shake of our joined hands.

"I need to tell you something."

Closing my eyes briefly, I hope he can't see the disappointment on my face if he says there won't be a next time.

"I'm not rea—" Mateo expels the air from his lungs in a deep sigh. "I'm not ready for tonight to end." His thumb glides over my hand.

A small smile tugs at my lips as my heart soars with joy combined with relief. "Me neither. What'd you have in mind?"

Signaling to the left, Mateo veers the truck, detouring from the route to my house and takes us fifteen minutes along the southbound highway before finally exiting to a small coastline town.

"I haven't been here in years," I comment as I step out of the truck.

The sound of gentle waves crashing onto the shore fills the quiet night.

Mateo takes my hand and leads me to the sand where I immediately kick off my shoes while he does the same.

Walking barefoot along the beach, we make our way to the wooden pier that juts out over the ocean. I release his hand and lean on the railing with bent elbows. Against a moonless sky, a million stars sparkle in the distance.

"It's so peaceful, isn't it?" I ask, glancing to the side where he mirrors my position.

He hums in agreement as he looks up to the sky before snapping a quick picture of me with his phone.

"It's going to be dark," I tease.

"I'd still see you."

"If you go could anywhere in the world, where would you go?"

Shrugging, he says, "I'm not sure. I've not traveled much. I thought about joining the military when I was younger because I wanted to travel."

"Really?" I ask, surprised at this revelation. "You don't strike me as a military man."

"Yeah, I don't take orders well."

Mateo's hands find my waist, spin me around and lift me up onto the wide railing.

"Don't let me go!" I yelp, linking my fingers together behind his neck.

"Never." He tilts his head up and kisses me.

I relish the feel of his warm tongue in my mouth and my fingers run through his silky hair as I widen my legs, inviting him to move closer. A flutter rises in my core and I shiver.

When Mateo finally brings our kiss to a close, I press my forehead against his. "I love kissing you."

Grabbing the back of my head, Mateo plunges his tongue into my mouth once again, devouring every moan that escapes. "I could kiss you all night."

I smile and hum my pleasure.

"Where would you go?" he asks.

The answer flies out of my mouth quickly. "Back to Africa. Someday I'll get back there. I love those people."

"How long were you there?"

"Almost eight months."

"And you came home because of your grandmother?"

I nod.

"What'd you do there?" he asks, inquiring about my time in the small village.

I grin. "I can tell you I didn't do *this.*" I pull his face closer, putting an end to the conversation.

An hour slips by as we kiss until our lips are swollen and our jaws sore. He groans and complains about how hard he is while I reveal how wet I am.

"We could always do something about this problem," I whisper in his ear.

"Don't tempt me," he growls, removing me carefully from the railing.

"I don't know what it is about you that's making me this crazy." I snake my arms around his waist and hug him. "Gram was right. I do like you."

"Good...because I like you, too. A lot."

He kisses the top of my head. "I should probably get you home."

Quiet sounds of old love songs escort us back to my house until Mateo pulls into the driveway and shuts off the truck's engine.

My phone vibrates with an incoming text message. After responding curtly to my uncle, I note the time is after midnight.

"I didn't realize it's so late. You're going to be tired tomorrow."

"It *is* tomorrow and sleep is overrated," he comments with a cheeky grin.

"Can I ask you to do me a favor?"

He angles his head to look at me. "Whatever you need."

"Please don't wake me up too early."

"I probably won't be here too early anyway. I'm going to be up for a while longer."

I tip my head with confusion. "It's late. Where are you

going?"

He looks down at the bulge in his jeans.

"Ohhhh...gotcha."

"What are *you* going to do?" he asks suggestively.

"I'm probably going to finish what I started earlier today."

"Can I watch?" He teases suggestively.

"Oh my God! Is sex all you ever think about?"

He nods proudly. "I am a man. It's how our brains work."

I roll my eyes. "I was thinking about you earlier today when I was...writing...on paper...with a pencil."

He smiles at me then speaks with a low and sexy voice. "Me, huh? What exactly were you thinking about?

"Everything. Anything." *Sex.*

"You write sappy love songs that rhyme, don't you?" His fingers squeeze gently as his words tease.

Mortified and slightly offended by his insinuation, I take a moment to respond, inhaling quietly, thinking about the hundreds of pages I've written over the past few years.

I close a second hand around his where my thumb circles slowly. As if I'm sitting in a confessional at church, whispered words reveal my secrets.

"Wait a minute...how did you know I write songs?"

Guiltily, Mateo looks away and immediately I know Gram has something to do with it.

"Don't always believe everything she says. You never know what's going to come out of her mouth these days."

He smiles warmly as if to soften the blow of my grandmother's betrayal. "You didn't answer my question."

"Yes, I write love songs, but they're not always romantic. I write about experiences. Good ones, bad ones, happy times, sad times. Sometimes I write about beauty and pain. Other times I write about desperation and triumph. Everything I write is from the heart. It's organic and raw."

He offers a quick subtle nod. "You seem very wise for your age."

"Oh, yeah, I'm really an owl," I reply through quiet, surprised laughter, remembering my mother saying similar words to me many years ago. "I've heard that before. My mother used to say I was an old soul in a little girl's body."

Mateo's body shifts, angling himself so our lips are only a breath away. My eyes wander, slowly moving over the structure of his cheekbones, his full eyebrows, the small scar on his forehead until they meet his. My heart quickens with anticipation when he casts a look of pure understanding mingled with heady desire.

I can hear nothing but the sound of our shallow breathing.

With deliberate and slow movements, Mateo caresses his face against mine, touching my skin lightly with his warmth, allowing his lips to slide along my jaw and travel effortlessly to the sensitive spot below my ear.

A flutter rolls in the pit of my stomach, and my hands tighten around his. A delicious tension builds between us, forcing me to clench my core and suppress the need for release.

"Mate—Oh," I yelp and toss my head back when he sucks my earlobe into his mouth and clamps down gently with his teeth before adding in a swirl of his warm tongue. The simple act leaves me wanton and desperate to rip my clothes off.

When his lips finally meet mine, each touch is soft and sensual. He pulls his hand from my grasp and cradles my head, deepening the kiss which elicits a moan of desire.

I struggle to speak against his lips. The invitation to follow me upstairs to my bedroom is quashed when he flies and pins me against the leather seats. My legs fall wide, welcoming the hard length of his body pressing into mine. My greedy hands roam over the thin cotton T-shirt covering his back, and my fingers yearn to claw at his skin.

His mouth continues to pleasure mine. With each roll of his tongue, Mateo adds a swivel of his hips into my heat. I feel his erection strain against his jeans, begging for release.

Mateo releases a distorted curse, breaking apart the joining of our mouths. Not wanting to forfeit this kiss, I smash my lips against his once again, desire making me desperate.

"Cat," he sighs heavily and curses again. "We have to stop." He drops his forehead onto mine. "Not like this."

I pinch my lips closed, refraining from telling him to shut up.

"I don't want to fuck you for the first time inside my work truck."

My head lolls to the side and a smile spreads across my face. I feel my face flame bright red. An eruption of giggles fills the cab.

"What's so funny?"

"For being so talented with words, you're not very original." I pinch my lips and constrict my eyes slightly. "It sounds so primitive...Neanderthal-ish."

Mateo exhales sharply and shakes his head. "Never in my life have I been shut down because of the word *fuck*. Most women love to hear it."

A pang of jealousy riddles my body at the idea of him with other women.

"Lucky for you, I'm not most women." I waggle my eyebrows playfully.

"Lucky for me is right." Mateo lowers his lips and kisses me slowly. "What would you prefer? Make love?"

I gauge the reflection in his eyes and see lust looking at me. This—whatever this is— is a temporary issue of lust and desire. It's about getting what you can't have. It's about the chase. It's about putting my body out of misery.

"Come to think about it...fuck is fine."

The dark driveway illuminates suddenly when the spotlight attached to the house goes on, and I feel as though I'm sixteen years old again being called in by a watchful guardian.

"Guess you've got to get in the house," he chuckles. "I don't want your grandmother to get mad at me." Lifting his body, he moves to sit in the driver's seat.

"Gram wouldn't get mad at you. She'd love any man who agrees to date me."

From my peripheral vision, I see him stiffen subtly.

"Not that we're dating," I stammer in correction. "Bad choice of words."

Sensing my agitation, Mateo reaches for my hand reassuringly. "Not a bad choice of words. I..." he pauses, "just didn't expect you."

A thousand different emotions begin to rise and lodge themselves in my throat.

"Thanks for dinner." Anxiety and sudden nerves taint my quiet voice.

"Thank you for coming."

I meet his eyes and smile at the humor reflected in them.

"To dinner," he adds. "Thank you for the dance and the kiss."

"Yeah, sure. No problem. Anytime," I quip, reaching for the door handle to remove myself from the awkward situation.

"Hey." He reaches for my hand and I turn back. "Let me walk you to the door."

My lips tighten. An adamant refusal moves my head quickly from side to side. "No, that's okay. You don't have to do that."

Ignoring me, he retorts, "I wasn't asking for your permission."

He exits the truck and walks over to my side before I hop down.

"A gentleman opens the door and always walks a lady home." With a smirk, Mateo offers his right arm.

"Did you just make that up?" I ask, linking my elbow with

his as I walk alongside him.

"No, I heard it in a movie once."

"At least you're honest. I wouldn't want anyone to accuse you of lying or worse—plagiarism."

"Never!" he boasts, stopping at the back door. "I'm too *original* for that." A bright and playful smile stretches from ear to ear as he leans in to place a soft kiss on my cheek.

My eyes close and I relish the feel of his lips on my skin.

"You have the softest lips," I murmur, reopening my eyes to find him staring at me. "I said that out loud, didn't I?"

He nods and brings his mouth close to mine, letting his tongue slide across my bottom lip. "I bet your lips are really soft, too."

Goosebumps dot my arms, and I shiver just thinking about his mouth on me *there*.

"Go inside, Cat."

I nod in agreement as I reach behind me for the door handle. My fingers curl around the knob but find resistance.

"It's locked," I mumble.

"Don't you have a key?"

Rendered speechless from his kiss, I nod and bend my knees to reach beneath the mat, my fingers searching blindly because my eyes remain fixed on his. With the metal key in hand, I begin a slow ascent. My gaze travels down his body and lands on his midsection, lingering at his groin where I detect the firmness and see the strain against his jeans.

Do not touch I silently admonish myself until I come to a full upright position.

"That's not a very good hiding spot." He smiles devilishly, letting his eyes shine with humor.

"I don't have anything to hide and nothing in this house is of much value."

"I beg to differ," he retorts, his eyes roaming down the length of my body.

"I think I need to go inside," I stammer.

Nodding, he takes a step closer and lowers his lips to my ear, causing the tightening of my core to resume. "I think you're right."

"I'll see you tomorrow."

"Yes, you will." His voice is marked with conviction, his hazel eyes filled with promise.

Chapter Four

MY ATTEMPT TO SLEEP IN WAS THWARTED BY MY excitement to see Mateo again. Without the sound of early morning hammering, I slept like a baby. After waking up and showering before Mateo and his crew arrived, I threw on a white sundress and strappy sandals and even applied a swipe a pink lip gloss while the Pandora app boomed with my Sixties Rock Station. Hoping to look presentable and somewhat normal, I ran curl product through my hair and prayed it'll help contain the wild, nearly bleach-blond mane in this humidity.

I stand before the mirror hanging on the back of my door and nod. *Presentable. Normal.* A rap to my bedroom window draws my attention and I see Mateo in the mirror's reflection. I turn immediately and walk quickly, almost skipping, to the window.

"What are you doing?" I ask after lifting the window and looking down to the driveway where two men work, carrying bags of material. "And why are you looking in my window?"

"I had to see you," Mateo replies with a grin.

Excitement floods me although skepticism also rises. "I was on the way downstairs to see you."

"You really should close your curtains," he warns.

I tip my head and grin. "I don't usually have men looking through my bedroom window."

"Move that." He nods his chin, pointing to the small lamp on the bedside table.

Once the light fixture is placed on the floor, I watch carefully as he maneuvers his long legs followed by the rest of his body. A smile spreads across my face at the sight of this beautiful man struggling to climb through my bedroom window.

Mateo cracks his neck when his work boots touch the hardwood and he stands completely.

"Good morning," he says, taking a step to close the gap between us.

I look up and smile. "Good morn—"

My face is suddenly cupped by two tanned hands and a soft kissed is placed on my lips. He inhales quietly and kisses me again, adding in a gentle lick of his tongue. I raise my hands; one finds his waist while the other glides across his back. The contact ignites my body and I pull him closer and guide us back a few steps. He follows my lead until the back of my legs hit the cotton sheets of my bed. Our lips separate and he looks down at me, searching my face while his thumb caresses my cheek eventually sliding over my closed lips. I know what he sees. He sees a woman drenched with lust, desire in her eyes and wantonness in her expression.

And he responds.

Pushing me back onto my bed, Mateo covers my body with his. I am wonderfully sandwiched between the softness of my comforter and the ropes of hard muscle beneath his warm skin. My legs widen, allowing him full access to my core. His hands roam over my neck and shoulder as his mouth crashes into mine. The heat between us is palpable and the chemistry undeniable. With desperate kisses and tiny nibbles, he embarks on a southbound journey, exploring my body for the first time. The straps of my sundress are yanked down, exposing the soft ivory skin of my breasts. Attention is given to each one when he opens his mouth, taking my hardened nipple in and massaging it with his supple tongue.

A quiet moan emerges as my lips part and I struggle for air, each breath is ragged and desperate.

My hands grip the nape of his neck and slide into his silky damp hair, attempting to return his lips to mine. Sensing my need for his mouth, he kisses my breast for a final time then dots my neck and jaw with tender kisses before ravaging my mouth.

Our tongues move with desire, tangling as our bodies had done when we danced at the restaurant.

Leaving his lips pressed against mine, Mateo brings our kiss to a slower pace and then finally to a close. My eyes open slowly, my brain registering the predicament we're in.

"What are you doing?" I mumble breathlessly against his lips before clarifying, "What are *we* doing?"

I notice a glimmer of humor in his eyes when he responds. "I don't know about you, but I'm on a coffee break."

"Coffee break? What time did you get here?"

"Seven."

"I thought you just got here," I breathe.

He shakes his head. "Nope. I've been sitting on the roof. You were sleeping soundly before. I didn't want to wake you."

A combination of embarrassment and thrill flies through me. "You saw me sleeping?"

"I already told you I had to see you."

"Where's everyone else?"

"They went to get coffee."

Returning his lips to my neck, Mateo nibbles his way and fuels my need. Without the distraction of his lips kissing mine, I feel the full weight of his body and my deep inhale reveals my arduous effort to breathe.

"Whoa!" I yelp when Mateo rolls over and pulls me on top of him. "You're making me dizzy."

A cocky grin tugs on his cheek and he whispers in my ear, "Just wait. You're going to see stars when I'm done with you."

I gulp.

His hands grip my straddled legs and push the linen material to expose my thighs while his thumb brushes lightly over the soft cotton that covers my buzzing flesh. I close my eyes and give in to the darkness.

"Do you have any idea what I want to do to you?" His voice is low and filled with promise.

"I have some ideas."

Skimming his lips over my skin, he murmurs, "Where should I start?"

Anywhere I want to scream, but knowing his workers will be back shortly, a wave of disappointment washes over me. Time isn't on our side.

I hide my face in my palms then drag the heel of my hand around my face and cover my mouth, embarrassed by the impending question. The words linger on my tongue before I blurt out, "Can we please have sex soon?"

His eyes widen with surprise then turn dark, hooded and lustful.

"It's just. I'm really attracted to you and I haven't had sex in a really, *really* long time."

A small smile transforms into a wicked grin across his handsome face.

"How long?" he asks, his voice low and raspy.

I debate how honest I should be and decide to be vague. "A *long* time."

Narrowing his eyes, he asks, "Are we talking weeks, months or years?"

"What does it matter? Long is long."

He releases a chuckle. "Not true. There's long and then there's *long*."

I join in his amusement knowing he's no longer referring to time.

"Close to a year," I confess, pulling my eyes away from his and look at my journal peeking out from beneath my pillow. "You?"

"What about me?"

"When was the last time you had sex?"

A slight shake of his head is his response.

"You're a virgin?" I squawk in disbelief. There is no way in hell this virile, gorgeous man is untouched.

Deep laughter fills the room and echoes off the walls. "Hardly."

"Don't make fun of me!" I slap his arm playfully and lean down to bite his cheek, grazing his skin lightly with my teeth. "I'll bite you."

"Please do," he waggles his eyebrows and growls, throwing his hands back behind his head, ready to enjoy the show.

"I'm serious!" I eye him with a severe look as I fight a smile.

"What's this?"

His hand moves beneath my pillow, and he pulls out my journal.

"*That* is private," I declare, reaching for the pages upon pages of words that chronicle my life's experiences and journey.

Respecting my comment about privacy, he asks if he can look. "Only if you don't mind."

I search his eyes, looking for some shadow of mistrust and when I find none, I nod, giving him permission to glimpse into my soul. "They're my experiences written as song lyrics."

Quietly, he turns to a random page, reads then turns to another. I watch his eyes move from left to right as he studies the words that express my greatest dreams to my deepest regrets and everything in between.

Bewildered hazel eyes flash up. "You wrote this...all of this?"

I nod, not sure if I should be flattered or offended by his reaction. "Every last word."

"This is *really* good. It's amazing, actually." He blinks as if he's thinking about something before speaking again. "Cat, do you know how many artists would kill for words like these? I can feel every emotion here. I feel your happiness and I feel your anguish, too."

"Like I said, they're private thoughts and they're not for sale."

His forehead wrinkles. "Who said anything about selling them?"

Shaking my head as resolve appears on my face. "I've been approached before."

"Really?" he asks with intrigue.

"You don't believe me," I state quietly while anger brews inside, straining my voice.

Sliding a hand to caress my face, Mateo responds. "It's not that I don't believe you, but you're sitting on a goldmine and you don't even know it."

"What I know is my experiences are mine. I don't want to share them with the world."

He shakes his head as if he doesn't understand but doesn't push the issue.

After releasing a heavy sigh, Mateo searches my face. "I need to know something..."

"What?" I ask, finally realizing I'm still straddled over his lap. I move to lie next to him, and he shifts his body to face me, placing the journal between our bodies.

"Who hurt you?"

A wave of sadness spreads through me, remembering the day everything changed. "Someone I never would have expected." My voice emerges quiet and shallow. "But he can't hurt me anymore. He has no power over me."

"Can I borrow this?" He holds up my journal and immediately my suspicion kicks in.

"Why?" I demand as adrenaline races through me. "Why do you want it?"

A hand is slowly raised and his fingers move the wayward hair from my face. "I want to put this to music for you."

My body goes rigid and my breathing hitches. My head moves from side to side, denying his request. "I can't...you can't..."

"I can't what?" he questions softly.

"My journal is everything to me. I'm not ready to share that with anyone."

He nods. "Fair enough."

"And you wouldn't know how I envision it."

"Then tell me." His fingers curl inward as his knuckles slide down my cheek, caressing the soft skin gently.

I hum the melody I created for several of the songs. Slowly, he catches on and mouths the words to match each note.

"I like that transition there. What about this?" he offers before slightly changing the melody.

I smile at his contribution. "That's nice. *Really* nice."

From my window, I hear his name called several times followed by a loud whistle.

"Coffee break is over."

My eyes widen, realizing the other men will see him climbing out of my window.

"Maybe you shouldn't go back through the window."

"Maybe I should stay here all day." His eyebrows move playfully.

"I would love that!"

"I'll talk to you later." He kisses me again.

"Are you leaving for the day?"

"No, but I'll be thirty feet up in the air. I'll need to concentrate so I don't fall off the roof."

"Please be careful. I don't want you falling and ending up in the hospital."

He notes the color of my dress and says that I could be his naughty nurse.

"Yeah, and I'll shove a catheter right up your—"

"Damn, *mamacita*!" He winces and I laugh, scrunching my nose playfully.

"Want me to make you lunch?"

He gazes away for a moment before returning his attention to me. "Not today. I'm leaving at twelve."

"Are you going to that other job?"

He hums in confirmation as he manages to squeeze his big body through the small opening of my window. Standing on the ladder, he smiles sheepishly.

"I'll call you later. It might be late though."

A pleased smile etches across my flushed cheeks. "You can sing me a lullaby."

Mateo laughs, responding that his words would definitely *not* make me fall asleep.

My pulse quickens and warmth travels to my core, igniting a round of quick flutters.

"By the way, Cat...you might want to get a curtain for the bathroom window."

I gasp and ask with narrowed eyes, "You didn't happen to take a picture, did you?"

"No." He smiles. "But I like that little tattoo on your back. What is that?"

I constrict my eyes and reach for the decorative pillow, hurling it in his direction as he continues to descend.

"That's it," I race to the window and poke my head through, shouting after him. "I changed my mind. I don't want to have sex with you."

Every man stops what he's doing and looks up to my window. Mateo finally steps off the ladder when his work boots touch the asphalt in the driveway and he tips his head back to look at me. "Liar liar panties on fire." He adds a wink to his childish words.

Embarrassed and frustrated, I slam the window down and rattle the frame then plop on the bed. I lay there with a grin on my face until a knock on my door forces me to my feet.

"It's open," I call out as the door swings open and smacks against the adjacent wall, the door knob connecting with the hole that's already there, making it a little bigger. A scowl stares in my direction.

"What the hell was that about? And why the fuck was that guy climbing down from your window?"

My uncle's glare is met with pinched lips and a dramatic eye roll. His disheveled clothes and unshaven face match his sour mood.

"You realize I'm not ten years old, don't you?"

"Oh, I realize. Maybe you should so you can start acting like a responsible adult."

A torrent of muffled profanities flies from my lips when he yanks the door shut.

"I heard that," he yells back.

Reaching for my phone, I sit on my bed and text Mackenzie, needing to vent my frustration. My uncle's constant mood swings have me wondering why he moved back here if he's so miserable. No wonder his wife left him.

My phone chirps and I read her text. `Forget about him. Tell me about your Latin Lover.`

I respond, `He's not my lover... yet.`

`It's about damn time! ;)`

I end our exchange when my grandmother barges into my room, waving an envelope in the air with a huge smile on her face.

"It's here, Cat! It's here."

I rise to my feet and accept the parcel.

Gram follows my lead and sits on the bed beside me. My heart thunders in my chest as I look at the return address label. Philadelphia isn't too far. I can hop the train and come home on weekends to visit Gram. If things work out, Mateo could come down to visit me. The idea of not seeing him every day makes me a little sad, but this is a great opportunity for me.

"Open it! What are you waiting for?"

Using a pencil, I wedge it between the adhesive seal and retrieve the contents. I skip the greeting and read quickly, perusing the four paragraphs.

"Well?" Gram asks with anticipation.

"I did it," I whisper. "I actually did it."

"I'm so proud of you, Beth! I knew you could do it."

My mouth opens and my heart plummets as I utter quiet words filled with sadness. "Thanks, Gram, but I'm Caterina, your granddaughter, remember?"

"Of course, you are. I know that!" she responds indignantly.

While I should be jumping for joy, my emotions are caught in a firestorm. Disbelief and elation battle against worry and grief. As happy as I am, I don't want to leave my grandmother, knowing her mental health is deteriorating rapidly, much faster than her doctors had predicted.

My eyes well with moisture and I wipe them, refusing to cry when Gram exits the room, calling her dead husband's name. I place the envelope on the bedside table and again grab my phone to share the news with my best friend.

Walking downstairs, the smell of something burning seeps through the air and causes my footsteps to hasten.

"Dammit, Gram!" I mumble as I turn off the burner and remove the pot of burnt garlic and onion. Cooking is the only thing that makes her happy these days and I know she would feel badly if she couldn't do it anymore. Contemplating the options, I prepare a cup of coffee and grab a slice of cherry nut bread from the tray, but I immediately spit it out when egg shells grind between my teeth. Standing at the kitchen window, I watch the clouds drift by. Thoughts consume me as important decisions will need to be made.

A soft knock on the back door calls my attention. I turn

to see Junior standing there.

"Can I use your bathroom?" he asks.

I smile. "Sure. It's down the hall, first door on the left."

I climb the stairs and close my bedroom door, once again rereading the letter while debating if I should tell Mateo the news. From the back of my closet, I retrieve a small box of pictures and old journals, memories from my former life when my mother was still alive and Gram had her memory.

"Hi."

I startle and drop the small booklet filled with songs my mother and I composed together.

"You scared me," I say, walking over to greet Mateo's face peeking through the window frame. Mesmerized by the sight of him, I almost forget to inquire about my window. "Did you just open my window?"

"Maybe," he replies with a devilish grin.

"That's a bit stalkerish," I comment even though I'm secretly thrilled. "You're not some crazy killer, are you?"

"I'm not a killer..." I see humor etched on Mateo's hot and sweaty face. "But I am crazy about you." The sound of his words alone sends a buzz of adrenaline, causing my nipples to tighten as my mind forgets about the past, sending my mind straight to the gutter. I comment on his face.

"Is this what you look like after sex?" I push his dark hair away from his forehead, leaving the silky damp strands wayward.

I think I've rendered him speechless because he simply stares at me with a grin on his face.

"Maybe."

"Why are you at my window again?"

He leans in and rests his elbows on the window frame. "I'm leaving so I wanted to say goodbye." I turn my head and glance at the clock, noting it's not even eleven thirty.

"You could've texted me."

"I don't want to text with you and besides I wouldn't be

able to do this."

He reaches for my hand and pulls me toward the open window. I bend my knees to meet him at eye level. His lips close over mine briefly. Not once does his tongue slip in and tangle with mine.

His gaze shifts away from my face. "Is that what your Gram was hollering about?"

I follow his line of sight and look at the large envelope sitting on the bedside table.

"Yeah." I nod. "She's pretty excited for me."

"Why? What's it for?"

"I got into grad school and I've been offered a really great opportunity to work in Africa," I answer slowly. "I'm not sure if I'm going to go yet."

"Which grad school?"

"Drexel," I murmur. "In Philly."

His lips tighten and I detect a hint of disappointment on his face.

"So you're leaving soon?"

I shrug, offering no verbal confirmation.

The scale of life is unbalanced. There are too many reasons not to go and each one adds weight, tipping the gauge against me.

I answer his silent queries. "I have a lot to consider."

"Dame un beso," he commands with a sexy smile before puckering his luscious lips.

Leaning into the open window, I kiss him.

Mateo descends for a final time and I watch him answer his phone as he climbs into the cab of the truck. My fingertips graze my lips, missing the soft touch of his and immediately I sigh, knowing my heart is growing attached. A movement in my peripheral catches my attention and I look over to see Junior peering up at me with a look of disappointment on his face. I wave at him, but he exhales heavily and turns away.

After a quick text to Trina asking if she needs me to work today, I grab an Uber across town for a few hours.

The antique bell on the door rings when I push it open. Trina looks up and smiles.

"Hi, doll."

My eyes scan the mountain of newly consigned items, mostly clothes and shoes, and wonder how it's all going to fit in her small shop.

"These were donated, but don't worry, I'm not keeping it all. Some people think my store is called Trina's Trash." Her laughter is light and humorous. "It may not be Nordstrom's, but I have decent things, don't you think?"

"Agreed," I say, picking up a pair of Ann Taylor linen pants which still have the tag on them.

I spend the next few hours rummaging through the pile, sorting the "trash" from the "treasure."

A group of teenage girls come in, sifting through the racks to find one-of-a-kind, Bohemian style clothing. Too bad for them, I already grabbed all the good stuff.

"Hey there," I call out in greeting but get no response. I stifle a sarcastic comment because I know this type. Rich girls who think it's cool to shop for "vintage" clothing but whose daddies have enough money to buy Trina's entire shop.

"Phoebs, look at this!"

Her blue eyes widen and twinkle as if she sees stars. "That looks exactly like what Chloe wore last week in New York."

"Oh, my God. I adore her. I can't wait for her new album. Rumor has it she's working with some hot new guy," a girl with long dark hair says.

Her petite friend suggests it might be Shawn Mendes while the other girl with blonde curls squeals when she says Harry Styles.

"Oh my God, can you imagine Chloe and Harry together?"

"That would be amazing, but I still can't believe they broke up. I loved ChloRo."

I keep my head down and listen as I hang the shorter dresses on plastic hangers. I roll my eyes at the stupidity of combining celebrity couples' names.

"God, she's so beautiful. I love everything about her," the blonde gushes. "She's so talented. I heard her new album is really emotional."

Continuing the task of putting away the new shipment, I scroll through and click on the *Lifehouse* station on Pandora as I push one ear bud into my ear.

Trina offers a smile to each girl as they step up to the register.

"Did you find everything okay?" she asks as she does to every single customer. It's standard protocol for her.

The girls ignore her and continue to chat amongst themselves, only stopping momentarily to hand over their credit cards and sign the receipt. I feel sorry for Trina as she continues to be extremely polite, folding their purchases neatly and placing them in the pink gift bag that bears her shop's name. I remember the conversation about why she spent money on the bags when she could just as easily use recycled grocery bags.

"It's my name. I want people to know how I do business. Sometimes your name is all you've got" is what she'd said.

And how true that is!

Some names are so much more than just a name. A family name can build you up or tear you down. Rockefeller. Kennedy. Kardashian. Sheen. Gates. Madoff. Steinbrenner.

Creed.

Around the same time I was leaving my name behind, others were jumping at the opportunity to join and take the family name.

After looking through the tall storefront window, Trina

decides to close early. Business is slow *and* the sun is shining. She finds any opportunity to soak up vitamin D, inevitably turning her leathery skin darker.

"Please use sun screen," I plead, looking at myself in the mirror, eyeing the freckles dotting my ivory skin.

"You need a tan. Then you'd really look like a California beach babe."

I smirk and roll my eyes. "I've got a little color," I retort, "but I'd rather not get skin cancer, thank you very much."

"Can you put these things on my tab?" I hold up a new journal, a pair of oversized sunglasses and a big floppy hat that still has the tag attached. "It's amazing what people give away. Must be *last season*," I say, rolling my eyes before I rip the tag off with my teeth.

"Sure thing!"

We exit the shop together but part ways when she hops into her car and I continue to walk down the street. It really is a lovely day and since I have nowhere in particular to be, a stroll through the park sounds like a good idea.

Sitting on the park bench, I take small bites of the gyro I bought from the street vendor and take in my surroundings. Mothers push plump babies in strollers along the asphalt paths while a dog chases after a tennis ball. Agile children reach across and swing their legs, moving easily across the monkey bars. I adjust my hat and push my sunglasses up on the bridge of my nose then extend my legs in front of me, crossing one ankle over the other. It's a beautiful summer day.

The heat on my face reminds me of long days in Africa.

The squeal of children's laughter is soon replaced by melodic, soft sounds of an acoustic guitar wafting over from beneath a huge oak tree. The musician, a young man rocking a messy man-bun, strums slowly, stops and pulls the pencil from behind his ear to jot something down on a piece of paper. After plucking the strings, he stops again, looks around then erases what he'd just written only to replace it with something new. I recognize the smile of satisfaction on his face. There's a sense of peace and harmony in the soul when things fall into place, when the perfect word combination matches the number of syllables needed and the story begins to tell itself.

My phone vibrates with a message from Mackenzie, asking if I can cover her shift at the bar tonight. My fingers hesitate to respond because I was hoping to relax and possibly ask Mateo to meet up, but she's my best friend and there have been plenty of times she's filled in for me when I had issues with Gram.

Hot date? I ask.

The three dots move across the screen and then stop before the word Yep appears.

I'm jealous. And while I am happy for my best friend, a hint of envy bubbles. She's got an extensive list of ex-boyfriends. Guys love her, but she usually ends up breaking their hearts before they break hers. I don't know how she does it or why for that matter.

My gaze moves back to the musician, my feet tapping to the easy rhythm. Retrieving a pen in my bag, I open up to a blank page in my new journal and scribble a few words of my own as he continues to play.

I love music. I love everything about it. I love the melody, the beat that keeps the timing, the intricacies of the chords and the words. The words are everything to me. I close my eyes and create my own story to go along with his music. When I reopen my eyes to write the words onto the page, a surprised chuckle escapes because Mateo's name appears several times.

"Oh, no. I'm in deep trouble," I whisper to myself when a shift in the melody reminds me of Elvis Presley's *Can't Help Falling in Love You*. Falling for Mateo isn't something I should do, but it may already be too late.

Returning my thoughts to the paper and pen, I continue

to write. Memories flood my mind as I remember the past. Thoughts of my mother consume me. The hours we spent together, moving the notes around to create the main riff followed by the hook. I loved coloring in the small ovals after she played the new song on the piano. She was amazed at how easily and quite naturally the structure and cadence came to me; she'd said it was in my blood. I'd learned to play the piano from watching her, but after years of piano recitals, I played my last concerto and shifted my focus and my passion to the words.

My thoughts. My secrets. My confessions. My heart.

Once my father stopped and actually took notice of what I was creating, he introduced me to almost every record label he was connected to. I was considered by many to be a prodigy. Many compared me to this generation's top songwriters, but I didn't want to share my thoughts with anyone; they were for me and me alone. The spotlight wasn't something I ever wanted...unlike others who thrived on the attention.

Picking up my phone, I mentally chastise myself for torturing myself for checking social media. Facebook, Instagram, Twitter. It's all for show. Who cares what you ate for dinner. Who cares where you're vacationing. Who cares that your kids are driving you crazy. Who cares that you and your sister had a falling out. Who cares that a new album is coming out.

As much as I say I don't care, I guess I do because I tap the blue icon. Morbid curiosity gets the best of me when I click on her profile. I raise my eyes to look around making sure no one is watching me. Images of her and her friends smiling on the beach in Cabo appear. Photos of her sitting in front of the cameras at the television station are followed by more of her dining at Soho's newest restaurant. Finally, images of her standing next to a man whose face is blurred with the caption *Turning Up the Heat* or the other *Spicy Summer* suggest the pop star has a new love interest— already. Poor

Ronan, he never had a chance.

My phone rings, but I decline the call. My father's constant calls have become a nuisance. I switch the ringer to silent and push him to the back of my mind. *Out of sight, out of mind.*

"Hi."

I draw my attention away from the screen and look up to see the musician standing before me with clear green eyes and his guitar strapped diagonally across his chest. I slip my phone back into my bag.

"Hello," I reply, closing my journal and setting it down beside me.

"Mind if I sit?"

I smile because he sits before I can answer.

"I'm Caleb."

I smile and offer my name to which he responds with a raised brow.

"Caterina," I clarify.

"That's a really pretty name."

"Do you come here often?"

My forehead wrinkles and my lips purse. "That's a terrible pickup line. I would imagine a musician could do better than that."

He smiles sheepishly. "I wasn't trying to pick you up." His leg brushes against mine when he readjusts the instrument.

I notice the long scar running the length of his thigh down to his calf.

"It looks worse than it actually was," he says with a grin. "I was an adventurous kid."

I nod and smile tightly.

"I used to race motocross. I was really good, too," he says, perhaps reminiscing his glory days, "but I landed the wrong way." He runs his hand along the scar. "And I broke my leg." His fingers pull the hem of his shorts to expose the wound further. "Here," he points high on his thigh, "here," he slides his fingers to his knee, "and here," he taps his shin.

I hiss between my teeth and wince. "Ouch! That's really awful. I'm sorry that happened to you."

"Eh, that's alright." He shrugs then taps his guitar. "That's how I discovered this baby right here." His expression changes when he strums the strings. "Lulu's been right there with me."

"You named your guitar?" I ask skeptically with a hint of amusement.

"Yep. I was tired of watching TV and playing video games. I really couldn't do anything so I picked her up, taught myself to play and she became my best friend. I never rode a bike again after that."

I laugh lightly at the humorous expression beneath the overgrown and unkempt scruff covering his face. "So it's not really a good thing when someone says 'Break a Leg,' huh?"

"Guess not."

Caleb slides his thumb over the strings and strikes a chord with his other hand. His fingers moved effortlessly, creating a pretty melody.

"You're good."

He smiles at the compliment. "Do you play?"

Shaking my head, I tell him I used to play piano.

"We should start a band," he proposes with a grin.

I chuckle and counter his offer. "Only if we play in the dark. I don't like the spotlight."

"Is that why you're incognito?"

"What? I'm not—"

"C'mon...you've got the 'big hat and even bigger sunglasses thing' going on. Who are you hiding from?" he asks with a playful grin.

I run my fingers along the woven edge of my hat. "I just picked these up today at work."

"And where would that be?" he asks nonchalantly.

"Trina's Treasures right up the street."

Caleb chuckles then turns away, looking at a bus as it comes to a stop at the park's main entrance. "There goes my ride. Guess I'll have to wait for the 3:30 bus."

"Three-thirty?" I shriek, standing quickly and tossing my journal in my bag. "Sorry. I would offer to give you a ride, but my car is kind of out of commission at the moment. Apparently leaving the top down in the rain isn't such a good idea." I shrug my shoulders and smile. "Who knew?"

Caleb rises and stands next to me, extending a hand. "It was nice to meet you."

I slide my hand into his and return the sentiment. Aside from the obvious lingering connection of our hands, I observe how soft his hand is. It's nothing like Mateo's big, rough and callused hand.

Maintaining eye contact, he adds, "Maybe I'll see you here another time."

I look away and smile tightly, knowing our paths probably won't cross again because this park isn't a place I visit often anymore. Years ago, my mom and I would come here almost every weekend to check out local artists.

With a final wave, I walk in the opposite direction and search the bottom of my bag for my phone to call an Uber. The screen is covered in notifications of missed calls and text messages. I look at Mateo's name and the number four in parentheses. A smile appears on my face, wondering why he's called so many times in a short span of time as I tap the screen to return the call.

My smile morphs into a frown when my call is sent to voicemail.

I respond to my uncle's text, telling him that he'll have to figure something out because I have to cover Mackenzie's shift at the bar. As much as I love my grandmother, I'm not her only caregiver, and he needs to step up and do his part—unexpected trips or not.

When I arrive at home, the construction crew is gone,

Johnny's gone and so is Gram. I look at the dry erase board for some indication of where everyone has gone, but it's blank.

Knowing it's going to be a long night, I climb the stairs and collapse on my bed after switching the ringer back on and setting an alarm for a short nap. My breathing is steady and I sigh, falling into a deep sleep within minutes. My heartbeat quickens and I smile when I see Mateo in my dreams.

Chapter Five

"WHAT TIME DO YOU GET OUT?" MATEO ASKS, worry tainting his deep voice that I'll be taking an Uber from work. "It's not safe."

"Two-thirty. I'll be alright," I laugh into the phone, enjoying the protective tone in his voice.

"I'll pick you up."

I roll over in bed and look at the clock. "No, that's too late and you have to be here early in the morning. It's fine, really." I hear a car door close and wonder if my uncle changed his plans.

"How was your day?" I ask, releasing a loud yawn as I stand up and walk to the bathroom. I reach in, turn the knob to start the shower and step out of my clothes.

"Busy but good. I called you a few times. What'd you do all day?"

"I worked for a bit, but Trina closed the shop early so I went for a walk and had lunch in the park."

"Lunch? With who?"

"Myself," I drag out slowly. "I had the best gyro ever."

"Please tell me you didn't eat street meat."

"I did and it was delicious." I smile, wiping steam from the mirror with a quick swipe of my hand. "Hang on a sec." I set the phone down and brush my teeth quickly.

Our conversation continues for a few more minutes until I inform him that I really need to jump in the shower and get ready for work. After insisting that I'm torturing him with the image of my naked body, Mateo, grudgingly, disconnects the call.

After tapping the Pandora app to Alicia Keys radio, I step into the shower, letting the hot water spray down on me as I shampoo and condition my hair. My head bobs along to the music while the lyrics emerge from my lips. Carefully I slide the razor over each leg, leaving the skin smooth and soft. Soapy hands lather my body, caressing every swell, gentle curve and hidden space. I notice the song changes so I pull back the curtain, dry my fingers and turn the volume up higher. Matching her word for word and note for note, I step back into the shower and belt out *Girl on Fire*, singing in complete harmony with my idol as my fingers tap the imaginary keys on the tiled wall.

Feeling my fingers prune, I turn off the shower, grab an oversized towel and wrap myself up. Between the lotion, gobs of curl product and heavy makeup I only wear for work, I think I've added an extra pound to my weight. I grab my phone, turn the volume down, and walk into my room.

I scream and clutch my towel when my eyes, wide with shock, land on Mateo's long body reclining on my bed. His elbows are bent behind his head, his legs crossed at the ankle and a huge roguish grin covers his face.

"What are you doing here?" I screech as my cheeks burn with embarrassment and lust at the sight of him in jeans and a black T-shirt. He looks delicious enough to eat.

"I missed you," he says, patting the side of my bed. "Sit."

A ball of jumbled nerves lodges in my throat, and I swallow hard. Licking my lips, I find my mouth is suddenly parched, all of the moisture pooling below my navel in between my legs. I look down at my towel and suggest that

I get dressed first.

With a look of pure desire, Mateo narrows his beautiful eyes and shakes his head slowly, patting his thigh. "Come here." I hold his gaze and stifle the small chuckle at his double entendre.

I glance at the clock on the bedside table then turn to grab a pair of lacy boy shorts from the top drawer of my dresser, looking at him in the mirror as I speak. "I have to get to work and we both know what's going to happen if I walk over to you."

Bending my knee, I slide my leg through one opening when a hand suddenly reaches between my legs and stops me from proceeding. I feel Mateo rise and stand behind me. Our eyes meet in the mirror as he closes the gap between our bodies, pushing his body flush with mine. When he leans forward, his erection strains against his jeans, and I can feel it at the small of my back. Without looking away, Mateo holds my attention as my hair is brushed aside and his lips find my neck.

"Beautiful..."

I break the connection when my eyes close, giving in to the feel of his proximity. I inhale the scent of his cologne. What feels like a thousand tiny kisses form a path to my chin as his hands slowly move over my towel and massage my breasts. Reaching for the corner of the thick cotton towel, he yanks it down in one swift motion. My eyes open and I stiffen, realizing my nakedness is on full display.

"...doesn't begin to describe you."

The kisses resume while his hands commence on a wandering mission, slowly exploring my flesh. Relishing his touch, I moan quietly and roll my hips. His reflection reveals his warm smile as he moves to nibble on my ear. Gently lifting one before the other, he guides my limp arms to the nape of his neck, allowing my fingers to find the soft tufts of his black hair. Now having full and unrestricted access to my breasts, Mateo rolls my nipples between his thumb and two additional fingers.

"Mateo—" I whisper breathlessly as my core screams for attention. "Please."

"Please what, baby?" he asks, meeting my eyes in the mirror.

"Touch me." The longing and desperation in my expression is primal and raw.

Pulling away just far enough that I can still feel the heat emanating from his chest, Mateo covers my hands with his as he places them on the edge of my dresser. "Hold on."

Tracing a slow line up my arms until his fingertips reach my shoulders, the contour of my back and waist is caressed. With his firm hands on my hands, he lowers himself so his lips float near my backside. I shiver when I feel his soft tongue lick slowly before placing a chaste kiss. His quiet moans cause my core to buzz with anticipation of having him in me, joining our bodies as one.

Light strokes of his tongue mixed with roaming kisses give way to gentle bites.

"Turn around," he orders and I comply immediately without a second to reconsider what I'm doing or what *he* is doing.

Kneeling before me, Mateo gazes up at me. Revealed in his eyes is a starved man, consumed by unadulterated desire. "Open," he commands with a raspy voice, guiding my legs apart before slowly moving in to taste me.

I clench my fingers tightly to prevent them from covering my face and blocking my ears because I want to watch. I want to listen. With each swirl of his tongue against my hot flesh and every pull of my nub with his teeth, we both elicit sounds of pleasure. Adding his fingers to the wonderful combination, Mateo brings me closer to the edge until I fist his dark hair, cry out his name and orgasm.

Resting his lips against the smooth skin, he offers a final

kiss before standing completely. My eyes flutter open slowly and gaze up at him and notice his glistening mouth. Cradling the back of his head, I lower his face and meet his lips.

"More," I breathe. "I want more."

He groans. "I do too, but I can't give it to you right now."

Disappointment floods me and I look away only to have my chin pulled back to meet his kiss.

"Thank you," he mumbles against my mouth.

I grin. "I think I should be the one saying thank you."

"The pleasure was all mine."

Maintaining eye contact, I slide my hand down his chest and cup his stiffness. "Your turn."

He looks away for a moment before he returns his eyes to mine. "Next time."

Determined to return the favor, I unbutton his jeans and find the zipper.

A firm grasp stops me. "You have to go to work."

I glance at the clock and gasp, realizing just how long he was down there. I reach for my phone and open the Uber app.

Mateo takes my phone out of my hand. "I'm driving you."

My attempt to decline his offer falls dead on my lips when he kisses me again. "Stop fighting me."

I grin and release a defeated huff.

"I want to do things for you, to you and with you."

His words fill my ears and I nod slowly, giving him permission to do whatever he wants.

"I think about you all day, every day."

"Me, too," I confess, thinking about the page I filled earlier today with thoughts of him.

"Get dressed," he encourages as he sits on the edge of my bed.

I retrieve the black lace from the floor and pull on my shorts. The matching bra and the fitted T-shirt cover my chest.

"That's what you're wearing to work?" he shrieks.

I nod while curiously raising an eyebrow. "It's what I always wear to work. All the girls do...even in the winter."

"Turn around." He motions with his index finger.

After a quick spin, I see the expression on his face and I laugh. "What?" I ask.

"Your tits and ass are practically hanging out."

I roll my eyes. "You've seen me at work before."

Nodding his head obstinately, he insists my shorts weren't *this* short last time.

"Jealous?" I tease as I walk over to him.

He slides his hands around my waist then down to my ass. "I don't want anyone staring at this."

"Have you seen Mackenzie? Trust me... no one is looking at me."

"I only see you."

My belly flutters at his sweet words.

"And besides, I don't want to share you with anyone."

Smiling, I slide my feet into sneakers and toss my heels in my bag before offering a kiss and telling him that we need to leave so I won't be late for work.

I call out for my grandmother or my uncle but get no response. Running my fingers along the top of the piano, I tap a few keys before I walk past.

"Do you play?"

My eyes meet his. "Not anymore."

I jot a quick note, telling Gram that I'll be at work.

"Why did you stop playing the piano?" he asks, following me out the door.

"It wasn't fun anymore."

Mateo opens the passenger door and helps me in, walks around the front and then climbs into the cab. Once on the road, he slides his hand across the leather seat and takes a hold of mine. I look down at our laced fingers and smile, reminiscing about the way he pleasured me only a short time ago.

With a quick tap on the steering wheel, he turns on the radio and Colbie Caillat's voice sings about falling in love. We smile at each other and I realize, as I much as I hate to admit it, I'm falling for Mateo. Fast and hard.

Life is all about timing and this timing is all wrong. I might be leaving in a month.

"I like her," I comment to break the awkward silence.

He shrugs. "She's okay."

I purse my lips at his comment as I dig through my bag, quickly tossing the six-inch stilettos out to answer my phone.

Mateo eyes my heels and smiles. "You should've had those on earlier."

I grin and shiver at his suggestion until I see the number on my phone and mumble, commenting that he's a pain in my ass.

"Your uncle?"

"No." I shake my head. "My father." I toss my phone back into my bag.

"I take it you don't get along." His thumb rubs a small circle over my skin.

"It's a long story."

Mateo glances at the digital clock on the dashboard. "We've got fifteen minutes."

Remaining quiet for a few seconds, I finally shake my head and open my mouth to speak. "Parents are supposed to love and protect their kids not feed them to the wolves."

The grip on my hand tightens and his expression turns deadly. "Did someone tou—"

"No! Nothing like that." I reassure him with a smile. "He's a selfish man."

"Do you see him often?"

We stop when the traffic light turns red.

"I try not to." I chuckle darkly. "He's been badgering me for weeks now that I'm home from my trip. He wants to see me before he hits the road again. He travels a lot for work."

Shifting his body, Mateo looks directly at me. "I can go with you if you decide to go."

A warm smile tugs at my lips and I welcome the feeling of protectiveness. "Thanks. I may take you up on that offer."

"I won't let anyone hurt you."

I nod quickly and accept his words, pulling me away from thoughts about how different my relationship with my father was when I was little.

"By the way, you have got a set of powerful lungs."

"What?" I chuckle. "What are you talking about?"

"The shower." His hazel eyes widen, suggesting I know exactly what he's referring to. "Alicia Keys…"

My shoulders move, implying my indifference. "Oh that. Yeah, I sing a little."

"A little? If I didn't know better, I would've thought she was in your bathroom! Why didn't you tell me?"

I offer a dubious look as a response. "It's not that important."

"Cat, you play piano, you write lyrics *and* you sing?"

Our eyes meet.

"That's a trifecta in the music industry," he states with a smile.

I sigh, wanting to wipe the excited expression right off his face. It's one I've seen a million times and one I despise.

"That's not who I am. It's not who I want to be."

"But you've got talent. You could be bigger than Chloe and you've definitely got more talent!" he counters.

"Chloe?" I squawk angrily at the comparison. An ache forms in my chest because I feel the tension between us rising. He, like so many others, is going to point out all the opportunities I'm missing or how much money I could be making.

"Chloe Creed…," he states her name with an obvious tone then continues to remind me of who she is as if I didn't know.

"I know who she is." I pull my hand from his and press the heels of my palms into my eyes, momentarily forgetting that I have dark makeup on. "I know *exactly* who she is," I murmur, looking out the window, feeling grateful we've arrived at the bar.

"I didn't mean to upset you. I'm sorry if I did." He takes my hand once again.

I release a quiet breath. "It's fine. You're just not the first person to say these things to me."

The seat belt strains against his chest when he leans over to kiss me. "I'll see you later." I close my eyes when he brushes a curl away from my face. "I'll be thinking about you."

"Thanks for the ride and the—" I shut my mouth before I say "orgasm."

"Anytime, mamacita. *Anytime.*"

The bar has been busy and loud since the doors opened and my tip jar is overflowing. I was asked to cover a bachelorette party until Lou gets in. A group of young women drink and dance in the private VIP room on the second floor before joining everyone else downstairs. While pouring drinks and popping bottles of expensive champagne open, I look through the tall glass windows that encase the plush room. From this vantage point, I can see everyone on the main floor. The dance floor is packed with partiers enjoying a night out or perhaps just the need to blow off steam, each moving to the beat of the music and stepping on everyone else's feet. It's nothing like the dancing Mateo and I did at the Cuban restaurant. While hot bodies gyrate closely to one another, it doesn't feel intimate.

"Sorry I'm late," Lou offers as he steps behind the bar.

I smile compassionately, knowing how difficult the situation is for him. "No worries."

"How are they?" He tips his chin to the few women who've returned to the room.

"Good." I eye the jar overflowing with fives, tens and a

few twenty-dollar bills. "They're having a great time!"

"Let me know when I can return the favor."

"I sure will," I answer as I wipe down the bar.

"Here. This is yours." Lou reaches for my hand and shoves a wad of rolled cash at me.

"No way!" I shake my head.

"Cat—"

"Lou! We always split tips. You know that!"

"Not tonight." His eyes close for a brief moment before he reopens them and nods once.

I fold the money and slide it into my back pocket, leaving my butt to appear voluptuous on one side. Walking toward the balcony which leads downstairs, I scan the bar once again. Filling with excitement, I smile when I notice Mateo standing near my usual bar. He looks out of place because while everyone is hot and sweaty, he is the picture of perfection. Every single strand of his dark hair is in place, revealing his gorgeous face and exposing those incredible eyes which move across the bar in search of something or someone.

"Hi." I place a hand on his slim waist as I move in behind him. "What are you doing here?"

Mateo glances over his shoulder then turns when he notices me standing there.

I detect a sense of relief in his gaze as he leans down to kiss me. I return the brief moment of affection then pull back.

"I came for you."

I suppress my laughter as a grin stretches across my face, loving his play on words.

"Oh yeah, well there's no PDA allowed here."

He laughs and motions to all the people on the dance floor whose bodies display much affection in one form or another.

"I'm *working* though," I counter.

My eyes drag down his body and I lick my lips at the sight of him, dressed casually with perfectly fitted jeans, dark boots and a black T-shirt.

"What are you drinking?" I ask, stepping behind the bar.

"Whatever you've got."

My cheeks flush hot with the memory of how he savored my body hours earlier.

He grins wickedly, confirming my suspicion of his dirty thoughts.

I grab a tall tumbler and fill it with the same beer he ordered last time. "You're so bad!"

"You have no idea."

"I don't get off for another hour." I toss back as I walk away to take a drink order.

With his curled index finger, he calls me to come closer. I tiptoe over the bar and give him my ear while I inhale the scent of cologne.

"I don't think I can wait that long."

My hot flesh constricts with uncontrollable need and desire.

My manager calls my name and reminds me that I have thirsty customers waiting.

"You're going to get me in trouble." I pull back and smile.

"That's what I'm counting on."

For the next hour, Mateo nurses a beer and remains at my bar, watching my every move and tossing lustful glances in my direction until I cash out and meet him out front.

He extends his hand and leads me to his truck.

"Thanks for picking me up, but I could've called for a ride."

"I don't mind and like I said, 'I came for you.' "

The laughter I suppressed erupts. "You think you're funny, don't you?"

"What?" He feigns innocence although his eyes twinkle with humor.

"The things you say. The words you choose."

He shrugs. "I told you I'm good with words."

"Yes, but what you *say* is not always what you *mean*," I point out.

His grin confirms my suspicion as a quick memory takes me back to the semester focused primarily on multiple meaning words and their many, oftentimes vastly different, definitions. An explosion of boldness and bravery shoots from my lips. "So did you *come* for me or not?"

"I certainly did." He clicks the key fob and the back lights flash, sending a flicker of illumination through the darkness.

I jab his stomach with my free hand. "You're going to drive me crazy!"

"That's what I'm counting on." Opening the door, he helps me in before he walks around to sit in the driver's seat.

I slide my hand along the smooth leather, my fingers inching closer to his thigh when I touch something.

"What's this?" I ask, lifting a manila folder.

Quickly, Mateo takes it from me and tosses it onto the back seat. "Work stuff."

He strains against the seat belt to kiss me.

"When's your next day off?" he asks as we drive along the quiet roads, passing only a few cars while most others are parked on either side of the street.

"Sunday, although I might go down to Trina's in the morning. We'll see if she needs me."

He glances sideways and smiles. "I'd like to take you out to dinner. We haven't had a real date yet."

I suppress the question floating through my mind of whether "dating" is what we're doing.

My body tingles with delight at the thought of spending time with him and of what might happen afterward.

"Does Sunday work for you?"

He nods. "I'll pick you up at nine."

"In the morning?" I shriek, turning to look for some sign

of jest but find none.

"Too early?" He laughs.

"Seeing as I probably won't get home until three a.m., I'd say so."

He considers my statement and agrees that I'll need my rest so he counters with twelve.

"Much better." I grin.

"I plan on spending the whole day and night with you."

A streetlight provides a moment of visibility in the dark cab when he turns right at the intersection near my road. On his face, he wears a hopeful and promising expression.

My tongue darts out to moisten my lips and I search for my voice. "What are we going to do all day and night?"

"I know exactly what I want to do."

"You're not going to take me on some wild adventure, are you? I don't do," I air quote, "adventurous."

"Why not?" he asks, pulling into my driveway and parking the truck in front of the garage.

"Apparently *that* gene skipped me."

"Well, some might consider traveling to volunteer in a remote village in Africa pretty adventurous, no?"

"Some might say so, but I wasn't there seeking an adventure. I was there to help. It wasn't about me; it was about them. No one paid any attention to me and that's exactly how I wanted it."

Silence rises between us, and I suddenly feel hesitant as though I've said the wrong thing. The circling of my fingers stills on his skin.

"You're an amazing person."

I shake my head slowly in objection to his compliment. "No, I'm not."

Needing to fill the quiet, I look at the addition to the house and ask when he thinks the project will be completed.

After humming in thought, he responds, "Seven or eight weeks."

"Just after fall," I comment. "Gram will be happy. She loves fall. It's her favorite season."

"Yours, too, huh?"

My eyebrow furrows in confusion. "How did you know that?"

"I learned a lot about you today."

"What are you talking about?"

Mateo pulls his eyes from mine and confesses that he read pages of my journal while I was in the shower.

Confusion mars my face as I waver between anger and fury.

"You had no right to do that. That's private!"

"I know. I'm sorry."

I run my fingers beneath my bottom lashes and wipe the moisture revealing my frustration.

"You have to respect my privacy. I'll tell you things when I'm ready to. Okay?"

He nods apologetically. "Don't be mad. It was there on your bed and I guess I wanted to get to know you better. That's all. I wasn't trying to be a dick."

"Not everything about me is revealed in there."

Mateo removes his seat belt and inches closer to me. The warmth of his breath tickles my face. "In that case, I can't wait to find out what's tucked away in here." His fingers slide across my black T-shirt and stop just above my heart. My pulse quickens and I wonder briefly if he's referring to my small breasts or the depth of my heart.

I find his gaze, his eyes filled with need as he leans in to join our lips. Moving of their own accord, my hands move quickly to the back of his head and grasp his hair, pulling him closer so that our bodies are nearly connected along the leather seat.

He drags his mouth away from mine only to slide his lips to my ear. "Is this real?" he whispers. The rasp in his voice speaks directly to my body.

"God, I hope so." I lower my hand, grab his ass, and raise my hips at the same time.

A moan escapes his lips. "I wasn't implying just *that*."

"Oh," I squeak quietly.

"I haven't even fucked you yet and I can't stop thinking about you."

Closing my eyes, I suppress a giggle at his word choice, secretly loving it, and pray this isn't a dream.

"There you go again."

"What?" he inquires, mildly offended.

"Saying all the right words."

"They're more than words, Caterina."

He tugs my hand from his backside and places it on his chest. "It's what I feel here."

I glance at the dashboard clock which reads 3:06. "I wish you could stay the night."

"Me, too, but I don't think your gram, or your uncle for that matter, would appreciate that."

"Are you kidding me? Gram would do somersaults down the street if she could."

"Somersaults?"

"And maybe cartwheels, too!"

A single kiss lingers on my lips.

"Gram has waited for a long time for this."

"You mean to tell me you've never had a boyfriend?" he asks skeptically.

I shake my head and my lips pop. "Nope!"

He cocks an eyebrow.

"Well, nothing serious. My father was super strict. He didn't want me to get distracted by anything or anyone. I never went to birthday parties for kids at school and I certainly never went to sleepovers like all the other girls did."

"That must've been tough."

"It was until I had enough and quit everything."

No longer feeling the stiffness of his erection against my

belly, I use my hands and push myself up. He takes the hint and moves to an upright position beside me. Guilt creeps in and settles within me for bringing up this heavy topic.

A chirp accompanied by vibration surfaces from his phone on the center console.

My eyes follow his movements when he grabs the phone and holds the side button, powering it off completely. After a second quick peek at the clock, I note the early morning hour and wonder who could possibly be texting so late. Jealousy mocks me.

"Was he mad?" he asks.

I blink rapidly, returning my attention to the current conversation. "Who?"

"Your dad."

I inhale deeply then yawn, nodding my head and widening my eyes. "My father was livid, but it didn't last long."

"Tired?" he asks, bringing a hand to caress my face.

"I am," I answer honestly.

Mateo tucks my head beneath his chin before offering a final kiss. "See you in a few hours."

I pull open the door handle, causing the overhead light to shine. After stepping down, I turn back to see him looking at me. "It's funny." I smile coyly. "I haven't known you very long, but I feel like I can talk to you so easily. I trust you."

"Sweet dreams, *mamacita*."

"Night." I close the door quietly and walk to the back door with extra light steps so I don't wake Gram.

Chapter Six

ROUNDING THE CORNER, THE KITCHEN LOOKS like a war zone. Pots and pans, along with flour and what seems like every other baking ingredient, are spread across the counter and table. The smell of homemade goodies wafts through the air. The house phone rings so I stop to answer it.

"She's not interested," I reply and disconnect the call. "These telemarketers are relentless."

Gram simply stares at me absentmindedly.

"Smells wonderful, Betty Crocker!" I tease, breaking off a small piece of cheese danish and popping it into my mouth, praying not to chew on egg shells.

"Oh, good morning, sweetheart," my grandmother says, greeting me with a warm smile and a massive hug. "I've missed you."

I return the embrace, wiping flour from her cheek and thank God for her state of clarity today. "I missed you, too, Gram. Where were you?"

Her body stiffens momentarily before she pulls back, breaking the connection of our affection. "I've been right here...haven't I?"

In that moment, I know she's coming to terms with her illness. The faraway expression, complete with clouded eyes, is proof of the severity and progression of her disease. The memory lapses and poor judgment are starting to take a toll. My heart aches for her.

"Sorry, Gram. I've been a little distracted." I don't want to upset her by telling her that she was gone without a trace the day before. Thankfully Elaine texted me when she found Gram walking in the park near the new housing development and brought her home safely.

Turning serious eyes on me, Gram speaks with soft but firm words. "I need you to promise me something."

"Sure! What is it?"

Her chin quivers and tears pool in her eyes. "Don't let me be a burden."

"Oh, Gram!" I throw my arms around my petite grandmother and hold her as a quiet sob erupts from her tiny frame. "You won't ever be a burden."

"I know what's happening to me." Her words along with fearful eyes speak volumes.

"It's okay. We'll face this thing head on." I kiss the purple streaks in her hair and stifle the emotion from pouring out.

"Knock, knock." Mateo's voice calls through the open door and he immediately asks if we're okay when he notices our expressions. "What can I do to help?"

My lips pinch and I smile half-heartedly as I blink away the tears in my eyes. "I've got it." My words don't seem to convince him. I reiterate my control of the situation, thanking him for his concern.

Silently, hazel eyes question me and I reply by closing mine briefly, finding much needed strength. When they reopen, I plead for understanding and he simply nods then leaves.

"He's very handsome," Gram says with a quiet voice while she's still wrapped in my arms. "Do you like him?"

My lips part. "He is very handsome, Gram and yes, I like him very much. We've become good friends."

Moving her head, my grandmother pulls back and looks up at me. "Do you think you'll marry him?"

I shake my head in disbelief and roll my eyes. "Oh God, Gram. Please don't start this nonsense again. It's too early in the morning."

"What?" she squawks, staring at me with a dubious expression. "Didn't I see him climbing out of your bedroom window a few days ago? He could use the stairs if he's going to stay over."

I swallow thickly and turn to pour myself a cup of coffee, hiding my guilty eyes and red blush. "He was just being silly." After adding cream, I stir the hot beverage and take a small sip.

A sly grin creeps on my grandmother's pretty face. "Is that what they're calling it these days?"

"GRAM!" I spit out, spraying coffee all over the window above the kitchen sink.

"If I were young and single, I would do whatever he wanted. He's quite a catch. And those eyes..." She fans herself and sighs dramatically.

"I didn't have sex with him," I counter. Although the truth is I'm dying to, practically salivating at the very thought of us together.

"Well, maybe you should."

And with that, my grandmother fills a tray with homemade cheese danish and walks out the back door.

I stand with my bare foot pressed against the inside of my other leg, imitating the tree pose I learned at yoga. Somewhere in the back of my mind is the vague memory of Mackenzie dragging me to hot yoga; I remember nearly passing out in the heated room. I smile at the recollection and sip the remnants of my coffee.

Watching my grandmother smile as she distributes the homemade pastry causes me to sigh heavily. I don't want to lose her to this disease, but I know it's inevitable. I vow to do all I can to help her for as long as she needs me.

I open the window when Mateo appears before me.

"Hi. Sorry about before."

"Is everything okay?" he asks.

I nod. "It's as good as it can be for now."

He smiles warmly. "I was going to sneak into your room."

My pulse quickens when I remember what he did in my room less than twenty-four hours earlier.

He grins and sinks his teeth into the danish, leaving a smudge of icing in the corner of his mouth. Using the tip of my index finger, I wipe the side of my mouth and suggest he do the same. Keeping his eyes pinned on me, I notice the tiniest sliver of his pink tongue dart out. It continues to emerge and slide across his lips until finally making contact with the icing.

"So good," he moans. "So sweet."

I lower my foot, stand straight and then cross my ankles, needing to quell the intense buzzing between my legs. I muster the power to restrain myself from reaching through the window, grabbing his face and kissing him wildly.

"Gram is one hell of a baker." When she's not leaving egg shells in the batter.

His eyes dance with humor. "I wasn't referring to the pastry."

I smile crookedly in response. "I know."

Our moment of unspoken passion is interrupted by the ringing of my phone. I pick it up, roll my eyes and shake my head. I answer Mateo's question before he even asks. "My father."

"He must really want to talk to you."

"I don't know what could be so important that he's hounding me day and night."

"Why doesn't he just stop by?"

A loud gasp releases and shock appears on my face. "Because my uncle would probably kill him...with his bare hands."

Mateo nods, comprehending the dynamics of my family before adding, "Every family has issues."

Needing to change the subject, I ask what time he's taking his lunch hour.

"I don't have chicken salad, but I could make you a sandwich."

He smiles in appreciation. "Actually, we already ordered lunch, but I'll share with you." He winks.

I hear the back door open and notice heavy footsteps.

"I've got to go." I blow a kiss, close the window and draw the flowery curtain, leaving Mateo's stunned face behind in the rectangular frame.

Turning to face my uncle, I ask where he's been. The small black duffel bag suggests his absence was for pleasure and not business.

"I had a few things to take care of. Why?" he asks sharply as he picks up a danish from the parchment-lined baking sheet.

"We need to talk about Gram." The seriousness of my tone secures his attention.

"What's going on?" He leans against the counter and takes another bite of pastry before setting it on the sheet as if he's suddenly lost his appetite.

Pulling him to sit with me at the kitchen table, the hard conversation about his mother's worsening condition ensues as I provide all the details.

"Assisted living?" he suggests then follows up with, "I can't take care of her."

"Johnny, she just poured her life savings into this addition. We can't put her in a home. She'll stay here with me."

"I can't ask you to do that."

"You didn't," I retort, pinning him with a serious look.

"Where is she now?"

I jump up, realizing Gram's been outside for quite some

time. I pull the curtain back and spot only the men working.

"Gram," I step outside in my cotton pajamas and call her name several times before looking up to the roof where Mateo and two others are. "Have you seen my gram?"

"She said she was going to bring Ronnie some pastry," Junior says casually.

"WHAT?" I screech and run my fingers through my hair, grasping firmly at the curls.

"Cat, what's the matter?" Mateo calls down to ask, his voice laced with concern.

I expel a deep breath from my lungs and look up, shielding my eyes from the sun. "Ronnie's my grandfather," I mumble, "and he's been dead for almost twenty years."

Mateo's eyes widen and his lips form an O. "I'll be right down."

"No." I shake my head. "I've got it."

The hurt look on his face tugs my lips down into a frown. "I'm sorry. I'll be fine. My uncle and I will find her. You...just work." I race back into the house to get Johnny who is sitting at the table with his face buried in his palms.

"What are you doing?" I ask with disdain. "Your mother's out wandering the streets and you're just sitting here?"

He drags his palms along his face as he exhales. "It's their anniversary."

"But—"

"She loved that man like nobody's business." A warm and genuine smile appears on his ashen face. "I'm sure she misses him...especially today."

"That's great and all, but don't you think we need to go find her?"

Uncle Johnny shakes his head. "She'll be back soon. She does this every year. Her cheese danish were his favorite."

"I didn't kno..." Sadness fills my heart, wishing Gram could have one more day with him.

"That's the thing about love, Cat," he mumbles. "Even

when you try to let it go, it doesn't always let you go."

In this moment, I don't see my mother's brother. I don't see my pain in the ass Uncle Johnny. I see a man who is struggling with unspoken turmoil.

I ask softly, running my hand over his shoulder. "Are you okay?"

He casts his gaze up at me and replies only with a sigh and a sad smile.

Johnny stands abruptly, picks up his bag and walks toward the stairs. "Let me know if she's not back in an hour."

My "okay" falls silent when I'm left alone in the messy kitchen. I set about cleaning and putting things away when the back door opens. "Gram?" I ask.

"No, it's me."

Mateo appears in the doorway and leans against the frame. The apprehension is clear in his eyes. "Did you find her?"

I wash my hands and dry them with a dishtowel as I respond. "No, but Johnny said she's okay. She went to visit her husband on their anniversary." The tightness in my chest causes me to look down.

"But I thought you said—"

"I did." My eyes sweep upward to look at him. "The cemetery is only a few blocks away."

"Come here." Strong arms widen and beckon me. My feet hesitate for a moment before closing the gap between our bodies. I swore I would never need a man to make me feel good or to comfort me, but the moment I wrap my arms around him, a sense of calm is restored in my soul. I know everything is going to be alright.

His chest rises with a deep inhale and falls with an exhale through forced lips. I tip my head back and look up, meeting his eyes once again. The sunlight filtering into the kitchen shines on him, making his warm and wonderful eyes appear more green than brown. With each lazy blink, they burst with unspoken concern and compassion for my predicament.

"What am I going to do with you?" he asks, cupping my face to tilt my head back, providing the perfect access to search my face before lowering his mouth to mine.

I grin against his warm lips. "I've got a few ideas."

A low moan vibrates in his throat, and I squeeze him harder.

"Wanna take a ride with me to pick up lunch?"

"Now?" I move back and look at my pink and white pin-striped pajamas.

Shaking his head, he replies, "In a little while" before dragging his gaze downward, letting his eyes travel the length of my body as he smirks. "Or you could be lunch."

"What would the other guys eat?"

He slides his hands down to my ass and gives the flesh a squeeze. "I don't know, but I'm not sharing."

My nipples immediately react. The feeling of my tight buds straining against the cotton awakens my desire for him and I long for Mateo's hands to roll them between his fingers. It amazes me how his touch, let alone his utterances, can have such a dramatic effect on my body, leaving me wanton and desperate all at once.

I glide my hands and find the nape of his neck, simultaneously pulling his head down and moving my lips to his ears.

"Please put me out of my misery soon," I murmur the whispered plea.

His nose skims my jaw line and his lips dot it with slow kisses. "Soon."

My eyes close and I fill my lungs with a quiet breath.

"I'll see you in thirty minutes."

Unable to speak, I swallow thickly and nod.

Without a moment of hesitation, Mateo detaches himself from our embrace and hurries back outside.

I glance at the clock and decide to give my grandmother

another twenty minutes before I send out the search party, remembering my uncle's assurance that she should be home in an hour.

Racing to the stairs, I take them two at a time and enter my bedroom. The white envelope on the nightstand glares at me, begging for attention and correspondence. I reach for it as I collapse onto my bed and expel a heavy sigh. Rereading the small font, I hold the thin paper between my fingers and wish there were an alternative, but deep down, I know there isn't and while some wouldn't agree with my decision, it's mine to make.

My fingers glide slowly over the round circles on my phone. With each tap, anxiety builds within me and finally explodes when I hear ringing. I wait and wait until the line connects.

"Hello?" a deep voice answers.

My mouth opens but makes no sound. I clear my throat and make a second attempt.

"Hello, Abimola...it's Caterina Ryan."

"Where are we going?" I ask, sitting alongside Mateo as I eye the tan carpenter pants that cover his long legs. I feel a sense of melancholy over how loosely they fit and I chuckle quietly.

"What are you laughing about?"

"I like your other pants," I state casually.

His cocked eyebrow implies a need for clarification.

"The ones you wear when you're not working. Like the ones you wore to the bar the last night."

He touches the material covering my thigh and squeezes my leg gently before gliding his hands upward, exposing my skin. "And I prefer this much more than the underwear you wear to work."

My laughter is laced with doubt. "First of all, they're not underwear—they're just *very short* shorts and we all know men love to see tits and ass."

"While that may be true, I don't particularly care about other men looking at your tits and ass."

"Awww! That's sweet! You've got that macho thing going on. I like it." I tease, adding a wink to keep the banter playful. My smile only hints at the immense pleasure his words bring.

"I don't know if it's a Puerto Rican thing, but I tend to be a little hot-headed and overprotective when it comes to my girls."

My smile falls. "*Girls*?"

"Yeah, I have a lot of cousins who are girls..." His eyes burn into mine when he adds, "and you. You're my girl."

The trepidation in me settles and my smile returns.

I slide my hand over his and intertwine our fingers, appreciating his soft grasp of affirmation.

I'm yanked from a moment lost in my own, private thoughts when the truck suddenly jars after hitting a huge pothole in the pavement.

"Shit! I didn't see that coming," he mumbles.

My phone rings as Mateo pulls into the small parking lot. I mouth that I'll be right in just before I answer the call from Gram's neurologist to confirm her rescheduled appointment.

Walking into the busy deli, I notice the upbeat, fast-paced Spanish music permeating throughout the small store. Customers stare at me, probably wondering what a blue-eyed blonde white girl is doing here. I ignore their murmurs as my eyes scan the space filled with shelves which are lined with Goya products. A variety of Caribbean fruits and vegetables fill the square bins.

I follow the sound of Mateo's voice and find him standing casually with his elbows resting on the glass fixture and a bright smile on his face. A curvy woman faces the back wall and appears to be packing a large paper bag. She says something in Spanish and calls him by the same name I've heard Junior use before.

"Yeah, it's good. I just wish I knew more about the schedule."

My mouth drops open when Iza turns around. She seems nearly as shocked as I do judging by the expression on her caramel face. Her eyes dart from me to Mateo and again she speaks in Spanish, tossing a hard look at him.

He turns to me and extends a hand.

"You remember Izabel, don't you?" he says with a grin.

I notice her eyes constrict as she hisses, "Don't call me that. You know I hate that name!"

"Hey," I say with a tight smile.

Mumbling beneath her breath in Spanish, Iza walks to the register and presses the keys forcefully.

Mateo's amusement ceases when he hands over the cash and tosses her a hard look, warning her with serious eyes and a subtle shake of his head.

An older man emerges from behind a swinging door and asks with a heavy accent, "Will we see you next week, Teo?"

Mateo releases the hold on my hand before stepping over to greet the man. They clasp hands firmly and bump shoulders.

"I don't know." He glances back at me. "I've got a lot going on right now, but I'll let you know." Mateo smiles at the man who simply nods in return.

"Where does he want you to go?"

"I fill in when his drummer isn't available."

"What?" I gasp then laugh. "You didn't tell me you played the drums."

Mateo shrugs. "I thought I told you."

I shake my head as I take the bag from Mateo. When we reach the truck, I peek inside the large paper bag before setting it on the floor between my feet.

"Nope. You didn't mention it."

"Sorry."

"What'd you order? You could feed an entire army with all the food in here."

He laughs lightly. "I'm tired of eating sandwiches for lunch every day and since today is my day to get lunch, I thought I'd get something different."

I feel slightly affronted about his sandwich comment especially after I offered to make a "sandwich" only hours before. He must notice my apprehension because he takes my hand in his and smiles.

"But if *you* made me a sandwich, I would eat it." His countenance turns dark and his eyes narrow slightly. "I would eat anything you spread before me and I'm sure I would love it."

My fingers curl and my knuckles graze my lips, stifling a lewd solicitation from escaping.

"You know you're killing me, right?" I groan, folding my legs over one another, allowing my dress to reveal the ivory skin of my inner thigh.

"You're playing with fire, *mamacita*."

"Good! I like things *caliente!*" I stress the word and feign an accent while fanning myself.

His amusement surfaces as deep laughter before he takes a sharp right turn into a vacant spot at the medical center. He throws the truck into Park and takes a hold of my face between his hands, forcing me to look directly at him.

From his full lips, a litany of beautifully rolled words seduces me. Staring into his eyes, I fall prey to the animal in him as he lures me in with carefully crafted utterances that force my tongue to glide across my lips. It's the most beautiful sound I've ever heard in my life.

I release a moaned sigh as his voice deepens and transforms into a hard, almost angry, tone. My body relaxes at the single utterance of "*querida*."

His lips crash against mine and his tongue enters my

mouth with a sense of urgency. Between passionate kisses, a continuation of mumbled declarations in his native language caress my lips.

"Mateo," I pant, placing a hand on each of his wrists. "Please—"

"You like that?" he murmurs against my face.

"Oh God—I love it, but I need more."

Hazel eyes full of promise scorch mine. "I will give you more...when the time is right."

After a final kiss, Mateo pulls into traffic with his hand on my thigh, a smile on his face and an erection in his pants.

I lead Mateo to the huge maple tree and pat the cushion of the makeshift porch swing that replaced the tire swing of my youth. Memories of Uncle Johnny playing with me, pushing me higher and higher before Gram yelled at him produce a smile and I tell Mateo about it.

"So you guys were close?" he asks, pulling a small container out of the bag after handing me a plastic fork.

Nodding, I reply, "We still are for the most part." I pull my hair back and point to the half inch reminder of the day. "Although he did give me this scar."

"How did that happen?" he inquires as he inspects the jagged pink line on my forehead. "Did he do that one, too?" His finger glides across to the other scar.

"No, that was in self-defense."

"Sounds like you played rough when you were a kid," he laughs, returning his attention to our food.

"I never started trouble, but I sure as hell finished it."

"Good to know." He winks. "Junior and I have had our share of fistfights over the years. It was usually over some girl. Sometimes I would just go after her because I knew he liked her."

"That's so mean!"

"And the uncle who scarred your head wasn't?"

"Not usually. He's going through something, but he's not been forthcoming with information. I hate that. I hate when people don't tell the whole truth."

I notice Mateo looks away for a moment and then glance sideways at me. "Maybe he's waiting for the right time. Maybe he's waiting to see how things turn out."

Removing the plastic lid, Mateo picks up something resembling a flattened and fried banana. He dips it in the garlic sauce then holds it out for me to bite.

"You first," I mutter, worried I won't like it.

He laughs and shoves the entire piece in his mouth, adding an exaggerated moan of delight.

I roll my eyes and take a small bite when a second piece is offered. I chew slowly as I decide whether or not I like it.

Waiting for my answer, Mateo asks, "So? What do you think?"

"It's okay." I smirk as I take another bite.

"You won't know if you like it if you never try it."

"Are you only referring to Spanish food?"

A devilish looks spreads across his face and his eyes travel down to my chest before drifting back to my face.

"Nope."

I ignore the tingling between my legs.

"It's not my fault really. My mom wasn't much of a cook."

He considers my statement with a wary expression. "I can relate."

"Your mom didn't know how to cook?"

Shaking his head, he replies, "She was never home that's why I lived with my abuela."

He smiles fondly. "She was four feet eight inches of attitude. You did not cross that woman unless you wanted to get clocked upside the head with her chancleta."

"A what?" I ask, my voice rising playfully.

"A slipper." Mateo widens his eyes, mirroring my shocked expression as he nods slowly. "Hispanic women are no joke!"

"Did your mom work a lot?"

A quick shrug of his shoulder reveals his indifference, but I detect an intimation of hurt in his eyes. "Yeah, on the streets," he states sarcastically.

I swallow hard. "Oh. I'm sorry."

"It was a long time ago," he responds dryly.

My phone rings and I reject my father's call once again. I set my phone down and tell him how my mother woke up one day and left. We hadn't heard from her until we received news that she was killed in a car accident."

I gaze into his hazel eyes and my heart aches. Beneath the apathy, reflected back at me is compassion and sorrow. Aside from our shared love of music, a sense of camaraderie grows between us. We each hide a painful past of being raised by our grandmothers after our parents abandoned us.

We continue to eat our lunch packed with surprisingly delicious ethnic food in silence before he asks a question I don't see coming.

"When are you leaving for Africa?"

I choke on the sip of water I've just taken.

"How..." I clear my throat. "How did you know about that?"

"You told me about it and..." A look of guilt washes over him and he tries to cover it with a gorgeous grin. "The letter was on your nightstand."

Anger swells, revealing itself in the form of a nasty scowl on my face. "And that was an invitation to read it?" I squawk, outraged that he took the liberty to read my mail. "Goddammit, Mateo. We talked about this!"

"I'm sorry. You had already told me about it and the letter was sitting there. I saw the word "Congratulations" and I was curious."

I push the inhaled breath out slowly through a small

opening of my lips and close my eyes. I need a moment before I spew misdirected words at him.

When I reopen my eyes, I find him with his head tilted to the side, silently asking for forgiveness complete with puppy dog eyes.

Detecting no malice in his gaze, I chuckle but can't hide the irritated sigh. "You need to respect my privacy. I won't tolerate you or anyone else reading or sharing my things."

His expression sobers. "I'm really sorry. I didn't think it was that big of a deal."

"But we talked about this!"

"No, you said not to read your journal."

"That's just semantics!"

Casting my eyes downward to mask the pain, I shuffle my foot along the grass beneath the swing. "I have huge issues with that."

"But you let me read your journal that day in your room. The things you wrote are really private."

My eyes snap upward and stare at him. "Don't you see?! I gave you *permission*. It's different."

A single hand slides to my face and pulls me close. With his soft lips against mine, Mateo offers a tender, sincere and final apology while accepting my absolution. Bringing our kiss to a close, I rest my forehead against his, my fingers grasping the tufts of hair touching the nape of his neck.

"I feel—"

I suppress the words on my tongue.

"What is it, Cat?" His fingers caress my cheek and I open my eyes and lean into his palm. His eyes seek for the completion of my thought. "What do you feel?"

My throat constricts and I swallow thickly.

"I feel like you should probably get back to work. I feel like we've been here for a lot longer than an hour."

Something similar to disappointment appears on his face before he offers a small smile.

"Thank you for having lunch with me," he says as he packs up the remnants of food and places it in the bag.

"Thank you for asking..." I reply with a smile of my own.

Walking alongside one another, we talk about superficial things until we reach the house and find Junior and the other men returning to work.

"I'll call you later," he says softly as if he doesn't want anyone to hear.

"Okay."

We part ways as he climbs the huge ladder and I walk into the house.

"How was lunch, sweetheart?" Gram asks when I find her standing at the kitchen window with a cup of coffee in her hand. I eye the beverage and the slice of toast smeared with a combination of yellow and purple before looking through the window, realizing she must have seen me walking back with Mateo.

"Lunch was nice," I respond, raising an eyebrow to question her lunch choice. "What are you eating?"

"Coffee and toast."

"I see that, but what's on your toast?"

The ringing of the house phone halts Gram's response.

"I don't understand why you keep calling this number. She's told you a thousand times she's not interested. Don't call again," I bellow into the phone and slam the receiver down. "They're so annoying."

I find Gram still looking down at the toasted bread in seemingly deep thought. "Honey mustard and grape jelly."

Disgust mars my face. "Oh, Gram! That's awful! Those things don't go together."

Picking up the slice, she brings it to her mouth and allows it to linger for a moment before she speaks. "Sometimes the most unlikely combinations go wonderfully together."

I look my grandmother straight in the eye, deeming her to be wise despite her illness. "I agree, Gram. I completely agree."

"He's the one, you know. You're going to marry him."

Gone is my wise gram replaced by the delusional one.

Ignoring her comment, I glance at the calendar and remind her that she has a rescheduled appointment for tomorrow at ten o'clock in the morning.

"Why was it rescheduled?"

My eyes travel to her colored hair and I smile coyly, knowing my words are deceitful. "I think you had another appointment that day. It's no big deal."

I can see the internal struggle reflected in her eyes.

"I'm going to head down to Trina's for a few hours. Are you going to be okay on your own until I get back?"

"Why wouldn't I be? I'm not a child," she barks with an angry tone.

I chuckle to mask my fear. "I don't want you flirting with any of the guys outside— that's all."

Popping my head back into the kitchen, I scold her. "And stop telling Mateo things about me!"

After ordering an Uber, I text Mackenzie as I wait at the end of my driveway.

A whistle grabs my attention as my best friend and I exchange text messages. I turn around and look up in search of the sound. Cupping my hand to shield my eyes, I see Mateo smiling down at me from his perch on the roof.

"Where are you going?" he asks, standing casually as if he weren't thirty feet in the air.

Worry races through me. "Be careful!"

"Afraid I might fall?" he taunts, balancing on one foot.

"Mateo! Stop it!" I grit, stomping my foot and huffing my frustration.

"If I fall, will you catch me?"

Even with the distance between us, I can see his serious expression, his eyes burning into me.

My heartbeat quickens and I can hear my pulse thumping

in my ears as adrenaline pumps through my body, forcing it to react immediately.

"I'll be here." My smile grows wider. "I'll catch you."

The Uber arrives seconds later and I wave a quick goodbye to Mateo.

When my phone alerts of a text message, I pull it out of my oversized bag, fully expecting to see Mack's name. I can't hide the surprise when another name appears.

"Mateo," I sigh as I read his message.

`You communicate better with the written word. Tell me what you feel. Be honest with me.`

I gaze out the window and think about my response.

My fingers fly across the flat surface, detailing my feelings for him. I know I've probably said too much and will likely scare him away, but he asked for my honesty so honesty is what he will receive.

I watch the dots move and then cease until four words materialize.

`The feelings are mutual.`

That's it? I think to myself. I practically wrote a book about my feelings and *that's* what he chose to write back.

My fingers prepare for a rebuttal but then freeze.

I've said too much. My own stupidity mocks me, repeating the torment.

Stupid, stupid me.

Chapter Seven

LATER THAT AFTERNOON AS I PREPARE TO CLOSE
the shop since Trina has already left for the day, I hear the small bell jingle, indicating someone has entered the shop.

"Hi!" I call from beneath the mountain of newly consigned merchandise. "I'll be right with you."

My weary arms drop the pile onto the counter and my eyes widen when I come face to face with Caleb, the musician from the park. He stands before me with a guitar hanging across his body and a man bun restraining his dirty blonde hair.

"Caleb!" I greet him with a smile. "What are you doing here?"

"Hey. What's up?"

My eyes dart from side to side, suggesting this is my place of employment to which he simply smiles.

"Our men's section isn't nearly as big as the women's, but you're free to browse."

"I actually came here to see you."

The word "oh" falls from my lips.

An awkward moment fills the space between us.

"Well, here I am."

"I'm working on a new piece and can't seem to get the riff

down. I was wondering if you might be able to help me out."

My surprise is evident on my face. "Yeah! I'd love to."

"Really?"

"When do you want to meet?"

"Uh...I kinda thought we could do it now...if you're not too busy."

I check the time on the old grandfather clock then look at the pile before replying, "We can do that, but first I have to hang up all these clothes."

He nods and waits.

Grabbing a few hangers, I set them down before him and grin. "Feel free to help."

As Caleb detaches the guitar from his body, his shirt rides up, revealing a line of hair on his abdomen. I look away quickly before he catches me ogling his midsection.

After every article of clothing is hung and arranged on the rack, Caleb follows me over to the front of the store where a floral-patterned loveseat sits.

"Show me what you've got."

Caleb scoots forward, adjusting the guitar across his body and smiles shyly when our knees touch. I ignore the contact and wait for him to strum the instrument.

My eyes close as I listen to the melody, my head bobs, memorizing each chord as it reaches my ears.

"That's good," I comment before offering some feedback.

Taking my suggestions, Caleb replays the riff until it flows seamlessly. When he sings the lyrics, the depiction of a beautiful story told in song is created.

Time slips by when I join in, harmonizing the melody until a knock on the front door interrupts the music.

I jump to my feet when I see Mateo standing there.

Unlocking the door, I open it wide and greet him with a small smile which he does not return. I feel unease creep in when he darts a glance at Caleb and then back at me, pinning me with a hard glare and a cold attitude.

"I came to pick you up," he states, explaining his reason for showing up at my place of work.

"Thanks, but I could've called an Uber."

"Well, I'm here now so let's go."

My face contorts into a look of confusion and my voice rises. "Excuse me?"

Caleb rises and slips the guitar over his body. "I'm gonna take off. I'll see you around, Cat. Thanks for your help."

Mateo opens the door but doesn't reply when Caleb says goodbye.

I stand there silently wondering who this man is.

"What time do you have to be at work?" he asks curtly. The tension in his body is visible and seems to escalate when his jaw ticks.

"I'm not working tonight."

"You didn't tell me that."

I gasp, responding that I didn't know I had to give him an account of my whereabouts.

"You don't get it, do you?"

"Get what?" I hiss.

"I want to spend every minute with you that I possibly can before I have to le—" He sighs, rubbing his palms across his face. "Did you not read my text?"

I chuckle darkly. "All four words?"

Mateo closes the space between our bodies and pulls me flush.

"Cat, what you wrote in that text message," he whispers quietly, "is the same exact thing I would have written to you."

My eyes fill with moisture as I stare into his hazel eyes.

"Really?"

"Every. Last. Word."

With that, he crushes his mouth against mine and erases the feelings of frustration and apprehension. My hands claw at the Billy Joel concert T-shirt covering his back, needing to feel the heat of his skin. My core throbs at the contact and

I moan against his lips.

"Come with me," he pleads with desire.

I nod and hum my agreement.

After rushing to get my bag from the back room, I lock the front door and follow Mateo out to the truck.

"Are you hungry?" he asks when we are both seated in the cab.

"No," I reply quickly.

"Good."

Mateo pushes the truck to reach a high speed as we travel on the highway and enter the next town over.

"Where are we going?"

Ignoring my query, Mateo exits the highway and pulls into the parking lot of a Marriott Hotel before he turns to me.

"If you don't want to, then we don't."

I understand what his words imply so I unbuckle my seat belt and answer with a passionate kiss.

Butterflies dance in my belly when we enter the cool room. I notice Mateo's hand matches mine; both are damp and sweaty. I can feel my pulse beating like a drum in my ear when I see the large plush King-size bed sitting in the center of the room. I startle at the sound of the door shutting behind me but am comforted by the circling motion of Mateo's thumb on my skin.

Leading me further into the room, Mateo stops suddenly and turns to face me. He reaches for my bag and removes it, setting it down on the desk chair. "You won't be needing this."

I gulp nervously, desperately wanting to move forward but completely fearful of how my heart will survive once this is over.

With nimble fingers, Mateo unbuttons the three small

circles in the front of my dress. His nose skims the skin on my shoulder as he gently pulls the zipper down. My eyes close when his fingers lightly trace a line from my fingertips and travel upward to the crook of my elbow, finally ending at my clavicle.

He moans his pleasure when he slides the strap down and replaces it with a kiss.

"Tell me," he whispers in my ear, sending chills down my spine.

My head lolls to the side. "Tell you what?" I mirror his quiet voice.

My dress falls to my feet and my strapless bra unclasped.

"Tell me what you wrote in that text message."

His mouth moves to the other side of my neck.

"Why?" I sigh.

"Because anyone can write words. I want to hear how you feel. I want to hear you say them."

Lowering his body, Mateo drags my bikini underwear down my legs and waits for me to lift each foot to step out of it. His hands skim the length of my legs, burning my skin with desire until one hand grabs my ass while the other skates around to the front, finding the heat of my sex. One kiss followed by several more, grace my skin as his fingers part me and caress the sensitive bud.

"Tell me," he demands, replacing kisses with gentle bites.

"I said I feel things for you I have no right to."

"Go on," Mateo encourages with a slide of his hand which makes me gasp.

"I said I feel as though I've known you forever."

"Continue." His tongue slides over the seam of my backside.

"Oh God, I can't think."

His fingers immediately cease their wonderful massage.

"Okay, okay...I remember." I smile.

"I said I feel like my heart beats faster when I'm with you."

"What else?"

"I said I feel a connection with you that I've never felt with anyone else."

"Yes," he breathes as he moves his hand from my ass and slides it to my breasts, tugging at my nipple.

"I said I feel like I can trust you."

Mateo's lips reach my ears. "There's more, Cat."

"I don't remember," I lie.

"Don't lie to me. Ever."

I release a small breath as saliva thickens in my mouth and I prepare to utter my final words, knowing it will change things once I've said them aloud. "And... I said I feel like you're someone I could fall in love with."

I nearly lose my footing when my body is spun around quickly and I come face to face with lust and desire.

Drawing me in with his eyes, Mateo's lips hover over mine, denying me the contact I crave. Instead he wraps his arms around my body and pulls me against him. The bulge straining against his pants seeks release as his hips roll.

Without a second thought, I yank the T-shirt from his body and freeze when I observe the perfection before me. Hot, tattooed skin covers thick layers of hard, ripped muscle of his chest. My fingers slide over the dips of his firm abdomen and move to the V that continues into his jeans. After placing a kiss on his chest, my hands grip his slim waist and move to his back. I drag my fingernails down his skin and utter a plea. "Please."

In no time at all, Mateo sheds his clothes and stands before me in his glory. My tongue longs to taste his entire body.

"What was my response to your text?"

Dazed and confused, I ask, "What?"

Mateo cups my face and looks at me. "What was my response?"

"You said," I stammer, "You said the feelings were mutual."

"A thousand percent mutual."

Slowly, he walks us backward until I feel the bed behind me.

"A thousand percent," he growls in my ear.

My nakedness is on full display when he lays me back on the bed. Bearing his weight with his elbows, Mateo widens the space between my legs and makes room for his hips. I feel the tip of his erection at my slick opening.

He takes a lock of my hair and secures it, allowing the curl to glide between his fingers before he twirls it, wrapping the blond strands around the tip.

"You're so beautiful."

My eyes close momentarily in response to his flattering remark before reopening slowly.

I want to return the compliment, but I'm completely speechless.

"This...you and me...this is happening..." he mumbles quietly, "so fast."

I nod in agreement and add a small crooked grin, acknowledging how crazy it all is.

Keeping his gaze locked on me, Mateo pushes himself up to a kneeling position. The raking of his eyes over my bare flesh makes me shiver and causes my nipples to pebble. With a raspy whisper, this gorgeous man utters a string of passionate words which are accompanied by gentle kisses down over the swell of my breasts. He continues to bathe me with tenderness as his lips taste the skin of my navel until he reaches my core.

"*Preciosa*," he mumbles as he parts my legs and kisses the highest part of my inner thigh. My fingers clench the soft cotton bed covering and my eyes stare at the ceiling, breathing my way through his delicious torment.

One slow lick of my wet flesh is soon followed by another. His long fingers are added and quickly disappear into my hidden place of desire, curling and searching for the one spot that will make me explode.

"Hold this pussy open for me," he orders as his free hand trails lower to circle the unchartered puckered ring.

I gasp at the unfamiliar contact, but immediately relax when gratification overpowers modesty.

Using my feet, I push myself up, angling my body to maximize the pleasure from his mouth. Muffled words of encouragement beckon me to orgasm. I close my eyes, writhe in complete bliss and come apart. My pent-up frustration and desire for him release in a wave of moisture and moans. Mateo's hot tongue continues to move gently, consuming my orgasm as it spreads throughout my extremities.

"Oh my fu—" With a quick yank of the throw pillow over my face, I stifle the vulgar words and bury my smile.

"You're completely drenched," he declares with a tone of amusement, disbelief and pride.

The bed shifts and I feel a layer of heat above me. He removes the pillow from my face and looks down at me.

"Why are you hiding your face from me?"

"I'm not," I mumble as I struggle to regain possession of the pillow.

"Don't hide from me. I love to look at your face. I want to look at all of you."

Mateo's eyes slip from mine and travel down my body before returning his gaze to my lips. He lowers his mouth and covers mine, pushing his tongue in and swirling it around, forcing me to taste the remnants of my release.

He moans something in Spanish against my neck then raises his head abruptly.

"Are you on the pill?"

I shake my head but quickly clarify that I am on another form of birth control.

"I don't have a condom because I didn't plan for this to happen tonight, but—"

I nod my understanding and disappointment fills me

that he's going to say we have to wait yet again to make love.

"Cat, I'm clean. I just had a physical last month and I haven't been with anyone else since I met you. I promise."

Gazing into his eyes, I see honesty. I see truth.

"I believe you."

My hands reach for the back of his head and pull his face to mine. "I trust you, Mateo."

"Gah!" My eyes widen and I cry out when he enters me, my body unprepared for the feeling of stretching and vigorous movements.

"Are you okay?" he pants in my ear then raises his body, withdrawing his length from my opening.

"God yes! I just didn't realize how...how big you are."

His eyes twinkle and his lips form a grin, beaming with obvious pride at my assessment.

"I'll go easy this time," he says, pushing himself once again into my core. "Better?"

I hum my pleasure and drag my nails up and down his flexed biceps. My lips find his chest and kiss a trail from one side to the other. As if receiving the consent to thrust deeper, Mateo pistons relentlessly, driving so hard into me, I think I might split in two.

Then with a feral, guttural groan, Mateo releases and pumps his violent orgasm into me before pulling out and expelling hot liquid onto my stomach. Sated, his body stills. With my legs wrapped around his ass, I prevent him from moving even if he wanted to. My hands glide over his back, feeling the sheen of sweat pouring from his skin. I pull him closer, hugging his body tightly.

Heavy, ragged pants infiltrate my ears as Mateo's heart begins to regulate, beating once again at a normal speed.

"I can't move." He chuckles into my neck as his nose skims the damp skin.

"Then don't."

My body immediately notices the absence when Mateo

pushes up onto his elbows and slides off of me. My core tightens as if begging for another helping of his deliciousness. The bed dips when he rolls onto his side and although my eyes are closed, I can feel the weight of his stare while his hands gently caress my breast. Slowly, he drags his fingertip upward until it rests at my hairline.

"You have a nice profile," he mumbles, causing my cheek to pull into a smile. Using the tip of his finger, he glides slowly, tracing a slow line from my forehead down to my nose and over my lips.

I remain still, enjoying the feel of his light strokes over my cheeks. Lovely words are whispered with each caress. I don't know what they mean, but I relish the beauty of the language and how they make me feel.

"You realize I don't know what you're saying, right?" My eyes widen, reiterating my obvious point.

He turns my head with a slight tug of my chin. I look at him and smile when I find a massive grin on his face.

"I know you don't. That's what makes this so fun."

Pouting playfully, I counter, "But you could be saying awful, horrible things to me."

Shaking his head subtly, he lowers his mouth, lingering his lips over mine. "Trust me, I'm not. You feel my words right here." He touches the skin that covers my heart.

I peck his lips quickly before jumping to my feet. "I need to jump in the shower."

"Why?" His dark eyebrow rises sharply. "I'm not done with you yet."

With my hands on my hips, I debate whether to shower or join him when I see his erection is stiff and hard, ready for another round. My eyes dance with delight when he rolls onto his back, crossing his arms beneath his head, putting himself on full, uncensored display for my viewing pleasure.

Maintaining eye contact, I take a few steps away from the bed and chuckle when he frowns.

"You're going to leave me like this?"

I round the corner of the bed and stop before proceeding to climb back onto it slowly, methodically. I lick my lips as if I am a starving, wild animal eyeing my prey. Mounting his body, I lead him into me and we find the perfect rhythm. With his hands on my ass, he thrusts upward as I ride him. Knowing he's close, I angle my body and take his dick into my hand and stroke him hard until he groans in ecstasy.

Having been satisfied and now weary, I collapse onto his chest and listen again as he utters sweet words in his native language.

"Now we take a shower."

After grabbing his phone from his discarded pants, Mateo follows me into the bathroom and fills the small space with music from an app. He sings along to almost every song as his hands roam freely over my body, washing away the scent of sex and sweat. Facing me, he pushes the hair away from my face when an upbeat song filters in.

Scorching hazel eyes meet mine as he matches Bruno Mars' words about it being a beautiful night and wanting to get married. I swallow hard. The intense look on his face scrambles with my emotions because my heart wants to accept the spoken words while my brain reminds me they are simply love lyrics from a popular song on the radio.

The song is interrupted by the ringing of his phone.

"Do you need to get that?"

He shakes his head. "What I need is right here."

When evidence of my hidden sentiments pools in the corner of my eyes, I reach forward and embrace him. I can't let him see me like this. I don't understand the feelings running rampant through my heart which make my pulse quicken and allow my thoughts to become wildly absurd.

"Come here," Mateo says, pulling me up into his arms as my legs wrap around his waist. I bury my face in the crook of his neck and let my tears mingle with the hot water that pours over our naked bodies. His hand cradles the back of my head as he shushes me. "Don't cry."

I smile weakly and lie as I wipe my tears with the back of my hand. "I'm not."

"I feel what you feel."

The deluge of emotions rushes forward and the water works begin again. My hold on his neck tightens as a quiet sob rips through my body.

Again, he attempts to quell my whimper.

"You're making me feel bad. Was the sex that bad?" he laughs in attempt to lighten the mood.

I toss my head back and come face to face with him.

"That was the best sex I've ever had in my entire life!"

He looks at me dubiously. "Really?"

"God, yes!" I reply then feel the joy slip from my face, wondering briefly if he's had a better experience with someone else...possibly someone like Iza. I scramble to stand on my own two feet and turn the faucet off, leaving only the sound of the music to remain.

"I didn't pay enough attention to you." He kisses my shoulder as I step out. I turn to look at him with a puzzled look on my face.

He moves around me and uses a small white towel to wipe the steam, allowing our eyes to meet in the mirror. "The next time I make love to you, I will take my sweet time."

"I can't wait." I bite my lip to suppress the smile at his word choice.

After getting dressed and spending a few more moments kissing, we walk out of the hotel hand in hand to find the moon has replaced the evening sun and is now shining in the dark night sky.

"Are you hungry *now*?"

"Starved!" I reply animatedly, bringing our joined hands up to my mouth and sinking my teeth playfully into his thumb.

"Don't do that! I'll drag you back inside that hotel."

I shrug casually. "Who says we have to go inside a room?"

Mateo unclasps our hands to start the engine and drives us to a small diner off the highway.

He asks about the grin on my face.

"This place doesn't serve spicy Spanish food," I answer his question.

"Punk!"

I laugh. "Aww, but you love this punk, don't ya!?"

His countenance turns serious as he looks at me pensively, his hazel gaze exploring my face until he says, "Let's go."

We walk in silence across the parking lot as the tension builds. We are seated in a large booth near the window. I move the paper placemat forward and notice the small jukebox mounted on the veneer tabletop. Spinning the dial, I stop at Bruno Mars' song and smile.

"I could listen to you sing all day. You should go on The Voice or something."

He acknowledges his talent with a quick nod which reveals a sense of confidence rather than arrogance.

"You could be the next Ricky Martin," I quip, spinning the dial once again before a waitress walks by, stating that she'll be right over.

"Ricky Martin?" he squawks, huffing his displeasure at the comparison.

"Yes! You know, 'Livin' la Vida Loca!' I bite the inside of my cheek to prevent a full blown grin from spreading across my playful face. "He's really nice, too."

Furrowing a brow, Mateo asks how I know this fact.

"I've met him a few times."

Mateo scoffs, rolling his eyes and looking at me pointedly. "Seeing someone in concert doesn't count, Cat.

Affronted, I reply. "I *did* meet him. Why would I make that up?"

"Fine. You met him, but please don't ever compare me to

him again."

"He sure can move his hips," I toss out.

I feel the weight of Mateo's stare, filled with challenge and memories of our time together just a short time ago. "I can move my hips, too."

The ache between my legs remembers.

I swallow hard when I meet his eyes, my tongue peeking through to lick my bottom lip; it, too, aches with remembrance. Sensing a shift in our light banter, I toss my hands in the air defensively. "Sheesh! All I'm saying is you have talent. You should do something with it."

"Are you kidding?" That eyebrow rises again. "Cat, people would kill for *your* talent! Hell, Alicia Keys would probably want to sing with you if she ever heard you."

She already has I think to myself. "I've met her, too."

"Ok, now I know you're lying," he laughs while I narrow my eyes.

The waitress saves me from providing an explanation when she sets down two glasses of water and takes our order.

Until our food arrives, we chat about insignificant things until my gram's name is mentioned.

"She's got dementia. It's been progressing rather quickly and my uncle and I have some decisions to make."

I nearly choke on the sip of water when he suggests an assisted living facility may be an option.

"I would never put Gram in a home. I couldn't do that to her."

"Then why put the addition on the house?" he asks, unaware of the wound he is opening.

I sigh. "She's in denial about my mother's death. When the car crashed, it exploded and she had to be identified by dental records. Gram doesn't believe she really died because we didn't have a body to bury and now that my uncle moved back, she wants to make sure there's enough room for everyone."

"Wow. I didn't realize she was that bad."

I tighten my lips and nod solemnly. "She has a few good days here and there."

"Here you go. One grilled cheese and onion rings," the waitress says, setting a plate down in front of me before she sets a turkey club sandwich in front of Mateo. I reach for the ketchup and squirt a small circle onto my plate, looking up when I notice the waitress seems to be lingering at the table.

"We're all set," Mateo says, dismissing her.

Picking up one of the triangle pieces of gooey cheese-filled toast, I dip it into the ketchup and take a small bite.

"Are you a singer or something?" she asks.

My eyes flash upward and look at Mateo who opens his mouth to speak but stops abruptly when he realizes she's addressing me.

"Weren't you on Star Search or one of those shows?"

Mateo looks at me expectantly as does she.

She narrows her eyes at me. "You look exactly like that little girl with an amazing voice. I think she played the piano, too."

I freeze mid-chew and smile weakly, shaking my head. With a mouthful of food, I lie. "I've heard that a lot."

"I wonder whatever happened to her," she says absentmindedly, shrugging her shoulder. "Well, enjoy your food. Let me know if you need anything."

Taking another bite, I remain quiet and keep my eyes cast down, avoiding Mateo's heavy stare.

"That was you, wasn't it?" he inquires quietly.

I take a sip of water then set the glass down, dragging my eyes slowly to meet his. I nod once and look out the window at the streetlight, remembering how the stage lights blinded me and I couldn't see anything or anyone in the audience. I found my father standing in the wing, encouraging me to do my best.

Rough fingers caress my hand and curious eyes beg for

an explanation.

When I don't respond, he simply asks, "What happened?"

My throat constricts and no words emerge.

"Cat, you can trust me, remember?"

I inhale a small breath and recall the events of my youth—my time in the limelight.

Mateo listens intently and asks questions which I answer honestly.

"What father would push his daughter into the spotlight for his own selfish gains?"

"Mine," I reply dryly. "Our relationship was never the same after I refused to be a pawn in his game. I was his ticket to the big leagues until he found someone else's coattails to ride on."

"He sounds like a bastard."

"Now you see why I don't answer his calls or want to see him."

"I'd probably punch him in the face if I ever met him."

Although an appreciative smile spreads on my face, I shake my head. "He's not worth it."

"I'm sorry that happened to you, but..."

I blink slowly. "But what?"

"You're," he breathes with exasperation mingled with hesitation, "incredibly gifted, Cat. You could do it now..." He reaches for my hand and rubs my knuckles. "On your terms."

I lock my eyes as my lips pinch together, displaying my adamant refusal. "I'm not interested in that life. It's full of snakes and liars."

After releasing a heavy sigh, Mateo mumbles quietly, "That's too bad."

The ride back to my house is quiet and somewhat awkward despite our intertwined hands and subtle smiles. I wonder what he's thinking about. Have his thoughts drifted back to the hotel when I nearly poured my heart out or is he thinking about the opportunity most would deem "once in a lifetime" that I forfeited.

"What are you thinking about?" he asks when he turns onto my street.

I grin. "Right now, I'm thinking about food."

Our heavy conversation at the diner diminished my appetite and left my grilled cheese nearly intact.

"Want me to turn around so you can get something to eat?"

Shaking my head, I reply that I can grab a yogurt or something that Gram made for dinner.

"I'm sorry you didn't eat. It wasn't my intention to deprive you of dinner."

"I know." I smile coyly. "I kind of worked up an appetite at the hotel."

Mateo parks the truck in my driveway and shuts off the engine.

"I'm not going to be around much next week. I have to be at the other job I'm working on."

I detect a tone of dismissal in his voice to which I respond with, "Oh...okay." In a matter of minutes, I can already feel as though he's distancing himself now that he's gotten what he wanted.

"Then I guess I'll talk to you when you get back." I add indifferently, hoping he doesn't notice the disappointment reflected in my eyes.

"I'm going to call you every day just so I can hear your voice."

My heart and lips smile in unison. "Yeah, okay," I remark sarcastically.

"What's that supposed to mean?"

"Nothing," I stammer. "I get it. I mean we had sex. It's no big deal. We both got what we wanted."

Shifting his body, he turns to face me and hisses. "Is that what you think?"

I stare at him blankly.

"You think I'm going to sleep with you and walk away so some other guy can step in and take you?" He shakes his head slowly, those eyes penetrating deep into my soul. "You're not getting away from me that easily."

"Please don't say those words if you don't mean them."

His hands cup my jaw gently before he says, "I mean them. Every last one. I feel what you feel, remember?"

"I'm gonna fall hard," I whisper after his lips touch mine. He smiles as my honesty surfaces.

"I'll be there to catch you."

With a final kiss, I exit the truck and enter the dark and quiet kitchen, bypassing the refrigerator where the stench of burnt food lingers in the air; luckily my stomach is full of butterflies.

Chapter Eight

A LIGHT TAPPING ON MY BEDROOM WINDOW rouses me from a deep slumber. One eye squints open as the morning sun filters in. I see Mateo smiling at me from outside the glass pane. My hair is wild, and my eyes sting from exhaustion. I stretch and roll over, burying my face into a pillow after having spent most of the night feverishly transforming my thoughts into lyrics.

After a second knock, I sit up and grab the sheet, covering my entire body so that only my face, dotted with freckles, shows.

His eyes light up with humor at my appearance as he pushes the window up then leans on his elbows. "You really should lock your window." Stepping through the open space, he sits on the edge of my bed, tugs at the sheet and laughs. "You look crazy!"

I cross my eyes and stick out my tongue playfully, adding to my insane appearance.

Mateo moves to whisper in my ear, his voice low and sexy. "Don't stick that tongue out unless you plan on using it."

My cheeks redden and I gulp. The intensity in his gaze is too much so I scoot around him and make a mad dash into the bathroom to freshen up.

Laughter erupts when I see myself in the mirror. I exit the bathroom in my white camisole and pink boy shorts, offering him a proper kiss when I reach him.

"Good morning," I growl after biting his earlobe. "You're here early today."

He glances at my clock and notes the time.

"GAH!" I yelp, jumping to my feet and confirming the time on the digital clock. "Shit! Gram has an appointment at ten!"

Running to the door, I open it wide and call out that we're leaving in ten minutes but get no reply.

Keeping my underwear and cami on, I shove my legs into a pair of linen pants and pair it with a loose button-down shirt, tying it quickly at the waist. I gather my hair into a low, sloppy bun.

"No bra?" Mateo asks as if he's horrified.

I chuckle and ask, "Have you not seen my boobs?"

Desire fills his eyes. "I certainly have. In fact, I believe I tasted them, too."

I slip on my sandals and walk to where he remains seated. "Stop it. You know what your words do to me." I offer a chaste kiss and open the Uber app on my phone.

Mateo follows me downstairs into the kitchen. I call my grandmother's name once again and practically have to cover my mouth when she emerges from the bathroom dressed in a fancy blue dress.

"Gram, where do you think we're going?" I ask, stifling my laughter.

"You said I have a doctor's appointment."

"You do at ten o'clock."

She tosses an obvious look in my direction.

"But you're all dressed up," I comment, noticing the gold wedding band on her finger and strand of pearls around her neck. A smile tugs at my lips.

"Then we're going to pick out my casket."

My countenance falls at her words and I breathe, "Gram." My heart sinks to the floor and an ache rips through it. "What are you talking about?"

"Caterina, I know I'm dying." My tiny grandmother steps toward me and caresses my bare face. "I don't want to be a burden to my children. I want to have my arrangements all set. In fact, I've already written my obituary." Her fuscia stained lips smile brightly. "All you have to do is fill in the date."

I cover her hand with my own and suck my lips in as my chin quivers. "Gram, please don't say things like this. It makes me sad."

"Beth, it's not my intention to make you sad, but I want you to worry about yourself instead of taking care of me. Go be the star you were destined to be."

The dam breaks and tears stream down my face. "I don't want to be a fucking star! I want to take care of you. You're my gram."

Inhaling quietly and maintaining her stoicism, Gram smiles. "You're going to shine. Everything is going to be okay."

She turns her eyes to Mateo who hasn't moved an inch. "I have already signed off for the final payment for the addition."

"But I haven't finished the job yet. I still have a lot of work to do. It's going to take some time." His challenge is met with a hopeful smile.

"You will, dear. In fact, I think you're going to be around for a *long* time."

Mateo follows me as I usher Gram out through the living room, she stops momentarily at the black piano and presses a few simple keys, glancing at me quickly from the corner of her eye.

"Needs to be tuned," she states casually.

I want to retort that it doesn't matter because no one

plays it anymore, but I don't. I simply nod and continue to lead her to the front of the driveway.

"How are you getting to the appointment?" Mateo asks, realizing my car is out of commission.

"Uber."

"Oh, hell no!" His face contorts from disbelief to anger in the blink of an eye. He slips two fingers into his mouth, emitting a loud whistle.

"What's up?" Junior calls from the second floor.

Mateo responds in Spanish.

"What are you doing?" I squeal, calling back as he runs to his truck. I shake my head and watch him back down the driveway slowly. I grab my grandmother's shoulders and pull her back when she doesn't move out of the way. "This way, Gram."

Mateo hops out and opens the passenger door for us, helping Gram in first and then me.

"Cancel the Uber," he demands.

Silently I do as he says, but remind myself to have a conversation with him later about his tone.

I provide the directions to the medical building and sit quietly beside my grandmother who is fiddling with her pearls.

"Ronald gave these to me."

I turn and smile at her. "I know, Gram. He loved you very much."

"I almost didn't marry him, you know."

My eyes widen with shock. This I did *not* know.

"What happened?" I ask, trying to keep her mind active even if she's remembering the past.

"He was torn between me and Margorie Hellerman. She had money and I didn't. Her father owned a successful lumberyard and Ronnie would've been set for life, but he chose love over money. He knew he'd have to work hard to provide for our family. I don't think he really ever loved her anyway."

I pat her lowered hand. "That's really sweet, Gram. I'm glad you told me."

She reaches for Mateo's free hand and places it on top of mine.

"Always choose love. It's the only thing that truly lasts."

And so for the last ten minutes of our journey to see my grandmother's doctor, who will no doubt have nothing new to offer, we drive hand in hand...all three of us.

"Thanks for waiting."

Mateo holds the door open for Gram and me as we exit the neurologist's office.

"How'd it go?" he whispers as we follow closely behind my grandma.

I shrug and mouth, "Same as always, although Dr. Rosenthal wants to try a new medication. He said and I quote, 'Currently, there is no cure for Alzheimer's. But drug and non-drug treatments may help with both cognitive and behavioral symptoms. Researchers are looking for new treatments to alter the course of the disease and improve the quality of life for many people with dementia.'"

Mateo looks perplexed that I was able to regurgitate all that information verbatim.

"He and I must've read the same website. He only added one other word." I press the elevator button before sighing quietly when Gram says she's not taking any more experimental drugs. "I'll stick with Namzaric and that's it."

I place my hand on her shoulder and rub softly as the double doors slide open. "That's fine, Gram."

After a short drive accompanied by an exchange of a few heated words and incredulous looks when Mateo agreed to drive Gram to the second destination, we arrive at Murphy's

Funeral Home.

"You don't have to do this," I say, shifting my body to face the sweet woman who practically raised me in my mother's absence.

Eyes that match mine crinkle, her crow's feet becoming even more pronounced as the seconds tick by.

"I will never be a burden to you or your brother." She pats my hands and says, "Out we go." Mateo is waiting at the passenger door, ready to assist, just as my feet hit the asphalt.

Needing a few moments to myself, I ask Mateo to wait in the truck. He doesn't need to be privy to all the gory details of the final arrangements.

"Actually, I do have a quick errand to run. I need to meet with the boss on the other job."

"See!" I whine. "You do have things to do. You don't need to play chauffeur for us."

His index finger rises and silences my lips before replacing it with a quick kiss.

"I'll be back in thirty minutes if not sooner."

I nod and step back, watching him climb into the truck and drive away.

"I'm so happy you two found each other."

I toss a side-eye to my grandmother. "Yeah, no thanks to you!"

"You would've found him anyway. I think you should keep him."

"Gram!" I laugh. "He isn't some stray dog."

"Did I ever tell you the story about Missy?"

I lead Gram into the funeral home as she recounts the tale of how she acquired her beloved dog.

Although I've heard the story a thousand times, maybe even a million, I smile.

"You might have, but tell me again."

Because Gram's health took a toll for the worse, Mateo and I cancel our date and spend the time at my house playing cards until he ups the ante to include strip poker.

"Later," I whisper in his ear.

I ignore my grandmother's constant demands for me to play the piano and roll my eyes when Mateo joined forces with her. I miss seeing him at the house and secretly hope this other project comes to an end soon. Thankfully, the other guys keep up their schedule and things are able to move along nicely.

By the time the following Sunday rolls around, I'm more than ready for our first "official" date despite spending almost all of our free time together and countless hours talking on the phone. He insists he doesn't mind dropping me off at work or coming into the bar to pick me up when my shift is over although he does voice his concern nearly every time about my shorts.

A knock on my door prompts me to call out, "It's open. Come on in." I exit the bathroom and smile when I see Mateo standing against the door frame, leaning casually on it.

"What's the matter? Didn't want to use the window today?"

He grins. "Not today."

My eyes travel from his blue Marlins hat to his Linkin Park T-shirt down to his board shorts and then widen, suddenly panicked that perhaps he's forgotten about our plans.

I run my hands along the soft material of my sundress and ask if I should change.

"Not at all." He steps forward and grabs my waist. "I like this dress...easy access."

I laugh and slap the tattooed imprints on his bicep, rolling my eyes and pursing my lips. "Is that all you think about?"

"When it comes to you? Yes, but only ninety-nine percent of the time."

"What's the other one percent?"

His hand moves up and cups my neck, drawing our faces closer together. He lowers his mouth and kisses me softly. "This."

I grin against his flattened lips. "I think those kinda go together, don't you think?"

He scoffs. "Not necessarily. I've fu—"

"Mateo Emmanuel Cruz! Were you just going to tell me about some girl you had sex with?!" I question, my voice bellowing with disbelief.

He looks guilty and his eyes blink rapidly, perhaps trying to dig out of the hole he's found himself in.

"No...yes, but," he stammers, "only because I meant you can do the act without actually feeling anything for the other person."

I narrow my eyes and consider his words.

"Good save!"

Before following me out, I notice Mateo scoops up my yellow bikini from off the floor. My plan to sit in the sun for a few minutes yesterday was foiled by the overcast skies.

"What do I need that for? Aren't we going to a vineyard?"

"Stop asking questions, Cat."

He ushers me out of my room with his hand placed lightly on the small of my back. Downstairs, I find my uncle playing Texas Hold' Em with Gram. A smile spreads across my face when I hear my grandmother humming the famous Kenny Rogers song about knowing when to fold'em.

"Watch her. You never know what she's gonna do next." My tone is light-hearted and playful, but when our eyes meet, he nods his understanding of the full implication of my words.

I realize in that moment that I'd never officially told my uncle about Mateo. I make an awkward and rather quick introduction to which they both respond, telling me they've already met.

Giving Gram a quick kiss on the cheek, she smiles and taps it again. I lean in for a second kiss, but she pulls away. "Not you." She smiles flirtatiously at my man.

Mateo returns the smile and leans in to kiss her cheek sweetly.

"Wow! You smell good!"

The normally tanned color of Mateo's face glows to a new shade of red as he coughs, covering his embarrassment with a chuckle. "Thanks."

"Be careful," Johnny utters a warning as we walk out the back door.

I don't bother to acknowledge him.

The summer sun beats down and although the air conditioning is on high, sweat drips down my neck.

"There's water in the cooler." Mateo tips his chin, pointing to the back seat of the dual cab truck.

I unbuckle my seat belt and turn around, but question him when I find nothing but a folded blanket.

"Shit! Do you mind if I stop home real quick to grab the cooler?" he asks, already switching lanes to get off the next exit as I secure myself in the seat.

"I don't mind. I'd love to see where you lay that pretty little head of yours at night."

He turns his face to me and cocks an eyebrow. "You didn't think my head was so little last night."

The thought of him thrusting and releasing in my mouth makes me blush.

I reach for the dial and turn on the radio, needing a diversion from the images of what we did in the wee hours of the morning when he brought me home from the bar.

One song ends just as a familiar one begins and I change the channel.

"Hey! That's a good song. It's got great lyrics. I've heard

she writes about personal experiences...kind of like you."

I nod once and look out the window as Chloe Creed croons about how people shouldn't mess with karma because her payback is a real bitch.

We drive through a neighborhood riddled with graffiti and several low-income housing complexes. I immediately question the look of apprehension marring Mateo's face when he parks the truck in front of a two-story building.

"I don't mind waiting here," I offer before he opens his mouth to speak. I don't want him to feel embarrassed or ashamed for living in what some might call the "ghetto."

"Actually, I'd feel better if you came in." He turns off the engine. "This isn't the safest neighborhood for someone like you."

"Someone like me?" I scoff.

"A white girl."

I feel a sudden sense of rage combined with hurt that I wouldn't be welcomed here simply because of the color of my skin.

"Did we just travel back in time to 1961?" I ask with no attempt to hide my derision.

"What?"

"West Side Story," I reply, pulling the lever to open my door before I step onto the sidewalk. I slide my hand into his when he extends his hand. With a weak smile, he leads me up the creaky and worn steps that are in desperate need of repair and repainting.

Spanish music and the aroma of spices waft through from behind a door that is ajar. A black cat, old and skittish, dashes down the steps and into the house when Mateo tries to pet it.

"That's Pedro."

I laugh. "Pedro doesn't like you very much."

"That's because I took her kittens and found them a better home last year."

"Pedro's female?" I screech through laughter.

He nods, pushing the door open. "I'm not sure who's home so..."

"It's fine." I give his hand a small, reassuring squeeze.

Following him in through the unlocked door, he calls out for someone in Spanish. A tiny woman with olive skin and short white hair emerges from what I presume to be the kitchen.

Her lips form a smile, but it doesn't reach her dark brown eyes.

They exchange a few words and I stand there quietly, reminding myself to ask him what "Matito" means.

Addressing me by my full name, he introduces me to his aunt, Tia Juanita.

I step forward and offer my hand which she takes after wiping her palms on the dishtowel she has been holding.

More Spanish words are uttered and I smile shyly when I get the feeling they're talking about me.

Mateo excuses himself to get the cooler.

"Where're you from?" she asks with a broken accent.

"Darien," I reply as a moment of inexplicable shame washes over me. She looks at me as if I had a choice to grow up in an affluent suburb.

Her lips tighten in disapproval.

"That's a long way from here."

Just as I prepare to tell her that Bridgeport actually isn't that far from Darien, I realize she's referring to our socioeconomic differences.

"Ready?" Mateo asks, walking in with a blue cooler.

"It was nice to meet you," I say, smiling at his relative who again wipes her hands on the striped towel. I fear she may rub off a layer of dark skin with the force she's applying.

Tia Juanita mumbles something to him and he responds swiftly. I want to kick myself for taking French as an elective in school instead of Spanish. At the time, my father had insisted I take "a useful language," but I was rebellious and fought him tooth and nail on everything.

Mateo exhales sharply, expelling a tension-filled breath from his lungs.

"That wasn't so bad," I offer, rubbing his arms in comfort.

Silently, Mateo looks in the side mirror and maneuvers the truck onto the crowded street. The window slides down and he tosses his arm up into the air, waving at someone behind us. I turn quickly and see Iza sitting on a park bench, watching several shirtless men play basketball with a makeshift hoop. She lowers her hand and shakes her head when our eyes meet.

"What's the deal with Iza?" I ask, needing some answers.

"What do you mean?"

"Did you date her?" Maintaining an even voice is no easy task.

I notice he swallows thickly and looks out the window. "Me and Iza...that was over a long time ago."

Jealousy spikes in me. "Clearly not for her!"

"Nah, she doesn't want me."

I huff in disagreement.

"She needs my help, but I'm not really in a position to help her right now."

My chest rises and falls as anxiety races through me. "And what exactly does she need help with?" My eyes fall to his lap.

He grins roguishly and places my hand on his growing erection. "Only for you, baby. No one else."

DiGrazia Vineyards welcomes us with its rolling hills and sprawling grounds. Couples lounge on the grass, relaxing on open blankets while sipping a variety of wines, cultivated from plentiful grapes.

"This is beautiful." I remark as I drape the small blanket on my forearm and follow Mateo to an empty spot away from others.

Taking two corners each, we stretch out the soft material and sit. I can still feel the hidden tension in Mateo's body so I lean in for a kiss, offering a gesture of thanks for our date.

"I'll be right back."

Mateo returns a few minutes later with two glasses and a bottle of white wine. We enjoy a light lunch, nibbling on fresh fruit, wedges of cheese, thinly sliced pepperoni and Ritz crackers.

Between selfies with his phone and passionate kisses, we pass the time talking about sports and music legends. We talk about how different our childhoods were, but how we believe that we have the ability to create or change our own destiny.

"Excuse me," Mateo stands and jogs over to where an older woman clears off a nearby picnic table. He asks to borrow a pen and promises to return it shortly, but she smiles and tells him to keep it.

He looks out toward the rows where grape vines abound, flops onto his hard stomach and writes quickly on a crinkly paper napkin.

"Following the path forged for me
...may or may not be my destiny."

Handing me the pen, he waits for me to begin. I mirror his position and close my eyes, carefully considering my words before pressing my pen down onto the napkin.

"While others see a future in the spotlight,
I put up a strong fight
Cause' that's not where I want to be,
It's not my destiny."

We pass the paper napkin back and forth, each writing another line to complement the one before. When I set the pen down, Mateo reads what we've co-written, smiles then scribbles a single word at the top. *"Destiny"*

"It's perfect."

"What do you want in life?" he asks, sitting up and resting his elbows on bent knees.

I roll onto my back and stare at the bright blue sky dotted with white fluffy clouds.

"I want to be happy. I want to make my own choices. I want to have children and grow old with the man I love."

He looks down at me and smiles.

"How about you? What do you want in life?"

"Mostly the same things, but I want to make something of myself. I don't want people to cringe when they hear my name. My family and I have done some stupid things to tarnish our family's reputation. I want to fix that."

"Is that why you didn't want me to see where you live?"

He shrugs, lifting his Marlins ball cap and running his fingers through his dark hair. "I don't want to be that poor kid from the projects. I work hard...I earn an honest living. I'm determined to change who I am."

"Well, if it makes any difference I love who you are." I counter, adoration dripping from my lips.

When I turn to look at him, his expression is serious, all signs of playfulness now gone.

"What's wrong?" I ask nervously as a shiver runs through me.

"Cat, I know this is going to sound crazy, but..." he hesitates, "I think I love you."

A roar of laughter rips through me and I toss my head back, guffawing hysterically as tears pool quickly in my eyes.

"What is so funny?" he grits through his teeth.

"Oh, God! I'm sorry. I really am." I wipe my eyes and try to gain my composure.

"Seriously, Cat. What's so funny?"

I rise up and sit back on my haunches to face him, removing his ball cap before taking his smooth face in my hands just as he's done to me so many times before.

"Here's the thing." I stifle the giggle and try my hardest to maintain a solemn expression. "You said you *think* you love me. I'm not really sure how that works."

He makes an attempt to speak, but I place my hand over his mouth.

"I, on the other hand, am completely, ridiculously in love with you."

"You are?"

I smile because for as much confidence as this man appears to have, he seems awfully insecure at the moment.

"Mateo, I love you. There's no question in my mind. There's no doubt in my heart. I don't say those words often and I don't take them lightly because my experience with love hasn't always been..." I swallow back the emotion threatening to rise. "It hasn't always been kind to me."

The sun reflects in his eyes making them appear more green than brown. Deep longing and compassion fill his gaze.

"Love was selfish and cruel. Love was cold and calculated. Love took but didn't give. For a long time, I didn't believe love really existed until I met you."

His lips meet mine for a gentle kiss.

"I think I loved you early on, but I didn't believe it. I mean, really...who falls in love after only a few weeks?"

"Me," he breathes, mirroring the hold I have on his face. "I fell hard and fast for you."

My body flies as Mateo rolls me onto my back and hovers over me. With gentle, slow sweeps, he brushes the wayward, loose curls away from my face. I fully expect him to push his erection forward, tempting me, seducing me, but he doesn't. I question his lack of enthusiasm.

"Baby, you stir every part of me." He rolls his hips and smiles. "But this," he says, placing my hand over his heart, "this beats wildly for you."

I caress his face and comment how handsome he is. I

take strands of his hair and slide them through my fingertips before I drag my fingers to his lips. I can't help but wonder why some people are blessed to have straight hair and an unblemished complexion while I'm stuck with wild curls and a freckled face.

"I love that you're naturally beautiful. You don't smear your face with all that makeup crap except for work."

I smile at his words.

"You're the beautiful one," I counter and then continue, "but you're a good person, too. You're kind, compassionate, helpful, patient and honest. All of that is probably just as attractive as the rest of you."

Mateo shifts his weight and rises up, tugging me gently to stand next to him.

"Do you trust me?" he asks as he reaches for the blanket.

Without reservation, I reply. "You know I do."

Bending at the knee, he lifts my body and holds me close to his chest as a husband would to his bride as he carries her over the threshold.

"Where are we going?" I giggle when I see the humor on his face.

"You'll see," he replies, carrying me through a path to the outskirts of the vineyard where the descending sun dances at the horizon.

My bare feet touch the soft sand, damp from the abutting lake. The fresh water is pristine, unblemished and inviting.

"Let's go for a swim." He yanks the black T-shirt off and tosses it back onto the grass.

"I don't have my suit. I left it in the car," I protest as he unbuttons his shorts.

"Who said anything about needing a bathing suit?"

A lustful blush reddens my face when the last things I see are Mateo's rounded globes enter the water. A few moments later he reappears in the distance, whipping his head to the side, causing his hair to stick up.

"Come on!" he calls out to me.

I look around and see no one. Swallowing down the ball of nerves, I undress quickly and dip my toes in the cool water.

"It's cold!" I screech as my nipples harden.

Mateo slips beneath the surface of the water only to reemerge in front of me.

"I've got you, baby." He guides me out to deeper water and smiles when I scream and wrap my legs around his waist.

"Oh my God! I think there's a snake!" My body tenses at the thought of what else might be swimming in here. "Something touched my leg!"

Waggling his eyebrows suggestively, Mateo laughs and says, "That was just me."

We kiss and swim and swim and kiss some more until only a sliver of orange can be seen in the darkening sky.

After using the blanket as a towel, we find our strewn clothes and get dressed.

"That was really fun!" I lean in to hug him. "Thank you."

"I want to do so many things with you. We should do something different every chance we get."

I lick my lips before speaking. "I don't usually take chances, but I will with you."

The small white lights strung around the property guide us back to the vacant spot where only the blue cooler remains before we pack up and head to the truck.

"Do you mind if I make a quick stop? I need to grab something for the other job I'm doing."

I smile. "I don't mind at all."

A conversation surfaces about how his favorite baseball team scouted him when he was a teenager, but that his poor choices and a juvenile arrest eradicated any real chance of signing with them.

"Imagine how different your life would be if you had signed." An overwhelming feeling of loss smacks me out of nowhere. Just thinking about how destiny could have led him on a different path, never providing an opportunity for us to meet saddens me.

"I could say the same to you." He glances at me quickly.

"Baseball could have opened doors for you. Music would have trapped me in a dark and lonely dungeon."

We drive through a wealthy neighborhood in Greenwich until we arrive at an incredible gated property.

Although it's dark out, my eyes take in the sheer size of the home. "Wow! This place is massive," I shriek, looking at the brick mansion before me as Mateo enters a code to open the wrought iron gate.

"How do you know the code?"

"I did a lot of work here last year."

After silencing the truck's engine, Mateo asks if I'd like to come in.

I shake my head. "No, thanks. I'd rather just wait here. My dress is still damp and I need to text my uncle to see how Gram is doing."

"I won't be long."

He disappears, entering the residence through a side door, and I look at the huge four-bay garage that looms ahead. I can only imagine the sleek and expensive vehicles it houses.

I'm surprised when my uncle responds almost immediately to my text message. His willingness to do his share in his mother's care has increased greatly in recent days. I don't know what to attribute the change to, but I'm glad he's stepping up his efforts.

Social media is packed with the same nonsense as usual so I close the app.

Mateo opens the door and climbs into the truck, placing a sealed manila folder on the top of the dashboard.

"Everything okay?" I inquire when I notice his expression is hard.

"Yeah, it's fine. I don't like being told what I have to do or having someone think they can dictate my schedule."

"Me neither." I scoff and nod my head in agreement, remembering how rigid my parents were with me. Between the constant piano lessons, voice lessons, recitals and auditions, I was left with very little time to do the normal things most kids were allowed to do.

We arrive back at my house almost an hour later and I'm faced with disappointment when Mateo declines my offer to come in, saying he's got a few things to prepare for the other project.

"Call me when you get home." I close my eyes and press my lips against his, but quickly reopen them when I feel tension radiating from him.

"Are you okay?"

He hums a dull response as he rushes to return my kiss goodnight then leaves quickly when I step out of the truck. No added sweet words. No affirmation that he loves me. Just nothing.

Chapter Nine

"MORNING," I HUFF, GREETING MY FAMILY WHO are sitting at the table enjoying Gram's homemade muffins. I pour a cup of coffee and look out through the kitchen window at the dark gray sky. I hope the expected forecast of rain all week changes. Even if it does, the materials are soaking wet from the buckets of rain that fell in the early morning hours.

I would've expected to get a call from Mateo since he never called last night, but it's been radio silence since we left Greenwich.

"Can I use your car today? I have a couple of errands to run."

After debating for a moment, my uncle agrees with a quick nod of his head, but says he's got a meeting and won't be back until one-thirty.

"Are you going to fix your car soon?"

"Yeah... probably."

Gram rises when the house phone rings.

"Ma, just let it go. It's probably those telemarketers again. I swear I'm going to turn the land line off soon."

"It might be important," she argues, walking over and putting the phone to her ear. "Hello?"

"What's up with you?" my uncle asks, setting his coffee down next to the opened newspaper.

"I deferred for a year," I whisper, bracing myself for his wrath.

Three, two, one.

"You did WHAT?!" His voice screeches and I wince from its sound.

"Shhh! Be quiet! I don't want Gram to know yet."

Scowling at me, he asks if it's because of my boyfriend. He doesn't even try to hide the snarl when he says Mateo's name.

"No, of course not!" I retort, thinking about how much I would miss him if I left. I don't know what I would do if I couldn't see him every day. "Gram isn't well. I need to be here for her."

My uncle seems to consider my words.

"No offense, but no one except for me, gets to decide what I do and don't do."

Gram reenters the kitchen and drops an f-bomb.

"Mom!"

"Gram!"

"Oh, that asshole keeps calling here, trying to get information about you."

"What asshole?" Johnny asks.

Gram turns to me and motions with her chin. "Her father."

My jaw nearly hits the tiled floor and I bellow, "What? Why is he calling here?"

"He said she won't return his calls. I asked him if he knew where Beth is." My heart aches at the sound of my mother's name.

"Mom, Beth is gone, remember?"

Her chin quivers before she storms off in a huff.

I climb the stairs quickly and reach for my phone. In the middle of the screen, I see a missed call and voicemail from

Mateo.

Tapping the glass, I call my father's cell phone and wait with bated breath while it rings.

"Caterina, sweetheart," he says sweetly. "I've been waiting for your call."

My jaw tightens and my teeth clench, my words releasing slowly "So you've resorted to calling my grandmother?"

"I couldn't reach you any other way."

I sigh in frustration and sit on the edge of my bed. "Maybe that's because I don't want to talk to you!"

He remains quiet on the other end of the line for several moments.

"I deserve a second chance, Cat. Give me that opportunity."

"You don't deserve anything!" I challenge. "Especially... not after what you did to me."

"I did what I thought was best for you."

"What?! How could you—" My voice cracks.

"Come see me and we'll talk." His voice is eerily calm and I quiver as if I'm walking into a lion's den. "I have something important to tell you."

"I can stop by the office on Thursday morning," I suggest because his office building isn't too far from Trina's shop.

"No, you'll come to the house Thursday night and have a meal with me."

"Fine," I respond, knowing he will get his way as he always does. "Who's going to be there?"

"Just us. My girls are away for a few days. I'll text you the address."

"You moved?" I gasp with surprise that he sold the house I grew up in. He and my mother designed the house and it was gorgeous.

"It was time to expand."

My phone rings in my ear and I see Mateo's face.

"I've got to go."

"I'm looking forward to seeing you Thursday at six-thirty,

sweetheart."

Disconnecting the call, I switch over to answer Mateo's call and nearly break down in tears at the sound of his voice.

"What's the matter?"

I exhale a deep breath. "I just got off the phone with my father."

"Your father? Why?"

I lie back on my bed and pull the blanket up, tucking it beneath my chin, comforting myself. "He's asking for a second chance at a relationship with me, but I don't trust him."

"Do you want me to go with you?" he asks quietly.

"Maybe. My father is kind of an asshole." I smile at Gram's use of the term regarding him.

Mateo's voice is raspy and his breathing slow.

"Are you okay?" I add in that I was worried when he didn't call last night.

"I'm sorry. I had a lot on my mind and I had to rework some things for this project."

"Like what? Measure stuff or pick out tile and carpeting?"

"No, it was more like rereading the fine print. I don't like when people think they can change the terms of an agreement. It'll be fine, I'm sure."

"What are you going to do today since it's raining?" I ask, hoping he'll offer to come see me. "Guess you can't work at your other job either, huh?"

"Nope. I can't do that one by myself either."

"I could help." I smile into the phone, imagining myself on the roof nailing down shingles.

"You could probably do this job better than anyone I know."

The hours since I've seen his face have been too long. "I miss you."

"Are you in bed?"

I nod then voice my response. "Yes...and I'm lonely."

"I'm coming for you."

A goofy grin extends from ear to ear. "I'll be ready and waiting."

Shuffling my feet, I dance my way to the bathroom and think how happy I feel because of this man. This man who hammered and drilled his way into my life and now fills my heart with immense love and unspeakable joy.

I set Pandora to my favorite station before I step into the shower. A thick, soapy lather washes over my body, cleansing me of the betrayal of my father. My fingers massage my scalp with melon-scented shampoo.

Over the sound of the water running, I hear the intro to one of my favorite Alicia Keys songs. I wipe my eyes, step out to raise the volume and return quickly to the hot water. Humming quietly as I remember the feel of my fingers gliding effortlessly over the black and white keys, I smile and pull the shower head down, turning the water away from me.

"Some people live for the fortune..."

The lyrics roll off my tongue as if I had written them myself.

"But everything means nothing if I ain't got you..."

My eyes fill with tears that fall and burn my cheeks.

"With no one who truly cares for me..."

A sob rips through me and I drop the shower head, my body crumbling to the floor as a war rages in my heart. My once incredible love for music is now permanently overshadowed by my hate for that life.

I cry for the little girl in me who never had a fighting chance. I cry for the woman in me who gave up everything she loved.

The music continues on, moving from one song to another within the same genre.

I drag my palms away from my face when I hear the most beautiful voice in the world call my name.

Inhaling deeply, I cry, "I'm here" as I attempt to stand on

weak legs. My red-rimmed eyes meet his when Mateo pulls the shower curtain back.

"Baby, why are you crying?" Panic drips from his voice as he wraps one arm around me while the other turns off the water.

Burying my face in his chest, I swallow the volcano of sorrowful howls until the powerful emotional roller coaster comes to an end.

He graces my forehead with a thousand tiny kisses and my fingers clutch the soft material covering his back.

Despite finally having gained my composure, I grit, "I hate him. I hate him so much."

"He can't hurt you anymore. I won't let him."

My body is wrapped in a towel and I'm guided back to the comfort of my bed.

He asks for the details that led to my emotional distress.

"You know how some parents take things away when their children misbehave...but they eventually give it back." I air quote, "Kind of like 'the punishment fits the crime,' but in this case, he extinguished something I don't think I'll ever get back."

Those gorgeous greenish eyes watch me carefully.

"He stole my love of music and then he betrayed me."

"I'm sorry he did that to you," he sighs compassionately.

"And now he's trying to weasel his way back into my life."

I wipe the last of my tears and shake my head.

"I don't want to have anything to do with him, his new family or that life. Nothing. I don't want to be associated with them in any way, shape or form."

"I don't blame you."

Mateo lies beside me, spooning the length of my bed when exhaustion overrides strength.

"Cat, you have to know that you have a gift. I mean, I've never seen anyone with your talent who isn't topping the music charts. Did you hear that Chloe Creed is still looking for backup singers? You wouldn't have to be in the spotlight..."

"Mateo, please!" I cry. "I don't want to be out there. I've seen what it does to people. They try to change you. For years my mother would brag about my talent and tell me how important it was to my father. She used to tell me how disappointed he would be if I didn't play a song right. They both, but my father in particular, tried to make me into something I'm not and when I didn't fit his mold, he was done with me and then he left me."

He runs his fingertips lightly along my arm up to my shoulder as he whispers in my ear, "No one is saying you have to cut a record deal." He chuckles and continues, "but do *something* with your natural ability."

"Music used to make Gram so happy. She loved when I played for her."

"Then play! Play for her." He pins me with those eyes. "Play for me."

My eyes cast downward as a sheepish smile peeks through my expression. By the manner in which he sighs my name, I know he senses my ambiguity and reservation.

"You know what..." The determination in his voice steals my attention away from my journal sitting on the bedside table. "Don't play for your gram. Don't play for me."

My eyebrows furrow, an indication of my confusion.

"Play for *you.*" He kisses me softly. "Play for the love in your heart. Play for the feeling you once had when you only felt love and nothing else. Play for *you*, Cat."

The simplicity of his words causes joy to emerge from the quietest parts of my soul. I rise quickly, pull on a pair of yoga pants and an old concert T-shirt. My damp hair is scooped up into a low knot and secured with a pencil. I extend my hand to Mateo which he gladly takes and allows me to guide him downstairs until my bare feet stop once we've reached the destination.

We eye each other knowingly and his smile encourages

me to continue.

I pull the shiny black seat out, lower myself down then pat the small space beside me, asking him to join me. I smile at him and place a kiss on his cheek, silently thanking him for this gift. I draw in a deep breath, giving my fingers a moment to pause before reacquainting themselves with the black and white keys.

My eyes close as I exhale and a silent thought consumes me before my lips move to whisper. *Hello, old friend. It's been awhile.* With my long fingers spread across the keys, I play an E chord before transitioning from a B6 to a C sharp minor 7 while my other hand provides bass with B and E octaves. I smile at the sound that fills my ears.

I open my eyes, roll my neck and raise my chin, trying desperately to force away the image of my father hovering over me. I groan quietly as I push him far from my mind even as his words seep into my ears; to this day, his words still remain with me.

Again, Caterina.

You can do better than this, Cat.

They won't love you if it's not perfect.

I pull my hands from the keys and look at Mateo, my expression falling in defeat.

"You can do this," he whispers encouragingly. "Remember, you're playing for you."

I nod and tuck a lock of loose hair behind my ear and return my fingers to the keys as I swallow thickly. My right hand moves slowly, gliding from key to key, creating a melody while my left offers a complementary chord. *Ah, how I've missed you.*

Continuing with natural ease, the instrument before me comes to life, weaving an intricate and beautiful tale of love.

My lips part. A quiet muffled utterance attempts to emerge, but everything freezes.

"Only do as much as you want to," Mateo says, leaning

over to whisper in my ear.

His encouragement is all I need and so with a nod, I try again, my fingers playing the familiar riff once again.

"Ahhhh...some people live..."

The anguish I'd suppressed for so many years releases in my own rendition of Alicia Keys' *If I Ain't Got You* as my voice fills the living room of my grandmother's home. Turning my head, I look at Mateo and smile. His eyes shine with rapt attention and awe. My voice becomes stronger, more confident as the tears stream down my face when the final note is played. My shoulders round and I bow my head, giving the sense of relief and freedom to reign within me.

My chains have been broken; *he* no longer has a hold on me.

Mateo's arms wrap around me and pull me close, burying my cheek against his hard chest.

"Baby..."

I grip his back and smile inwardly.

"That was amazing."

And it *was* amazing— the moment of liberation was unlike anything I've ever experienced before.

"Thank you."

He kisses my head before shifting his body to look at me. His fingertips gently wipe the moisture from my face. "Thank *you*." A smile widens on his face. "Thank you for sharing that with me."

In my peripheral vision, I see Gram enter the room so I turn to look at her and catch her wiping her face.

"Gram," I sigh, rising to meet her by the door. "Don't cry."

"Sweetheart, that was the most beautiful song I've ever heard you sing."

I squeeze my grandmother gently, silently thanking her for the years of love, support and encouragement after my mother left and my father forfeited me.

Mateo joins us and my gram slides an arm around each

of our waists. "You two are good together."

I couldn't agree more.

"Ready, Ma?" Johnny asks as he walks in, taking notice of our attachment to one another. His eyes move quickly to look at us then a grimace tugs at his face and an eyebrow rises in question.

"Where are you going?" I ask, thinking perhaps I'd forgotten an appointment.

"She wants to look at a car," my uncle replies in her stead.

"A car?" My high-pitched screech reflects my apprehension. Gram shouldn't be driving a car anymore.

"For you...for school."

I toss my uncle a hard look and roll my eyes because he knows I've deferred.

"Gram," I brush back the purple-tinted hair away from her face. "I appreciate that, but you don't need to get me a car. I don't need one. Save your money."

"How will you travel home to see me?" I see the panic in her eyes.

"There are trains, buses, and cars. Don't worry about that now, Gram."

"Well, since I'm already dressed, I might as well go." She smiles sweetly, dislodging herself from our group gathering before turning to Mateo. "Take care of my girl."

"Always," he replies.

Once the back door shuts, Mateo grabs my face, pushes me to the wall and crushes his mouth against mine, our teeth clashing and our warm tongues lapping. He gives just as much as he takes. The spark in my belly ignites to an inferno as my core rages hot with desire.

"Upstairs," I mouth against his lips.

Scooping me up in his arms, Mateo races through the living room and up the stairs to my bedroom, closing the door behind us with a quick kick of his foot.

Our clothes are shed immediately, revealing our

complete nakedness and uncontrollable desire for each other. His massive erection teases my wet core when he lays on me and spreads my legs wide.

"I need you," I pant through ragged breaths.

His tongue leaves a trail as he tastes my neck and jaw before he whispers in my ear. "I need you, too."

Plunging deeply, pushing himself into me, Mateo fills the void. The slick walls of my core tighten and squeeze, clenching desperately to heighten the experience. My legs wrap around the lower part of his back and cross at the ankles. Moving together, we find the perfect rhythm of hard, fast thrusts combined with slow and gentle swivels of his hips. A coating of sweat moistens our bodies, making our skin glide easily as we continue to make love.

"I love fucking you," he groans, climbing high, pressing forward toward his release. "I love it all."

It takes a moment for his words to infiltrate the silent screams of pleasure in my head. Grasping the nape of his neck, I pull his mouth closer. "I love it too." I smile at his use of the word and bite his lip.

I feel my orgasm building, rising slowly through my body until my nails dig into his skin and I cry out, savoring the moment of incredible bliss.

"Oh, my God! I feel that. I feel you coming on me," he announces on a deep moan before a string of frantic curses flies from his lips. His eyes slam shut and his face contorts as his orgasm erupts, spurting hot and heavy into me.

I finger the strands of dark hair that kiss his neck then brush the damp hair back away, providing me with an unobstructed view of his gorgeous face.

"I love you," I whisper.

He opens his eyes slowly and stares at me with eyes filled with love and so much more.

"Love isn't a strong enough word to tell you how I feel." He slowly imitates the light brushing of hair away from my face, the pencil which secured my hair is now long gone, lost somewhere in the chaos of entangled bodies.

He kisses my forehead then my closed lids. "Don't ever forget that you are the center of my universe."

My eyes open at his statement and a lump forms in my throat.

"Are you going somewhere?" I ask quietly, suddenly overcome with the sense of an impending goodbye.

"I have to travel a bit for this job, but I want you to know that how I feel today is the same way I'm going to feel in fifty years."

"How long will you be gone? Is Junior going too?"

"Hopefully just a few weeks and no, it's just me."

Apprehension riddles through me as I prepare to ask more questions.

"Don't worry about it now. I'm not even a hundred percent sure that I'm going. We're still working out the logistics."

We lie together, enjoying the peace and quiet.

"Te amo," he utters quietly into my neck before kissing me.

"I *te amo* you, too." I smile, knowing I've probably said the sentiment incorrectly, but based on his radiant smile, he doesn't mind.

"Lyin' here with you so close to me," Mateo sings softly. "It's hard to fight these feelings..."

"Is that Lady Antebellum?" I ask, running my fingertips along his bare chest.

He nods and smiles. "It's a perfect song for us, don't you think?"

The rain holds off for a few days then begins again on Thursday morning which meant Mateo was free to work on his other project because that one is indoors. Every time I ask him about it, he says he'll show me when it's finished. I can't help but detect the hint of apprehension when he explains that the experience is great for his portfolio and will open so many doors for him. He's on the fast track to leaving his old life behind.

I call his cell phone several times to confirm that he's going to accompany me to my father's house, but it goes to voicemail every time. I watch the seconds turn into minutes as time ticks by. I quell the feeling of anger because Mateo knows how important this meeting is for me. He must have a good reason for not being here. Begrudgingly, I tap the Uber app and order a car. Thirty minutes later, I arrive at the address I'd given Cheryl, my driver.

Stepping out onto the driveway, I stand there for a few minutes, deciding if I should cancel and go home or buck up and face my father. My eyes scan the decorative stones and I notice they are bordered with the same bricks that cover the house.

I walk over to the keypad, press the "TALK" button and wait when it crackles in response.

"Come in, Caterina," the ominous voice orders as a small gate begins to open. I look around, quickly determining there must be a camera because my father apparently knows I didn't drive a car.

My feet walk slowly up the long driveway and I stop when I see two cars— a shiny red Dodge Charger and a black Range Rover with a customized license plate.

The front door opens and the heavy woman, wearing a black dress with a white apron, greets me.

"I am Patricia."

"Cat" I reply.

She smiles warmly and escorts me into the immense foyer where a very robust man waits for me. We look nothing alike; no one would believe we are related. The buttons of his white, tight-fitted dress shirt strain against his protruding round belly and the collar seems to be cutting off his air supply.

One could only be so lucky I think to myself.

My father extends his arms, offering an embrace, but I am completely repulsed by the sweat stains under his pits. The image produces a bitter taste in my mouth and I scowl.

"Don't do that. You'll wrinkle prematurely," he reprimands me.

"I only have two hours so let's get this over with." I step into his home and shiver at the near freezing temperature, regretting not having worn the cardigan I decided I didn't need. "Nice icebox," I remark sarcastically, trying to get a rise out of him. Suddenly I'm fifteen years old again, rebelling against the weight of my father's tyranny.

"I'm glad you came. We have a lot to talk about." He leads the way into the formal sitting area where a huge floor to ceiling fireplace maintains a quiet roar. "It's warmer in here. The Mrs. likes the cooler air."

I chuckle dryly, "Fitting."

Taking the seat adjacent to his, I wait for him to speak again. I do not want to initiate any conversation with this man.

"How's school?"

"I graduated."

He nods thoughtfully. "Are you working?"

"Yes."

I see his jaw tick in response to my curt answers.

"How's Violet?"

"She still despises you."

He raises a glass of clear liquid and takes a healthy chug before a noise from somewhere, perhaps the basement, garners his attention.

"It's just your sister and her boyfriend messing around in the studio."

"She is *not* my sister," I spit with a hard glare etched on my tense face. "And I thought you said no one else would be here? You lied to me."

He ignores my accusation and smiles warmly as if reminiscing of days passed. "You always did have your mother's spirit."

"What did you do with her things when you moved into this place?"

The expression on my father's face softens further; I think he's lost his damn mind.

"It's in storage. I couldn't part with it. Cat, I loved your mother just like I loved you..."

I want to scream that his "love" is greedy, cruel and selfish. I want to tell him that his "love" robbed me of my joy and then my freedom.

"I'll be right back." The burly man rises, leaves the room and comes back a moment later with a manila envelope in his big hand. He sits down and places the sealed packet on the coffee table in front of me.

"What is this?" I ask, disregarding the look on his face.

"CT scan results."

"For what?"

"My doctor found a small tumor." He points to his head.

He drops the bombshell just as a door opens and I cringe at the sound of voices approaching. I don't need a confrontation with either one of my father's "girls."

"Hey, Randy? Matt and I were about to order—" the petite blonde calls as she rounds the corner. She freezes mid-stride and her eyes spring wide in surprise.

I leap to my feet and shoot daggers in my father's direction.

"No, it's okay. I've got to get going," the voice of my angel reaches my ears when Mateo enters the room two steps behind her, looking down at his phone.

Chloe shrieks, "Cat?! Why the hell are *you* here?!"

Mateo's eyes flash upward and find mine as the color

in his face immediately drains, turning his beautiful tanned skin a morose shade of gray "Cat?!"

I open my mouth to speak, but no words emerge; they're lost in a sea of betrayal, tossed back and forth between anguish and regret.

"Baby, what are you doing here?" he stammers. His shocked expression matches Chloe's perfectly as he walks towards me.

My brain struggles to process the scene before me as Chloe pulls Mateo back, purring his name softly.

My eyes fall to her hand locked around his forearm before they look at him.

Mateo is here with Chloe and she's touching him.

My fucking father set me up. I turn to look at him. "You're a bastard."

There's a flurry of commotion as each one of us tries to figure out how the others are connected. Even the housekeeper rushes in.

"Baby," Mateo calls again, breaking away from Chloe's clutch.

The voice that escapes from my lips is low and lethal. "What the fuck are you doing in my father's house?"

He gasps. "Your father? *Randy's* your father?" He turns to look at my estranged parent and calls him a mother fucker.

Standing several inches above Mateo, my father glares at him. "I don't know who the hell you think you are, but no one speaks to me like that and certainly not in my own goddamn house."

Chloe reaches for Mateo's arm once again, and I feel my insides set ablaze with jealousy.

"Matt baby, what's going on?" her voice softens to a kitten's whisper.

My heart pounds against my chest wall when he doesn't remove her arm nor does he move away from her.

"Do you two know each other?" she hisses like the snake

that she is.

Mateo's terrified eyes lock with my angry ones, yet neither of us speaks.

"Cat, why are you looking at Matt like that? You're acting like you own him?"

"He's my..."

"Your what?" Chloe prompts, mocking me.

The hazel in Mateo's eyes darkens as they fill with guilt then close.

My world, my hopes, my dreams—my love for this man—have all just been turned upside down and obliterated, left to die in a pile of rubble and ruins.

My chin quivers and I fight the tears as I continue to stare at him. He tilts his head lightly and sighs my name. The emotion in that single utterance is packed with everything we once had, everything we once shared. "Please," he pleads, stepping closer as his nostrils flare. He forces a swallow before he spews more words of deceit. Lies upon lies fall from his lips as he begs for the chance to explain.

My body is frozen solid and I vaguely hear my father demand how Mateo knows me.

Sensing my resolve, Mateo rushes to me and takes my rigid hand in his. His touch sends sparks straight to my heart. Whispered Spanish words roll from his mouth when he switches to his native tongue, making declarations he knows I don't understand. The look on his face implores me to not only listen, but to *feel* when he places it on his heart.

"*Mi corazon,*" he murmurs, choking back unshed emotions. "*Mi corazon es tuyo.*"

As if my hand were a thousand-pound cinder block, it falls heavily and smacks against my leg covered in ripped jeans.

"*Te amo siempre*" is his last declaration.

I reach into the darkest part of my soul, where years of betrayal and hurt reside, despite having recently been shed with light from what I thought was love, and I cast swords of hate, blades of fury and whips of rage at the man pleading before me.

Vacant eyes accompany my calm and murderous tone. "You lied to me. I hate you."

Mateo reaches for my arm. "Baby, don't do this. Not here." He yanks off his Marlins baseball cap, pulling wildly at his hair before he looks around at Randy, Chloe and the housekeeper who are watching with engrossed attention. "Don't. Do. This."

His chest heaves and his eyes mist as he makes demands he no longer has the right to. "Not now. Not like this."

"You. Lied. To. Me." I murmur through clenched teeth. "Every word you said was a lie." The broken words reveal the depth of my agony.

"Cat, I didn't lie to you. I promise," he pleads.

"You're no different than he is." I flash disgusted eyes at my father. "You're a manipulator and a user, but most of all, you're a liar."

A flicker of rage rises in Mateo's eyes. "I didn't lie to you."

My chest rises and falls, my breathing becoming more pronounced as his false words reach my ears.

"I didn't mean to hurt you. If you just let me expl—"

"—Fuck you! You can all go to hell," I hiss, my eyes laser-pointing at his.

My eyes rake condescendingly up and down his body as if he were a piece of trash. "You're just a fucking poor kid from the projects who lies and cheats to get what he wants. You're pathetic."

He staggers back a step and gasps quietly as if I had stabbed him in the heart. His eyelids close and the single tear that was teetering on the edge falls when he drops his head dejectedly. The pain in his eyes is nothing compared to the anguish in my heart.

My instincts push me toward the front door and I run

down the driveway. My head is spinning and my heart reeling. Banging my fists against the wrought iron, I cry out, choking my way through unstoppable tears as I escape from the mob of conniving liars. I have escaped from them. Every last one.

Running far from the Creed home, I find a tall shrub and vomit when my late lunch protests in my stomach. I feel so lost—so broken— in this moment. Everything I believed, everything I felt...it was all a lie. Mateo knew exactly who I was when he pursued me. I thought I was some random girl he'd met; I was a pawn in his game of life.

Game over.

The deep purr of a car's powerful engine closes in from somewhere behind me, and I turn to flag it down. My eyes are blurred and I can hardly see straight, but I step into the road and wave my arms. "Please," I wail. "Please help me."

With tires burning and smoke clouding the air, the car comes to a screeching halt.

"Please, help me!"

The driver's door flies open and Mateo runs to me. "Jesus Christ, Cat!"

He wraps his arms around me just as my knees buckle under the weight of a heavy and broken heart. I writhe in his embrace and release another torrent of earth-shattering sobs.

"Let me go! Don't touch me! I hate you!" I scream, continuing to fight against his hold as I attempt to free myself.

"Baby, come with me. You're going to get hurt in the middle of the road."

"Fuck you!" I bellow, collapsing completely onto the asphalt. I have no more fight in me.

I am completely broken.

Bending down, he scoops me up and carries me to the passenger's side of the sporty vehicle I'd noticed in the driveway earlier. He mumbles a curse when he realizes he doesn't have a free hand.

"I'm going to set you down, Cat. Don't let go." My body shifts and slides down against his chest. I keep my head low and my eyes lower. I don't move. I can't move. I am frozen as if I were made of stone.

"You need to get in the car."

I finally comply because my knees have weakened once again and I just want to get home.

Soft red leather framed by black provides refuge for my weary and trembling body. Through blurred vision, I glance around quickly and notice that everything is shiny and new from the dashboard to the paper floor mats.

I turn my head away from Mateo when he gets into the car.

"One day. One fucking day," he spits out, flinging his ball cap onto the top of the dashboard.

The movement frightens me and I clutch my bag with my left hand and cup my right over my face, willing the subsequent round of tears and the putrid bile to remain at bay. When my body shudders, Mateo places his hand on my leg as he had done so many times before.

"I'm sorry. I didn't mean to scare you." His fingers rub a small circle, attempting to comfort me. "Please look at me."

I keep my gaze out the window and make no move to look at him.

"You have to give me the chance to explain everything."

Rage swells in me at the idea that he thinks I owe him anything.

"You have to at least give me that."

My eyes follow him when he reaches beneath his boots, reaching for the paper mat and then grabbing a pen from the glove box.

The two objects are placed on the small center console between our seats. "Write something. Anything."

I continue to sit there, quietly falling faster and deeper into the abyss of my own mind.

He huffs in exasperation, mumbling that I need to "listen with my heart" as he drives the fast monster of a car toward the highway.

For nearly thirty minutes, we travel in total and complete silence except for my relentless sobbing, the four times his phone rings and the three chirps indicating a text message; none of which he answers.

I practically jump out of the car when he comes to a stop in my driveway, but he cuts the engine quickly and follows behind me closely, begging for me to stop and listen.

Shaking my head subtly, I warn Johnny not to ask questions; I don't plan to explain any of this mess right now. Detecting the tension, my uncle steps in front of Mateo and prevents him from following me upstairs.

"You hurt her?" The question sounds more like an accusation.

I hear Mateo exhale loudly as I climb the steps leading up to the second floor.

"Not intentionally, but yes."

I can only imagine how Johnny's thick brows furrow. "What'd you do?"

"I withheld something important...but I didn't have a choice."

Footsteps shuffle and I hear my uncle's warning, "Do not make me remove you physically from this house."

With each step, their voices diminish. Without the strength to make it to my bed, I lie on the floor with my cheek against the hardwood. Through the heat vent, I hear Mateo and my uncle talk.

"I love her so much."

"Then you shouldn't have lied."

Mateo yells, insisting that he didn't exactly lie.

"Were you completely honest and truthful?"

"No. Fuck! What a mess!"

Things remain silent for several minutes until Mateo

speaks.

"Can I ask you something?"

My uncle's response is swift. "Sure, as long as you don't ask to see her right now because that answer is no."

"How the hell is Randy Creed Cat's father? She doesn't even have his last name and he's never mentioned having another daughter besides Chloe."

"Not anymore. She changed it when she was eighteen. She hates the bastard. She suffered years of emotional abuse from someone who supposedly loved her and then he had her put away after my sister died."

"Put away?" Mateo inquires. "What? Where?"

A flood of tears rages from my eyes as I remember the day my father left me there, insisting it was best for everyone.

"Fuck! I had no idea."

I hear what sounds like a head or a heavy hand hitting the kitchen table.

"John, you gotta let me go see her. I need to fix this."

"I'm warning you. Don't make me come upstairs. My niece can be a pain in my ass, but I love her. She's like my kid sister."

I crawl to the door and push the lock button on the handle when I hear him run up the stairs. The creaky floorboard announces his arrival at my door and his attempt to open my door is foiled by the lock.

"Cat, please open the door," he begs as he knocks lightly.

I curl into a fetal position and cry silently.

"Are you really going to make me go through the window?"

I hear the light tone in his voice, but it doesn't make me smile. It makes me sad because everything I believed was— and still is— a lie.

Sighing heavily, Mateo utters. "Baby, I'm not leaving until you talk to me. I'll sit here all night if I have to."

From the small space beneath the door, I can see Mateo's dark jeans as he sits there against my door.

Minutes tick by slowly.

"Cat, I know you don't want to talk and that's okay, but will you at least listen?

I blink and listen to his voice. The voice I loved so much, but now burns in my ears.

"Remember how we talked about creating our own destiny?"

I remember that conversation so well, its contents seared deep in my brain.

"I got into a lot of trouble when I was a kid, but what I didn't tell you was that I ended up in juvenile detention for a few months. After that, my grandmother sent me to live with my aunt and uncle in New York. They didn't have much except a two-bedroom apartment in the projects."

Guilt rears its ugly head when I think about how I threw that in his face earlier today.

"I hated living there and I swore that I was going to do something better. I was going to have a better life, but not too many people are willing to give a Puerto Rican kid with a rap sheet a chance. I needed a chance—one single chance—to change the course of my life."

He breathes in quietly and sniffs.

"My uncle's friend had gotten the renovation project at Randy's house last year."

I cringe at the mention of my father's name especially after today's events.

"That's when I met Chloe. I became friendly with her and dropped a few hints about my interest in music. Once the project was over, she invited me to her studio to feel things out."

The idea that he was hers before he was mine disheartens me.

He clears his throat. "We kept in touch every so often, but she was busy recording her single and then she went on tour." The words flow from his mouth as if he'd prepared this speech. "Iza and I were trying hard to push the demo we'd recorded in Spanish, but no one was interested."

So that's the connection. I remember she'd said she hadn't heard from him in a while and that he was going to be...a star. The pieces start to fall into place about when he said she needed his help.

"I'd started working here and I met you..." He chokes back a sob. "...and you changed everything for me. I hope you know that. Not that I expect you to believe a word I say after what happened today."

My throat aches as if a thousand razors were slicing through it.

"That night at the bar when I took the champagne to Chloe for you, I was convinced this was destiny calling. She and Ronan had broken up and her team was looking for someone to fill his shoes."

His phone rings once and then goes silent.

"We talked about our mutual love of music and you even encouraged me to do something with it. That's what I'm doing, Cat. I'm doing something with it to fulfill my destiny. Oh baby, I wanted so much to tell you especially when I realized I'd fallen in love with you, but I couldn't. I'd signed a nondisclosure agreement. Darcy didn't want the world to know that ChloRo was done yet. She had this crazy idea that people wouldn't know the difference in our voices."

He releases a quiet breath before continuing.

"Junior thought it was stupid for me to pursue this. He said I was chasing a dream. But if we don't chase dreams, who will?"

He bangs his head lightly on the door. "I wish you'd let me see you."

I remain still.

"I had to manage both jobs at the same time without giving anything away. It was part of the NDA. If you think about it, I didn't lie to you. I just didn't exactly say where my other job was. You assumed I was working on another house. Cat, I didn't think I was hurting anyone and even with what you told me about your father and your love-hate relationship with music, I never in a million years would've made the connection. I mean, you don't even have his last name."

I think about how jealous Mateo had been the night he came to Trina's and saw me with Caleb. How could he possibly think it's okay that he's been spending all this time with Chloe?

"The rain this week threw off my schedule and I had all intentions of going with you to see your father, but then Chloe called and wanted to go over some new stuff we've been working on. I didn't realize how late it was and by the time I did, I was going to call you. But there you were... right in front of me. I didn't know what was going on. I didn't know why you were there. Everything just got so out of control and I saw the look in your eyes. I knew what you were thinking. I knew you thought I'd betrayed you, but I didn't. I couldn't even imagine what was running through your mind as you talked to your father and then saw me come in with your sister."

"Please believe me when I tell you that I had no idea you were related to them. You mentioned your father had been in the music industry, but I didn't really think much of it."

He curses quietly, groaning about how low the battery is on his phone. After a few seconds, a sweet melody drifts through the air when he slides it under my bedroom door.

"You've been sleeping a while and I've been watching you. Baby can't you see what you've done to me. Tell me what I feel is true," he sings along to the notes. "My life was drifting aimlessly until you came along with your sweet smile and trusting eyes. From the depth of my heart come only words of love, never lies. For all I have I give to you, let's start forever right here, right now. I am yours this I vow."

Sorrowful tears stream down my face as I listen to the words.

"I wrote that song when I realized I'd fallen in love with you," he says before adding, "And my God, I am so in love with you." I detect a key change in the music, and he sings again. "And while it's true we still have a lot of learning to do, I'll spend every day loving you."

"Cat, I'm not a perfect man. I fucked up and I know it, but I beg you to open the door. I need to see you and tou—"

I reach for the door and turn the knob, unlocking it with a soft click.

"I love you from the north to the south and the east to the west. I'll give you my heart until there's nothing left. Please—" His voice cracks then comes to an abrupt halt as he stifles a cry.

Mustering the strength to pull myself up, I stand and open the door slowly, meeting his red-rimmed wet eyes full of remorse and apology.

"Baby, I am so sorry."

We reach for each other at the same time, our arms embracing, pulling our bodies close as one as we cry together.

"I can't lose you," he whispers into the crook of my neck. "I can't."

A hiccup precedes my words. "You should've told me from the start. You lied to me and I have a huge issue with lying."

"I realize that now. I'm sorry."

My fingers run through the hair at the back of his head. "You really didn't know Randy was my father?"

Mateo pulls back. "I swear to God, I had no idea. It was purely coincidence that I worked on his house and yours."

"I don't know if I can do this. They're horrible people."

I try to blink away the tears in my eyes, but it's no use. My body quivers and I bury my face in my palms and cry, releasing ugly, gut-wrenching sobs. Enveloping my body in his arms, Mateo guides me to my bed and pulls me onto his lap, but I move to sit next to him instead.

"I'm so angry with you. You broke my heart today."

Mateo moves quickly, dropping to his knees before me. "Please tell me you still love me."

Drawing my hand to his face, he sighs. "Feel this." I absorb the softness of his face and look at him, acknowledging the remorse in his eyes. "Remember what we have. Remember who we are." He drags my palm down over his heart. "Feel this?" The rhythm of his heart is wild and unsteady. "My heart aches at the thought of losing you—especially over this. I'm trying so hard to better my life, a life I want to share with you."

His tongue slides out to moisten his lips before he sucks them together and with a swift swipe of his hand, he mops away the fallen tears.

"Look...I love you. I mean I *really* love you. And while I'm not asking you to marry me today because I have nothing to offer you... someday I'm going to get down on one knee and ask you to spend the rest of your life with me."

I ball my free hand into a tight fist, resisting the urge to caress his face.

"I need a minute." I shrug from his hold and walk to the bathroom to wash away the salt stains from my face. Sad blue eyes, full of hurt and confusion, stare back at me.

A tiny voice in my head warns me to take some time and allow myself to process this.

When I walk back into my bedroom, I find Mateo sitting with his elbows resting on his knees, his fingers laced together and his head bowed low. He moves slowly, dragging his head up to look at me. The expression of desperation on his face hurts my heart. Inhaling sharply, he fills his lungs with a broken and ragged breath.

I sit beside him, careful not to make contact with our legs.

"I'm gonna need some time."

"Time away from you isn't what I want."

I tighten my lips and grumble in disbelief. "This isn't about what you want right now."

"But you're asking my heart not to beat."

I close my eyes.

Silence, woven together by the hand of misery and threaded with despair, blankets us.

"You are the sun, the moon and the stars. Everything bright in my world."

Moments slip by as my tremors settle, and my tears subside.

"I have something else to tell you," he reveals quietly.

My chest constricts in preparation of this next revelation. I slowly reopen my eyes and stare straight ahead.

"They asked." He scoffs. "Actually, they didn't *ask*. Darcy scheduled me to go on tour with Chloe. I'm not ready to go on tour. I hardly know what the hell I'm doing most days. They're going for maximum exposure."

I hang my head and screw my eyes shut once again.

Combating in my brain are varying thoughts, each waging a fierce argument for victory.

Half of me selfishly wants to ask him to give up his dream and settle for a life with me, but the other half knows I should let him go so he could pursue a better life. His own words support the latter.

Moments later, I reopen my eyes with resolve shining through them.

"How long will you be gone?" And just like that, the decision is made to let him go.

"Four months."

I gasp but speak no words.

"I won't go! I'll stay here with you. Just say the word, Cat." I can hear the panic in his voice.

Murmured words reply firmly. "I would never ask you

to do that. *Never*." I take a breath when my voice falters. "I would never take away your choices...that would truly make me my father's daughter."

Overcome by emotional and physical exhaustion, I crawl into my bed and turn away from Mateo. I feel the bed dip and his body contours against mine.

"I never meant to hurt you," he whispers before he kisses my shoulder.

"I want to believe you."

Mateo shifts in bed and then returns to spoon me.

A slow rhythm, the combination of a piano and a violin, draws me in, encompassing the quiet as music spills from his phone. The rasp of a Spanish woman's voice soothes my broken heart. She sings a slow, hauntingly beautiful song as if she knows my pain.

"What is she saying?" I ask quietly.

"She's singing about loving a man and all the joy he brings to her."

He pulls my hair back over my shoulder and caresses my cheek. "She begs for time and promises not to let him down."

My eyes close and I relish the gentle feel of his lips when he kisses my skin.

"She loves him very much and wants to grow old with him."

I reach up and take his hand in mine, clutching it tightly against my thundering chest.

Chapter Ten

MY EYES FLUTTER OPEN AND I ROLL OVER IN MY bed. My body feels stiff and my throat aches when I swallow. I reach up to rub my face and realize I'm still fully dressed in my ripped jeans and oversized peasant shirt from last night.

Like a freight train, the memories crash into me. The house. Randy. Chloe. Mateo.

The pieces become clearer when my brain fills with recollection.

Turning my head, I squint as the morning sun filters in and I notice the time is only a little past six.

How will I face him? What will I say?

I decide in that second that I'm not ready to face him.

After a quick text to Mackenzie and an arrangement for an Uber ride, I pack a bag and head down the hall to my uncle's room. I knock softly and wait for him to answer. Needing to quickly inform him of my plans before my ride arrives, I turn the knob and find the room empty.

The bed is unmade; the black duvet left haphazardly on the floor and his keys and wallet which he usually leaves on the side table are gone. I scan the room for his sneakers thinking perhaps he's gone out for an early morning run.

I close the door and rest my head against it.

"Beth?"

Gram's voice startles me as she climbs the top step carrying two cups of coffee. The mention of my mother's name confirms her mental state.

"No, Gram. It's me, Cat."

"Why are you up so early? Where are you going?"

"I'm going to Mack's house for a little bit, but I'll be back soon." I hate lying to my grandmother, but I need this time to sort through my feelings.

"OK, dear. I was just bringing Ronnie his morning coffee. Don't you have to get ready for school soon?"

She shuffles slowly into her room, leaving the door wide open.

"Here you go, my love."

When my phone rings and Mateo's face along with his beloved Marlins hat appears, I choose to send it to voicemail. I mentally remind myself to grab my charger from my room since I only have four percent battery left.

"Gram, who's with you? Is Johnny in there?" I ask, tossing my bag onto the floor near my bedroom door and stepping into her room.

Standing in front of the dresser, Gram stares at a portrait of my grandfather in his full military uniform. I stand silently and listen as she tells him that she's going to be with him again very soon.

"Gram!" Confusion and anxiety riddle through me.

Through the light casting in from the picture window, I can see her eyes are clouded and distant.

When a car horn beeps, I run downstairs, apologize to the driver for my cancelled fare and head back into the house.

Sighing quietly, I enter the small room. "Hey, Gram. How about you tell me about how you and Gramps met?" I guide my grandmother to her bed and listen as she retraces the details of their love affair yet again.

A few minutes later, Mateo appears in the doorway and

answers my silent question.

"The window."

I sneer and roll my eyes. "Most people use the door, you know."

A sad expression covers his freshly shaven face.

"I tried, but it was locked."

"It was? Was my uncle's car in the driveway?"

He shrugs. "I didn't notice."

My eyes rake over his body and I realize he's not dressed for construction work; he's dressed for this "other" project.

"Why are you here if you're not working today?"

"Can we talk for a minute?" he implores, standing outside of the door, willing me to come out.

I set the cup of coffee down and rise. "Gram, I'll be right back."

As Mateo follows me, I pick up my bag and toss it onto my bed.

"Going somewhere?"

I ignore his query and turn to face him. "Why are you here?"

"I needed to see you."

"You just saw me a few hours ago when you slipped out of my bed."

His eyes soften. "I left you a note. You looked so peaceful. I didn't want to wake you."

"Where'd you go? Chloe's bed?" I snide.

It was a childish and immature thing to say, but the insecurity of not being good enough takes hold and rattles my common sense, but more importantly, my heart.

With a furious gaze, Mateo glares at me and draws in a deep breath. His eyes close for a moment and then reopen. "I don't want to fight with you."

I bite my tongue instead of spewing regrettable words.

"Look, Chloe texted me late last night and said Darcy wants us to run a few more songs."

I respond with indifference. "Then you should go."

"Cat, please. Don't be like this with me."

I exhale a deep breath.

"I don't know what you thought was going to happen. Am I just to congratulate you for this opportunity and ignore the fact you're cavorting with my enemies?"

"You're acting like I planned this. Like I had some underhanded scheme going on."

I stare at him.

"I thought we settled this last night," he says with a sigh.

Closing the space between our bodies, Mateo pulls me close and squeezes tightly. "I love you."

I close my eyes and absorb his words.

"I want you with me for this...right by my side. This is my chance...my chance to make something of myself. To reclaim my family's name."

I sigh and reopen my eyes. "I don't want to hold you back."

"You're not going to," he counters, tipping my chin upward and kissing my lips lightly.

With uncertainty evident in my voice, I whisper, "I don't know."

"I don't want to do this without you."

I narrow my eyes and spit. "You were going to do it regardless. This was already set in motion before you even met me."

"Exactly! And now that I have the best two things that have ever happened to me, I want them both. It's like I won the lottery and I want to share it with you."

"Money is the root of all evil," I mumble and step away when his phone rings.

He connects the call. "Hey, I'm on my way. Yeah...no problem." He chuckles quietly. "It's fine. Want coffee?"

I stand there with my heart lodged in my throat as I listen to the light, playful tone in his voice.

He slides the phone into his back pocket and looks at me. "I have to go."

I nod, trying to maintain a supportive and confident façade. This is his dream. This is his chance to change his life.

"I see it."

"What?" I ask.

"I see what you're trying to hide. Your eyes..." He moves closer and lowers himself to make direct eye contact. "Your eyes don't lie to me."

I shut my eyelids from revealing the truth. "Go."

After a hard kiss, he sucks in a deep breath. "I'll call you later."

I sit on my bed and listen to the sound of him jogging down the stairs and then closing the back door.

Wondering why my best friend hasn't texted me back, I look at my phone and realize it's dead so I reach for the charger and that's when I discover Mateo's note.

C,

You are my girl. The one and only. You have my heart. Never forget that. You are the sun, the moon and the stars. Everything bright in my world.
Te amo.

I glance at the clock and call my uncle. It rings three times before he picks up; he clears his throat when his voice emerges groggy and raspy.

"Where are you?" I ask, foregoing a polite greeting.

"Cat, what's the matter? He bellows, "It's early as fuck."

"When are you coming home?"

I hear a playful moan in the background.

"Listen! Tell your tramp to give you five minutes! You need to come home. I'm going to Mackenzie's for a few days.

I need some time to think and I can't do it here."

"*Where* are you going?!" he hisses into the phone and then tells his companion to hang on.

"Mackenzie...you know, my best friend?!"

"Yeah, I know who she is."

"Glad we cleared that up." I pinch my lips in annoyance. "Gram isn't well today and you need to take care of her."

"Shit. Alright...give me a couple of hours."

"Fine."

Frustrated, hurt and just plain angry, I send a text to Mackenzie once more.

`Mateo and I might be breaking up. My uncle is an asshole.`

"Hey, Trina! Sorry I'm a little late," I call, dropping my bag off in the back. "It took me a while to remember how to drive stick." I chuckle under my breath, thinking about the grinding gears on my uncle's sporty car.

She smiles brightly, "It's okay. Since when do you drive stick?

"Since forever. My uncle taught me when I was a kid."

"Interesting."

I hide the confusion on my face at her comment. Like her shop, you have to know Trina to really treasure her.

"I almost didn't have you come in today. I don't expect it to be all that busy today or tomorrow."

"Why is that?" I ask, removing articles of clothing from a donation bag.

"There's that big music festival down in the park."

My eyes reveal my surprise. "I didn't know." Something tells me my boyfriend might know about it though.

"Some guy came in looking for you the other day."

"Me? What guy would be looking for me?"

"Average looking hippie with a ponytail."

I laugh at her accurate description of my new friend. "That's Caleb. I met him in the park. He's a musician. Nice guy."

"He asked for your number, but I wouldn't give it out."

"Good thing!"

Since Trina's prediction that the day would be quiet, she flips the "Closed" sign and tells me to have a good weekend.

After a quick text to Johnny checking to see how Gram is, I take a stroll to the park. A gaggle of children, all wearing matching T-shirts, follow their camp counselor to the picnic table, forcing me to find a spot on the other side of the park.

By the main entrance, I see the final preparations being made for a temporary stage. Scaffolding displays the multitude of lights and the sound booth is arranged offstage. Various food trucks are situated just beyond the roped-off area. Several cars and trucks fill the vacant parking lot.

"Hey, you!" I hear moments after I sit on a bench. I turn to see Caleb walking over.

Sliding to my left, I invite him to sit down. "What's up? How's it going?"

He smiles. "It's going." The guitar is swung across his chest and now rests against his abs. "I finally got it." He strums the strings and plays the riff he'd been struggling with.

"Nice! That sounds really great!"

"I had trouble with another part, but I figured it out. I actually went to see you at that Tricia place, but she said you weren't working."

"Trina," I correct politely. "Trina's Treasures."

"She said you only work a few days here and there."

I nod.

"Do you work somewhere else?"

Suddenly, I feel slightly uncomfortable with his questions about my places of employment.

"I bartend, too." My curt response is followed by awkward

silence.

"Are you coming down for the festival this weekend?"

I shake my head. "I hadn't planned on it."

"You should come. It's all local musicians. I think there's an art show on Sunday."

"Cool," I reply, thinking about one local musician in particular.

Caleb quickly rises to his feet and swings the guitar over his shoulder. "I should give you my number so we can meet up."

I glance up, the sunlight blinding me so I use my hand to shield my eyes while Caleb waits expectantly.

With quiet reservation, I withdraw my phone from my bag, tap the digits he provides and press DONE.

"Now call me so I have yours."

I'm not in the habit of giving out my number especially to the drunk guys at the bar, but I feel foolish saying no. Reluctantly, I tap the green circle.

His phone rings. "Got it." He smiles. "I've got to catch my ride. Maybe I'll see you tomorrow."

"See ya!" I wave goodbye as he turns away before I tap the social media app.

"Hey, Cat?"

"Yeah?" I look up.

"You look really good without the big sunglasses and floppy hat that hide your face."

A coy smile tugs at my lips.

I close the app and allow my finger to hover over Mateo's name. I want to talk to him. I want to hear his voice, but...I know where he is.

Spreading my arms out over the old painted bench, I stretch my legs out and angle my face toward the sky. The sun's rays sprinkle my nose and cheeks with sunshine and my eyes become heavy.

Children's laughter rouses me from my catnap and I

glance around. I notice the stage is now littered with people walking back and forth, practicing a choreographed routine. The petite blonde, front and center, is hard to miss as she waves her arms in the air and cups her hands to form a C. The few teenage girls standing on the grass raise their crossed arms and cup their fingers into a C.

C.C.

Chloe Creed.

Commanding the stage, Chloe sings along to the recording and performs for the small crowd gathering to catch a glimpse of the rising pop star. One would think the six-inch stilettos are an extension of her legs as she dances and gyrates so easily. When the song ends, Chloe turns around and peeks over her shoulder, shaking her ass then blowing a kiss to the crowd. It's her signature move. She smiles and thanks everyone for their hard work.

I continue watching carefully as the production director reviews a few things with her. I see Chloe turn her head and with a quick wave of her hand, she summons someone to the stage. I jump to my feet when Mateo, dressed in black jeans and a fitted V-neck, walks out onto the stage and stands beside her, listening to the tall redhead as she moves about the stage to the different markers. He looks terribly uncomfortable and nervous.

Wishing I had a floppy hat to conceal myself, I dig into my bag and settle on a pair of scratched sunglasses. I walk cautiously around the perimeter of the park, trying to maintain a low profile.

All the performers step back into place as does the star of the show. Each one moves perfectly, succinctly to the sound of Chloe's voice and the music. A surge of jealousy rages through me when Mateo is directed to stand behind Chloe and hold her at the waist. While swaying side to side, she turns her head away slightly and raises her arm up to caress the back of his neck intimately, seductively.

My body trembles and goose bumps line my skin.

He crosses his arms over the front of her thin body and twirls her in one swift motion. She loses her footing and nearly topples over before he catches her.

My stomach rolls and I feel like I'm going to be sick.

Mesmerized by the scene unfolding in front of me, I continue to walk forward as they begin to practice the song again. The young girls who now surround me sing along and chant how much they love Chloe and Matt.

I have to look away. I don't want this image in my head.

"Catrina?" A voice calls as if she's speaking to me and then a hand touches my shoulder.

Turning my head, I see Iza standing beside me.

"Oh hey. It's Caterina, but everyone calls me Cat."

"You here to see 'Teo? He's doing good, right?" she says, her face beaming with pride.

"Actually." I sneer. "I didn't even know he was performing."

"He just told me this morning. I'm so excited for him. He's been waiting for something like this for a really long time."

I smile tightly and nod.

"I've got to go to work. I switched with one of the other girls so I can come tomorrow night."

"Tomorrow night?" I ask.

"The music festival. Tonight they have some local bands, but tomorrow... Mateo is going to shine."

Iza leaves me with a smile and a heavy heart. I feel completely blindsided by all of this.

Turning toward the park entrance, I notice a shiny red car parked next to a Range Rover. I duck under the makeshift barricade and walk alongside the car. Inside I see several manila folders on the passenger seat and a black Marlins ball cap on top of the dashboard. Could this really be Mateo's car?

I walk toward the back of the stage and hide behind a

tree, watching Mateo, Chloe and two other men as they walk over to a food truck.

With my phone in my hand, I press the call button. Raising my hand to my ear, I take a deep breath as my heart pounds in my chest and my head feels slightly dizzy. My anxiety is at an all-time high and only the sound of Mateo's voice will calm me. I watch him reach into his back pocket, look at the phone and hesitate before silencing it, sending my call to voicemail.

I gasp and call back. I mutter a string of vulgarities as he repeatedly rejects my call.

Screw you, Mateo Cruz! Screw you!

Feeling completely distraught, I call for a ride and cry while the Uber driver reassures me that I'm going to be just fine.

"Everything happens for a reason, darling," the middle-aged man says before I close the door to his gold Chrysler Town & Country.

I walk into the house through the front door and find my uncle playing cards with Gram. I offer a quick hello and dash upstairs before either has the chance to see my face.

Reaching for the cord to charge my phone, I see the note Mateo left this morning. The black words contrasting against the stark white paper mirror the day's events.

Actions speak louder than words.

I shower quickly and straighten my hair. After rummaging through my bottom drawers, I squeeze into a pair of black shorts and pull on a tight T-shirt. My reflection in the mirror is astonishing. Heavy, dark make-up frames my eyes, making the blue appear brighter and my lips pop in deep red.

With a roll of my eyes and a smirk, I ignore the smattering of missed calls from Mateo and the single text from Caleb. I bound down the stairs, call out that I'm leaving and hop into the Uber.

Mackenzie and I exchange a few texts and she apologizes for her absence. It's her way of easing into a face to face conversation.

"Hey, Lou!"

"Hot damn! Who are you and what did you do to my sweet, innocent Cat?"

I waggle my eyebrows and plump up my cleavage, a vain attempt to make them appear bigger than they really are. While some women are blessed with great boobs or a curvy ass, I was blessed with narrow hips and small breasts.

"You look like you're going to pounce on someone. Maybe we should call you Lioness."

Mack walks in a few minutes later and has the same reaction. "Oh my God! Look at you! Who did your eye makeup?"

"I did." I beam proudly.

She cocks her arched eyebrow questioningly.

"Seems I paid attention after all," I say, referring to the hours of tutorials she'd given me over the years.

The bar is packed. Every college student is here to enjoy a last hurrah before heading back to their respective campuses for the next year. Others are celebrating the start of great internships or new jobs. I don't miss how their wandering eyes rake down my body and I certainly can't complain about the extra bills they toss into my tip jar.

Several hours later, Mateo walks in, looks around to find me and then sidesteps through the maze of people dancing until he's standing at my bar.

I swallow hard, forcing the multitude of emotions, ranging from hurt, anger to love, from surfacing.

"Hi, beautiful." Looking equally beautiful, Mateo leans over the bar and waits for me to meet him half way for a kiss.

As much as I don't want to, I do. I tiptoe and use the bar as leverage to hoist myself up, pressing my lips to his. I relish the quick contact.

"What the hell are you wearing?" he asks, eyeing my cleavage as a dark expression appears on his face when I return to my upright position. I twirl in a small circle.

"My uniform."

"That's shorter and tighter than usual, no?"

I pull the tap and pour a beer for him, quickly moving down to serve a guy with sharp, handsome features.

"What can I get for you?"

"Heinekin. And I'll take some of that, too" he says, motioning to my chest with his chin as his eyes meet mine.

I return the sly smile he gives when I take his money.

"What's your name?" he asks.

"Cat. You?"

"Sean."

As I hand back his change, Sean grabs my hand and kisses the top of it. Apparently, he doesn't care about how filthy my hands are from rinsing glasses, spilling alcohol and wiping down the bar counter.

"Good to meet you, Sean."

I know Mateo is watching me like a hawk. His gaze is thick and heavy.

Making my way back to where he stands, I ask how his day was, giving no indication that I already know.

"Busy." He sips the beer. "I called you several times this afternoon."

I counter with a snarky response. "Interesting. I called you several times today, too, but it went to voicemail every time."

His beautiful face wrinkles with curiosity. "Are you mad at me?"

I mix a martini for a woman who is holding an empty glass, silently asking for a refill.

With the shaker in my hand, I ask, "Why would I be mad at you? Should I be?"

The façade I'm trying desperately to maintain is quickly

waning.

The frustration is clear when he sighs and rubs his palm over his face.

"Cat, I need to talk to you."

"Sorry. I'm working," I state sarcastically.

He's forced to stand by while I wait on more customers.

"Chloe is performing at the music festival tomorrow," he yells over the music.

"Good for her," I snip.

"She asked me to perform with her."

"Good for you," I reply dryly, biting back the emotions and trying to keep my voice even.

He narrows those gorgeous eyes on me and suddenly he reaches over the bar to take hold of my wrist. "Come with me."

"Stop! Mateo, I'm working!"

"I need to talk to you now."

"I think the lady asked you to stop."

I turn to see Sean standing there, rushing to my defense.

"Mind your fucking business. This is between us," Mateo spits harshly.

"Cat?" Sean asks, waiting to see if I corroborate Mateo's statement.

I open my mouth to speak, but Sean's fist makes contact with Mateo's cheek, sending a spray of saliva in my direction.

"Stop!" I scream.

Mateo shakes his head, quickly recovering from the sucker punch and pounces on Sean, throwing punch after punch until the bouncers yank him off.

Aside from the single unexpected assault, Sean never gets another hit in.

A commotion ensues as both men are quickly escorted outside just as Chloe and her entourage make their way in.

I yell, asking one of the other bartenders to cover for me while I follow Mateo out.

Like a raging bull, Mateo paces back and forth on the concrete as Sean receives a quick physical assessment to determine if he needs actual medical assistance.

"What the hell did you do that for?" I yell.

Both men respond simultaneously with anger in their eyes.

"He grabbed you," Sean bellows.

Mateo hollers, "He sucker punched me!"

"I told you to stop," I say, pointing my index finger at Mateo before I point to Sean. "And I didn't ask for your help."

I breathe a sigh of relief when both men decide not to file any charges against one another. Sean mumbles incoherently as he walks down the street then turns the corner.

After some begging and pleading, I persuade the bouncer to let Mateo sit in the break room while I continue my shift.

I lace my fingers with Mateo's and lead him back into the bar, but we're stopped by Chloe who narrows her eyes at our joined hands.

"Matt, what the hell just happened?"

"Nothing. I'm fine."

She scoffs. "You don't seem very fine. Look at your face." Her small hand reaches up to caress his bruised cheek.

He pulls away and scowls. "I said I'm fine."

Chloe's eyes dart back and forth between the two of us. "You better take care of that by tomorrow. I don't want anything or anyone fucking this up for us."

She walks away without another word and heads for the VIP lounge.

Entering the small break room, I order Mateo to sit while I get something to reduce the swelling.

"Here." I stand in front of him and cradle his head, gently pressing the ice pack onto his cheek.

He reaches for my waist and turns so his unblemished cheek is flush against my breasts.

A deep sigh expels from his lungs. "Baby, what are we

doing?" he asks, covering my hand on his face. "What's going on here? I don't like the way this feels."

My resolve diminishes.

"I saw you today. I saw you in the park."

He pulls our hands down and looks at me.

"Why didn't you say anything? I didn't know you were there."

Shaking my head, I sigh heavily. "I saw you perform with Chloe and I..." My voice cracks. "I also saw you reject my calls over and over again."

Mateo rises to his feet and wraps his arms around me.

"Baby, I'm sorry. It was busy and I was with important people."

My heart splinters at his words.

"Am *I* not important?" My chin quivers.

His eyes soften. "You know that's not what I meant."

My eyes fill with moisture.

He runs a hand through his hair and exhales, "I'm new at this and half the time I have no idea what I'm doing. Darcy said I need to network and make some good connections."

I stare at him and furrow my eyebrows, taking a small step away from him. "I called you seven times in a row. Seven! Who even does that?!" I throw my hands into the air. "What if it was an emergency?"

He looks guilty. "I don't know. I guess I wasn't thinking." He brings a hand up to touch my face. "Baby, I'm sorry."

A single tear, filled with so much despair, drops. "You seem to be saying that a lot lately."

"*You* are the most important thing to me," he whispers, lowering his mouth to mine as he wipes the tear.

I shake my head in disagreement.

"Yes, you are!" he counters.

The sound of cheering wafts into the room as one of Chloe's most popular songs begins. I swallow thickly and suppress the feelings of anger and resentment from rising.

Seemingly attempting to resist the urge to listen when she announces his name as a guest performer at the music festival, Mateo searches my eyes and my lips. "Why do you have all this extra shit on your face?"

I force air through my lips in exasperation and smile weakly, looking away from him.

He moves away for a moment to eye my body.

"And why the hell are you wearing practically next to nothing?"

I smile tightly, returning my gaze to him. "I wanted to make you jealous."

He chuckles. "That isn't very hard to do. I wanted to punch my cousin in the face when he said you were hot. It was one of the first days we worked at your house and you were wearing a black bikini top and sitting on that big swing in the backyard."

I remember the day.

"Or when I found you sitting in the shop window with that weirdo."

"Caleb isn't a weirdo," I lie, knowing he is a little odd.

"Is that his name?" he asks, nodding subtly with a quizzical brow as if storing that information.

"Regardless, I didn't want anyone looking at you before and I certainly don't want them looking at you especially now that you're mine."

The door opens and Lou pops his head in, saying that I need to get back out there.

I nod. "Okay. I'll be right there." I turn to Mateo. "Please stay here." I look around for a clock but fine none. Turning his wrist, I see a Rolex sitting uncomfortably just below where the colorful ink comes to an end. "Is this new?" I ask, silently commenting how stupid it looks on him.

"It was a gift."

Something in his voice suggests there's more to the story.

"From Chloe," I state the obvious.

He shrugs. "She's a little OCD about being punctual."

"She is her mother's daughter," I remark with a smirk.

His fingers move to remove the watch, but I stop him.

"I have another hour left. Can you stay out of trouble for sixty minutes?"

He grins and his eyes twinkle with mischief. "I'll try my best."

"Keep the ice on your face. You need the swelling to go down for tomorrow."

After a quick kiss, I exit the room and return to a long line of thirsty people at my bar.

While I pour drinks and watch Chloe from afar, my mind is back in the break room, thinking about the man I love. When the final call is made and the lights go on, Marco, the DJ, announces through laughter as people make their way to the exit. "You don't have to go home, but you can't stay here."

"Hey," Mackenzie calls, reaching for my shoulder as we walk behind the double doors. "What the hell happened tonight?"

I sigh. "Oh, Mack. I've got so much to tell you."

"Are you guys really breaking up?"

"The hell we're not!" Mateo chimes in, causing us both to turn in his direction.

I've been caught and I know it.

Quick introductions are made between my boyfriend and my best friend.

"Nice to finally meet you," Mack says with a smile.

Mateo looks at her pensively. "Have we met before?"

"Uh...no," she stutters. "I don't think so."

"Weren't you at Cat's house a few times last week or was it the week before?"

"Um...I might've stopped by," Mackenzie replies, turning to look at me. "But you weren't home."

"That's weird. No one mentioned it. Johnny hasn't been

home a lot. I think he's got a new flavor of the month."

"I miss you. Please carve some time into your schedule for me," Mack teases, knowing she's been equally unavailable.

"Massages?" I suggest, thinking about my sore muscles after the few recent nights with my insatiable man.

Her eyes widen with delight, and she moans. "Oh my God, yes! This guy I'm seeing knows what he's—"

"We're leaving!" I raise my hand and silence Mack's description of her boy toy's sexual expertise.

Mateo escorts me out to his car and opens the door.

"So this is your car?"

"Nice, right?" A smile beams from ear to ear.

"Yeah, it is." I lower myself and secure my seat belt, wondering if this is another gift from Chloe.

"I'd been saving up for it...and then I got an advance from Randy."

I cringe at the mention of my father's name.

"Shit," he sighs. "Sorry."

"It's okay. It's one of those things we're going to have to deal with amongst many others."

"There's a lot we're going to have to learn along the way. This is new for both of us."

I shake my head and mumble quietly. "That life isn't new to me."

Mateo presses the button and the engine roars to life. He revs up the motor and smiles. "I love that sound," he says with a crooked grin.

"Just promise me you'll be careful with things you receive from the Creeds; their "gifts" usually have strings attached."

He leans over to kiss me. "I will."

The drive home is filled with details about his day and the music festival. He insists I have to attend, but I don't know if I'm ready to see him on stage with Chloe just yet.

"I've been waiting for this opportunity for a long time. I want you there."

I smile to myself as I think about how Iza used the same wording.

As the departure date for the tour looms ahead, we talk about what it's going to be like. Bouncing ideas back and forth, we make several promises of things we consider non-negotiable while he's on the road with Chloe.

"Separate rooms!"

"Are you kidding me?" He rolls his eyes. "I'm going to pretend like you didn't just say that."

"And you have to pick up when I call."

"But what if—"

I shake my head adamantly. "I don't care if you say, 'Cat, I can't talk now. I'll call you back.'"

"Okay. And we have to talk at least once a day. You know I hate texting with you. I want to hear your voice."

"You have to be completely truthful with me no matter what it is or how insignificant you think it might be."

"And you have to come visit me every four weeks."

I squawk. "What? I can't go visit you on tour. *They'll* all be there."

"You wouldn't be going to see them! You'll stay with me in my room."

I cover his hand with my own. "We'll see. Gram isn't doing so well."

"We're going to be okay, right?" He turns his palm up and intertwines our fingers, squeezing gently.

"I hope so." I raise our joined hands and kiss his knuckles.

We arrive back at my house, and he walks me to the small landing.

"It's late. You should probably go home and get some rest." I whisper as I turn the key to unlock the door.

"Or I should follow you into your room and fuck you."

I shiver at his sexy counter offer. Playfully slapping his chest, I make a face at him although I find myself becoming accustomed to the arousal that accompanies his use of *that* word.

"You'll have to be quiet."

"I'm not the one who screams my name." He walks me backwards into the dark kitchen and kisses me as we climb the stairs awkwardly.

He shushes me when a muffled laugh conceals my amusement at missing a step. I grab the front of his shirt and nearly pull him down on top of me.

"You're going to wake your grandmother up."

"She won't mind. She loves you almost as much as I do."

I close the door quietly behind me.

"I need to take a quick shower."

Understanding my silent invitation, Mateo removes my clothes and then his own.

Hot water rains down on our naked bodies as we kiss, letting our tongues play.

"I'm going to have blue balls when I'm on tour," he says, littering my neck with kisses.

His hands slide down my back and cup my ass.

"I'm going to miss this."

I moan into his chest as one hand skates around to my front. "God, I'm really going to miss this."

He parts my desperate and throbbing core, sliding one then two fingers in, massaging rhythmically until he squats down and kisses the bare flesh. With a combination of forceful licks and gentle nips, Mateo devours me and I explode. His mouth continues to pleasure me until I push his face back.

"No more," I pant raggedly.

Standing tall, Mateo strokes his dick evenly, hissing with pleasure when I sit on the small seat and lick the tip with my soft tongue. My other hand moves beneath to cradle his balls, slowly extending a digit to reach his tight ring. I look up and see nothing but pure, unadulterated lust in his eyes. I see the temptation in his hard gaze, challenging me to press on and enter his body as I've never done before.

He moans and his head lolls to the side. He gulps when I push in further. I look down at my fisted hand and see a bead of white liquid shoot out. I part my lips and suck, using my tongue as encouragement, wanting and needing him to finish his release in my mouth.

Mateo grunts, exhaling a deep breath as he pulls me up to meet his mouth. He pushes the hair away from my face and kisses me. His tongue swirls in my mouth, tasting the remnants of his orgasm.

"What the—" he sighs. "I can't even..."

I smile at his inability to complete a sentence.

"I lov—"

"I know. You love me."

"I need to s—"

"Sit," I say for him.

I kneel before him and rest my hands on his strong thighs as he continues to regain his composure.

"Listen, I love you. I'm so proud that you're following your dream. I'm happy you have this opportunity...I just wish it weren't with *them*. I know if the tables were turned, you would be there to support me."

He smiles in appreciation.

Continuing, I say, "I don't want there to ever be anything between us. Nothing at all."

He nods.

I kiss his fingertips and lick my way up his arm over the colorful etchings.

"What does this one stand for?"

Looking down, he smirks. "That one stands for a lapse in judgment."

I hum in curiosity.

"I've made some stupid decisions in my life."

"Haven't we all?" I ask, wondering what he's referring to exactly.

"I guess. But meeting you, falling in love with you... that was the best decision I've ever made."

I laugh. "You decided to fall in love with me?"

"I tried to fight it. I knew the path I was headed on and I didn't want some girl tying me down."

My expression reveals the hurt he's caused.

"But you're not just some girl. You're my girl. And loving you, having you by my side...I want that forever. I won't ever let you go."

We fall asleep in each other's arms, our bodies entwined with one another for a few hours until the sun rises.

"Hey, you need to get up." I rub his shoulder to rouse him from his slumber.

"But I don't wanna work today," he complains playfully, rolling over onto his stomach, revealing his tight ass.

"You have to. How else am I supposed to watch you perform?"

"What?" He darts up and faces me with wild and messy hair. "Seriously?"

I smile and nod. "I can't wait to see you shine."

Chapter Eleven

"ARE YOU *SURE* YOU LIKE THIS ONE?" I ASK GRAM,
confirming her final choice after she dragged me for nearly
three hours up and down the aisles of Lowe's as she perused
the selection of bathroom vanities and matched plank tile
that would complement the paint color for the new bathroom.

"What do you take me for? A cuckoo bird?" Gram asks,
shaking her head at me with a scowl on her sweet face.

"Of course not, Gram!" I laugh while Johnny rolls his
eyes.

"Ready, Ma?"

We make our way to the register to pay for the tile and
paint just as my uncle receives a phone call.

"Will you be taking the vanity home today?"

I shake my head. "No, the contractor will pick that up on
Monday. It's in the computer already."

"Are you remodeling or building a new house?" asks the
cashier with long dreadlocks as she scans the carriage full of
materials.

"My daughter is coming home."

The cashier smiles politely. "That's great."

"Some people think she's dead." Gram taps her heart.
"But I know better."

I huff and offer a tight-lipped smile and wave at my uncle to hurry up.

"$1, 381. 45. Will this be on your Lowe's card?"

I shake my head.

My uncle steps up and swipes the debit card from the checking account he manages for his mother while he continues his conversation.

The cashier asks him to swipe it again and says, "Sorry. It's been declined. Do you want to try it again?"

Annoyed, Johnny swipes it again and once again it's declined.

"Hey. I've gotta call you back."

"Ma, did you write any checks from this account?"

Gram shrugs her shoulders.

The man waiting behind us vents his frustration with a heavy huff.

After pulling out his own debit card and swiping it, my uncle turns a bright shade of red when his card is also declined. I tell him that I would pay, but that I don't have that much money in the bank.

"You *should* have that much money."

I ignore his comment.

"Here." He hands over an American Express Black card and my eyes widen.

The transaction is finished and a long, printed paper is handed over.

"Thank you." Taking the receipt, Johnny pushes the cart to the store's exit.

I guide Gram out and secure her in the backseat of his car.

"How do you have that card?" I question as he loads the tile and paint into the trunk.

"What are you talking about?" he snaps, heaving as he lifts the heavy boxes.

"That was an American Express Black card. You need to

make lots of money for that."

"Okay," he states as if wondering why I care.

"I thought you lost your job." I narrow my eyes at him.

"I didn't *lose* my job. I left my job. There's a difference."

He slams the trunk shut, ending the conversation.

The drive back to the house is quiet. The only sound comes from the radio.

"Gram, that's the festival Mateo is performing at tonight." I turn and look over my shoulder.

Deep red lipstick is smeared across her lips and half of her chin.

"Gram!" I yell. "What are you doing?" I reach for the tube of MAC lipstick and groan. "Where did you get this?"

"Right there," she says, pointing to the space on the floor between her feet.

I huff and turn to face my uncle. "Nice. *Real nice.* At least we know your new girlfriend uses good lipstick."

"What?" he demands in confusion.

"It's MAC." I hold up the black tube of lipstick.

"Mackenzie?"

"The lipstick," I correct.

He looks at me as if I have three heads and mumbles incoherently before ending with, "Whatever, Cat."

"I'm going to the music fest tonight so I won't be home until late."

"Well, I have plans," he gripes. "Besides, you went out last night."

"No, I didn't," I argue. "I was working."

"Well, you wouldn't have to work if you had allowed me to do my job years ago."

"You know what?" I blink rapidly, my voice oozing with exasperation. "I'd rather be dirt poor than take a single penny from him."

"It's not *taking.* You earned it."

I toss his words back. "Whatever."

Several hours later, my phone rings just as I step out of the shower. I answer quickly and walk to turn down the volume streaming from my computer.

"Hi, handsome!"

"Hola, *mamacita*."

I smile at the pet name Mateo's given me.

"What are you listening to?" he asks with feigned rebuke in his voice.

My finger freezes on the keypad. "Nothing," I drag out as a smile tips my lips.

"Don't lie to me." He teases. "Are you listening to *Despacito* again?"

I silence the music with a click of the mouse.

"Maybe...I can't help it. He reminds me of you."

"WHAT?!" he screeches in disbelief. "Oh, baby. I think we need to break up."

"Ay bendito, papi."

He laughs hysterically into the phone. "Do you even know what that means?"

"No, but I know this gorgeous and extremely sexy Puerto Rican guy who might."

"Is that so?" His voice drops to an even sexier rasp.

Changing the subject before my hands find their way between my legs, I ask about the festival.

"What time are you going on?"

"Right around nine," Mateo responds. I can tell he's distracted by his hesitant reply.

"Are you okay?" I ask, wrapping my body up in a towel.

"Yeah. I'm good."

"You don't sound so good. You sound nervous." I wish I could be with him to kiss away his fears and anxiety.

"I'm a little nervous, but I guess it's more for Iza."

"Iza...why?"

"One of the singers tripped on stage and hurt her ankle so they needed someone to fill a ten-minute slot. I talked Randy into giving it to her."

"Wow! Good for her." I stand and look out the window where Gram is walking around.

"Wait 'till you hear her. That girl can sing."

Mateo misinterprets my silence and tries to clarify his statement as if he offended me. "I mean she doesn't sing like you do. You've got so much talent and you're beautiful."

I chuckle. "It's okay. I'm not jealous of Iza...not anymore."

"What are they having you wear?"

"Ball crushers."

I laugh. "What?"

"You're not going to believe me until you see me. The jeans are so tight, they crush my balls."

"I can kiss them and make you feel better."

He growls, "Don't say things like that. There's no room in there for a stiff dick."

"The girls are going to go crazy for you!"

He tries to downplay the exuberance of the wild fans.

"I've got to get going, but I'll see you tonight. I'll look for you."

"You can try, but you won't see me. The lights on stage are really bright." I step away from the window when Gram reenters the house. I drop my towel and rummage through my drawers looking for my ripped jeans and off the shoulder blouse.

"Cat, even if I were sailing along the ocean on a moonless night, I'd still find you."

An eruption of giggles releases from my lips. "Where do you come up with this stuff?"

"I told you. I'm good with words."

"I hope you mean those words."

"Every single one of them."

We exchange words of affection and disconnect the call.

"Hey, Gram!" I call when I hear her footsteps on the stairs. "I need you to get dressed. We're going out."

Her face beams as she squeals with delight. "Are we going to a party?"

I chuckle quietly. "Sort of."

"Will Ronnie be there?"

Sadness consumes me to think dementia is stealing my grandmother away from me.

"No, Gram. He won't be there."

Following closely behind her, I walk into her room and open the door to her closet.

Bags upon bags greet me. I pull out a few articles of clothing and notice the tags.

"Gram, have you been shopping from the TV again?"

She hums distractedly.

"Gram!" I call again and repeat my query.

"My friend Valerie told me to get those."

"Valerie?" I question, never having heard that name before. "How do you know this Valerie?"

"She works at QVC."

My uncle is going to have a fit and demand she return all these purchases. No wonder her bank account is low.

I match a pair of grey linen pants with a three-quarter length top and set out her sandals. She adds a long silver necklace and looks simply adorable when she's finally dressed. I make a mental note to get her on the scale in the morning because her pants are really loose and she weighs next to nothing.

"Did you lose weight, Gram?"

She doesn't reply as she retreats into her own mind.

A quick Uber ride delivers us to Veterans Memorial Park. I use Gram's age to my advantage which allows the driver to drop us off closer to the entrance.

It seems everyone in town is here to listen to the talented

musicians. My grandmother and I walk around looking at all the different tented booths where local artisans sell their ware. My eyes scan the vast space, hoping to catch a glimpse of Mateo. I just want to see him. I just want to see his smile.

I convince Gram to have tacos for dinner so we walk to the end of the line at the food truck and wait.

She asks questions about random things and I respond to the best of my ability. I don't know what happened in the 70s or early 80s. I wasn't even a thought in anyone's mind yet.

"What year did John Denver release Take Me Home?" she asks.

I laugh. "Who's that?"

"Beth, you're never going to be famous if you don't know him."

My heart plummets at the mention of my mother's name. "Umm...I'm not sure."

"But he's your favorite."

"Gram, I'm not—"

"1971," a deep voice states.

I turn to see my father standing behind us with a careful smile on his face. I swallow hard and look away, remembering how disastrous our last meeting was.

"Hello, Violet."

I glance at him and scowl. "She's having a good night. I'd appreciate it if you left her alone."

"You haven't answered my calls."

"I have nothing to say to you," I grit.

"For the record, I didn't know you and Matt were together and as far as I can tell, he had no idea you are my daughter."

"Were," I correct.

When the line moves up, Gram tries to walk away.

"No, Gram," I say, guiding her back in line gently. "We need to stay here."

"Matt said she's not doing so well."

I snap my head in his direction. "First of all, his name

is Mateo and secondly, neither of you has any business discussing my family."

"I am your family."

Fuck you I want to scream.

I order our dinner and reach for my bag but quickly realize it's not on my shoulder. I mumble quietly, wondering if this day could get any worse. Digging into my pockets, I pray that I'll find a crumpled, washed bill. I come up empty.

Humiliation washes over me when Randy steps forward and hand over a twenty.

"You don't have to do that."

"I want to."

I quickly explain that I must've left my bag in the Uber.

Releasing a huff, I accept his offer and remark that I'll send a check in the morning.

He orders a few things from the menu and waits alongside me.

"You always did like tacos when you were little, but you only put cheese on them. Nothing else."

I grimace. "How would you know? You were never even home." I immediately regret falling for his manipulation and taking the brief trip down memory lane.

"Beth was good about keeping me updated about everything you did. How you forced yourself to practice well into the night, how you forfeited going to birthday parties or playing sports." He chuckles sardonically. "I mean, I couldn't imagine what kid would say no to a trip to Disney because she wanted to participate in a talent show."

I close my eyes and suppress the bile at the mere mention of those recollections. Forced to sit on a hard bench and deprived of sustenance until I got a song right. My fingers ached for hours on end and my mother's insistence that my father would be angry haunted me daily.

Randy Creed is a master manipulator.

"Gracias," I thank the dark-skinned Hispanic man in his

native tongue as I reach for the cardboard tray. His returned smile suggests he appreciates my efforts.

"Come on, Gram."

My father reaches for my forearm when it's clear I have no intention of speaking to him again before I leave.

"Cat, you have to realize we're going to be in each other's lives because of Matt."

"No! That's where you're wrong," I hiss. "My relationship with Mateo is none of your business and what he does when he's with you people, is none of mine," I lie. I will be damn sure to know his every move. It's my obligation to keep him away from my father's deceptive web.

Sitting at a picnic table alongside a young couple, Gram and I eat our pork carnitas in silence. She's lost somewhere in her own mind and I'm lost in a pit of despair and regret.

"I have to use the bathroom," Gram states.

I glance around the park and notice the restrooms are on the opposite end.

"Come on, Gram. This way." I help her to her feet and guide her across the grass.

The line is long and Gram is impatient. She fidgets with her long necklace and shoves her hands into her pockets.

"Thanks." I sidestep a heavy woman and lead my grandmother into the large handicap stall.

"Make sure you squat."

Gram pulls her pants down and sits bare bottom on the seat.

I palm my face in disgust. When I drag my hands down, I notice something sticking out from one of her pockets.

After handing her some balled up toilet paper, I reach down and pluck the bills from her pocket.

"Two hundred dollars?" I squawk. "Gram, where'd you get these?"

She flushes the toilet then looks at me. "The nice gentleman gave them to me."

My father. I want to find him and shove the money down his throat.

Walking off my annoyance, my mind returns to Mateo. *He* is why I'm here. This night is about *him*.

As the performers take the stage, the MC takes a moment to thank Creed Records for sponsoring the event and reminds everyone how honored we should all be that Chloe is the special guest.

I'm exasperated yet thrilled.

Gram and I move closer to where the crowd either stands or sits on outspread blankets. I sigh in frustration because along with my bag, I also left the beach blanket in the car. Gram doesn't seem to mind for the moment as she kicks up her heels to the upbeat tempo or sways to the romantic ballad.

Almost an hour later, I can see how weary my grandmother has become. If we sit back where we were, I won't have a good view of Mateo's performance, but asking my tired grandparent to stand for another hour isn't an option either.

"Are you Catrina?" asks a gangly looking young man.

"Caterina, yes." I reply, wondering how he knows my name.

"These are for you." He sets down two folding chairs and opens them up, gesturing with his hand as if they were a queen's throne.

"Where did these come from?"

"The boss sent them over."

I roll my eyes and sigh, knowing exactly who the boss is. "Thanks."

"Enjoy the show," he says as he walks away and heads around back to the staging area.

The MC announces the next performer who hails all the way from Caguas, Puerto Rico and brings her own flair to the meaning 'hot mama.' "Please welcome Iza Guzman!"

My eyes widen in surprise when Mateo sits on the

stage with a drum between his legs. A single tap on a drum followed by two consecutive ones brings the music to life as Iza, wearing a tight, short red dress, turns around, flashes a huge smile and thanks the audience for coming out tonight. The crowd goes wild for her.

Taking in the whole scene before me, the band continues to rile the crowd up with its style of music. Several other men play various wooden instruments while Iza sings.

Gram taps her thigh, keeping up with the tempo of the music until the song ends and a slower one begins. Only the strum of a guitar is heard as the music transitions and the band moves off stage. Mateo stands and walks to the side of the stage only to return with a green-tipped microphone.

With my eyes glued on them, I watch as they stare at each other, swaying slowly, harmonizing a beautiful slow song. They mirror each other's stances and sing as if no one else in the world exists.

Anxiety builds in me and my heartbeat quickens. Their performance is quite intimate—too intimate for my liking.

As the song comes to an end, Iza wraps her arm around Mateo's waist and leans in for a hug. He drapes his arm over her shoulder and kisses the top of her head.

My dinner rolls in my stomach when they bow with clasped hands then walk off stage to thunderous applause.

I should stand and offer my praise for an incredible performance, but my heart feels so heavy that I'm cemented to the plastic seat.

In my peripheral vision, I see Caleb walking over sans his ever-present guitar.

He greets me with a warm smile and a quick peck on my cheek. "You made it!"

"Hey." I pull away quickly.

"And who's this?" he asks, gesturing to my grandmother.

"This beautiful lady is my sweet grandma." I cup my mouth and whisper, "But she hates to be called that." Caleb chuckles when I speak louder and say, "Right, Gram?"

She hums and looks away.

"Are you enjoying the show?"

I nod and reply with an excited, "Yeah, it's great. Who knew this city had so much talent?"

"That last girl." His eyes light up. "Man, was she hot or what?!"

I laugh and playfully tap his chest. "You're a typical guy."

He holds my gaze for a moment too long and I look away.

"I texted you the other day."

"Sorry I had a lot going on."

He immediately understands my implication when I motion with my chin in Gram's direction.

Our conversation is interrupted by the MC who screeches into the microphone, asking if everyone is having a good time. The crowd screams louder when he says he can't hear them.

"Now for our final performance tonight, please welcome singer-songwriter, the beautiful and extremely talented Chloe Creed."

Anyone who was sitting is now standing and a roar of cheers moves across the crowd like a tidal wave.

For ten minutes, Chloe performs flawlessly. Each song is on point as her voice rises to hit every high note or dips for the low ones. No one can deny her incredible range. I listen to her sing her popular songs, detailing experiences of a lifetime.

"Thank you so much! I love you guys so much! And now I want to introduce you to someone who is super special to me. I love him so much and I know you guys will too! Please welcome my man, Matt Cruz!"

I jump to my feet and crane my neck to see over the influx of signs being held in the air, declaring their love for Chloe and "Matt." Silver glitter outlines the words, "Crushin' on Cruise" while wild teenagers scream out, asking Matt to marry them or to "cruise" into their beds.

Mateo, wearing a white T-shirt and dark skinny jeans and black boots, takes the stage. His smile is huge and radiant; I can tell how much he loves all the attention. I remember loving it for a little while, too.

"Thank you! I wanna give a shout out to Creed Records for giving me this opportunity. I am so blessed to work with Chloe. To my girl C, I love you, baby!"

The audience responds with a chorus of "Awws."

My heart swells with immense joy at his words and my smile matches his. I whisper quietly, "I love you too, baby."

Mateo transforms into a star. He shines as if he were born to do this. Drawing the crowd in with a curl of his finger, he continues to seduce them with a swivel of his hips. Women and girls clamber to touch his extended hand as he moves along one side of the stage while Chloe commands the other.

Together, they are a charismatic musical match made in heaven.

I stand and clap wildly, placing my fingers in my mouth to whistle in appreciation for a job well done. Happy, proud tears stream down my face for him.

The MC thanks everyone for coming out tonight and reminds us to come back for tomorrow's art show.

"Maybe we can meet up for coffee this week. I'm working on a new song."

Distracted, I smile and nod, listening half-heartedly to Caleb before he says goodbye.

"Come on, Gram." I guide her up gently and lock my hand with hers. We are like salmon swimming upstream as we make our way to the staging area. I want to hug Mateo and tell him how proud I am of him.

My poor grandmother is practically dragged behind me until the crowd clears. I see Mateo standing beside Chloe signing autographs and taking photos. Again, he seems to be in his glory.

"I have to pee," Gram says, tugging on my hand like a child. I sigh and roll my eyes, looking around for a bathroom.

"Give me ten minutes. Can you hold it for ten minutes?"

We move closer when the fans have finally dispersed.

I can't hear their exact conversation, but suddenly Chloe turns venomous eyes on him and screeches something about her being the star of the fucking show. He looks stunned and seems to be apologizing to her.

I want to rescue him —save him from the wrath she inherited from her mother.

Pulling my phone out of my back pocket, I call him. I watch as he makes no move to answer his phone.

She tries to walk away from him, but he pulls her back and his expression softens. He lowers his face to hers, placating her until she smiles and nods.

I dial again.

"Beth," Gram whispers.

I turn around and notice the linen material between my grandmother's legs darken.

"Oh," I breathe. "I'm sorry, Gram."

Rushing to find the nearest restroom, I abandon my efforts to reach Mateo and call my uncle instead.

"She's soaking wet! I can't take her home in an Uber!"

I listen to his shouts that I'm selfish and reckless.

Screeching to a halt, Johnny arrives a short time later with his light brown hair messy, his casual clothes disheveled and his frustration and anger directed at me.

"Slow down!" I hiss. "You don't need to drive so fast!"

My phone rings with an unknown number, but I don't answer it. The caller continues but receives my voicemail each time.

I open my mouth to ask my uncle for help with Gram but change my mind when I notice the tight hold on the steering wheel that leaves his knuckles white. I struggle to get my grandmother out of the back seat where she's fallen asleep yet manage to walk alongside her into the house.

"I've got her," my uncle spits as he scoops her up in his arms and carries her up the stairs into the bathroom. I follow closely behind and hear him tell her that she's going to be alright.

"I'll take it from here." I nod my appreciation before I begin the task of caring for my aging grandparent.

Once she's settled for the night, I shower quickly then collapse onto my own bed and try Mateo's phone once again. I feel disheartened that he hasn't even started the tour and he's already managed to break one of his promises. I grab my journal, pour out my feelings then cry myself to sleep.

I startle awake to the sound of my window opening.

"Hey," Mateo whispers.

My legs swing off the bed and my feet land with a hard thump.

"What are you doing?"

"The backdoor is locked and my phone died."

I turn on the lamp and smile when he climbs through the window and tosses a backpack onto the floor.

"You could've borrowed someone else's phone to call me."

"I did. I called you several times from Chloe's phone, but you didn't answer."

"Oh," slips from my mouth and I cringe at my own idiocy for sending all those calls to voicemail.

Mateo kisses me and my fingers caress his face. His skin feels damp and coated.

"What is on your face?"

He blushes in the dim light. "Stage makeup. I tried to wash it off, but it's like...polyurethane."

I roar with laughter and hug him tightly. "I was mad at you."

"Why? What did I do now?" he asks genuinely.

"I thought you sent my calls to voicemail again," I confess.

"No, my phone died," he reassures me. "Did you make it to the show?"

My face lights up, beaming with so much love and pride. "Yes!" I kiss his lips. "You were magnificent. You're a natural up there."

"Really?" he asks without a hint of sarcasm.

I nod enthusiastically. "Your voice didn't falter at all and you definitely know how to work the crowd and everything."

He kicks off his shoes and follows me into bed.

"Those girls are crazy! Did you see their signs?" He laughs.

"I did, but they spelled your last name wrong."

An odd, almost wary, look passes over his face which prompts me to inquire about it.

His response floors me.

"Darcy thought "Matt Cruise" sounds less..." He air quotes. "*Hispanic.*"

"That's ridiculous! You *are* Hispanic!" I state angrily. "I hate that bitch!"

Silence settles in as we wait for the tension to subside.

"Those crazy girls aren't going to care if you're black, white or purple! They'll fling their underwear at you regardless."

His face contorts to one of repulsion.

"I don't care. I only want *your* underwear." His lips meet mine for a warm kiss as he reaches down to caress the soft cotton between my legs.

Biting my bottom lip, I inhale and exhale quietly through my nose, trying to maintain my composure and refrain from ripping his clothes off immediately.

"I went to Lowe's today," I blurt, needing to change the subject so I don't concede to my body's desire.

I tell him about everything we picked out and the odd situation with Gram's and Johnny's debit cards.

"Then he pulls out an AMEX Black card. Crazy, right? I mean who lives with their mother yet has enough money for a card like that?"

"Maybe he's saved a lot of money."

Mateo kisses my neck and caresses my core again, attempting to move us to a more intimate conversation.

"Are you attracted to them?"

"Who?" he breathes as his teeth nip my ear.

"Iza and Chloe," I say, further explaining how evident the onstage chemistry is between them.

"No, I'm not attracted to either of them. I'm insanely attracted to you." He kisses my forehead. "In fact, I thought about you the whole time."

I tweak his nipple through the cotton shirt. "Liar."

"I did!" he insists, pushing the hair away from my face and looking directly at me.

"You need to keep your distance though. Chloe is possessive; she's going to treat you like she owns you," I say thinking about the heated conversation I witnessed earlier.

Mateo shrugs, suggesting he can handle the pop star.

"She's used to getting her way."

"Too bad she's not in charge of me."

I inhale quietly. "Chloe is—"

"A co-worker. We only work together. It's no different than when I work here with my guys. We work, we do the job and we get paid. End of story."

I roll my eyes. "Not exactly the same and you know it."

"Well, that's how I see it."

"Chloe is a liar who steals things. Don't trust her."

Minutes later, he asks what I'm thinking about when he realizes he's dominated the conversation about life backstage and the feeling of adrenaline that ran through his body.

"I didn't know you were going to perform with Iza."

"I wasn't supposed to, but when she asked, I couldn't say no. I kind of owed it to her."

"She really loves you."

He shakes his head. "Not in the way you're thinking."

"And Chloe said she loves you, too."

"Nah, those are just words. She didn't mean anything by it."

"I have a confession," I whisper as I look away.

Mateo shifts his body so that I'm now lying on top of him. "Tell me."

"Watching them touch you was really hard. It's going to take some time for me to get used to that."

"It's just a dance. You have nothing to worry about."

"True, but some dancing is like having sex with your clothes on."

He challenges me, but I remind him about the first time we danced at the Cuban restaurant.

"Okay. Point taken."

"I understand it's all part of the show, but it's tough to watch."

"I get it," he concedes. "I wouldn't want some other guy's hands all over you either."

I push myself up and straddle his abdomen before yanking off my camisole, exposing myself to him.

His hands skate up my thighs and brush lightly over my waist until they reach the swell of my breasts. Taking my nipple into his mouth, he moans his delight. Barriers are stripped away as we join our bodies as one.

"Te amo," he sighs, weary and sated.

"I *te amo* you, too."

Chapter Twelve

MATEO AND I TRIED TO MAXIMIZE OUR TIME together, knowing his departure date for the tour was quickly approaching. I'd cut my hours at Trina's so I could be home to have lunch with him on the days he worked at the house. Some days he had to leave earlier than expected so his crew ate the lunch I'd prepared for him. I'd filled another journal with my deepest feelings, my intimate thoughts and my heart's desire.

After every shift at the bar, Mateo, faithfully, drove me home despite having worked late into the night at the studio with Chloe. Mateo was keen and could sense my unease even when I didn't voice it; never in a million years did I think my path would once again cross with theirs. He'd often offer a conciliatory smile when he had to answer Chloe's call even though it had only been hours since they'd last spoken. She knew he was with me and she didn't like it. The few arguments we'd had were quickly resolved; neither of us wanted to waste the energy and preferred to resolve our issues between the sheets. With reassuring words and gestures of his love and devotion, Mateo convinced me that I had his heart.

Today, the man I love, the man who stole my whole

heart, will climb into a sixteen- passenger van with the man I hate, the man who broke my young heart to travel across the United States for four long months.

"I can't believe you're leaving already." Time is one of those things you can never have enough of. "I'm gonna miss you like crazy," I breathe quietly into the crook of his neck.

"I'll miss you more," he squeezes my bare ass. "Sometimes I wish you hadn't deferred grad school. You would be busy down in Philly and Caleb might get the hint to leave you alone. I might have to set him straight the next time he texts you."

I push up onto my elbows and look down. "First of all, I will miss you more because the person who stays always misses the most. They're left to face everyone and see everything that reminds them of the absent person. Secondly, grad school will be there next year. I need to be here now and lastly, Caleb is harmless."

Mateo laughs. "That was a mouthful."

I grin and shimmy my way down his hard body. "I love having a mouthful of you."

His phone rings just as I finish pleasuring him.

"Shower with me," Mateo offers, gazing at me with tenderness in his eyes.

"Promise you'll visit me."

"I already told you I will." I kiss his cheek softly.

Inhaling sharply, Mateo releases a heavy breath.

"Sing your heart out and stay true to who you are. Got it, Mateo Cruz?!"

He nods. "Got it, future Mrs. Cruz."

My nose wrinkles when I realize my initials will one day be as they were before.

"What's that face for?"

"If I marry you, my initials with be C.C. again."

"And?"

"Those are Chloe's, too."

"Not really because that's just her stage name."

I rise and follow him into the bathroom.

"Thank God for small miracles."

"I can't believe it's been three weeks already. Where are you?" I ask, rolling over in bed, noting the late hour on the clock.

"Somewhere in Indiana," Mateo replies with a yawn.

"And Missouri is next?" I know it is based on his tweets and other comments on social media. My heart soars every time he tweets, "C, you have my heart. I love you!" It reminds me of how very much I am loved.

He hums an affirmation before telling me about the fairgrounds and the smaller venues they've played in. His only complaints, aside from missing me, are the food and sleeping arrangements. "Life on the road isn't as glamorous as it seems."

Quiet, steady breathing indicates he's fallen asleep.

"Baby, go to bed. You're exhausted."

"What?" he says as if startled. "I'm okay." He yawns once again.

"I love you."

"Te amo."

Between Gram's appointments and my uncle's frequent absences, I'm left to bear the burden alone. Junior and his team have been working hard to finish the project and only have a few weeks left. Mateo calls every day even if it's only for a few minutes before he falls asleep.

"I'll only be gone for three days," I counter when Johnny argues that now isn't a good time for me to visit Mateo.

"I wasn't asking for your permission or your blessing. I'm

going."

I storm out of the kitchen and sit at my piano as the house phone continues to ring.

"Are you going to answer that sometime today?"

"Why? It's probably just another charity or some pledge drive looking for more of Gram's money," Johnny replies as he walks up the stairs, stomping his bare feet like a petulant child. "I'm going to shut off the land line. There's no point in having it."

I release a small breath as I place my fingers on the white keys. Note by note the song I've been working on comes to life. I struggle to reach the high note and decide to move the key change earlier on. I can't wait to surprise Mateo with it.

Two days later, Mackenzie drops me off at the airport for my flight to Tennessee.

"I can't believe we haven't hung out in forever," she sighs. "Whatever happened to beverages with boys?"

"We found *men*! Not that I've met yours yet..." I say with a hint of mild accusation. "Is this new one even of legal age? Is that why you won't let me meet him?"

Mackenzie rolls her beautiful green eyes and ignores my comment. "I'm going to miss you."

"We'll still see each other at work when I get back, right?" I say with a smile.

"I'm moving in this weekend," she confesses.

"What? Since when?" I screech.

Chuckling quietly, she reveals, "Since my guy rented a Penske truck to help me get settled in." She can't hide the sadness that sweeps over her face. "Promise you'll come visit me!"

It seems everyone I love is leaving me.

"I will. Please promise me you'll stop in to say goodbye to Trina. I think she might've missed a few mortgage payments since you stopped shopping so much."

Mack laughs. "Yeah, I've been trying to cut back on my

spending."

I slam my hand against the dashboard dramatically. "WHAT?"

"Seriously!" she screeches as she maneuvers her car into the departure lane.

"So you're giving up your fancy lipstick and expensive mascara?"

"Have you lost your damn mind?! I still need to look good!"

We share hugs and kisses before I wave goodbye and pull my carry-on suitcase behind me.

The flight to Tennessee gives me enough time to finish the song I'm working on and take a quick powernap. The next stop on their tour is an amphitheater in Music City in the heart of Nashville. That's what's nice about this city; everyone loves music.

Mateo's schedule has him doing something every day, but my flying here to meet him works best for everyone. He and Chloe have been rehearsing some new song and they're hoping to get into a recording studio since Randy pulled a few strings. He also somehow managed to get a local radio station to interview them about Chloe's new album. I didn't want to be a burden so I told him that I'd grab a cab and meet him at the hotel. After a quick check-in, I'm free to wander around the city I used to frequent with my parents.

I touch base with Johnny to inquire about Gram. He tells me she's okay for the time being. I wander the streets, pick up a few souvenirs to bring home and grab a bite to eat at Arnold's Country Kitchen. With my belly full and my wallet light, I meander back to the hotel. I shower, shave and relax on top of the king-size bed until my eyes drift to a close. The clicking noise jolts me awake and I look to the window.

"No window today, baby." Mateo laughs, capturing my reaction on his phone when the sound reaches straight to my heart. "I'm coming through the door."

I nearly tackle him to the floor as I run to him. My towel loosens and eventually falls at my feet when my arms snake around his neck and pull him toward me, kissing him desperately as if he were my last breath.

"Oh my god, I've missed you so much!" I mumble against his lips. I squeeze his back and hold him tightly. "I feel like I'm dreaming."

His hands smooth my damp hair away from my face, exposing my bright eyes and wide smile that seem to hypnotize him. He can't take his eyes off of me. "Let me look at you."

"You are looking at me," I reply with a grin.

Mateo steps away and rakes his eyes over my body, locks his fingers with mine and spins me around slowly. "Simply beautiful."

Kissing our way to the bed, we reacquaint our bodies with gentle touches and passionate embraces.

"I'm not gonna be able to let you go in a few days," he says seriously, his eyes revealing truth and conviction.

"Well then...you better enjoy me while you have me."

Undressing quickly, Mateo loves me with his mouth and fingers, taking the time to pleasure me, preparing me for the onslaught of what I know will be rough and hard. It's what we both want; what we both need.

"I need to watch," he pants, turning me over onto my knees. "God, I love doing this to you."

Consecutive, long and deep thrusts penetrate me and I cry out in gratification, begging him to give it to me harder.

I scream his name and orgasm, continuing to move until he finds his own release in me.

Hot and sweaty, he collapses on top of me. I love the feel of his body on mine. His warm breath, wheezing in my ear and telling me how much he's missed fucking me sends shivers down my spine. His hand moves and outstretches over mine and he laces our fingers together before sliding his thumb over my ring finger.

"I'm working on making a name for myself and when I do, I'm going to marry you." He places a chaste kiss on my cheek before creating a trail down my back with his lips, leaving sweet kisses in its wake.

An ache pierces my heart and I close my eyes.

"I can't breathe," I sigh quietly.

Mateo shifts his long body and removes his weight from me.

"Sorry."

I turn to face him and glide my fingers over his face. "It's not that I couldn't breathe because you were on top of me. When you say those things, you take my breath away."

A garland of Spanish words is spoken to me by the man I love. I don't have to know what they say to feel his adoration.

"Mateo, I love you just the way you are. Your name, your past...who you are...you're perfect to me."

"I want to provide for you."

"I don't need to be *provided* for. I only need you."

An embrace lingers between us, neither wanting to be the first to let go until his phone rings.

"I wish you didn't have to answer that," I grumble quietly.

He nods in agreement, kisses the tip of my nose then reaches for his phone.

"An hour?" he questions. I can see by the look on his face he isn't happy.

Exhaling, he simply responds, "Fine."

His eyes, riddled with apprehension, gaze at me as his lips move.

"How would you feel about going to dinner in an hour?"

I gulp. "With *them*?"

Sitting on the edge of the bed, Mateo hangs his head. "We don't have to go."

I sit up alongside him and rub the curve of his back, hoping to dispel the tension in his muscles.

"Baby, you have to go. I can wait here."

He shakes his head. "That's not right. You came here to spend time with me not to sit in a hotel room by yourself."

From the tips of my toes, a sense of determination rises in me. I won't let the Creeds keep me away from him—not for a minute. I slide my hand into his and smile tightly. "I don't really want to go, but I will for you."

"Really?" he squawks, turning to face me with a look of surprise mingled with appreciation. "Thank you!"

"Just don't leave me alone with any of them."

With a slight tipping of his head, he agrees.

"Chloe seemed genuinely happy for me when I mentioned you might be coming for a visit."

"She did?" I squawk, my eyebrows rising to my hairline.

He nods. "They're actually not as bad as you think they are."

I freeze and my face contorts into a hard scowl. "You don't know them like I do. You have no idea what they're capable of. Trust me."

Mateo takes a hold of my face and draws me in. "I won't let them hurt you."

We arrive at Etch Restaurant shortly before seven. My hold on Mateo's hand is like a vice grip until he returns a gentler squeeze, reassuring me everything will be just fine. Already seated at the head of the long wooden table, I find the president of Creed Records sipping a hefty cocktail. To his right is his superstar, Chloe and to his left, sits his former business partner now wife, Darcy. They appear to be having a heated discussion.

"Hey, guys," Mateo interrupts by way of a greeting.

"Matt." My father nods briefly, but when his eyes land on me, they widen and he jumps to his feet. "Caterina! Sweetheart!"

The vice grip returns and threatens to break every bone in Mateo's hand.

The burly man strides over and reaches for an embrace, but Mateo blocks his attempt.

"She's my daughter," Randy hisses.

"But she's *my* girlfriend and tonight...she's *my* guest."

"You've got a set of balls on you, kid," my father spits, glaring at Mateo.

I glance at Darcy and Chloe who both wear an expression of shock.

"Boys, put your dicks away and come sit. This is supposed to be a nice dinner," Darcy chimes in with a playful smile and a roll of her eyes. "How are you, Cat? Have you been well?"

I force a tight smile and nod. "I'm fine, thanks."

"And your grandmother? How is she?"

Oh. you know, dementia has stolen her mind and she thinks I'm my dead mother. Remember her? How could you forget? You had an affair with her husband. I internally cringe at my silent, snarky response, but verbally, I provide a more appropriate answer. "She's fine."

"And Johnny? My gosh, how is that handsome devil?"

"He's fine." I stare at her and exhale, wondering why she's asking about my family. It's not like they were friends after what she and my father did.

"How long are you in town?" Chloe's mother turned manager asks. "Matt should've told us you were coming. We would've sent a car for you."

I notice Chloe's torso jerks subtly and she blinks. "Yeah, it's cool you're here. Maybe you could help us with some stuff we're working on."

Why? So you could steal it again? The silent words inquire yet my lips never move.

Mateo sits beside Chloe as if providing a barrier between *them* and me and keeps his arm draped across the back of my chair. His fingertips circle my bare shoulder then rest on the black material just a bit lower.

Darcy asks the waiter for another martini then turns her attention in our direction. "So how exactly did you two meet?"

All eyes zoom in on us.

Mateo recalls the story of our meeting including the joke about our chicken salad which he still has never eaten.

"Wow! What a small world, huh?" Darcy concludes sweetly.

"Do you still play the piano?" my father asks, piercing me with his eyes.

I glare at him and throw daggers into his heart and lie. "No, I stopped playing a long time ago."

A look of shame and guilt stretches across his face. "I thought maybe you would've found each other again."

Slowly, I turn my head from side to side. "You can't bring something back from the dead."

I notice Darcy stiffen momentarily. "My gosh, Cat. It's amazing how much you look like your mom. The resemblance is uncanny."

I draw up expressionless eyes and remark, "Yeah, I get to see my dead mother every time I look in the mirror."

"Please stop," Mateo whispers. "I'm begging you."

"Sorry." I smirk. "I just finished reading Stephen King. Gloom and doom, death and misery are on my mind."

My father chuckles darkly. "Ahh, Cat. You were always so good with words."

The road crew arrives shortly after. Drinks are poured and delicious meals are enjoyed. Aaron, a man with salt and pepper hair and wrinkled skin, sits to my right and talks my ear off about life on the road and his years in the music industry. I smile and feign interest.

"You look really familiar," he says before asking what my name is again.

"Cat Ryan."

My father looks over and inquires. "Since when do you go by your mother's last name?"

"Since I legally changed it."

His nostrils flare. "And when was that?"

"The day I turned eighteen." *A few years after I left Norwich Academy* I want to add. A red flush covers my father's face, prompting Darcy to place her hand on his forearm. With gentle wisps, she soothes him while tossing me a harsh look, silently demanding that I stop my belligerence.

I cast my eyes down in submission and silently apologize, acknowledging that I'm an adult who is behaving like a child.

A group of overly enthused teenage girls, celebrating a Sweet 16, prance over to the table and beg for pictures with Chloe and "Matt."

Mateo shifts his body as he and Chloe lean in toward each other for the photo. They rise and join the birthday girl for a more intimate picture. I watch him transform into "Matt Cruise" right before my very eyes and a feeling of wariness nudges in my belly.

"Ohmigod! Is it true?" squeals another party guest. "Are you and Chloe really dating?"

Mateo's eyes widen in surprise, and he swallows nervously. "C has my heart. Always has. Always will." He glances at me quickly then returns his attention to the estrogen-filled girls.

"Excuse me," I say to Aaron, needing him to move his legs so I can stand and rush into the bathroom.

"Cat," Mateo calls after me but is silenced when Darcy says, "I've got her."

I slam the stall door shut, slide the lock and sit on the toilet with my face buried in my palms. Using slow breaths in and out, I calm myself down as jealousy and rage course through me. I've seen the pictures on social media, touting Mateo as Chloe's hot new man, but I assumed they were referring to onstage. These girls clearly think there's something going on offstage.

"Cat?" a soft voice calls. "Honey, are you okay?"

I wipe my eyes, rise and unlock the door and find Darcy

standing by the sink.

"I think I ate something that didn't agree with me."

Her reflection in the mirror indicates she doesn't believe me.

"You can tell me the truth," she encourages although her eyes say otherwise.

"The *truth*?" I ridicule, my voice oozing with contempt. "Since when are you interested in the truth?"

Darcy tilts her head, eyes me carefully before exhaling. "I thought we buried the hatchet a long time ago. Let's not rehash the past, okay? Oh, and I'm really sorry for bringing up Beth. I've just never seen two people look so much alike as you and your mom. She was really beautiful, wasn't she?"

A few of the teenage girls push through the door, giggling hysterically, gushing about how excited they were to have just met Chloe and Matt.

"Oh, he's gorgeous!" one girl squeals.

"I know! How old do you think he is?" the other asks, walking past me to an empty stall.

Their conversation continues as shouts through the confines of the small space.

"I can't believe he let me touch his abs."

"Lucky Chloe gets to lick them!"

I close my eyes as their words settle, causing nausea to turn my stomach. I reopen my eyes, adjust my headband and stare at myself in the mirror while the two girls quickly wash their hands and leave.

"You know this industry. You know how the game goes."

I look down to wash my hands and ignore Darcy.

"Matt obviously cares about you," she states with a sigh.

"He loves me," I hiss, meeting her eyes in the mirror once again.

"Then it'll all work out."

"Come back soon. We wouldn't want to have to send out the search party again," Darcy suggests connivingly, subtly reminding me of my failed attempts to run away when I was young.

Sighing deeply, I pull the heavy door open and walk down the dimly-lit hallway toward the table.

"Kitty Cat," my father calls as he leans casually against the wood grains on the wall.

I physically cringe at hearing my childhood nickname. The memories it evokes have been long suppressed. Memories of my 5th birthday party and the box which held the small kitten resurface. Images of my beloved daddy rolling a ball of red yarn in the living room make me quiver. I close my eyes and dispel the scene of my younger self sitting upon my father's back, playing "horsie" until my mother reprimanded us, citing her fear that I would be injured. I force those flickers of my past down before they threaten to crack open the sealed vault.

"Don't call me that—ever again," I spit through gritted teeth, continuing on my way even though he murmurs that I can go to him if I need anything. "And by the way..." I stop and dig into my wallet, grab some cash and hand it over forcefully, "Gram doesn't need your money.' "

"Violet was always good to me when your mom and I—"

My jaw tightens at the mention of my mother.

"Aren't you going to ask how I'm feeling?" he chides.

"You look perfectly fine."

"You, better than anyone, know that looks can be deceiving."

I narrow my eyes and realize I've, once again, engaged in a conversation with him.

Randy Creed is a master manipulator.

"I'll be home next week for a meeting so please come by the house. We didn't finish our conversation. I don't know how much time I have left and now that we've found each other again, I don't want to lose you."

"You don't need me. I'm nothing but a pathological liar

who craves attention. A menace to the Creed family name. Aren't those the words you used to describe me?"

I walk past the giant of a man and rejoin Mateo who is talking quietly to Chloe. My eyes catch the movement as he removes his hand from the back of her seat.

"You okay?" he asks, sliding a hand beneath the table to gently rub my thigh.

I nod and reach for the tall glass of water and notice my hand is trembling wildly.

He leans in and whispers, "You sure?"

"Yeah. I think I'm going to head back to the room. I'm a little tired from traveling today." I force a smile, but it doesn't reach my eyes. I stand and without looking at anyone in particular, I voice my gratitude for the meal and say goodnight to everyone.

Mateo excuses himself and follows me, calling my name as I continue to walk to the front of the restaurant.

"Hey! I'm talking to you."

I thank a man for holding the door open.

Releasing a deep breath, I startle when Mateo catches me by my waist, pulls me against his chest and wraps his arms around me. "What's wrong?" he asks when his lips reach my ear and he guides us away from the crowded entrance.

I hate the opposing feelings warring inside of me.

My head hangs and I close my eyes. "I shouldn't have come here," I confess.

Spinning me around, Mateo reaches for my face, caressing my cheeks with his thumbs. "Don't say that."

Eyes full of regret and disappointment look up and meet his soft and worried gaze.

"I want to be supportive, I really do, but this...this is so much harder than I thought it was going to be."

Remorse transforms his features.

"I'm sorry, baby."

"Don't be. This is what you have to do. I get it, but I don't want it in my face. Seeing you with them...it's just hard. Not to mention the girls all think you're with Chloe."

Mateo reaches into his pocket when his phone rings and he grimaces.

"Who's that?" I ask, wondering if Chloe is already looking for him.

He sighs, "Iza. I'll call her back tomorrow."

"I saw her last week at the bar. She came in with Junior, but they didn't stay very long."

He slides the phone back into his pocket then hums. "He didn't mention seeing you."

I shrug. "I see him almost every day so I'm sure it wasn't worth mentioning."

A vibrating noise and a chirp emit from his phone, again interrupting our conversation.

He reads the text message aloud. "Headquarters Beercade in ten." His lips pull down into a frown and his eyebrows furrow while he taps a response. I stand there wide-eyed, gawking at him.

"What?"

I screech, "You're texting?"

"Yeah?" Laughter laces his question.

"But you always said you hated texting with me."

"I only hate texting with you because I'd much rather hear your voice."

I twist my lips to the side and narrow my eyes. "But you text with Chloe?"

"I don't really care about hearing *her* voice."

I rush to put my arms around him and squeeze. "I love you." I exhale quietly. "Go do what you have to do. I'll wait for you back in the room." I glance up and smile, but I can see the debate in his mind.

"Only if you're sure?"

I nod and assure him it is even though it's not. I came to Nashville to spend a few precious days with *him*— not to run around the city with them.

A quick wave of his hand hails a cab for me before he kisses me goodbye.

"I won't be gone long."

I lower myself into the back seat as he leans in for a final kiss and whispers, "We didn't have dessert." He winks, and I smile.

Shortly afterward, I fall into a deep slumber.

Rolling over, I see green numbers reveal it's just past two o'clock in the morning and the cold space beside me in bed is still empty. I check my phone for any missed calls or perhaps text messages, but I only encounter a blank screen.

I click on the small lamp then fumble through my bag, taking out my journal to jot down a few random thoughts that keep circling in my mind. Having recently filled the last page, I sigh and grab the hotel notepad to write on. When my eyes grow heavy, I close them once again.

"Morning, *mamacita*," Mateo utters quietly, spooning me from behind. My eyes struggle to open as I look at the clock. I turn my head and see his handsome face greeting me with a smile. "Sorry about last night. Things ran late."

I mumble my complaint at the early hour and argue that I'd much rather sleep than hear lame excuses.

"Can't. I have to be at the radio station in two hours."

Screwing my eyes tightly, I growl, "Good. Then do yourself a favor and go back to sleep."

He peppers my neck with kisses and his hand moves around to massage my breast. "I'd much rather do you."

Pushing the uneasy thoughts about last night to the back of my mind, I roll over and welcome him into my body.

"No, thanks," I counter sarcastically when he offers for me to tag along for the interview.

"We're going to do an acoustic set of some new stuff."

I wiggle my finger back and forth playfully. "I'm good."

Standing in front of the mirror, I pat my face dry after a

hot and steamy shower and ask what time he'll be back.

A white fluffy towel is secured snuggly just below Mateo's waist. We stand side by side, each preparing our body for the day ahead. I move and step behind him, staring at the perfect planes of his back as my fingers slide north along his arms until they reach his broad shoulders. The warm yet hard flesh is wedged between my fingers and I massage gently, eradicating the tension I feel.

"Not too long. A couple of hours at the most," he says, tilting his head to the left then to the right.

"Okay," I respond, thinking I'll have enough time to put the finishing touches to the song I've written for him.

I ask the concierge for the local radio stations and scroll through my phone until I find Lightning 100. The morning team announces they'll be interviewing pop radio's rising star, Chloe Creed, in ten short minutes.

After purchasing a bagel and a large coffee, I sit by the pool and wait for the segment to begin.

My excitement wanes when Chloe and her new beau, Matt Cruise, are introduced. One of the two on-air personalities comments about the rasp in Chloe's voice and annoyance runs through me when she comments suggestively that "We had a late night" which only prompts the other personality to inquire about the nature of their relationship. Her responses are coy and somewhat cryptic.

"So Matt Cruise, any relation to Tom," the first man asks through a chuckle.

"Yeah, you're a name pop music hasn't heard before... where the hell did you come from?" the second man chimes in with a chuckle.

"I've—" Mateo starts but is quickly interrupted.

"He's my hidden gem."

There's a moment of awkward laughter.

"Tell us a little about yourself, Matt."

Mateo chuckles lightly, but I know it's forced. His past isn't something he enjoys talking about.

"Growing up, I bounced back and forth between New York and Puerto Rico. My family has always been into music so I guess you could say it's in my genes."

DJ Easy, the radio personality, continues to badger him with questions about musical influences.

"I love music. Doesn't matter what kind, where it's from or what it's played on."

"Cool! We have a couple of questions from some listeners. Do you mind?"

I smile, knowing he's likely got a roguish grin plastered on his face. "Not at all."

The DJs banter back and forth until they agree on a question.

"If a woman's body were an instrument, what would it be?"

"What kind of question is that?" Chloe laughs, chiming in as if rushing to his aid.

"I've got this," he assures her. "Um...let me think about that." Mateo says. "Maybe a drum so I could bang her hard."

I roll my eyes as everyone on air laughs at his crude reply.

"I'm just messing with you guys. I think I'd have to say a piano," Mateo offers seriously, his voice dropping to a sexy purr. "The inner workings of the piano are extremely intricate. Touching the combination of the right keys together creates a beautiful sound. Each stanza would guide my fingers as they slide over every key, finding the perfect cadence. And like a song, her body would ebb and flow with the rhythm, building gradual momentum before finally exploding with a powerful crescendo."

My eyes close. The recollection of those words causes my core to tighten and moisture to pool in between my legs.

"I think every woman in Nashville just fell in love with

you!" the DJ teases.

"So is there a special lady in your life? I mean, come on, let's face it...you've got the looks of a magazine model."

The other DJ laughs and points out the awkwardness of the last comment. "Dude, have you got a thing for Matt Cruise?"

A rumble of light laughter comes through the speaker.

"I'm secure enough in my own masculinity to appreciate a handsome guy," DJ Easy retorts with humor.

"There is one special girl in my life. C has my heart. Always has. Always will."

And just like that I fall even more in love with Mateo Cruz.

The conversation finally shifts to their tour and music. I release a sigh of relief.

"We bounce ideas off of each other. There have been times we worked straight through into the early morning hours. We're in constant contact. Right, Matt?"

He clears his throat and hums in agreement.

"All work and no play?" a man asks. "Pity."

"So we understand your father has really built quite an empire at Creed Records. That's a long way from his humble beginnings."

"He's great! He works really hard to recruit new talent and is looking to branch out to other genres. Everyone can relate to music whether they understand the lyrics or not. It's all about how it makes you feel."

Her words, although cheerful, sound well-rehearsed and insincere.

"We're looking forward to hearing this new single you've got coming out."

I can only imagine the expression on her face.

"Omigod yeah, we're so super excited to drop it here first."

"Cool! Can't wait!"

After a commercial break, Chloe and Mateo sing about

a cat and mouse chase between two eventual lovers. It's a beautiful banter which highlights each of their range and ability as they tell their own version of events of falling in love. They sing together and harmonize perfectly. I listen to the unfamiliar words until one phrase catches my ear.

Dubbed the "hottest new thing," Chloe and Mateo thank the radio for their sponsorship at tomorrow night's concert and remind everyone to come out and see them perform live.

An hour later, my phone rings.

"Hey, baby," Mateo croons in my ear. "What are you up to?"

"Hi," I say, grabbing the edge of the pool towel to shield my eyes from the bright sunlight. "I'm sitting by the pool. You?"

"I have a photo op luncheon and then I'm done for the day."

"Okay," I reply, hoping he doesn't suggest I come along again.

I hear a flurry of commotion in the background and it sounds as though his muffled voice is conversing with someone else.

"I'll let you go." My response is curt and it doesn't go unnoticed.

He sighs heavily. "I'm sorry, babe. I didn't think I'd be this busy that's why I asked you to come now. Every time I turn around, they've got something else planned."

"I get it," I mumble.

Another gorgeous day accompanies me as I take in the sights and absorb the city's vibe. I pay the fare and tour the city on the hop-on hop-off Old Town Trolley and listen as the driver details Nashville's history. With only a few dollars left to my name, I head back to the hotel and nap.

A freshly showered Mateo slips into bed beside me and drapes his arm over my side. I awaken to the contact and shift my weight, causing my journal and pen to fall to the floor.

Nuzzling into the crook of my neck, he exhales a breath of exhaustion followed by words of confirmation.

"What do you want to do tonight?" he asks, covering a yawn with his fist.

I flip onto my side to face him. My fingers reach out to lightly stroke his face, causing his eyes to close.

"You look so tired."

His eyes struggle to reopen.

"You're working so hard." I run a hand through his damp hair and kiss his forehead.

Steady breathing indicates he's fallen asleep.

For the next three hours, I alternate between staring at him and dreaming of him. He consumes my every thought.

Mateo finally awakens when his phone rings. He rolls over to answer it with a weary voice.

"No, we're not going. I already told you I have plans with Cat."

A female's harsh voice suggests she's not happy.

"I know that...you keep reminding me...maybe later... Okay."

A blank expression greets him when he turns back to me.

"You have to go, don't you?"

"No," he states unwaveringly. "You have me all to yourself tonight— I promise."

After two rounds of hot shower sex, we finally manage to get dressed for some time outside of the hotel room. We exit the building through the pool area since a few girls have been spotted hanging out by the main entrance, hoping to see Chloe, but more likely, Mateo.

An Uber ride leaves us on a busy corner street in Hillsboro Village.

"I can't believe you gave up tickets to see Darius Rucker," I say, shaking my head, knowing how much Mateo admires him, especially his ability to cross genres.

Mateo smiles and kisses the top of my hand which is enclosed in his. "It's not like I've never seen him in concert back when he was Hootie."

"I know, but those were great seats!" I offer.

He stops as we wait for a car to pass.

"Would you have enjoyed the show knowing everyone else was going to be there?"

I narrow my eyes playfully. "You're so smart! And I'm glad you're being careful with their gifts." I look down at his bare wrist. "Where's your watch?"

"In my suitcase." He shrugs and pulls me along when the road is clear.

"I'm starving," he declares.

"But you just ate," I reply suggestively with a laugh.

"And it was delicious!"

A red blush covers my face as Mateo pulls the door open to a restaurant and we join the long line.

"My abuela used to always let me have flan before dinner."

"What's that?" I ask, wrinkling my nose at the sound of the word.

"You've had it before. It's like egg custard. It's sweet and creamy."

I bury my face in the palm of my hand, dramatically covering my eyes as embarrassment washes over me. When I look up and find him staring at me with humor on his face, his eyes, partially hidden by the low brim of his Marlins hat, dance with amusement.

My mouth pops open and I gasp. "Mateo Cruz, you are so bad!" I can't contain my delight when this side of my man emerges.

He bends down slightly to whisper in my ear. "Baby, I could write a million songs about loving you."

Standing behind me, Mateo drapes his arms over my shoulders as we continue to wait.

A multitude of square tables welcome hungry diners for

a meal. Wooden wainscoting separates the painted walls where plaques of recognition, old photographs and sports memorabilia abound.

"Where are we?" I ask, having missed the sign as we entered.

"Brown's Diner. They supposedly have the best cheeseburgers around."

"This way, ya'll," a perky redhead leads us to a table while Mateo guides me along by my shoulders.

We decide on cheeseburgers, fries and beer from a local brewery.

Scanning the packed restaurant and taking in the atmosphere, Mateo comments about the photographs of famous singer-songwriters.

"Ever listen to Loretta Lynn?" he asks, turning his attention back to me.

"Um...I'm sure I have. My parents always had some kind of music on. They listened to a lot of different genres when I was growing up."

Mateo gazes at me pensively for a moment.

"What?" I ask as the waitress drops off the ales. I take a sip and lick my lips. "So good!"

"That's the first time you've ever mentioned your father in a positive way."

I set my beer down and look away, apprehension rushing through me.

"Cat, I'm sorry. I didn't mean to upset you."

Sighing quietly, I return my eyes to his. "It's fine. I try not to think about it. Things really started to change between us when Darcy and Chloe came along."

We struggle to return to the light-hearted moments since the mention of my father has soured my mood. Mateo's eyes and tight smile apologize for tainting our evening together.

"What time is your flight tomorrow?"

"Noon."

"I can't believe you came all this way and can't stay to see the show." Disappointment mars his face.

"I know, but I came to see my hot boyfriend, Mateo Cruz, not skinny jeans wearing 'Matt Cruise,' the musician on tour."

"Maybe you can stay next time."

I detect some sadness in his expression.

"I will next time for sure. I promise."

Our cheeseburgers and fries seem to disappear shortly after they were delivered.

Mateo settles the bill and asks what I'd like to do next as we exit the diner.

"I don't care. I'm just happy to be with you. I've missed seeing you every day."

Climbing into the cab, I ask the driver to give a suggestion of what to do.

"You like music?" he asks.

"Yes," I reply enthusiastically.

"There's a show at Cheekwood's Swan Lawn. It's a mix of song and symphony. You never know who's going to show up."

Mateo and I grin at each other.

"Sounds perfect."

Arriving after the show has begun, we find an empty spot on the lawn. I sit between Mateo's bent legs, mirroring his position and rest my head on his chest. My eyes observe the lights reflecting off the building that shine brightly in the moonless night as several musicians perform their original songs.

"This is so beautiful," I comment.

"The building needs a new roof," he replies, causing me to look back at him quizzically.

"That's what you're thinking about?" I laugh.

His hazel gaze looks at me lovingly. "I'm thinking about you going home tomorrow without me..." He brushes my hair to the side, tucking the long strand behind my ear. "I miss the day to day with you."

I shift and turn around to face him.

"I miss you so much, but I understand this is important to you. Some days I want to call you a thousand times just to hear your voice. I've never loved or needed anyone the way I love and need you."

He rolls me onto my back. "You are the most important thing in my life. You *then* music. Don't ever forget that."

A single chaste kiss evolves into a raging wildfire of passion until an "ahem" forces us apart.

"Do you mind if we head back?" Mateo asks, panting against my lips as his erection presses into my belly.

"Not at all!" I grin.

Our backseat intimacy is disrupted by a phone call from Chloe, telling him to stop by a club.

"I'll see if she wants to go," he responds before covering the phone and turning to me.

I'm furious and annoyed at the interruption, but even more so at the insinuation that he should really stop by to make an appearance.

I don't want to share him. Tonight he is mine.

"Go," I huff. "I'll wait back at the room."

After studying me for a few seconds, he tells Chloe that he'll call her back.

"We don't have to go."

"Mateo, this is what you're here for. I get it...but I was hoping for one night with just you."

He removes his ball cap and runs his fingers through his hair.

"An hour. We'll go for an hour and that's it."

Even though he doesn't voice it, I know he desperately wants to go. It's a good opportunity for him to network and I don't want him to ever resent me for holding me back.

"Fine. An hour," I state with a firm expression on my face.

After a few text message exchanges with Chloe, the

driver reroutes us toward Printers Alley. A quick Google search lists the club as a local hot spot for aspiring musicians.

"Over here," my father calls as we step out of the car. He greets us with a wide smile which I don't return. My grip on Mateo's hand becomes firmer as the seconds tick by.

"*This*," my father continues, "is the place to be tonight."

I want to rebut and beg to differ, but I don't.

Once cleared by the bouncers, Mateo and I follow Randy into the club called Sambuca then are led to a private VIP lounge.

"Hey you," Chloe sings as she kisses Mateo's cheek while keeping her eyes on me. "Hi, Cat."

Keeping my face from revealing anything but indifference, I reply with a curt "hey" and decline her offer for a cocktail while Mateo says he'll have a beer.

The room is dark and the music pumping. I tag along, holding on tightly to Mateo's left hand, as Chloe introduces him to several music executives. Some are longtime friends of my father's whom I recognize even though they are now old and bald.

"Caterina?" I hear someone call my name. "Caterina Creed? Holy shit! Is that you?"

I am yanked from Mateo's grasp and clutched against a sweaty man. The stench of alcohol weighs heavily on his breath and makes my body stiffen.

"Let me go!"

My father is at my side in an instant.

"Benny, what the hell are you doing? Leave my kid alone, will ya?" he jokes.

I cringe at his response and give him a side-eye dirty look.

"You don't remember me?" he asks with glassy eyes and a drunken smile. "I'm Bada Boom Benny." He raises his hand up, pretending to play the drums. "You used to sit on my lap and play the drums with me."

Mateo jumps in and shakes his hand, introducing himself when he notices my reaction.

Benny's fat fingers take a hold of Mateo's outstretched hand. "Mateo? What are you... Spanish?"

He nods once as his chin rises with pride. "Yes, I'm Puerto Rican."

Benny narrows his beady eyes. "You look Sicilian."

"No, sir. One hundred percent Puerto Rican."

Randy joins the conversation and tells Benny that Matt is working with Chloe. "He's quite talented. He sings in English and Spanish. The girls love him!" He turns to Mateo with pride beaming. "I think I have a star on my hands."

"Thanks, Randy," Mateo replies to the compliment. "Excuse us."

We walk toward the corner so we can have a few moments to ourselves. Leaning down to whisper in my ear, Mateo apologizes for Benny's behavior, but says I must've left quite an impression on him.

"Music was my thing. I could pretty much pick up any instrument and make it sound good." I smile tightly, suppressing the memories from long ago.

Chloe steps up and hands Mateo a bottle of beer.

"We're going to sing a few songs," she says while taking a sip of her cocktail.

"Now?" Mateo shrieks, protesting before further complaining. "Come on, seriously? Don't you think we should save it for tomorrow night?"

"Matt, you have to take every opportunity and run with it. Maybe you don't really want this after all."

Her passive aggressive tone doesn't go unnoticed when he pinches his lips and huffs.

"Cat and I were just leaving."

"I wasn't asking," Chloe says, narrowing her eyes before turning to me. "You don't mind, do you? I mean if you don't want him to, just say so. You don't have to lie."

I cringe internally as I slide my hand around to his back and lean into his chest. "If Mateo wants to sing, then he'll sing. It's up to him."

"That's what I thought." A wide grin stretches across Chloe's face. "Be ready in twenty."

Grimacing, I look up at him. "So much for an hour, huh?"

"Baby, you could've said no!" he counters as if this is my fault.

"And you could've said no to coming here in the first place." I hiss, stepping back to put some distance between us.

A quick glance around the crowded room, I find Darcy watching us carefully. I see Chloe stabbing her index finger into Randy's chest, probably filing some sort of grievance before they both look in our direction.

"I'm going to the bathroom." I stomp off and ignore his calls for me to stop.

Rushing past the crowd, I bypass the bathroom and step outside through and open door. I take in a much needed deep breath despite the humidity in the air. From the huge outdoor speakers, live music emerges.

I find a vacant bar stool and sit, close my eyes and bury my face in my hands. I fight to steady my breathing; each ragged pant is an indication of my anxiety level. A million questions swirl around in my head.

What am I doing here? Why does he want this so much? Am I holding him back? Should I let him go?

A gentle hand to my shoulder prompts me to look up. I inhale sharply at the sight of Darcy before me and then roll my eyes.

"Trouble in paradise?" she asks softly, misguided concern in her eyes.

"I'm fine." I stand. "I just needed some fresh air."

"Matt was worried you might miss their performance."

I scoff and shake my head in anger, knowing that his performance supersedes my feelings or whereabouts.

"I'll be—"

"I know this—"

Darcy and I speak at the same time. I insist that she continue.

She smiles tightly. "I know this must be hard for you. You could've had this, but you gave it all up. I understand this life isn't for the feign-hearted. The constant spotlight, the scrutiny of the public eye, the loss of privacy. Surely you realize how talented he is, don't you?"

I stare at her contemptuously then look away as she continues to speak. "I never wanted this life. I wanted to write until you and your viper daughter stole that away from me."

Ignoring my accusation, she continues. "Randy has big plans for Matt...and Chloe. They make a great team. I hope he means enough to you that you won't jeopardize his chances."

Tossing a hard glare, I open my lips to speak. "I'm in love with Mateo *not* Matt."

"Is there a difference?" she asks sharply with a raised eyebrow.

"Yes, there—"

I suddenly realize she's baiting me and I refuse to fall into her trap.

"I just want you to be careful. We all know how easily words can be misconstrued."

I hear the warning. "Noted."

"Shall I tell Matt you're here or that you're going back to the hotel?" she asks.

"Neither. You don't need to speak for me. You might twist my words again," I reply sharply.

She smiles as the devil himself. "It's good to see you've found your voice again. Silence didn't suit you well."

Darcy walks away and heads back inside while Chloe and "Matt" are introduced. A cover of Shawn Mendes' song Stitches filters through the Bose speakers as they sing alternately, each adding their own personality to the song.

I type a quick text but wait before sending it. Debating whether to leave or not, I close my eyes and listen as the music changes, morphing into one of Chloe's hit songs. The familiar words send a wave of frustration and regret through me. I blink away the moisture in my eyes and wipe away the few tears that drip.

With a quick wave of my hand to stop a cocktail waitress, I ask for two martinis and two shots of Fireball.

Another song highlights their talent.

I sit quietly and take in the atmosphere. A group of people stand together in a small brood, clinking glasses and dancing to the music. A couple cuddles in the corner and his hands roam up her dress, pleasuring her with no regard for time and space.

"Here you go." The waitress sets down the drinks and places a cocktail napkin across from me as if I am waiting for a guest.

The song Matt and Chloe performed at the music festival comes on and I lift the glass to my lips. In one swift gulp, I finish the cocktail and follow it with a shot.

"You're missing the show," remarks a deep voice.

I turn my head and see my father standing there watching me. My smirk combined with the returning of my attention to the empty shot glass suggests I'm not in the mood for him or his lies.

"Waiting for someone?" he asks, eyeing the full martini glass on the table.

The shot glass rolls slowly between my fingers, the liquor tempting me to lose myself for a little while.

"What happened to us, Cat?"

Again, he is ignored.

Randy pulls out the vacant seat in front of me and sits. He laces his hands together and I notice that his diamond studded wedding band sparkles in the artificial light. It's the most ostentatious piece of jewelry I've ever seen on a man.

His eyes follow mine and he covers his ring finger with his other hand.

"Darcy insisted on this." He chuckles. "I guess she wants to make sure people know I'm a married man."

I choose the martini and finish the cocktail in three hard gulps, wiping my mouth with the back of my hand. "Funny. The last wedding band didn't stop you from cheating."

"Is that what *this* is about?" he asks, motioning between our bodies. "What happened between me and Beth was just as much her fault as it was mine."

I narrow my eyes. "I don't give a shit about that."

"Your mother and I became very different people who wanted different things. Then it became clear that she wasn't well and...I couldn't handle it so I started working more and keeping my distance."

I pick up the shot and toss it back, my face scrunching at the burning sensation in my esophagus. I roll the second shot between my fingers.

"What do you mean she wasn't *well*?" My fingers freeze and his eyes flash to mine. "She was terrified of you. You wanted us to be perfect. You pushed and pushed until you broke us!" my voice screeches as liquid courage fuels my anger, bolstering the years of pent up resentment.

His face contorts to one of confusion. "What the hell are you talking about?"

"All those years...I sat and had to be perfect. Nothing I ever did was good enough. You pushed and pushed me. And then you...didn't believe me when it mattered most. And let's not forget how you sent me away! What kind of father does that to his own daughter?"

I scoff, grabbing the shot glass and raising it to my lips, but a quick hand stops me.

"What's going on here?" Mateo asks, breathing raggedly

as if he'd just run a marathon or two. He looks between my father and me.

"Oh, you know...me and Daddy Dearest were just strolling down memory lane," I say sarcastically as I narrow my eyes at my father.

"Are you doing shots?" Mateo asks incredulously.

I ignore the judgment I hear in his tone.

I hold up my index finger. "A shot. I only had one. When you add "s" to a word, it implies more than one. You should know that. You're *good with words*." I toss back the second shot with my free hand and raise two fingers. "Now I've had two *shots* and a martini."

"Did you do something to her? Why is she drinking like this?" Mateo looks at Randy with venom in his voice.

"Fuck him! He can't hurt me anymore. I already told you —"

"Cat—" my father cuts in.

"Let's go. We're leaving," Mateo commands, guiding me gently by the nape of my neck. The contact of his warm hand confuses me.

"This conversation isn't over," Randy says, shaking his head while pushing away from the tall table to stand. "I think you've got some of your facts wrong, kid."

"Fuck you! You're the goddamned liar. Not me!"

The two men exchange a quick word and, each nods his head.

"I shouldn't have come here," I state as we wait for a cab.

"But I wanted you here."

I challenge his words with a nasty scowl on my face.

Climbing in clumsily, I sit in the back of the cab and curl my body into a semi-fetal position on Mateo's lap. Moments later, I rise up and ask the cabbie for his name.

"George, you know what?" I ask with slurred words. "I don't like when people steal from me or tell lies about me. And I didn't like being sent away."

Mateo tells the cabbie not to mind me before he turns to me. "You're drunk, baby."

I shake my head even though it only makes the spinning sensation worse.

"I'm not just drunk." I turn, fall face first into his sweaty chest and sigh heavily. "I'm miserable, too."

"Are you going to be sick?"

Mumbling, I continue, "You're going to be a star and forget all about me. You're going to marry Chloe and be famous."

Mateo's arm wraps around my back, and he laughs. "How am I supposed to marry Chloe when I'm going to marry you?"

"Because you're...you're a liar just like them."

A loud ringing startles me awake. Fumbling for the receiver to answer the phone, my fingers follow the sound.

"Hello?" My voice is scratchy and sore. "Hello?" I call a second time.

The line goes dead.

I drop the receiver and return my body to its former position with one arm and a leg dangling off the bed. Slowly, I reach for my pounding head and allow the darkness to reclaim me. Sensing the absence of Mateo's body wrapped around mine, I open one eye and glance to my side. My forehead wrinkles with curiosity as to why he's sleeping with his back to me.

Shifting my position, I press my body flush against his back and feel his steady breathing. I slide my leg in between his bent ones and run my hand beneath his arm, splaying my fingers across his bare chest. He exhales quietly and laces his fingers with mine.

"I love you," I whisper as I place a single kiss on his bare shoulder.

Sleep finds me until my alarm beeps, reminding me that I need to get up for a late morning flight. I slip out of bed and trudge over to the shower. A couple of Ibuprofen and a greasy breakfast sandwich should ward off this hangover.

Mateo enters the bathroom while I dry myself off.

"Why didn't you come in the shower?" I ask, running my fingers through my hair as he brushes his teeth.

He looks at me in the mirror. "I'm tired. I didn't get much sleep," he says, reaching around me to turn the shower back on.

"Are you mad at me?" I ask when a sullen feeling overcomes me.

Tired circles of hazel stare at my eyes and then fall to my lips. "I'm just tired, Cat."

I nod and leave him to shower. I dress, pack my suitcase and check in with the airline. Perturbed that Mateo is wasting time on a lengthy shower when we have so little time left before I board my nonstop flight home, I walk down to Starbucks in the lobby and order breakfast to go.

"Caterina," my father calls.

I roll my eyes and pretend not to hear him.

"I thought about what you said last night and I really think we need to talk. Got a minute?"

Because I have to wait for the food, I concede and sit down.

"How much do you know about your mom's dreams of stardom?"

The quick flash of my eyes suggests I don't know all that much. Johnny always says she had her head in the clouds about music and fame.

"Look, your mom and I realized early on that you had a talent. It was something pretty miraculous and we knew the potential you had to be a star...something that Beth always wanted. But you can't be a star without exceptional talent and..."

"And what?" I hiss, huffing loudly.

"Beth didn't have it. She worked so hard to get better, but it wasn't a God-given gift like yours."

I look around the small coffee shop and consider his words.

"In her eyes, *you* had to be a star. She wanted everyone to know your name. Her name."

He answers a text and sets the phone back down on the table.

"I'm not sure where you got the idea that I was the one pushing you."

My lips purse and I blink, looking away from his remorseful face.

"Ask Violet if you don't believe me. They used to fight all the time. Your grandmother just wanted you to be a kid, but Beth wanted you to be a star."

"Order for Cat," the barista calls with my food.

"I've got to go." I stand.

"Please call me when you get home. I really want to clear this up. This resentment you have towards me."

Anger rises in me. "You took their side and practically locked me up! How could I not resent you? I hate you!"

"Cat, for the love of God, when are you going to stop this nonsense? When are you ever going to admit that no one stole from you?" Exasperation coats his words. "It was a bad time in your life. You had just lost your mother and you were...acting out. You needed help and Darcy tried to be there for you, but you wouldn't give her a chance."

He looks up at the scar on my forehead and I know he's remembering the incident between Darcy and me. She had been tormenting me, saying horrible things about my mother and I snapped. I flew into a rage and went after her, but she'd backhanded me across the face so hard I fell down and cracked my forehead on the corner of the kitchen cabinet. I reached for a knife to defend myself, but she grabbed it, stabbed herself in the arm and called for my father's help. It was my word against hers. I'd jumped to my feet and reached for the knife when he accused me of lying, but he restrained me until emergency services arrived.

"And Chloe, how do you think she felt living in your shadow? And then you accused her of stealing your songs? Come on, enough is enough."

I have to practically pick up my jaw from the floor as my heart thunders in my chest.

"Order for Cat?"

I walk up to the counter and get my food before I turn back to my father. "This is the last time I will ever speak to you so listen well. If you do anything to fuck up Mateo's career, I will find you and..." I suck in a deep, ragged breath, "No amount of restraints will hold me back from hurting you this time."

"You need help, Cat."

The elevator ride is slower than molasses. I feel agitated and frustrated. I can't wait to get my bags and head home.

Because my hands are full, I kick the door lightly and call Mateo's name, hoping he is finished in the shower. I wait and kick again. My eyes bulge and my jaw drops when Chloe opens the door in a tiny camisole and even tinier boy shorts. Immediately my gaze turns to Mateo who is standing there with a towel low around his waist. A million questions swirl around the room wordlessly.

"Cat," Chloe says, opening the door wide for me to enter like it's *her* room.

"What are you doing here?" I ask, directing my question at her then my boyfriend as I walk past him to set the food down on the desk. Everything in the room looks the same except for the strewn papers which are now sitting in a neat pile on the bed.

"Chloe came—"

Jumping in, Chloe says that she came to see if I had any

tampons.

I scoff. "Tampons? *Really?*"

I notice Mateo's eyebrows furrow and he looks uncomfortable...or guilty.

"Yeah, I just got my period." She wipes her forehead dramatically. "Thank God! I thought maybe I was pregnant." She looks at Mateo and laughs flirtatiously. "That wouldn't be so good, huh?"

"I don't have any, but I'm sure the pharmacy across the street does."

I grab my backpack and heave it onto the bed, tossing in my journal that looks like it's been through a war zone.

From my peripheral vision, I see Mateo open the door. Chloe steps through and then turns around to speak to him quietly through the small opening. He nods somberly and finally closes it.

Walking over to his suitcase, Mateo drops his towel and slips on a pair of black boxers, jeans and a T-shirt.

Tension builds, creating a thick barrier between us, as I sit and eat my breakfast, keeping my eyes on him while he moves around the room.

"Your coffee's getting cold."

He nods but doesn't stop picking up the rest of the shredded pieces of paper off the floor.

"Why aren't you dressed?"

Mateo ignores me before he eventually tells me that Iza called.

"Are you upset with me?"

He finally freezes and tosses me a hard look.

"Okay," I draw out slowly. "Can you at least tell me what I did to upset you?"

"You really shouldn't drink so much if you can't handle your alcohol," he spits in an unfamiliar tone.

"I wouldn't have had so much to drink if we didn't go to that stupid bar," I counter.

"Oh, we're back to that? Do you want to add any more to last night's list of why this trip sucked so bad or how much you regret coming to see me? Or maybe you want to drop another bombshell."

I choke on the bite of egg sandwich. "Bombshell?"

With hurried legs, I cross the room and grab his arm, sliding a gentle touch down over his ink until I lace our fingers.

"I'm sorry for whatever I said last night. I was clearly drunk. I didn't mean it."

He turns to me with pain etched on his face. "That's the problem. You meant every word."

I reach up and caress his face. "I'm sorry."

His free hand moves to cover mine and he turns his head to kiss my palm.

"Baby, I love you. I'm doing the best I can here."

I whisper, "I know." And it's true. I do know how tough it is for him. I remember it all too well.

"Are you going to tell me what I said to hurt you?"

His eyes close and he forces a swallow, gently pressing his forehead against mine.

I sigh.

"I hate knowing that's what happen—" his voice falters. "I wish you had told me sooner."

Anxiety spikes in me.

"Oh God, babe! What did I say?"

Searching my eyes carefully, he breathes as his chin quivers, "Everything."

I pull back and look at him with wide, anxious eyes.

He nods solemnly, answering my silent query. "You told me everything."

A tiny whisper emerges, fear filling my words. A rush of adrenaline explodes in me and my chest tightens at the thought of revealing what I've stifled for so long.

"Everything?"

"Including Norwich Academy."

An agonizing lump forms in my throat and I struggle to speak. "Now you know...now you know why I hate them so much."

"You poured out your heart until it bled."

He pulls me into a tight embrace, blanketing me in his warmth and unconditional love.

"I would never hurt you like they did. *Never.*" The honesty, full of determination, rings in his declaration, prompting my fingers to grip the material covering his body as I weep quietly.

"I know that...I know that...I know that." With each assurance, my voice weakens.

Chapter Thirteen

"IT WAS AWFUL," I COMPLAIN AS I FLIP OVER AND rest the back of my head on Mackenzie's lap with my feet extended over the edge of her loveseat. My best friend runs her fingers through my hair, pulling at the curls.

"You're going to frizz my hair." I announce, spooning another helping of ice cream into my mouth.

"Cat, your hair is frizzy! You really should do something with it."

I roll my eyes and ignore her.

"Let's color it!"

Mackenzie's hair color used to change with each breakup; it was her way of reinventing herself and leaving the old Mack behind. But there's only so much that can be done with her shade of red.

"I'm not coloring my hair. Mateo and I didn't break up."

After the trip to visit him in Nashville ended disastrously with me confessing in a drunken tirade about the demons I face and the skeletons in my closet, Mateo asked for a few days to clear his head. I know I dumped some heavy things on him especially given the fact he's working with the very same people who tormented me and ruined my life when my privacy was invaded, shared with the world and I was sent away to live in a residential facility. An overnight trip to see my best friend in New York is exactly what I need.

"When was the last time you talked to him?" she asks, separating my hair in three sections to start a loose braid.

"Three days ago."

Amazed that I answered without breaking down, I sigh. "I miss him. I miss the sound of his voice. I miss his smell."

Mack hums. "I know what you mean."

Her reply causes me to turn and look at her with a puzzled look on my face.

"And who might you be thinking about?" I sing-song.

She snaps out of her daydream. "What?"

"Give it up, sister! What's your new guy like?"

Her eyes dance with delight.

"He's great. His schedule right now is busy, but he always makes time to see me. We get along really well."

"I wasn't asking about your dentist," I retort with a chuckle.

"I think you'd like him. You have a lot in common."

Declaring her to be a nut job, I return to my previous position and voice my concerns.

"I can't believe I haven't met him yet," I state. "What does he look like? Is he hot? Does he have a job?" Memories of Mack supporting her last boyfriend swirl around in my head.

"He's gorgeous so yes, he's hot. And...he's in between jobs right now." She looks at me warily.

"Mack!" I screech. "Why do you fall for gorgeous losers?"

"He's not a loser. It's complicated right now. He's got a million things going on."

I detect a hint of sadness in her voice.

She nudges me to sit up so she can finish the long braid. "There. Wild hair tamed."

I run my hand over my hair and breathe. "Oh God. You know I can't go out in public like this."

Mack laughs. "Well, you better throw on a hat because

I've got to get going to class and you've got a train to catch."

After gathering my overnight bag, I follow Mackenzie down to the sidewalk. With quick hugs and promises for another visit, we depart. She reaches for her phone and says, "Hi, baby" as she crosses the street.

I can't help but wonder if she's paying for her loser boyfriend's cell phone.

I board the Metro North train and settle in for the ride home. I miss Gram. And I kind of miss my uncle, too. As crazy as he drives me sometimes, he does mean well. I was grateful he took the initiative to hire a home health aide to spend a few hours a day with his mother.

A few phrases materialize in my head and I write them down in my journal so I don't forget. My mind has been all over the place since Mateo asked for some time to process the situation.

I scroll through Facebook, passing the time looking at meaningless videos and shared recipes. I click on the other icon to open another social media app. I don't know why I bother; it's usually the same crap.

My thumb freezes when I see them. A picture of Chloe exiting a hotel room as Mateo stands there in a towel. The look on their faces is an intimate one. *Son of a bitch!* Someone snapped a picture of Chloe leaving his hotel room in Nashville. I remember the shorts, but I don't recall seeing the folded papers in her back pocket.

Smothering the crackling of my heart, I close my eyes and pray that when I reopen them, there won't be an abundance of additional photographs of my boyfriend and the pop star.

Fucking paparazzi.

Insecurity wins out and I look at every image of them on the road, sitting side by side in the back of the van with Chloe's head resting against Mateo's shoulder while he stares out the window. Another image shows them rehearsing on stage. The last one is of Chloe wearing Mateo's Marlins ball cap. Even I have to admit, he looks annoyed.

Needing reassurance to quell my worried heart, I call his cell phone, but it goes directly to voicemail. I know he's asked for a few days, but I need to talk to him. I debate whether to leave a message when my second attempt to reach him goes unanswered. I want to call back a thousand times just to hear his voice.

"Hey, it's me. I miss you. Call me. Te amo." I smile sadly as I disconnect the call.

Please God, don't let them steal this away from me, too.

I plant a big fat kiss on my grandmother's cheek when she greets me at the door.

"Hi, Gram! Oh, I've missed you!" I say with a huge smile, pulling her small frame up into a hug.

"Beth! You're home! I knew you would come back to me."

The smile on my face drops when I meet my uncle's cautious eyes and he nods subtly. I wave my hand in front of my nose and scrunch my face, trying to terminate the odor wafting in the air.

Johnny rises and whispers as he walks past me. "She burned eggs this morning and left the burner on."

I cover my mouth and hold my breath.

Placing an arm on his mother's shoulder, my uncle offers a gentle reminder. "Mom, this is Caterina, your granddaughter. Beth isn't coming home." The tone in his voice is gentle as he placates her.

He warns me with his eyes that she's deteriorating fast.

"Gram, did you make muffins?" I ask, clearing my throat after it falters with emotion.

Her gaze is empty and far away.

Johnny shakes his head quickly, sending a warning my way.

I grab the corn muffin, peel back the paper baking cup and take a tiny bite, complimenting Gram with exaggerated moans.

"So good, Gram," I lie as I chew the salty muffin and force myself to swallow the morsel.

When she turns to speak to my uncle, I spit the adulterated muffin in the trash.

Johnny leads Gram upstairs to nap.

I sit at the kitchen table, check my phone and then rest my head on the surface.

"How are things with you?" my uncle asks as he breezes back into the kitchen and tosses the rest of the baked goods away. "Obviously she's not doing well."

"I didn't realize it was going to get this bad this fast."

"Her form of dementia is fast progressing."

My gaze drops as does my heart.

"She'll need twenty-four hours a day care soon and it's not something you or I are capable of taking on."

The house phone rings and Johnny rushes to answer it.

"Stop fucking calling here! Take this number and shove it up your ass! It's on the "Do Not Call List!" he seethes, slamming the receiver down.

I cock an eyebrow, silently voicing my query at my uncle's tone and harsh language.

He paces back and forth with his hands on his hips.

"I'm about to disconnect that phone. There's no reason to have it! It's been ringing nonstop and my mother swears Beth calls her. She doesn't understand that my sister is fucking dead!"

My uncle's eyes fill with moisture as his chest covered in a white Yankees T-shirt rises and falls. "Seeing her like this is killing me, Cat. It's killing me. I know I'm going to lose her soon."

The emotional rollercoaster of my life just plunged me down into a ditch of despair and I am overwhelmed, suddenly giving into a fit of hysteria until strong arms wrap around me.

I cry into my uncle's arms, my heart splintering into a thousand tiny pieces. "She can't die... She just can't...I need her."

"I know, kid. I know." I feel his chest shudder when he inhales sharply and he rubs my back.

Running up the stairs, I collapse onto my bed and sob, remembering how good my grandma has always been to me, how much she's always loved me, how she supported me when my parents' marriage fell apart, how she comforted me when my mother died and how she came to visit me when no one else did. She has always been on my side, never wanting anything in return.

After taking a long hot shower, I find my grandmother sitting on the couch, staring at the muted television. I sit beside her and caress her hand.

"Gram, do you remember when I used to sing for you? Would you like me to sing for you again?"

A hazy gaze meets my eyes as a small smile touches her lips.

Sitting at the piano, I splay my fingers out against the keys and bring Amazing Grace to life. By the last verse, tears flow endlessly down my cheeks, accepting the fact that the next few months may be the end for her.

When my fingers cease to move, I look at Gram who simply smiles at me.

Chapter Fourteen

"HEY, TRINA!" I REACH OUT AND HUG HER LEAN frame, thanking her for allowing me to take some time off to visit Mateo and tend to my Gram.

"It's been busy. We just got about six bags of donations of fall clothes. As always, you get first dibs."

I smile, beaming with excitement to check out the new outerwear as I walk to the back to put my bag away. I roll the bin with hangers over and begin the task of hanging up dresses, sweaters and shirts.

"It's so crazy how people give away brand new things," I comment. "Don't they appreciate what's in front of them?"

"Good question."

A voice startles me, and I look up to see Caleb standing there with a smile on his face.

"Caleb! Hi," I say, dropping the sweater and going around the long counter to greet him. "How are you?"

"Yeah, long time no see. I'm good."

I realize I've been backed into a corner and I feel foolish for not responding to his text messages.

"Sorry. I've been dealing with my gram and—"

"Your boyfriend's on tour with Chloe."

"How did you know?"

"I saw the way you looked at him when he was on stage at the music fest... and then it's been all over social media."

I inhale deeply and frown. "Yeah, it kind of sucks right now."

"We could grab lunch in the park and talk about it," he suggests.

Unable to gauge his intentions, I decline his offer, citing my need to be home right after work to care for my grandparent.

"Do you need a ride?"

I shake my head. "Caleb, can I ask you a question? And I need you to be honest, okay?"

He nods once.

"Why are you trying so hard with me when you know I have a boyfriend?"

A nervous chuckle escapes. "Man, you don't mince words, do you?"

I smile tightly and shrug unapologetically.

"If I'm being *honest*, I'm not interested in you that way. I mean you're pretty and all, but I..." he stammers, "I know who you are."

"What do you mean?"

"You're Caterina Creed, right? You were destined for great things in the music industry and then you just disappeared."

My eyelids close then reopen. "That's not who I am anymore, Caleb. That girl is long gone."

"That's a shame. You could've been a huge star."

"I know, but —" Not wanting to forfeit my privacy by divulging my personal issues, I offer a word of thanks instead.

"Would you mind taking a look at some new music I've been working on?"

"Sure...as long as you come with no other expectations."

A bright smile stretches across his face. "I promise."

Caleb leaves soon after we settle on a day and time to meet to review his new music.

"You have a thing for musicians, don't you?" Trina asks, looking at me with a playful expression.

"No, I only have a thing for Mateo, who happens to be in music. When I first met him, he was a regular guy doing the addition at my house," I clarify.

"How are things going with him?" she inquires carefully.

"Good... although I haven't talked to him in a few days. Why do you ask?"

"You seem a little sad, that's all. Maybe you should go to lunch with that nice musician. Might make you feel better."

I furrow my brows. "Going out to lunch with Caleb isn't going to make me miss Mateo any less. In fact, it'll exacerbate my sour mood because nothing he says could ever make me feel like Mateo does."

Later that night my shift at the bar flies by and Lou comments on my dismal demeanor as he asks if I'm okay.

"I'm just tired," I lie. *I miss Mateo. He is the air I need to breathe* aren't exactly things I would reveal to my coworker.

"Hey," Carolyn calls. "A few of us are going to the Tree House for a round or two. You in?"

I wipe circles onto the bar after cleaning up and decline her offer.

"C'mon, Cat. You can't sit around and mope because you and your boyfriend broke up."

My eyes flash upward and meet hers instantly. "We didn't *break up*." My tone implies she's obviously mistaken about the status of our relationship. "He's on tour and he'll be back soon."

The straightening of her lips and the crease in her forehead prompts me to inquire.

"What makes you think we broke up?" My stomach rolls with a sudden bout of nausea.

"Don't get mad at me, okay..."

Carolyn taps her phone and opens Instagram. "Here."

I take the device slowly and glance at the screen.

There in bold, brilliant color is an image of Mateo sitting alongside Chloe with his arm draped over the back of the seat; his eyes are serene as he looks at her with a beautiful smile on his face. The next image shows her hand on his thigh. I shiver, allowing my finger to move along to the next picture. I gasp and stifle the bile from spewing in my mouth as I stare at a photograph of Chloe wearing his Marlins hat and playfully riding on Mateo's back with her legs clamped around his waist. Unable to bear much more, I scroll to the last picture. It's an intimate image taken of the two of them sitting in the back of the van. Leaning against the window with a fist curled beneath his chin, Mateo appears to be in deep thought as Chloe sleeps with her head resting on his arm. Perhaps he's scheming, devising a conniving plan to deceive the woman who waits for him back at home.

I hand Carolyn's phone back, thank her and walk back to the break room.

My body begins to convulse and my hands fly into my hair, yanking and pulling wildly as betrayal and stupidity ridicule me for thinking I was enough. Thinking the love he proclaimed we had was enough to see us through the temptations of *that* world.

Mateo Cruz is a liar. His words are meaningless lies.

Retrieving my phone from the locker, I tap the screen for what feels like a thousand times, trying to get something other than a black screen to appear.

I rush into the bathroom and vomit in the sink, rinsing my mouth out quickly as tears stream down my face. My mind continues to conjure up the images of Mateo and Chloe.

After scrubbing my face with cold water, I stare in the mirror at the dark circles under my sad eyes. The woman in the mirror stares back and then speaks to me, reminding me of the love Mateo and I have. Reminding me to believe what I know is in my heart and not what I see.

My eyes close for a moment.

Breathe. Just breathe.

I arrive home shortly before three o'clock in the morning. My silence and disinterest suggested I had no intention of joining the Uber driver's forced conversation of trivial and meaningless things. A confused heart garnered all of my attention.

The house is dark and quiet. The sound of the light rain falling against the roof and the old grandfather clock ticking in the corner of the living room create a somber rhythm. I tiptoe up the stairs and avoid stepping on the wooden floorboards near my door for fear they may squeak and wake up Gram whose recent nights have been restless.

"I've been waiting for you," a voice calls from the darkness that engulfs my room.

I scream. One hand reaches for my chest while the other flicks the light switch on.

"What are you doing here?" I shout, no longer caring about keeping the volume down.

"I missed you," Mateo says, his voice sweet and sexy. "I had to see you."

I stare at the man I love and see truth revealed in his hazel eyes as he moves away from the corner chair I recently picked up at Trina's. His jaw is now covered with a light scruff and his eyes droop with weary. Walking to me with open arms, Mateo engulfs me into a tight embrace, cocooning me in his warmth. His chest shudders against mine when his lips kiss the top of my head.

Involuntarily, my arms rise and my hands slide upwards to grip the sweatshirt that shields his body from the chilly autumn air. I turn my head and rest my cheek on his bicep. Our breathing pattern becomes in sync as we hold each other wordlessly.

The feel of his body against mine makes my heart race. It sends an alert to every ending, telling them to wake up so they could experience everything as well. His hold on me is intense and I struggle to breathe while the feelings I bite back slowly ascend until they release in a single full-blown sob.

"What's wrong?" Mateo moves his body back just enough to look down at me. "Why are you crying?"

My mouth opens, but no words surface.

Cupping my face in his palms, Mateo bends to meet me at eye level. Through blurred vision I see his grave expression and worried eyes.

"Cat, what's going on? Is it Gram?"

I bow my head, plastering my face with my palms in pain and agony because I don't know how much more my heart can take as emotions duel inside and slice the vital organ beating wildly in my chest.

After several attempts to utter a word, I find the strength to speak. Removing my hands from my face, I drag my tear-filled eyes up to meet his. "Why are you here? Are you here to break up with me in person?"

"What?!" he shrieks with disbelief. "Why would you say that? Why would you even think that?"

I hiccup and swipe my fingers across my cheek to mop up the wetness spilling from my eyes. "I saw the pictures."

His eyebrows furrow. "I don't—"

"Don't lie to me! Don't you fucking lie to me!" I grit through my teeth. "I saw the pictures of you and Chloe."

"We haven't taken any pictures aside from promos." His tone is soothing and placating. "I honestly have no idea what you're talking about."

I reach for my phone but quickly remember the battery died while I was working.

My lips tighten into a hard line and I force a swallow,

shaking my head in disbelief and casting my eyes away from his.

"Baby, look at me."

"I can't," I mumble.

"Why not?" he asks quietly, trying to mask the hurt in his tone.

"Because your eyes...are deceitful. They're hiding something."

He sighs heavily.

"You're here to tell me something, aren't you?" I raise my chin, preparing for the truth.

Mateo reaches for my hand. "Come sit with me."

I free my hand from his grasp. "I don't want to sit."

Without permission, he again takes my hand and leads me to my unmade bed. I sit but leave a noticeable amount of space between our bodies.

He angles his body to look at me. "It's three o'clock in the morning. We're both exhausted. I don't have a lot of time and the last thing I want to do is fight with you."

Leaving my fingers laced with his, I look up and demand he tell me why he's here.

"I didn't want to do this over the phone..."

"What? Just tell me already!" I snarl.

"The tour's been extended." He looks at me with hazel eyes full of caution and tenderness.

"Extended? How long?" I ask, instantly hating that our separation will be more than I bargained for.

Mateo runs his index finger and thumb across his eyebrows then drags his hand over his face. "Another three months."

"Why?"

He shrugs. "Darcy scheduled more shows, but they're out west. Flying back and forth isn't an option so we're going to stay on the road."

"Unbelievable," I spit.

"We're doing really well. I'm getting my name out there fast. This is what we wanted."

"*We?*" My chin quivers. "This isn't my dream. It's yours." I blink away a tear. "I don't want that life, Mateo."

"But I want—"

"I think you and I want different things," I murmur sadly.

"I want *you!*"

I challenge his words. "You want me so much, yet you didn't call me for days."

"I can explain that."

Unwilling to accept his answer, I continue. "The Mateo I fell in love with, the guy who woke me up with loud banging, the guy who took me out to simple places, the guy who consumed me would never have done that."

"Baby, I am that guy."

"No, that guy would've never gone all these days without contact. He wouldn't have made me suffer while waiting by the phone just to hear his voice."

His eyes move slowly and scan my face.

"You made promises and you broke them."

Wrapping his arms around me, Mateo pushes me back onto the bed and looks down at me. "I'm sorry. I'm sorry for hurting you. That was never my intention."

I want to believe him, but my skeptical heart cautions me.

"I think about you constantly. Not a moment goes by that I don't think about how much I love you. I miss you so much."

"Could've fooled me." I shift my body so we lay on our sides facing one another.

"I'm the fool," he says, releasing a breath and raising his hand to caress my face. "I don't know what I was thinking. I was so busy with the shows and then I spent every spare minute writing and recording."

"You're recording on the road?" I ask skeptically.

"Darcy has us working nonstop to get some new songs

written. We're just recording demos."

Something about the look on his face piques my curiosity.

"What?" My question sounds like more of an accusation. "I know there's more."

"Things have been a little strained between me and Chloe since Nashville. It's like she's trying hard to make..."

"You two a couple?" I complete his sentence.

Guilt washes over his face before he presses his forehead against mine. "It's complicated. Darcy thinks we can expand the fan base if we go with that angle, but you *know* you have my heart."

"Do I?"

"Of course!" he promises softly.

"The pictures all over social media seem to tell a different story," I hiss, clenching my jaw in anger.

His lips slide to my ear. "Baby, you know that Chloe means nothing to me. You know how much I love you."

"Explain the pictures then. They're so... *intimate*."

He scoffs. "Intimate pictures?"

"Don't be coy! I only saw a few and you looked awfully comfortable with Chloe on your back or Chloe asleep on your arm."

"We didn't take any intimate pictures. The photographer wanted playful images. They're all staged right down to the position of my hand under my chin."

Retorting quickly, I pin him with a hard glare. "Well, they suggest a lot more than just two people being playful. They're downright flirtatious."

With a quick nod of his head, Mateo concedes, confessing he understands my point and promises to be more careful with his actions.

"She's been acting really weird the past few days."

"Who?"

"Darcy. She's been trying to push the "couple" angle and forcing us to write love songs rather than the pop music

Chloe is known for."

A moment of recollection hits me. "Not all of Chloe's songs are like that. *Darkness* is a more serious, sadder song."

"How do you know about that song? It's not one of the ones the radio stations play."

"It's probably a little too dark for the radio, but it is on her album," I clarify. "So is *Rebellion.* I wrote those songs after my mother died."

Mateo's eyebrows crease and he blinks several times. "You did?" he asks dubiously.

"You don't believe me?" I challenge. "My mother had just died. I was in a really dark place and I poured my heart out writing song after song."

Processing my declaration, Mateo stares at me as his fingertips glide over my face. "Are you sure it's the same song?"

Angered by his question, I step back. "Did you not listen to a word I said in Nashville? Or are you just like everyone who didn't believe me?"

"I'm not saying I don't believe you, it's just...I thought she only used one of your songs."

"No!"

"Cat—" Mateo sighs, looking at me sympathetically.

"Don't you do that! Don't look at me like I'm crazy and don't you dare say I need help!"

"Baby, I wasn't going to say that."

"The Creeds are liars. They all lie and steal! They're rotten sons of bitches and I hate that you're involved with them!"

Pulling me close once again, Mateo rests his forehead against mine. "Baby, you need to calm down. I'll talk to Chloe when I get back."

"You will do no such thing!" I squawk. "She'll just deny it and make me look like the liar."

"Can you prove you wrote the song?"

"Of course, I can! I have kept every single journal, every

single napkin, and every single scrap piece of paper since I was eight years old. They're in a box in the back of my closet."

"That's interesting because I asked Chloe the other day about some of the lyrics and she said that her mom helped her then she got all defensive. Apparently, Darcy was nominated for a Grammy a few years ago."

I nod. "I've heard." *Only a million times.*

"A Grammy. That's huge!" he sighs dreamily. The longing on his face indicates a prestigious award is on his radar. "I wonder what category."

"Chloe didn't mention that?"

He shrugs and shakes his head.

"She was part of a songwriting team whose song was included in a film soundtrack."

"That's impressive," he declares.

Childishly, I sneer. "Too bad she didn't win."

"The vile woman you described isn't at all like the person I see."

"What you see is a lie. She is a horrible person."

I angle my head and glare at him. "I don't know who I hate more over there."

I slide my arms under his and reach around to hold him tightly, my face nuzzling in the crook of his neck. A single kiss to his warm skin ignites the kindling between us.

"Sometimes I wish you didn't have this dream," I confess selfishly, looking up at his face.

He stills. "I want to make something of myself. I need to do this."

"I wish we could go back to the way things used to be."

"You deserve better than that," he breathes as he kisses my lips.

I return the chaste kiss.

"This isn't about me and we both know it."

His mouth crushes against mine and his tongue slides against the seam of my lips, beckoning them to part so the long-lost lovers can reunite. Twisting and sliding together, our tongues rejoice, engaging in a sensual dance as our clothing is stripped away, one article at a time.

Salty tears—tears of joy and tears of hurt— flood my eyes.

Hovering over me, Mateo's lips move from my mouth to my neck then over the swell of my breasts where his teeth bite gently on my hardened nipples. His hand travels south of my navel and circles my buzzing flesh with his thumb while pumping two fingers in and out of me. There is no need for foreplay; my body is ready and desperate for him.

"Please. I need you in me," I beg.

"I need to taste you first." He settles himself between my legs and devours me until I grab a pillow and cover my face, screaming out in pleasure when I orgasm.

"I love you so much," I cry when he enters my slick body. "I will always love you."

A combination of slow and hurried thrusts plunge deep into my core as he repeats his confession of unwavering love for me.

"Do you really have any idea how much I love you? How much I've missed fucking you?"

When my hand grips his ass, Mateo fulfills my request for more.

"Like this?" he inquires roughly. "Is this how you want it?"

"Yes!" I howl.

Feeling as if I'm going to split in half, I dig my nails into Mateo's back as he sinks deeper and deeper into the welcoming abyss of my core. Thrusting passionately, he reaches the point of orgasm, buries his groan in my neck and comes hard as warm liquid fills me.

Moments later, when our heartbeats have regulated and our breathing less ragged, Mateo looks at me.

"Don't *ever* doubt my love for you."

I suck my lips inwardly and smile tightly.

"I want to believe you. I want to believe we're strong enough, but..."

"But what?"

"I know what that world does to people. They're vindictive liars."

"It won't happen to me," he says confidently.

Mateo swathes my naked body in his and for the first time in weeks, I sleep peacefully in the arms of the man I love.

After a quick shower together, Mateo puts on a pair of jeans and a green V-neck sweater, the color almost matching the light hazel of his eyes this morning. I slip on my black yoga pants and the Columbia sweatshirt I bought when I visited my best friend.

"Columbia? Is that new?"

I look down and nod. "I got it when I went to New York to see Mack." I hear the click as he takes a photo of me.

"Oh," he says, "I didn't realize you went for a visit."

"You would've had you called me."

His expression drops, and I instantly feel guilty for the spiteful jab.

I'm quick to apologize, but lighten the mood when I demand that he stop taking random pictures of me because I look awful in them.

"You look beautiful in them. Every single one."

He takes my hand and leads me through the quiet house. We walk the new addition as he inspects the work that's been done in his absence.

"I'm impressed," he says with a trace of humor. "Junior actually did a good job."

I laugh. "Why? Did you think he wouldn't?"

He shrugs. "He's been known to cut corners here and

there, but everything here looks perfect."

"He said he'll be done next week."

"If you weren't already mine, I'd slow down the job just so I'd have an excuse to see you every day."

His comment makes me smile.

"What time is your flight back?" I ask, wondering how many hours I have left with him before he has to leave.

"Six- thirty."

He follows me down the stairs and into the kitchen where Gram is standing over the sink rinsing a coffee cup as she looks out through the window where colorful leaves fall from the trees.

Mateo holds his fingers to his lips and sneaks behind my grandmother.

The sound of his quick kiss to her cheek is replaced by the sound of a slap as her hand makes contact with his cheek.

"Gram!" I bellow, reaching for her hand before she can strike again.

Stunned, Mateo's eyes widen and he moves away from her, looking at me for an explanation.

"Don't hit!" I reprimand my elder. "Gram, this is Mateo. You remember him, don't you? He's the nice man who's doing the addition on the house."

Mateo can't hide the perplexed look on his face.

Mumbling quietly, Gram says Beth is coming home soon.

"Stay right here," I whisper to Mateo as I lead Gram back to bed for her morning nap.

I return several minutes later to find Mateo sitting at the kitchen table with a cup of coffee in his hand and a slice of breakfast pastry on a napkin.

I tip my chin to his light meal. "I wouldn't drink or eat that if I were you."

He stops chewing. "Why?" he asks, looking down carefully.

"You'll likely get a mouthful of coffee grounds at the

bottom or chomp on egg shells."

Covering his mouth with the napkin, he spits the food out.

"I didn't know she'd gotten that bad. She's going downhill fast."

I nod sadly. "You have no idea."

"Why didn't you tell me?"

I stare at him pointedly and stifle the urge to comment again about his recent lack of communication.

Pouring out the pot of coffee Gram made, I set a fresh pot to brew and drop two bagels into the toaster.

"Can I ask you a question?" I ask while opening the refrigerator to retrieve half and half and cream cheese.

"You know you can ask me anything."

"Why'd you avoid me after Nashville?"

Mateo clears his throat and sighs heavily.

"That last night...you dropped a couple of bombshells on me and I needed time to process it all. I couldn't believe luck would have me working with the very same people who hurt you."

I cast my eyes downward.

"You told me about your relationship with your mother and how you felt after she died. You told me how you blamed your father for so many things. Then you started crying when you told me how close you and Chloe used to be when you were little kids."

Immediate memories of Chloe and me as young girls who loved to sing and dance together at the studio when her mother was my father's business partner flash in my mind. Chloe had been the only other child I spent time with. She always wanted to be the lead singer while I was happy to sing backup. It was around that time music, while opening doors for her, was locking me in a dark and lonely dungeon.

Mateo walks over to where I stand at the counter, smearing cream cheese on the toasted bagel as tears stream down my face. He stills my trembling hand and forces me to look at him, tucking loose strands of wild hair behind my ear.

"You also told me about meeting Abimbola at Norwich and how much he helped you. I never knew just what an important part he played in your life. You never talk about him."

He saved me.

"I'm sorry," I utter painfully as I swallow the lump in my throat. "I'm sorry I brought up the past. I should just leave it where it is, but seeing them, knowing you're with them, brings all those painful memories to the surface. I'm sorry for everything."

He raises his hand and cups my cheeks, wiping away the moisture with his thumbs.

"Why are you apologizing to me?"

"Because I'm not as normal as you thought I was."

Shaking his head slowly, he lowers his face. "*Normal?*" he chuckles. "Who the hell is normal?"

"You are!"

"Baby, we've all got our issues."

"So why not talk to me about it all? Instead you shut me out...like I did something wrong."

"I didn't mean to shut you out. I was processing. I even talked to Randy about it and—"

"You did what?!"

"Not like that! I didn't go into details. I just told him I was thinking about leaving the tour because I had things to take care of at home."

"You were going to leave the tour because of me?" I'm horrified at the notion of standing in the way of his dreams.

"Not *because* of you...*for* you. You are the most important thing in my life."

"What? You can't!"

"I didn't," he states, forcing a small smile. "I realized that leaving the tour would probably be the end of the road for my career and I couldn't do that to us. I want you to be proud of me."

I throw my arms around his neck. "I am proud of you. I am so very proud of you!"

His eyes crinkle when he smiles. "I'm going to marry you. You know that, don't you?"

I nod and my heart soars when he places his hands on my waist and his lips at my ear, quietly singing Bruno Mars' song *Marry You*.

"Ahem."

Mateo and I look at my uncle as he walks in the door, glowering at us with a hard expression on his face.

"I need to talk to you." He points to Mateo. "Now."

"What for?" I demand, dropping my arms to my side.

"It's okay, baby. We'll just be a minute."

Mateo follows my uncle outside, and I'm left flabbergasted and confused as I fight the urge to stand at the door and eavesdrop.

Moments later, Johnny walks through the kitchen wordlessly. His heavy footsteps echo through the house.

"What was that about?" I ask Mateo, who slides his phone back into his pocket.

"He just wants to make sure everything's good."

I narrow my eyes. "*We* are none of his business."

"Let's go get something to eat. I'm starving."

I point to the bagel. "You don't want that?"

"I worked up quite an appetite after this morning," he whispers, pinning me with a sexy grin.

I look at my bare feet. "Let me grab my shoes."

Dashing upstairs to my room, I slip my feet into shoes and grab my phone, quickly deleting a text message from Caleb before stopping at my uncle's room to let him know the home health aide will be by shortly.

Stepping onto the driveway, I notice the shiny red car. "When did this get here?"

"I drove it here last night."

I grimace, remembering how distraught I was when I got home.

We drive away from my home toward his neighborhood with our fingers laced as light conversation flows easily between us.

"Are you sure you want to leave your car parked here?"

Mateo shuts off the engine and nods. "We won't be long."

I follow him up to the second-floor apartment and after a quick knock, the door opens and Mateo is pulled into a massive hug by his Tia Juanita.

"Matito! *Ay, Dios mio!*" She lavishes his face with a million kisses before she turns to me and smiles. "*Hola, mi amor.*"

Hello, my love? I reply with a smile that hides my surprise at the warm reception.

While she prepares a delicious Spanish omelet, Mateo explains that he's only here for a quick visit, but that he had to come see her. Since Mateo speaks primarily in Spanish, I conclude that he's providing details about his experience on tour. When he mentions Chloe's name, a scowl appears on her face, and she waves a dishtowel in the air.

On the table in front of us, two dishes, covered in eggs and bacon, are set down along with two glasses of orange juice.

"*Gracias,*" I say.

His aunt rubs my shoulder and mumbles quickly in Mateo's direction.

In between bites, Mateo translates her broken English side of the conversation for me.

"You no have to speak por me," his aunt says. "She understand me."

I smile and nod, trying to agree with her although it is difficult.

Mateo excuses himself when his phone rings.

I rise and bring the dishes to the small sink.

"Matito love you. He love you muchisimo."

A smile forms on my face. "I love him, too."

"Tia," Mateo says, thanking her in Spanish followed by a hug and kiss. "We've got to go."

She hugs him tightly, making the sign of the Cross on his forehead before she does the same to me.

Back in the car, I ask about her mention of Iza.

"I guess Iza was looking for me. Have you seen her?"

I shake my head. "Not recently."

"Where are we rushing off to?" I ask as he maneuvers through the busy and crowded streets toward the highway.

He swallows nervously.

"I need to stop by Randy's for a minute. You don't have to come in if you don't want to."

My stomach tightens. "I don't want to."

"Fair enough."

"Crap!" I palm my forehead when I remember I was supposed to work at Trina's.

She picks up after the fourth ring.

"Hey, it's me! I'm so sorry I didn't show up."

I continue to explain how Mateo surprised me for a quick visit.

"He did? Again?" I ask, lowering my voice. "Okay, no that's fine. I'll talk to him."

After disconnecting the call, I put my phone away and allow my eyes to linger out the window before I turn to face Mateo's questioning eyes.

"Who's *he* and what did *he* do?" Jealousy taints his voice.

I huff. "Caleb came by the shop again this morning."

"Again?" he shouts.

"He comes in often and wants to talk music. He's somehow figured out who I used to be and is hoping I can help him in the industry. Aside from you, I don't want anything to do with them or the music world."

"I think his interest in you might be a little more than

just about music," he counters.

"No. I asked him point blank."

Mateo laughs. "Of course you did."

"Not that it would matter because I'm only interested in you." I lean over as the seat belt strains against my chest to kiss his cheek and slide my hand to his groin.

"Don't get me started," he warns.

"I need to take what I can get while you're here." I smile and waggle my eyebrows suggestively.

"You can always visit me again."

I smirk. "No, thanks."

When we arrive at the home of Randy and Darcy Creed, I choose to wait in the car. I scroll through Facebook and check my email, all of which is useless and meaningless.

Moments later, Mateo retreats from the house with my father following behind. When our eyes meet, Mateo issues a silent apology as my father stops and waits for me to lower my window.

"Hello, Cat."

I ignore him, keeping my eyes focused on the garage in front of me.

"I found a box of your mom's things."

I turn to look at my father and shoot daggers at him. "Throw them away for all I care."

"Cat, you know I can't do that."

A sardonic chuckle emerges through my pursed lips. "Why?"

"Because she's my w—"

I glare at him. "Wife? No, she stopped being your wife the day she found you screwing Darcy in your office."

"That's not—"

"We're leaving now," Mateo interjects. His tone is clipped and protective.

My father shakes his head sadly as he fumbles through a sorry excuse for his unfaithfulness.

"Randy, I'll talk to you later."

The anger in me erupts and I bang my fist on the dashboard.

"Whoa! Easy, babe!"

Mateo reaches over and caresses the pummeled leather, telling it he's sorry for my rough handling.

I roll my eyes and laugh, conceding to the light moment.

"Sorry," I utter an apology to Mateo *and* to his car.

"She forgives you," he says with a playful grin.

"That man infuriates me." I clench my fingers into a fist but refrain from hitting anything. "One would think that having cancer would make you less of an asshole, but no... not him."

Mateo's head snaps in my direction. "Randy has cancer?"

"Yeah! He told me the day I saw you at their house."

"He does?" he asks again.

"I'm not making this shit up! God, stop acting like you don't believe me!"

"I'm just surprised that's all. No one has said a word to me."

Thirteen minutes of silence flow by as the tension builds between us until Mateo signals and pulls the car into the rear parking lot of a Kentucky Fried Chicken restaurant.

"You're hungry again?"

He laughs, putting the car in Park. "No."

After quickly removing his seat belt, Mateo practically pounces on me and kisses me long and hard, melting away the feelings of anger and apprehension brought on by the confrontation with my father.

"What are you—"

He swallows my words with passionate licks of his tongue in my mouth.

My hands find his hair, gripping tightly for closer contact while his hands slip into my yoga pants and reach for my sex.

Round and round his fingers go as he drives me wild

with ardent kisses until I open my mouth and cry out.

With ragged breaths and a final kiss, Mateo pulls away when my slick core assures him that I've come.

His lips reach my ear. "You needed that. Do you feel better now?"

"Holy sh— What...that was...why did..." My heart is pounding in my chest and I can't even form a coherent sentence so I settle on a single word response. "Much."

My eyes glance at his wet fingers and I open the glove compartment for a napkin.

With a grin and wicked eyes, Mateo slides his fingers into his mouth, swirling his tongue to lap up the moisture. "Finger lickin' good."

"Gah!" I laugh. "You're crazy! You know that?"

He nods. "Crazy for you."

Grabbing a pen from the center console, Mateo quickly writes on each of his palms before closing them into two tight fists.

"Pick one."

"Why?" I ask, skeptically.

"Just do it."

"Does one say 'blow job' and the other say 'car sex'?"

His laughter fills the space between us as he shakes his head. "Come on, I'm serious. We don't have a lot of time."

My eyes dart from his right hand to his left.

"This one," I say, tapping his left hand.

"Are you sure?" he teases.

I tap his right hand.

"Too late. You made your choice," he says with infectious laughter.

"Let me see. What did I choose?"

"Something I'm going to put on your left hand." Uncurling his fist and extending his palm out, he reveals the single word.

"Ring?" I question.

"We're going ring shopping." He stares at me, gauging

my reaction.

My mouth falls open. "WHAT? You're proposing to me?!" My eyes are rounded saucers of disbelief.

He shakes his head. "Not today, but I want to get an idea of what you like."

I toss my hands in the air, putting all ten fingers on display, wiggling them playfully.

"What's that supposed to mean? You want ten rings or ten carats?"

I grin and lightheartedly slap his arm. "No! I don't wear jewelry so I have no idea what I like. I guess something simple."

"We're about to go find out."

I kiss him hard on the lips. "I love you."

Our quick drive leads us to a jewelry store where we are greeted as we walk in with our fingers intertwined.

Alyssa, the woman at the counter, gushes over Mateo and then quickly adds that we make a "beautiful couple."

"Follow me this way."

Mateo beams as we walk toward the glass counter where exquisite diamond rings sit nestled in black velvet. Every cut imaginable smiles and shines, flashing its brilliance and clarity, hoping to be the one selected.

While I scan the rings, trying to see the price tag of each to no avail, Mateo pushes up the sleeves of his shirt and leans casually against the counter.

"Pick one," Mateo insists when I hesitate to answer the sales woman's inquiry as to which one I'd like to see.

"They're beautiful, but they look...expensive."

"Can we have a minute?" Mateo asks Alyssa before he turns to me. "What's the matter?"

"Mateo, I don't need a big expensive ring. I want something simple. We're not flashy people who need a piece of jewelry to stake a claim on one another." I say, thinking about Darcy's gaudy three carat solitaire or my father's diamond-studded wedding band.

I caress his face, loving the feel of his skin beneath my fingertips, promising myself to him forever. "I am yours."

"As I am yours."

He turns to kiss my palm before taking both my hands in his.

"If you're worried about the money, don't be. Things are good."

"It's not *just* the money."

"Then what is it?"

"I just want you. Nothing else."

He inhales while searching my face.

"Please don't be upset with me."

He releases the breath quietly, shaking his head. "I'm not upset. I think I fell even more in love with you. I didn't think that was even possible."

Alyssa returns and suggests we follow her to another case, but Mateo declines the offer.

Perhaps the fear of losing the sale is what drives Alyssa to blurt out that Mateo can apply for a store account if he's worried about a poor credit history.

His eyes snap to hers. "Excuse me?"

She stammers through an apology as her eyes fall shamefully to his tatted forearms.

"Alyssa, is it?"

The employee nods regretfully.

"Thanks for your help. We'll be leaving now and taking our business elsewhere. You have a nice day."

With his head raised high, Mateo leads me out of the store with a vow to never return.

"What a bitch!" he says after he slams the door.

"Easy! Take it easy on your car."

He chuckles at my comment and thanks me for being me.

"Let's head back to my place."

Mateo revs the engine and peels out of the parking lot, leaving a plume of white smoke in his wake.

After turning on the radio and lacing our fingers together, Mateo drives peacefully back to my house as he sings along to *Smile* by Uncle Kracker.

I glance over to look at him and my body begins to sway, matching his movements, as his head bobs to the rhythm of the music. His voice is smooth and sexy. His playful eyes sparkle while his luscious lips move to form each word of the song.

"You're pretty sexy, you know that?" I state with a smile of my own.

"Who me?" he asks, feigning modesty, but the winking of his eye assures me he knows the truth.

"Yes, you! And lucky for me, you're all mine."

We each lean in for a quick kiss and exchange the Spanish sentiment of "Te amo."

The driveway is empty and everything is quiet when we arrive back at my house. I check the time on my phone and realize our time together is dwindling and a moment of sadness passes over me. I hate saying goodbye to him.

I quickly read the note on the kitchen table and smile.

"Gram's getting her nails done."

"Alone?" he asks surprisingly.

Shaking my head, I tell him that Sarah took her and then smile wickedly.

Mateo pulls me flush against his body and I can feel his erection press into my belly.

"You know what that means, don't you?" I ask sweetly.

He releases a throaty hum, nodding his head up and down, moving down slowly toward my lips as his eyes pierce mine.

I relish the feel of his tongue in my mouth. Kissing Mateo is unlike anything I've ever experienced. My hands grip the soft, silky hair that touches the nape of his neck and

I bring our kiss to a close before opening my eyes to look at him.

"I have something for you," I whisper with a smile.

He rolls his hips, pressing his erection harder against me. "I have something for you, too."

"I just need two minutes." I bite my lip and grin.

"Two minutes? What the hell are we going to do for two minutes?"

"You are going to sit and listen." I reach up and lightly tap the tip of his nose. "I'll be right back."

My legs carry me up the stairs and into my room. I open the side table drawer and remove the single sheet of paper, giving myself a mental pep talk before heading back downstairs.

"No, I'd rather you not. I'll do it," Mateo grits into his phone before ending the call.

"Who's that?" I ask, breezing back into the room.

"Chloe. She wants to finalize a song, but I wrote most of it so I'd like to be the one to finish it."

I nod. "Speaking of songs." I grab his hand and lead him to the piano. "Sit."

After overcoming a sudden bout of nerves, I turn to face Mateo. "Before I met you, things were different. *I* was different. But now, I feel like I can do anything. There's nothing holding me back. Every day I wake up knowing you love me and every night I close my eyes knowing we have a future together. I didn't think it was possible to love one person this much, but I do. I love you with everything that I am and everything that I have." I choke back the rising emotions. "I wrote this song for you."

Mateo remains perfectly still as he looks at me; only his eyes move slowly as if memorizing the features of my face.

I smile, turning to place the sheet of music on the piano ledge and my fingers on the keys.

With three fingers, I create a chord followed by the

addition of several more. My mouth opens and the words flow effortlessly. My hands move along the majority of the eighty-eight keys, depicting a beautiful love story of two strangers who met and fell in love.

Streams of heavy tears pour from my eyes as I continue to sing through broken utterances.

"It was always you...always you..."

My fingers finally rest as the last note fades. My heart's desires revealed in the simple lyrics.

My head drops, and my body shudders with strong emotions.

"That was," Mateo's voice cracks and I hear him swallow then exhale sharply, "the most beautiful song I've ever heard in my life."

He drapes his arm around my shoulder and pulls me close, encouraging me to lean in. I close my eyes and inhale his scent, gripping the material covering his chest as the stifled feelings leak out.

"Look at me," he commands quietly and so I do.

I wipe my nose with the back of my hand then swipe at my eyes with my fingertips.

His hands cup my jaw, keeping me still so he could look directly into my red-rimmed eyes. Moisture spills from his eyes and leaves a trail of salty stains on his gorgeous face.

"I didn't mean to make you cry," I mumble, forcing a small smile.

"You do this to me. You make my heart overflow and spill out from my eyes. What I feel for you is indescribable...it's so much more than love."

I hiccup and take a moment to catch my breath as he continues.

"I am nothing without you." His thumbs mop away the moisture still dripping on my face. "You are the sun, the moon and the stars. Everything bright in my world. You are my goddess, my one true love, my forever."

My hands skate around to his back, crushing my body against his as if my life depends on it.

"Make love to me," I cry into his shoulder.

In one swift motion, I am scooped up, carried upstairs and gently placed on my bed.

As if he has all the time in the world, Mateo removes each article of clothing from our bodies with care before skimming the planes of my naked body with his tongue. He rolls one of my budded nipples between his fingers and smiles at the sounds I make.

"Querida..." A flurry of passionate Spanish words erupts from his mouth, making me squirm as he loves me with his fingers. With each movement, he hisses additional words that would make even a grown man blush.

I come quickly and beg for more.

Mateo obliges until he grunts and climaxes. His arms give away and he collapses onto me, my lungs filling with a gasped breath.

Against my chest, I feel the hammering of his heart as it beats wildly and erratically.

Mateo sprinkles my neck with light kisses until he reaches my ear. "It was always you...always you..."

He continues to repeat my words and I hum in sheer happiness.

"I can't breathe," I finally confess, prompting him to roll to his side.

"I'm sorry I get carried away," he sighs. "I can't ever get enough of you."

"Thank you."

"For what?" he asks, brushing the hair away from my face.

"For being you. For loving me. For this." I point to the space between our weary bodies.

I can almost see the gears working in his brain.

"What?" I ask, knowing him all too well.

"I have to tell you something. I have a confession."

My forehead wrinkles with apprehension.

"I wrote a song for you..."

"You did?" I ask, the swelling of my heart producing the biggest smile on my face.

"I told you...I think about you constantly," he releases a quiet breath.

"Then why the long face?"

His shoulders rise and fall before his eyes cast away and he speaks hesitantly. "Chloe saw it and wants to record it."

"What?" I shriek. "Well..." I stammer as my joy turns to anger. "She can't! I mean, you can't let her."

He takes a hold of my face and keeps me still, silencing me with his lips as his expression softens. "Shhh...she can't do anything without my permission."

"You don't know that. They'll find a way. They always do."

"Chloe and I talked about it, and I was adamant."

My eyes close and I exhale, feeling my body relax as the tension dissipates.

He offers another kiss and adds a smile. "This song, if I ever decide to do something with it, will only be for you because it's about you."

"I can't wait to hear it. Will you sing it for me?"

"I will when it's finished. I promise."

The sound of the back door opening provides the perfect opportunity for me to hide the disappointment.

Mateo offers a quizzical look. "Who's here already?"

We rise, walk to the kitchen and find Gram sitting at the table waiting for Sarah to prepare her late afternoon snack.

I bound into the room, greeting her with a kiss and an inspection of her glittery fingernails.

"Your nails look sparkly, Gram. I like that color!"

I toss a quick glance at Sarah when my grandmother doesn't respond quickly.

"How's it going?" I ask the woman who is pouring a glass of orange juice and placing a few butter cookies on a small dish.

"It was an interesting day. *We...*" she nods in Gram's direction, "perseverated on the color purple because it's Beth's favorite."

I sigh, nodding with understanding.

"I have to run out. I'll be back by six."

"Aren't you a sight for sore eyes?"

All eyes turn to Gram who whistles and catcalls, smiling flirtatiously at Mateo.

He approaches with a cautious smile and takes a seat to her right. "Hello, beautiful." He reaches for her hand and raises it to his lips, locking his eyes with hers while he places a soft kiss on her skin.

"And so charming, too," she gushes, batting her eyelashes. "Are you married?"

Mateo's eyes snap to mine. "Not yet, but I am spoken for."

Gram's countenance falls and she releases an exaggerated sigh. "That's too bad. My granddaughter sure could use a man like you."

He cracks a smile. "Tell me about this granddaughter of yours? Is she as beautiful as you?"

"She's radiant." Words of pride slip from her lips. "She's smart and talented. Oh, you should hear her play the piano and her voice...she's like an angel from heaven."

My heart bursts with joy at my grandma's words and tears threaten to fall once again.

"She sounds wonderful," Mateo adds, drawing his eyes away from her and looking back at me tenderly. "I think I would fall madly in love with her."

"You would make beautiful babies. Your dark skin and her blue eyes."

"I think you're right."

As if someone turned off the switch, I watch my beloved grandmother slip back into the darkness. Her hazy eyes lose focus and she descends into the depths of dementia.

"It was nice talking to you, Violet. I hope to see you again soon."

Mateo reaches for her hand, but she swats him away, calling him a name no proper woman should ever use. Mortified, I rush to his defense and beckon him to rise so we can leave.

"Oh my God! I am so sorry she said that to you. I'm so embarrassed," I cry when I'm seated in the front seat of his car.

"Baby, you don't need to apologize. She's not well; that's the illness talking. I know Violet loves me." He smiles and adds with a wink, "I mean, come on...how could she not?"

My smile widens until laughter erupts. "So modest."

"I speak the truth. You know my words are always true."

"We'll see."

After dropping his car back off at the storage lot, we greet his cousin Junior who is bringing Mateo to the airport.

"Thanks so much for doing this," I say to Junior, hugging him with genuine gratitude.

"Anything for this guy now that he's a big star and all." Junior elbows Mateo in the ribs. "Don't worry, I'll keep building houses while you chase your dreams."

My eyes dart back and forth between Mateo and his cousin. The quick exchange in Spanish leaves me feeling slightly awkward from the obvious tension.

"Don't bring lunch next time you come to work. I'll make you some of my famous chicken salad."

Junior smiles. "Cool. Alright, say your goodbyes. I've got to get this pretty boy to the airport."

Consumed by an overwhelming sense of sadness, I suddenly regret our decision to say our farewells here rather than at the airport.

Junior waves goodbye and waits in the truck.

My eyes remain cast down, fearful that if I look up into his eyes, I won't be able to let him leave.

"This isn't goodbye," Mateo says, drawing me close by my waist. "I'll see your beautiful face every time I close my eyes."

I drag my eyes up and smile. "And I'll see you in mine."

Tender moments slip by as we embrace tightly, wordlessly declaring our love for each other.

"I'll call you later. I might even text you." He says with a sorrowful grin as he blinks furiously, preventing moisture from spilling out of his eyes.

I can't help but smile. "You're going to text me?' I'll believe it when I see it."

Looping my arms around his neck, I draw my lips to his and offer a final passionate kiss before Mateo pulls away and walks to the truck while my heart splinters into a million pieces.

"Te amo," I whisper, knowing that although he can't hear me, he can feel my love.

Tears burst at the seams while I wait for the Uber. I cover my mouth and wipe my face when it arrives a few minutes later, and I have to clench my teeth to prevent myself from changing the destination route to the airport.

My phone chirps, indicating I have an incoming text.

`Te amo. I miss you already.`

`Te amo you too.` I smile as I tap the screen to respond to Mateo. `You took my heart with you.`

`And I left mine with you,` he replies. `Please consider coming for a visit.`

I hesitate with a response. `I'll think about it.`

Quiet moments slip by as the driver points the vehicle in the direction of my home.

`By the way, what was written on your other hand?` I ask, replaying his unexpected visit in my mind.

Three dots flit across and then an image appears of his open palm. `House.`

"House?" I gasp while my fingers rush to respond. `We`

`were going to look for a house?`

He sends back a heart emoji. And then three dots appear before his response does. `We're going to need a big house for all those dark skinned blue-eyed babies of ours.`

Chapter Fifteen

IT'S BEEN THREE WEEKS AND TWO DAYS SINCE my lips have touched his. Twenty-three days since our bodies were one. My desperate longing for Mateo has grown like a raging wildfire and only one thing can extinguish it. I dream about his face and his body at night while thoughts of him fill the pages of the new journal he sent when I briefly mentioned that I'd run out of pages in my last one.

I sigh, smiling sadly as we disconnect the brief call since he's heading into the studio to record another demo with Chloe. Although we FaceTime and talk or text nearly every day about the next time we'll see each other, it doesn't assuage the missing piece in my heart, the gaping hole that aches for him, his presence, and his contact. I want more than the hushed conversations through quick phone calls. I want to hear his voice in my ear when he's making love to me. I want to feel the fullness of him thrusting into me. I want to kiss his lips every morning and each night.

"Good mornin', Gram." I greet my grandmother with a hug and a kiss which she doesn't return. I look at my uncle with curiosity.

"Bad night," he mouths as a wave of sadness moves over his face. "Sarah will be here soon."

I nod, wondering how I didn't hear a thing, but with the extra shifts at the bar and helping Trina nearly every day, I fall into a deep slumber every night. After pouring a cup of coffee, I sit at the kitchen table adjacent to my gram.

Silence and awkwardness join as uninvited guests and sit amongst us.

"Have you figured out when you're going back to school?" Johnny asks as he sets his phone down.

"The university isn't going anywhere," I retort, annoyed with his constant badgering about when I'm going to resume my studies.

"I realize that," he snaps. "But you don't want to miss an opportunity either. You're a talented writer; you could travel the world as a journalist."

"I don't want to be a journalist. I want to write songs." I sip my coffee and peer at him over the cup.

"Write songs? There's no money in that!" he sneers then continues. "Oh wait...yes, there is, but you chose not to—"

I pin him with narrowed eyes.

"You act as if I had a choice. I was just a kid and it was my word against theirs."

"You had proof!"

"So did she! She copied everything I wrote into her notebook. Who would've believed me?"

"Anyone who knew you would have recognized your talent. You could've won." He leans forward and enunciates each word slowly. "...if you had let me do my job!"

"Please just drop it. There's no use in dredging up the past. It's over and done with. And besides, it's not like it's ever going to happen again because if it did, I would drag the Creeds to court and smear their name in the industry."

"There she is..." my uncle sings, nodding his head and welcoming my feisty side back. "There's my girl."

My phone rings and I jump to my feet to take the call, rushing out of the room with my coffee in hand, excited that he's calling much earlier than I expected since he and Chloe are recording more demos.

"Hi babe!"

The line disconnects, but he calls right back.

"Hello?" I bite my lip in anticipation, feeling slightly embarrassed about our late night exchange of sexy text messages. "Helloooooo," I call into the phone.

I can hear him breathing and talking to someone in the background.

"What do you want to do about it?" Chloe asks.

Holding my breath, I listen intently.

"I'm not sure. I feel really bad about the whole thing," he sighs, exhaling a hard breath.

"I mean really, what did she expect from you?" she heckles, undermining our relationship.

"A lot. I made promises to her...so many promises that I knew I shouldn't have made. I had no right to lead her on like that."

I feel the blood drain from my face and my knees buckle, forcing me to drop down to sit on the top step of the stairs. I curl my legs in and hold myself as I continue to listen to the words that decimate my heart.

"From the first time I met her, she seemed so needy to me. I don't know how you can even stand it."

"I guess she can be sometimes, but that's not fair. We used to be really close and I'll always care about her, but...I can't give her what she's asking."

Mateo sighs heavily and then continues to speak quietly about how he needs to let me down gently and he hopes that we can somehow remain friends in the end.

Hot silent tears flow from my eyes and I open my mouth to speak, but no sound or utterance emerges.

"Can't you just be honest and tell her how you feel? If she cares at all about your happiness, she'll stop trying to hold you back."

Because the meager contents in my belly threaten to rise, I reach for the railing and struggle to stand, needing desperately to get to the bathroom before I vomit on the staircase. The phone slips out of my hand and bounces on the hardwood floor.

Scrambling on my hands and knees, I retrieve the phone and crawl to the bathroom, lean over the toilet and purge what feels like everything in me, including my heart and my love for Mateo.

"You don't get it, Chloe. I made promises to her. Life changing ones and looking back, I was so stupid to say those things to her. I got her hopes up for nothing."

"Matt, you can't hold yourself responsible for this. Can I tell you something?"

There's a pause before she continues.

"I know she calls you all the time. I heard you talking to her the other day and she sounds really clingy. It would drive me crazy if someone borderline harassed me. Are you sure you want someone like that in your life?"

Through blurry eyes, I tap the speakerphone and continue to listen. My body convulses against the cold tile floor.

"Honestly, it is annoying that she calls me all the time. Sometimes she talks and I have nothing to say."

My gut wrenches as thoughts race to my mind. I think of the many nights I've listened to his silence only to be told "I wasn't sleeping."

"Do you want Randy to talk to her?"

I can hear air releasing from his lips. "No, she doesn't like him at all."

"You'll figure out what to do about her. I mean, you might want to consider cutting her loose."

"I know," he agrees. "But I don't want to hurt her. She's been through enough."

I close my eyes and grip the material above my heart, keeping it in my chest as it shatters into a million pieces.

What sounds like an exaggerated kiss mocks me.

"Hey, guys! Come on in. We're ready to start. Can someone grab me another towel?" Chloe calls. "We need to get this perfect. My mom knows what she's doing. She thinks this will be the one to put us on the map."

The intimation of remorse is all but gone from his voice. "It's pretty cool you've grown up around music. You know what you're doing."

"Not really...I just sing and shake my ass." She laughs. "My mother does the rest; she's the real mastermind."

Chairs shuffle in the distance.

"In case I forget to tell you, I'm glad you're working on this album with me. We're good together."

I can imagine the slight smile that tugs at his lips when he responds with "No problem."

"Hey Matt, do you believe in destiny?"

"I sure do. We have the ability to create or change our own destiny."

The room spins and the white walls close in on me, trapping me in my own skin, depleting my lungs of oxygen. Panicked, I gasp for air like a fish out of water as Mateo and Chloe sing together, creating a delicate harmony, detailing the inner musings of my soul. Throughout the song, each voice complements the other, revealing a deeply profound "once in a lifetime" love that neither expected nor is willing to forfeit.

My heart. My soul. My love for Mateo. My words. All of these things compiled together to be enjoyed by the world when they were only meant for me. The private place, deep in my soul is on display, bared for everyone to see.

Again.

My fingers clutch the phone, and I hurl it across the room, the screen cracks and webs before I rise and stomp on it, smashing it to bits as the sound of their voices cease.

"Cat?" Johnny calls, rushing into the bathroom. "What

are you screaming about?"

I turn lethal eyes on my uncle and snarl.

"What the fuck is wrong with you?"

My chest heaves and I yank wildly at my hair and pant like a deranged animal. My voice drops to a growl. "I hate him. I fucking hate him."

Then everything goes black.

Chapter Sixteen

"ARE YOU SURE YOU WANT TO DO THIS?" JOHNNY asks, handing me the legal-sized stack of papers. "Have you even talked to him?"

My eyes, dark and sullen, snap in his direction. "If you won't do this for me, I'll find someone who will."

"Cat, you know I'll do it, but I think you need to give him a chance to explain himself."

"EXPLAIN HIMSELF?! How can he explain this?" I turn my laptop to reveal intimate pictures of Mateo and Chloe showcased on every social media outlet. Images of them lounging by the pool, his hands smearing tanning lotion on her back and them recording their new single and finally singing together with their lips merely inches apart jump off the screen.

"Oh," my uncle utters a single word. "Maybe it's not what it seems."

"Like the pictures of your ex-wife screwing your partner in the back seat of his car?"

Johnny cringes in horror, and he winces in what I presume to be pain.

"Did you give *her* a chance to explain?" I bellow loudly, causing the ache in my throat to deepen.

"Leave that bitch out of this!"

We stand at an impasse.

"You thought you knew her, didn't you?"

Furious eyes warn me to stop. "You're treading on thin ice, Cat."

"I thought I knew Mateo, but I didn't. He's a fucking lying bastard just like my father."

He rubs his face with his palms. "All I'm saying is something doesn't feel right."

"Whose fucking side are you on?"

"Yours! You know I am and always will be on your side! For Christ's sake, you should've done this years ago."

There is an incessant knock at the front door. I wrack my brain wondering who it could be since most people usually use the back door.

"I'm coming!" I call, walking to answer the front door and yanking it open.

"Iza!"

A shocked expression greets her, and my words welcome her. My eyes look beyond her to see if she's alone.

"Hi," she says with a tight smile. "Is this a bad time?"

"No, not at all. Come in." I open the door wide and stand back to allow room for her to pass.

"I tried calling you, but it kept going right to voicemail."

My lips tighten and I drag my eyes upward as I close the door and follow her into the living room. "Yeah, my phone broke."

Iza glances around and notices my piano then looks at me. "You play?"

I shrug, choosing not to respond directly and deflect with a question of my own. "Is there something I can help you with?"

Pulling her eyes away from the piano, she looks at me. "Mateo said he couldn't get in touch with you. He got worried and asked me to check on you. He thought maybe something was wrong with your grandmother."

A scowl transforms on my face and I scoff. "He's worried? I seriously doubt that. He's an asshole who can go fuck himself."

Stunned, Iza's mouth pops open and she gasps in response before she flies off into a monologue filled with expressive Spanish words. "I'm so mad at him, but why are you? Why would you say that about him? He loves you."

I sneer, "He doesn't love me. He's a liar. Everything he ever said was a lie."

"Cat, I don't know what happened, but I know him. He sounded panicked on the phone. It's like he was desperate to talk to you. He said he needs to talk to you."

She reaches into her bag, retrieves her phone, and presses a single button. "I'm calling him." The sound of ringing wafts into the air as she extends her hand. She taps the speakerphone button and says, "Here. Please talk to him."

I glare at the offensive device and insist that she hang up, telling her that I don't ever want to speak to him again.

Then I hear his voice.

"Iza!" Mateo shouts into the phone. "Did you talk to her? Oh God, please tell me she's okay."

Iza and I square off in a staring match until I mouth the words "hang up."

Slowly, she raises the phone to her ear and speaks to him in Spanish.

"Cat, baby, I don't know what's going on, but I've been trying to call you for several days now, and you're not answering the phone. I need to talk to you. Please."

My pulse quickens, the blood rushing through my veins as my breathing becomes labored at the sound of his voice. Deep in the abyss of my heart, a million emotions ranging from hatred to love wrestle until deception and betrayal join forces and combust.

I snatch the phone out of Iza's hand.

"What do you want?" I scream into the phone.

"Baby, what's wrong? We haven't talked in days. Why are you being like this right now?"

With each inquiry, his voice rises to a higher octave.

"Why would you even try to call me? I'm needy and clingy and you need to cut me loose."

Mateo bellows across the line. "What in the hell are you talking about?"

"I'll see you in court."

I tap the circle to end the call and stare at the phone in my hand. The pit in my stomach grows larger and my heart turns to ice when it rings and vibrates immediately. Iza reaches for it, but I hold it away. "Do. Not. Answer. It." I glower at her. "At least not until you're out of my house." I hand it back to her slowly. "I'm serious."

A flurry of Spanish expressions, full with hand motions flying in the air, indicates her frustration with me. "I don't understand what just happened. Mateo might be *un pendejo* sometimes, but he loves you."

"He doesn't love me. He's a liar! Everything he ever said to me was a lie. He told me what I wanted to hear and he manipulated me."

For a moment the ringing ceases until it starts all over again.

Her eyes flicker downward, looking at her phone, perhaps verifying Mateo is the caller.

"He's not going to stop calling me."

"I don't care." *Although I really do.* The love I feel for Mateo Cruz isn't one that can be extinguished so easily.

"Can I use your bathroom before I leave?" Iza asks.

I realize she's come a long way to see me...at Mateo's insistence. The very least I could do is allow her some courtesy.

She didn't do anything to me; she's only guilty by association.

"Sure. It's down the hall on the right."

I watch her walk down the narrow corridor and hear the steady ringing of her phone.

I exhale the deep breath that filled my lungs with anguish. I'm so confused. Overwhelmed and perplexed by the contrast of his words and actions, my heart explodes with unshed emotion. Moisture fills my eyes, lingering for a moment before the dam breaks and hot salty tears gush down my face.

My shoulders shudder violently as I weep into my palms and gasp for air. When my legs can no longer bear the weight of my heavy heart, my body concedes, sliding down against the wall for support.

Iza returns to find me sobbing on the floor as though my soul is being ripped away from my body. She cries out to God, asking what is happening as she wraps her arms around me. Peeling my hands away from my face, Iza comforts me as she continues a one-sided conversation in her native tongue.

"It hurts so much," I stammer as broken words emerge from my trembling lips. "I love him so...so much, but I hate him at the same time. I hate what he's done to me."

Iza lowers herself to mirror my position on the floor.

"What happened? What did he do?"

I wipe the tears with the tips of my fingers and take a breath, preparing to provide a full account of his transgressions.

"Things were so good when he came for a surprise visit. We had the best time and then we went looking for a ring."

"A ring?" Iza shrieks unable to hide the surprise in her voice.

I nod. "I was shocked. I love him and want to marry him someday...well, I did want to before all this, but..."

"So what changed?" Her dark, arched eyebrows furrow.

"We talked or texted every day and things were great.

Then one morning he calls and he—"

Pain lances through my heart again.

"I don't think he meant to call me, but he did and I heard an entire conversation he had with Chloe about me. He told her that he misled me and that I was expecting too much from him. He needed to figure out a way to let me go because he made promises...life-changing promises—that he shouldn't have made. Chloe, that fucking bitch, told him to cut me loose."

Iza's face contorts into one of anger as her eyes darken and her upper lip curls, again uttering a sentence in Spanish. Her expression alone reinforces her resentment toward Mateo.

"Then it got worse..." I add, hiccupping as my tears subside.

Iza braces and anticipates for more.

"When I was in Nashville, I finished writing a song. It was something my mom and I had co-written before she left. It was one of the most beautiful songs I'd ever written. You see...I'd never really believed in love, but I guess I hoped someday to find it. I wrote the song about Mateo even before I knew he existed and when I finally found this love with him, the words were effortless because he is...was... my once in a lifetime love."

I see the confusion on Iza's face as she shakes her head. "And what happened?"

With my heart splintering I stammer, "He stole it and gave it to Chloe. I heard them singing it together."

I sob and thrash, kicking the floor with my heel. "How could he do that to me? He knows what they did to me once before and now, he's one of them."

Her eyes round like saucers as she screeches in Spanish. "Porque? Why would he do that to you?"

I shake my head and shrug my shoulders, weeping inconsolably. "Because...it's all just love lyrics and lies...that's what he's all about."

"But that's illegal. He can't use that without your permission."

I nod feverishly, proving my point. "Exactly. Especially when he knows how intimate those words are to me."

She runs a hand over her long brown hair. "I don't know why he would do that."

"He always told me how good he thought I was and that I should do something with my songwriting, but I don't want to. I lived that life, Iza. I don't want it."

"But Mateo could write his own songs with Chloe. She's written some really good songs over the last year. *Ay, Dios mio*, I can't believe he stole yours."

"You don't believe me? You think I'm lying?" I shriek, rising to my feet as something in me snaps. "You know what?! Chloe doesn't write shit! Her mother writes some of it and when she can, she preys on innocent children, steals from them and then has them sent away. Chloe has always taken credit for things she didn't do."

Iza retorts with another disbelieving response in Spanish.

"I heard them singing a song that they supposedly wrote together, but almost every line came from one of my old journals."

"Cat, I don't understand. How would they have your old journals?"

I inhale sharply, swiping at my face to dry it.

Iza drags me to the couch and forces me to sit.

I blow out a puff of air before I begin.

"Randy Creed is my father. He married Darcy after my mother divorced him and when my mother died, I lived with them until...until Darcy convinced my father that she feared for her and Chloe's life. She said I had serious mental health issues and needed to be placed in a residential facility."

"I'm so sorry."

"I tried to convince him that I was fine and that I was

being set up. Things started happening around the house and I got blamed. The final straw was when Chloe lied and said I stole her journal and copied it. It was the other way around. Darcy gave my father an ultimatum."

I drag my eyes to meet hers.

"He chose *them*."

We sit in silence as Iza takes a moment to digest this profound revelation.

"So Chloe has recorded and performed songs that you wrote but she took credit for?"

I nod. "I was in such a bad place so I spent a lot of time alone in my room—"

"—writing," she blurts out, completing my sentence.

"Later that year, when Creed Records took off, Chloe received recognition for the song called Loneliness."

"But you wrote it? Why didn't you say something to anyone?" she questions as Mack had so many times before.

"I tried, but it was my word against hers. I had my journal as proof, but she had one too."

I rub the back of my neck when I feel a deep ache surfacing.

I swallow. "My father—"

She snarls, cutting me off. "—is an asshole. I never liked him."

Her response elicits a chuckle from me as I move to sit cross-legged. "Join the club."

"So what are you going to do now?"

I raise my chin high. "I'm going to sue them, cut all of them out of my life and move on."

"Mateo, too?" she squawks, a look of sheer horror marring her face.

"*Especially* Mateo."

Moisture pools in her eyes. "You're going to break his heart."

My chin quivers. "Iza, he's already broken mine. But more

importantly, he broke my trust. And that...I can't forgive."

Tilting her head, Iza glances at me with pity and sorrow as a single tear rolls down her cheek. She mumbles words in Spanish and although I don't understand what she's saying, I know she feels my pain based on her tone.

"I'm sorry this happened to you."

Nodding slowly, I pinch the bridge of my nose and agree, but it's no use as a line of moisture trickles down my face.

Iza surges forward and wraps her arms around me, comforting me while once again speaking to me in the foreign language.

I grip the back of her thin sweater and cry, relinquishing the floodgates to my soul.

"You okay?" Johnny asks, waking me from my slumber on the couch.

My body was left exhausted after all the time spent detailing my story to Iza. She left with a promise to speak to Mateo even though I begged her not to.

"What?" I reply in a haze. I sit up and take a moment to gather my bearings. "Yeah, I'm just tired."

"Your eyes are puffy. Were you crying?"

I run my fingers through my hair and twist it at the nape of my neck, securing it with my hand. A single nod confirms his suspicion.

"Why don't you call Mackenzie and go for a visit or something?"

"I have to work tonight," I reply, briefly wondering why he would suggest I go visit my best friend. "And besides Mack's in New York, remember?"

"She's home this weekend—"

Puzzled, I ask how he knows this.

"I saw her," he begins, "at the grocery store."

If my mind weren't already flooded with a million other things, I'd inquire more, but I've got room for nothing else.

"What's that?" I ask, tipping my chin to point to the folder in his hand while my body remains in a fetal position.

"The papers."

He sits beside me and hesitates before opening the envelope. "We'll do this only if you're one hundred percent sure. I know I don't know Mateo well, but I think you should give him the benefit of the doubt and at least have a conversation with him."

"Why?" I seethe. "So he can lie to me more? No thanks!"

Brick by brick, layer by layer, misery builds and buries me into the darkest hole imaginable.

Chapter Seventeen

"WHAT THE HELL! WATCH WHAT YOU'RE DOING!"
a woman standing across my bar screeches when the martini
glass slips from my hand and splashes all over her red blouse.

"I'm so sorry!" I grab the white rag and mop up yet
another mess I've made over the past two nights.

"I've got this. Go take a break," Lou says, placing his
hand over mine, forcing me to abandon the task. "I wish you
would've listened and stayed home tonight."

"Is she new? She sucks as a bartender."

I hear her say as I hurry into the break room and lock
myself into the last stall of the small bathroom. The effects
of sleep deprivation caused by the recent events in my life
finally take its toll and wreak havoc on my body.

"Cat?" the voice of my angel calls with a soft purr. "Where
are you?"

Even his voice infiltrates my mind and plays tricks
on me. The hallucinations have not ceased in forty-eight
hours and I'm reminded of my time at Norwich Academy.
The first time Darcy came to visit me, she pulled her own
hair and slapped her face then called for help, crying that I
had assaulted her. Again, it was my word against hers. My
medication was increased and left me in a zombie-like state

for days at a time.

With my palm planted firmly on each side of my face, I look up and listen when I hear my name called once again.

"Go away!" I cry, forcing the voice in my head to retreat. "Go away! I'm not crazy! You're not real!"

"Open the door," he demands with a desperate tone.

I shake my head violently and wail. "You're not real!"

Strong hands grip the top of the door. "Open the fucking door before I rip it off its hinges."

I rise, realizing Mateo is actually here and threatening to destroy the barrier separating us.

Looking at his fingertips, I notice his nails are stained red, and anxiety rushes through me at the thought he may be hurt.

"Why are you here?" I scream. "I don't ever want to see you again so leave me the hell alone!"

"Open the goddamned door!" He bangs his fist on the door. "I want to see you. I want you to look at me and see what you've done."

"*What I've done?*" Anger spews from my lips as I reach down and slide the lock, opening the door. "You're the fucking li— Oh my God!" I gasp with horror when I see him. "What happened to your face?!" I clench my fingers to refrain from touching his wounds.

I weep as my eyes roam over the swelling of his left eye and the gash just above the bridge of his nose until my fingers touch the trail of dried blood stains at the crease of his mouth.

His chest heaves as he mumbles with ragged words, "This...this is... nothing." Covering my hand with his, he drags it down to his heart. "I'm so broken right here. So fucking broken."

Pulling me hard against his chest, Mateo holds me tightly, forming a cocoon around my body.

"Stop!" I flinch, stepping back into the stall. "Don't touch me!

"Look at me! Cat, you *know* me." His chin quivers as he pounds his fist against his chest. "You *know* what's in here. I. Am. Yours."

Stepping closer to me, Mateo stands before me bloody and bruised. Instinctively, I reach for him and sob, soaking his soiled shirt with hot tears.

A free hand cups my head, firmly tucking me into the crook of his neck while the other hand wraps around and his fingers spread across my back.

"Who did this to you?" I cry, hating that I've given in to temptation and am in his arms once again.

"He was trying to keep you away from me."

"Who?" I huff in confusion and disengage myself to look up at him.

"Your uncle."

"Johnny did this to you?" My voice screeches as I counter with disbelief. "I don't believe you."

His lips tighten before he speaks. "It's not a good feeling when people don't believe you, is it?"

I lower my eyes.

"I went to see you, but he wouldn't let me in the house."

"But he knew I was working..."

Mateo shrugs and winces. "He just kept telling me to leave."

"He knows what you did to me."

"Baby, I know what you're thinking, but you're so completely wrong. I don't know how things got so far off track," he says after several minutes pass by. "You are everything to me. I need you so much and I'm so sorry I hurt you."

"Do you really think saying 'you're sorry' is going to change anything. Everything that comes out of your mouth is a lie." I shake my head and cast my eyes away from his. "I know what you said about me. I heard every single word."

Mateo's hands move swiftly to cup my face, his fingers caressing my skin gently. "No, baby. That conversation you heard wasn't about you."

My eyes snap to his and darken. "You're a liar. I heard you with my own ears!" I counter angrily. "And the pictures? Am I wrong about those, too?"

Guilt tarnishes his face, his expression turning to one of remorse.

"No, but I can explain those."

I grimace and shake my head, refusing to listen to his excuses about Darcy's ideas to gain publicity for him and Chloe as a power couple.

"And you were willing to go along with her charade? At whose expense, Mateo?" I demand, waiting for his answer.

"Yours," he confesses, sighing heavily.

"That's right! Mine!!" It's my turn to beat my fist against my chest. "The woman you supposedly love. You don't love me! You love yourself. It was always about you. Your dreams and your goals. You're a selfish bastard like my father."

"You're right," he sighs. "I am a selfish bastard."

I step away to wash my face then grab several paper towels, using some to dry my face and the remnants of his smeared blood.

"You need to leave."

"Fuck that! I'm not leaving until you listen to me and we clear this up."

"Clear this up? There's nothing to clear up. I'm finally seeing you for who you really are."

"You can't possibly believe what you're saying," he exhales. "Give me ten minutes. That's all I'm asking for."

"I'm working!"

"Then I'll wait. I don't care." His fierce eyes meet mine in the mirror. "I'm not leaving, Cat."

"Don't you have a show to perform with your girlfriend?" I chide, tossing the paper towels into the garbage.

He looks at the deliberate space between our bodies.

"First of all, *you* are my girlfriend." He takes two steps forward, backing me into the corner. "And secondly, I left the tour."

"What do you mean 'You left the tour'?" I ask, looking up at him warily.

"I'm done. You are the most important thing in my life. Nothing matters more." He lowers his mouth and hesitates before kissing me.

I turn away, denying him the opportunity to manipulate me once again.

"Lies. Every word that comes out of your mouth is a lie." I shove him out of my way, but he reaches for my forearm and forces me to spin back around.

"I *never* lied to you," he hisses. "*Never*."

"So you chose not to tell me about the thing you have going on with Chloe? That's a lie of omission and it's still a lie."

"I was going to tell you the same night you overheard my conversation."

"How convenient!" I toss my hands in the air. "Lucky for you, I saved you the trouble."

Furious hazel eyes glare at me before my body is swooped up and tossed over his shoulder.

"Put me down!" I bellow as he stomps out of the bathroom, through the break room and out the back door beneath the flood lights. "I have to work."

"We need to talk."

Slowly, he sets me down on my feet and, without warning, I slap his face hard, ignoring the flash of guilt when red spittle flies from his mouth.

He looks down, spits a mouthful of blood mixed with saliva on the ground and wipes his mouth with the back of his hand before looking directly at me.

"I deserved that."

After walking over to retrieve the old metal folding chair used by employees on their cigarette break, Mateo points to it and orders me to sit. "Please," he adds when I refuse.

His expression is hard and serious, but softens when I finally take a seat and cross my arms.

"Don't say a word. Just listen," he says, lowering himself to squat in front of me with his hands spread across my thighs. For a long while, he just stares at me. As if mustering up the strength, Mateo inhales and blows the air out through his lips.

"Chloe is back with Ronan, but Darcy doesn't want anyone to know because she's worried about how it might affect the tour. So she came up with this plan to push the idea that Chloe and I are now a couple. She had us stage some pictures by the pool and my phone fell in."

I glare at him and say nothing although I want to explain that tanning lotion will do that—make your hands slippery.

"Of course, no one had a bag of rice nearby," he chuckles, but I don't share his moment of amusement. "My phone wasn't working right. Videos started playing out of nowhere. Apps would open up then close. The screen would go black and it would freeze. Chloe and I were about to record an acoustic demo when she asked me about Iza."

"Iza?" I ask skeptically. "Why?"

"Iza has been blowing up my phone, calling me nonstop, asking when she's going to record a demo. Three times a day she was calling or texting and it got to be too much. I made promises to her about recording I had no right to make. I guess I gave her the impression I had way more clout than I actually have. I'm no one at Creed Records. Just another expendable voice. I'm just a 'good-looking face with an okay voice' according to Darcy."

"It's hard for me to believe what you're saying. I know them. How do I know they didn't put you up to this?"

"*This*? How would me leaving the tour to be with you

help *them*?"

I shake my head. "I don't know."

Mateo lifts a hand to caress my face. "Querida, mi amor, you *do* know."

My brain processes his explanation as my hand rises to lightly trace where my hand connected minutes earlier. "I'm sorry I hit you."

Sorrowful eyes reach into my soul, offering sincere apologies.

"You think I wanted to pretend that Chloe and I were together? Hell no!"

"But I saw all the pictures. They were intimate."

"They were all staged for publicity. I was going to call you to tell you about them, but then Chloe wanted to head inside to record the demo and you know how that goes. As soon as we were done, I tried to call from my phone, but it wouldn't even turn on at that point. I called you from Chloe's phone, but it went to voicemail."

"Why didn't you tell me about Iza?"

"Because I knew how hard it was for you dealing with me being on the road with Chloe and I didn't want you to worry about me talking to another girl all the time. As much as you say you're not jealous, you are. I see it in your eyes. I hear it in your voice. I feel it in my heart."

My stomach rolls at the idea that he may be telling me the truth, but my heart is still leery.

"What about the song you recorded? I wrote that."

"I had no idea until you mentioned it to Iza."

"Iza told you what I said?" Anger rushes through me at her betrayal.

"No, *you* did. I was on the phone the whole time."

"What?"

"She knew you wouldn't talk to me so she called me from your bathroom and told me to be quiet. I put my end on MUTE so you wouldn't hear anything. You had no idea that

I was listening, did you?"

I shake my head. "No."

"Every time Iza spoke in Spanish, she was talking to me."

"She was?" I ask, remembering how expressive her words had been.

He nods.

"That last night in Nashville, you alluded to being betrayed by your father. You told me how he chose them over you. You also told me about going to therapy and how you tried to hurt yourself. I was devastated and couldn't imagine the world without you in it." He caresses my cheek. "Without realizing it, you confirmed everything when you told her about how Chloe stole your song and recorded it as her own."

My eyes close.

"You have to believe that I would never betray you like that. Baby, we talked about this, don't you remember? I know how important your private thoughts are. I don't know how Chloe got a hold of your words, but I intend to find out."

"I finished that song in Nashville."

"Isn't it in your journal?"

I sigh. "No, my journal was full so I wrote on a notepad instead."

My hands loop around his neck and our foreheads join together.

Detecting the questioning look in Mateo's eyes, I inquire about it. "Do you not believe me?" I swallow hard, preparing for his response.

He licks his lips before he speaks. "I do, but I also remember seeing Chloe and Darcy work on the song together."

My heart nearly stops. "You don't believe me. You think I'm making this up, don't you!?"

"No! Of course not. Your eyes have always told me the truth just like they are now." He caresses my cheek softly, sweeping his thumb over my skin.

"I can't believe the mess we're in," I whisper with a now raspy voice.

"I can't believe you think I could do that to you!" Mateo counters.

"You know I have trust issues. And hearing those words and then my lyrics come from your mouth, I nearly lost my mind." I cringe at my own careless words.

"Don't lose your mind," he says with a smile. "It's smart, creative and beautiful."

Mateo tilts his head, moving it so he can kiss me. "Baby, you are it for me! Everything I've ever wanted all rolled up into this amazing package."

We share a chaste kiss although our tongues slip out to greet one another for a brief moment and my fingers glide to the nape of his neck.

"We need to get you cleaned up."

"I hope your uncle isn't one to hold a grudge," he chuckles lightly as he slips his arms around my waist.

Looking up, I ask, "Why's that?"

"His face looks pretty much the same as mine."

My stomach flips at the sight of the extensive damage to Mateo's beautiful face and it hurts me to think I was the cause of such bloodiness and bruising.

I shoot Lou a text to tell him that I'm going home.

"Whose phone is that?" Mateo asks, motioning to the old iPhone in my hand.

"Gram's."

"What happened to yours?"

Shame washes over me. "I smashed it to pieces."

Draping an arm over my shoulder, Mateo guides me to the pickup truck and enquires about my grandmother as my hand slips around his waist.

"Not so good."

During the ride back to my house, I tell Mateo about

Gram's recent and rapid deterioration.

When Mateo parks the truck next to my uncle's car, the motion sensor light flickers on and I notice the broken pieces of red plastic.

"What happened?" I shriek.

"Your uncle took a bat to my taillight."

"Oh my God!" My hand flies to my mouth, covering the loud gasp. "I've never seen him act violently."

Mateo nods in remembrance. "He was pretty upset with me."

I note the late hour and pray my uncle is sound asleep.

No such luck!

Walking into the dark kitchen, I flick on the small light above the table and jump back when I see a dark figure sitting quietly in a chair.

"What are you doing? You scared the shit out of me!"

The chair scrapes loudly when Johnny rises to his feet, striding over to our direction furiously.

"Stop!" I hold my hand up when I notice his eyes are laser locked on Mateo's and his hands are fisted into balls of muscle. "Stop! Don't hit him!"

I push against my uncle's chest and heave with all my might. "He's with me."

"Are you fucking stupid?" he bellows, still glaring at Mateo.

I cringe at my uncle's harsh words.

"No! We talked about what happened!" I hiss.

"And you believe this asshole?"

"I love this asshole, okay?!"

With a pleading look, I beseech my uncle to understand my irrational heart. "I can't help it! I *love* him!"

"John, I would never hurt her intentionally," Mateo interrupts. "This woman is my entire life. I would give up everything for her. *Everything.*"

The tension between the two men I love is thick and

heavy.

"Can we please just sit and talk for a minute? I need to get him some ice and you need some, too."

For the next hour or so, the three of us sit and talk. I provide my uncle with a full account of everything that has happened recently. I have every intention of finding out how Chloe got my song and Mateo agrees with my plan to pursue the lawsuit.

Taking my hand in his, Mateo adds a few details and apologizes again profusely for his poor judgment in allowing Darcy to manipulate the situation and jeopardize our relationship.

"Never again. I've had my fifteen minutes of fame, but it wasn't worth the cost of losing you."

I bite my tongue and refrain from patronizing him; I know what those people are capable of and he undermined them and fell victim to their plotting and scheming ways.

"I think you need to return to the tour and pretend that everything is fine with you and Cat. You need to get closer to each of them to find out who's involved and to what extent."

The hair on my neck rises and I shiver. "I don't like that idea."

"I don't either," Mateo agrees.

My uncle looks at Mateo. "You might not have a choice. Does Chloe trust you?"

If Mateo thinks I don't notice the way his eyes look away from mine, he is sadly mistaken.

I narrow mine and question him. "What's that all about? Did something happen between the two of you?"

Setting his elbows on the table, Mateo scratches the back of his neck.

"C'mon, Cat. You know better than that," he replies with a voice filled with exasperation.

"You look guilty."

"Look, Chloe is going through some things and she

confided in me about them."

I hiss, "Like what exactly?"

"Like she's pregnant with Ronan's kid."

"Chloe's pregnant?" My mouth gapes wide open. "What's she going to do?"

He shrugs and sighs. "I don't know. She's talked about getting rid of it."

"*Getting rid of it*?" I flinch at his repulsive expression.

"Her words not mine," Mateo retorts quickly.

"See," Johnny says, reiterating his earlier words with a pointed stare. "She trusts you."

"As much as I hate to admit it, my uncle's right. You have to go back and act as if everything is okay. Go along with their charade to get some answers. And I don't want you to ever resent me."

"That's impossible!" Mateo declares before telling me that he doesn't think my father is involved. He seems to genuinely be perplexed about the deterioration of your relationship."

I clench my teeth. "That's bullshit. He knows exactly what he did."

While Mateo and I talk quietly, my uncle contemplates and finally says, "Okay, so here's the plan..."

Chapter Eighteen

"I CAN'T BELIEVE I SLEPT NEXT TO YOU ALL NIGHT and I couldn't touch you," Mateo complains as he nibbles and kisses along my jawline.

"Technically you slept next to me all morning," I say with a grin, running my hand over the dark hair at the nape of his neck.

"It feels like it's been forever since we've had sex."

"Yep." My lips pop with a loud sound.

"One little taste?" he asks, trailing a line of kisses down my chest and over my navel.

"Nope." Again, my lips pop.

My core tightens at the mere thought of his mouth on me, but I'm physically and emotionally drained. My eyes close as his fingers circle and tease my sensitive spot.

"You're killing me here."

"Babe, you have a fat lip and a swollen eye. I think you need to let that heal before you start using your mouth on me."

"What if I promise to only use my tongue?" He licks my bare skin.

"No—ahhhh!" I yelp when his tongue swirls around again. "You have to stop. Please! You have a plane to catch and I need to get in the shower. Johnny wants to leave by eleven."

"Can I at least shower with you?" Mateo pleads with puppy dog eyes.

"Yes, but we're only showering."

I hear him chuckle when I roll out of bed and head into the bathroom.

My willpower vanishes the moment I see his naked body step into the shower and feel his arms wrap around me, fondling my breasts and rolling my nipples.

"I've missed you so much," he growls in my ear, causing my eyes to close and my legs to part.

He grabs the bar of soap and smears it across my body, bathing me from head to toe, leaving no part untouched. His wet fingers linger between my backside, gliding a slow and sensual trail up and down my seam.

"Oh God," I moan.

I turn around and find his lips. With the soap now in my hand, I lather my palms and caress his colorful skin. After finishing the front half of his body, I ask him to turn so I can wash his wide, muscular back. My hands snake around his hips, circling his washboard abs, moving southward until I reach my destination. He moans his pleasure when I grip his thick cock at the base and begin stroking long and even.

"Cat..." he breathes.

"Yes, baby?""

"I need to fuck you." The desperation is clear in his voice.

"Then do it."

Mateo spins around to face me and crashes his lips against mine violently while our teeth clash and we elicit throaty moans. With hot water raining down on us, he lifts my body and I wrap my legs around his hips. He spreads his hands under my ass, and angles my body and impales me, thrusting as voraciously as a desperate and starved man.

After a series of hard plunges into my core, I scream his name as I release and he quickly follows after, spilling his seed against my throbbing walls.

He nuzzles my neck. "God, I love fucking you."

I squeeze my core muscles and milk him a final time before he slips out. "I love you."

He drags lazily, sated eyes up at me and smiles at me. "I want to be home with you."

"Good. Don't screw up again."

I stand on my own two feet although my legs feel like Jell-o.

"You know...if we're supposed to pretend that everything is fine, you really should come for another visit."

I clarify his words as we step out of the shower. "Everything *is* fine...with us. I can't leave Gram right now."

Although he smiles, I know Mateo is disappointed.

Wrapping a towel around my body, I move around my room, grabbing clothes to put on since the temperature has dropped in recent days.

"It's a balmy eighty degrees in South Carolina right now."

I glare at him then smile. "I'm trying not to hate you," I say as I walk into my closet to find my tall, brown boots.

"Hello?"

I poke my head around the corner and see Mateo on the phone.

"Um...yeah...no, I'll be there."

"Who's that? Chloe?"

He shakes his head.

"Darcy. She's wondering why I didn't answer my phone last night. She wanted to get a few pictures of us...at the beach."

I inhale sharply and release the puff of air, reminding myself to go along with everything given I know the truth, but a moment of insecurity threatens to mock me.

"She doesn't know you're here?"

He shakes his head quickly. "I didn't tell anyone I was leaving. I just left."

"Chloe's going to be furious if you don't get back in time for tomorrow's show."

"I'll handle her," he replies.

I nod and look away.

"Stop! I know what you're thinking and you need to stop."

Mateo walks over to me and bends down to meet me at eye level.

"I adore you. I worship the very ground you walk on. I am humbled to be in your presence. I am privileged to join my body with yours and I am honored to be the man you love."

I stare into his eyes and see every ounce of truth.

"Damn, you're good with words." I smile and whisper, "Thank you for the reassurance."

Walking downstairs, I find Johnny sipping coffee and Gram enjoying a glazed donut.

I kiss my grandmother gingerly and wish her a good morning, wondering what her mental state will be like today.

Mateo looks at my uncle and nods quickly.

"Sorry about your eye."

"Yeah, me too. But it's good knowing I can still knock down a younger guy."

I chuckle. "You're not that much older than Mateo."

He sets the cup down and grins crookedly. "Don't burst my bubble, alright kid?"

Following Mateo out through the back door, we stand at his truck, prolonging the inevitable.

"Do you think the plan will work?" I ask.

"It has to. You deserve some answers, and I'm going to help you find out who did this to you and to us."

He pulls me in close and expels a rush of Spanish words.

"*Te amo siempre*," I say, looking up at his stubbly jaw and kissing his chin.

Kissing my lips softly, he says, "*Te amaré por siempre.* You're mine forever."

My eyes fill with tears when he climbs into the truck's

cab.

"Call me when you land."

Scrambling to reach for the phone almost two weeks later, I answer an early morning call. "Hello?" My voice, raspy and low, doesn't sound like mine. "Hello?" I ask again when no one replies.

I glance at the clock and note the time is only half past seven. My eyes are puffy and my body stark naked. A quick recollection transports me back to the wee hours of the morning when Mateo sent me a slew of naughty text messages using his new phone. He was upset because he lost some of the recent pictures that hadn't been backed up to his computer. I reminded him that we have forever to make more memories and take pictures. Learning to let go of my trust issues, I knocked down the proverbial barrier and put my inhibitions aside with my sexually arousing text message responses which helped us each find our own releases.

Don't forget to delete these from your grandmother's phone he had said. I heeded the advice and erased them forever. I smile at the framed picture of the two of us and wish I could roll over in his arms and feel all the things he wrote instead of reading them. Torn between wanting him to glean whatever information he can to help build my case and wanting him home leaves me feeling a bit sullen.

Rolling over, I adjust my pillow and close my eyes, quickly going back to the land of slumber where Mateo and I exist in a perfect world without Chloe Creed. Mackenzie's suggestion to delete all social media apps from my phone was ultimately a good one but difficult to do. The constant stream of pictures kept me close to him when I couldn't hear his voice, but seeing the blond beauty beside him usually brought a round of nausea.

A week later, after growing tired of the endless telemarketer calls to my grandmother's cell phone, soliciting donations for various charities, I make the trip to the Apple store to replace my own. Grateful I had been diligent about backing up my iPhone, I still had over a thousand pictures.

"Hey, where's my car?" I ask, turning my head to look at my uncle who is working on his computer.

"It's being fixed."

"What? Why? It's not worth anything."

He pulls his reading glasses from his face and pins me with a hard look.

"I know that, but with Mateo gone, I don't want you catching a ride home from work so late with strangers."

I smile at his protectiveness. "I could always take your car since you're gone most nights anyway," I say with a suggestive smile. "How's the new girlfriend?"

A smirk eventually gives way to a small smile. "She's fine."

"When are you going to introduce me to her?"

His fingers resume tapping as he says nonchalantly, "You don't need to be introduced to her."

"Yeah, she'll probably be gone by next month anyway. You might want a new flavor for winter."

"Shut up, Cat." He shakes his head and then smiles, keeping his eyes on the screen.

"What are you working on?" I ask, walking over to stand behind him.

"Your case."

I drag the adjacent chair over and sit beside him so I can read his notes. Question upon question fly from my mouth until he stops, looks at me and tells me to be quiet because he can't concentrate.

"Then why are you working in the kitchen? Go use the

spare bedroom as your office now that Junior and the guys have finished."

Considering my suggestion, he says he just might do that.

"I want to go visit Mateo soon. Will you be around?"

My uncle shrugs. "I don't know, but between Sarah and Diane, they should be able to care for Gram for a couple of nights."

"I'm not sure how I feel about Diane yet. Last week when I got home at three o'clock in the morning, she was up cooking. Who does that? In someone else's house?"

"I don't know Cat, but she's here to keep an eye on my mother at night. It's better than leaving her alone, don't you think?"

I nod and concede. "I wish I didn't have to work nights."

"Hopefully after this, you won't have to."

Johnny angles the computer and shows me the figure he's seeking in the lawsuit against the Creeds.

"Holy shit! Where'd you come up with that figure? Did you pull it out of your ass?" I laugh, counting the number of zeroes.

"If you had been given proper credit for writing those songs, this would've all been yours from the beginning."

My eyes round and my lips form an O. While growing up, I'd never gone without; I never experienced the fear of not having enough of anything. Between music lessons and piano upgrades, traveling for performances and other expenses associated with my love of music, my father did whatever he had to do to make it all happen. Since my college education was paid for by my mother's life insurance, I'd never worried about money...until now.

A deep sigh reveals my angst. As angry as I am about the predicament I find myself in once again, I'm not sure a lawsuit is in my best interest. I feel like I'm David taking on Goliath.

"I've got your back, kid. I won't let anything happen to you. And we *will* win."

Johnny closes his laptop and exits the kitchen while I'm left to ponder what I would do with all that money.

A few days later, my uncle hauls my large suitcase from the trunk of his car and asks what I'm bringing.

"Mateo asked me to bring a few things he needed."

"Couldn't he have just bought new ones?" he asks.

"I'm sure he could have, but he asked me to bring these so I am. I'm sure he's got his reasons."

The trip to see his Tia Juanita was...interesting. I was surprised to see Junior and Iza sitting there eating rice and beans. When the invitation to stay for dinner was extended, I didn't hesitate. I've become quite fond of Puerto Rican cuisine and I enjoyed their company filled with stories about Mateo's youth and troublesome history.

"But he could sweet talk his way out of anything," Junior had said with a grin.

I'd mirrored his smile. "So he's always been good with words then and I'm sure having those eyes didn't hurt."

Mateo appreciated the time I took to get to know his family better and loved the photograph of me standing alongside his aunt. His text response indicated that he believes she loves me.

My flight to Tampa International Airport was relatively uneventful except for the screaming two-year old. Her temper tantrum reminded me of the time spent at my father's house when Chloe would scream like a lunatic and spew words of deceit that I was hurting her or stealing her things. Since we were both only children, the transition to having a sibling was difficult. The main difference was my mother raised me with discipline. As much as she wanted the sun and stars to revolve around my music talent, she was still the boss. Unlike with Darcy and her daughter, Chloe had behaved more like a toddler than a teenager.

After retrieving my luggage, my eyes scan the line of people waiting with signs for arriving travelers, looking for the driver my father sent. Mateo sent flowers and apologized for having shared my upcoming visit with my father who insisted a car be sent to pick me up. The phone calls to mend our relationship increased with fervor.

Above the crowd, I see a black Marlins ball cap and finally meet his eyes when the huge man in front of him steps to the side.

Mateo.

My heart races wildly at the sight of him and a wide smile spreads across my face when I notice the sign in his hand.

Mrs. Cruz.

With my arms wrapped around his neck, I pepper his skin with kisses and whisper in his ear, "You're crazy and I love you so much."

"Someday it'll be true," he says, pulling back to look at me before kissing me on the lips. "I've missed you."

"What are *you* doing here?" I ask, taking his extended hand as we walk through the sliding doors into the heat toward the sign for ground transportation.

"I couldn't wait to see you."

We stop at the taxi line.

"Didn't my father send a car?" I ask, looking at the people standing before us.

Draping his arm over my shoulder, Mateo pulls me in and kisses the top of my head next to wear my messy bun sits. "He did, but I didn't think you really wanted to use it."

And just like that I fall even more in love with Mateo Cruz.

Once we are settled in the cab, Mateo tosses a one-hundred-dollar bill on the front seat and smiles when he catches the driver's eye in the mirror.

The lanky driver grins and nods, turning the volume up on the radio.

Mateo pounces on me and devours my mouth, crushing his lips against mine and sliding his hand between my thighs. My protest ends the moment he massages my buzzing flesh through the denim. I orgasm within minutes.

"What the hell?!" I laugh as mortification sets in, realizing how desperate I must look in the eyes of the cab driver.

"I told you I was going to make you come as soon as I saw you."

He kept the promise he made on the phone last night.

"I thought you were kidding!' I quip, gliding my hand over his erection.

"When have I ever lied to you?" he asks, quickly rephrasing his question when I raise a dubious brow.

I kiss his lips once again to dispel the brief flicker of tension.

"What time is the show tonight?" I ask, opening the door when we arrive at the hotel.

"Eight, but I have to be there at five. Darcy always has dinner catered. Take this."

I look at the key card in my hand.

Pulling his hat low and slipping his sunglasses back on, Mateo takes two long strides and widens the space between us.

"You look like you're trying to hide yourself." I laugh, quickening my pace to keep up with him when he suddenly stops. Mateo looks directly at me and mumbles, "Room 522. I'll be up in five minutes." Then he walks away.

Realizing there's a group of girls gathered in the lobby, I understand what is happening. I nod, press the arrow and wait for the elevator. I text my uncle to let him know I've arrived safely and return Caleb's text, telling him that we can meet up when I'm back from my trip.

The quiet awkwardness of riding in an elevator with strangers shifts immediately when the door opens and I nearly collide with Darcy.

"Cat?" she shrieks, quickly trying to smooth away the shock on her face. "What are you doing here?"

"I'm visiting Mateo."

She steps aside to allow others to get on the elevator.

"Oh, he didn't mention it."

Adrenaline mingled with annoyance rush through my blood. "Probably because it's none of your business."

Darcy's eyes narrow into slits. "You little—"

"Cat!" my father calls, rounding the corner. "You made it!"

I quickly swing my backpack to my shoulder to minimize the contact when he reaches for a hug.

"You knew she was coming?" Darcy questions, her voice rising with disbelief and a hint of accusation. She steps into the elevator and glares at him. "We'll talk about this later."

My father stands there expressionless until he looks at me.

"How was your flight?"

"It was fine," I reply.

"How was the car service?"

A warm flush covers my face. "It was really good."

"I'm glad you accepted my offer."

"I didn't—" I retort, abruptly closing my mouth because I refuse to let Darcy or my father spoil my good mood.

The elevator dings and out steps Mateo.

"Hey," he greets my father. "I thought you would've left already. I just saw Darcy on my way up and she's pissed. She nearly ran right into me as I was getting on."

Surprise fills me when my father rolls his eyes. "I'll deal with her later." Turning his attention back to me, he asks if I'm going to attend the show.

Still undecided, I simply shrug.

"You should. It's a sold-out show."

Mateo tells my father that I had a rough flight and should probably go rest.

"Rough flight?" my father questions with a wrinkled brow. "I thought you said it was fine."

"I lied. It's what I do." The snarky response materializes from my lips before I can stop it.

"Cut it out, Cat," my father sighs. "I thought we were past all that."

Mateo guides me, taking my suitcase from my tight grip, and ushers me to his room, whispering naughty things in my ear which make my cheeks flame red.

The moment I hear the door click behind me, Mateo drops my suitcase and pounces. My eyes lose sight of the spectacular view through the window when my body is spun around, my face cradled and my lips ravaged.

"Oh—" I yelp, loving the unexpected but welcomed contact.

As if pouring gasoline on a kindling, a frenzied passion ignites between us. Our clothing is torn off, our desperate mouths crash and wanton bodies reconnect.

Mateo's mouth travels all over my body before settling between my legs. His warm tongue pleasures my sensitive buzzing flesh until all the nerves explode. Needing to be buried in my flesh, Mateo crawls up my body, spreads my legs wide and plunges in, causing me to howl at the contact. I adjust my position and make room, welcoming the stretch of my muscles as he pounds into me. Keeping his eyes on me, Mateo pours his heart into every thrust. I meet his movements perfectly, giving and receiving the unconditional and immeasurable love we share. I am going to marry this man.

With a final plunge deep into my core, I cry into Mateo's neck as I find my release.

"Oh my God! I can feel you. Everything tightens. Holy fu—"

My core continues to spasm, accepting the heat of his essence as he fills me. I spring my eyes open to find Mateo's eyes screwed shut, a look of pain combined with elation smeared across his tanned face.

Panting hard, I snake my arms around his neck and press my cheek against the slickness of his neck. Alternating between kissing and nibbling along his skin, I guide him back down from his high.

I run my nails over his broad shoulders then run my fingers through his damp hair, pulling his head back so I can look at him. Slowly, he opens his eyes.

"Can you tell I've missed you?" He grins, pressing his lips to mine.

"I guess I kinda missed you, too." I shoot back with a smirk.

"I'm serious." Propping himself up onto an elbow, Mateo traces the lines of my hairline, exposing my full face. My eyes fall to his full lips as he speaks. "As much as I love music, I love you more."

"Are you trying to make me cry?" I ask as moisture fills in the corners of my eyes. "I've turned into quite the crybaby over the last several months."

"There's nothing wrong with crying every now and then," he counters.

"Hah!" I slap his arm. "Don't tease me!"

The beautiful sound of Mateo's laughter fills my ears as he rolls off of me, sliding his arm over my ribcage while his nose skims my shoulder. "I've missed you."

I look to the side and meet his eyes. "I missed you, too."

Two quick knocks on the door elicit a growl from the man beside me who tells me to ignore it...until the incessant knocking becomes more forceful and determined.

"Coming!" Mateo calls as he stands, pulls on his shorts and struggles to get his T-shirt on.

He yanks the door open and Chloe barrels her way

through, her stride freezing when she sees me lying on the bed beneath the white cotton sheet.

"Jesus Christ. She just got here! Couldn't you wait ten minutes?"

I feel affronted; I want to tell her to fuck off and mind her business, but I lose the opportunity when Mateo beats me to it.

"Listen here," she grates, pointing a finger at Mateo's face. "This is *my* fucking tour. You're just along for the ride. I don't want you or anyone else," she turns to glare at me, "fucking it up for me."

Mateo swats her finger from his face and rolls his eyes. "No one is fucking anything up. The show will continue like it always does."

"It better!" Chloe tosses me a hard look once again before transforming her face into a softer expression when she returns her attention to Mateo. "You have so much potential. Don't throw it all away."

How I manage to stay calm and not physically attack Chloe is beyond me. I want to wring her neck with my bare hands.

"It's time for you to go," Mateo says, ushering her to the door. I hear the door open and Chloe say, "Oh, there's one more thing."

"What the fuck!" Mateo screeches wildly. His voice is tainted with pure disgust.

"A picture is worth a thousand words," Chloe yells as he slams the door shut.

I jump to my feet. "What happened?" I ask as I catch Mateo wiping his mouth with the back of his hand before he steps into the bathroom and splashes water onto his face and into his open mouth.

I giggle at the dramatic scene in the mirror. "What's the matter?"

He grabs the face towel and drags it down his skin. "She...

kissed me. She stuck her tongue in my mouth," he stammers.

My giggle turns into a snarl as my eyes widen with hatred. "I'll kill that bitch!"

Continuing to scrub his face, Mateo tells me how strangely Chloe's been acting lately.

I lean against the door frame and listen to him as he details her recent behavior.

"I don't know what's gotten into her."

My forehead creases and my stomach rolls, feeling uneasy before, like a lunatic, I burst into a fit of belly laughter.

"What are you laughing about?" Mateo asks curiously.

"You said she stuck her tongue in your mouth, right?"

He nods.

I gloat at the idea I'm about to reveal. "Your tongue just ravaged my pu—" My eyes spring open and I grin wildly as my index finger points to my vagina.

Mateo chuckles sardonically. "Oh my God. That is fucking perfect. How's that for Karma?!"

"Are you sure you don't want to come with me now?" Mateo tilts his head and asks, imploring me to change my mind.

I shake my head adamantly. "No. I really do want to nap, but I'll be there in time for the show. I promise."

Sighing quietly, Mateo leans in and plants a kiss on my lips. "I'll see you in a little while. Are you sure you don't want to come back stage and watch from there?"

"And run the risk of someone asking questions? No, thanks. I already bought a ticket anyway."

"It's a sold-out show," he states.

I grin knowingly. "I buy a ticket for all your shows."

"Why?" He laughs.

Shrugging, I peek up to look at him. "I want to support

you and…"

"And what?" he prods.

"Sometimes when things are bad with Gram, I just want to hop a flight and be wherever you are. Maybe someday I'll surprise you at a show."

With his lips once again on mine, Mateo mumbles. "I love you even more now."

An hour after Mateo leaves, I stand in the elevator with four overly excited college-aged girls who gush about my man. Cringing internally, I listen quietly as they detail things they'd do to him if ever given the chance. An awkward tight smile creeps on my face while I count the seconds until the door dings and finally opens. I know this is part of the industry; I've seen it a million times, but that doesn't make it any easier.

Wandering the streets of Tampa, I walk past the concert venue, glancing quickly at the historic building before turning right to search for food and find Original Grill Station, a small restaurant with outdoor seating. I am directed to a table for one, preview the menu and quickly place an order then tap on my phone, responding to Mackenzie's text messages followed by my uncle's. I call Sarah to check in about Gram and am happy to hear she's having a good day, trying her hand at a new recipe Sarah found on Pinterest.

"That's good to hear. Just please be careful. Gram sometimes confuses dish soap for olive oil." I laugh into the phone.

Our call is interrupted by Mateo's several calls and when I finally answer, he sounds annoyed.

"Hey baby. Sorry. I was on the phone with Sarah. How's it going?"

Mateo sighs heavily on the end of the line. "There's a

picture floating around already."

My face contorts with confusion. "What picture and where is it floating?"

Again, he exhales his frustration. "Chloe had a photographer ready to take a picture when she kissed me. It's all over Instagram."

Running my free hand over my face, I inhale slowly, taking a calming breath before I explode with anger. "This is so typical of her." I release the breath forcefully. "Time hasn't changed her one bit."

"I don't understand why she's doing this. She knows I'm with you. She knows I'm in love with you."

I smile as my heart swells. "Thank you, baby." I thank the waiter for my beverage and continue. "Chloe was always jealous. Jealous of my talent, jealous of my relationship with my father, jealous of my name. She did whatever she could do to take it all away."

"I'm sorry."

"For what now?" I ask inquisitively, wondering what he's apologizing for.

"I'm sorry I'm only realizing this now. I thought maybe you had over-exaggerated a bit when you told me how she was."

"*Over-exaggerated?*" I squawk and clench my teeth. "I'm going to pretend you didn't say that."

"Wait," he backpedals. "I didn't mean it like that. I believed you...I guess I didn't see how manipulative and vindictive she really is until now."

"Yep," I mumble, my lips popping at the end.

"I've gotta run, but I didn't want you to see the picture before I had the chance to tell you."

I accept my salad and nod my thanks to the friendly waiter.

"I appreciate that. Now go run along and pour yourself into those ball crushing skinny jeans."

Mateo laughs at my silly words before he disconnects the call with his own serious words of affection.

Having purchased a ticket online for tonight's show, I utter apologies and practically climb over people to get to my seat in the nosebleed section. There was no way in hell I was accepting the offer to stand backstage or sit in the front row. I'm not *that* much of a glutton for punishment.

The first twenty minutes of the concert, Chloe commands the stage, singing and dancing to her fans' delight. I have to give her credit; she can work the audience like no one else can. My heartbeat quickens when the lights dim and the silhouette of two figures, facing each other, illuminate on a riser toward the back of the performance area. Mateo's tall body is immobilized until the music starts and the lights flash.

Then he shines. His voice is perfect. His movements are perfect. His command of the screaming audience is perfect.

Mesmerized and completely enthralled by Mateo's performance on stage, I watch as my heart fills with pride for him. He was born for this; he truly is a star. He loves the limelight.

"Oh my God. We love you guys so much," Chloe gushes dramatically as the concert comes to a close. "This tour has been better than I could have ever imagined. Matt and I would love to show our appreciation and thanks for your support." She turns to Mateo and whispers in his ear as the camera zooms in, displaying his wide eyes and shocked expression. His lips move as he responds with one word. "No."

Ignoring him, Chloe turns to the crowd. "We have a special surprise for you."

Again, Mateo's countenance is hard, showing his frustration. The camera follows his every move and his beautiful face appears on the huge screen. I want to run to him, to offer words of comfort and to hold him in this moment.

The first few keys play softly on the piano and Chloe walks over to him, smiling up as she lifts a microphone and starts to sing "Once in a Lifetime Love."

My heart nearly stops. Slamming my eyes shut, I wrap my arms around myself as I shiver from the cold blood running through my veins. Slowly reopening my eyes, I watch with rapt attention as each word I wrote on that hotel notepad slips from Chloe's lips. She sings to Mateo, caressing his face softly as if *she* were his once in a lifetime love.

Staring at her, Mateo doesn't part his lips when it's his turn to sing. He's standing there, frozen like a statue. Hard. Expressionless. Cold.

Hazel eyes look out over the audience then search for the camera. When the attention is on him, he mouths, "I love you, C. You're my once in a lifetime love." Turning back to Chloe, he hesitates a moment before allowing his voice to depict the story of two strangers who met and fell in love, share a love beyond measure, a love beyond words, a love you only find once in a lifetime.

Hot tears run down my face and drip on my shirt.

Once again, my private thoughts have been stolen, used without my permission and exposed.

Betrayal and nausea wreak havoc on my stomach as bile rises into my mouth. The bitter taste forces me to run from my seat, again shouting apologies as I shove my way through to the nearest restroom.

I can feel the vibration of my phone in my back pocket, but I can't reach for it; my hands are busy holding my hair back as I vomit. The incessant ringing stops and starts again. I know Mateo is calling to apologize, but there is no need. I already saw it on his face and in his eyes.

Tonight, he saw Chloe Creed for who she really is.

After purging the contents of my belly, I rise and lean against the stall door, regaining my composure before heading out to wash my hands and face. A rumble of giggles fills the restroom as young girls clamber in; their lips flowing with words of amazement for the performance, but more importantly, Chloe and Matt's final kiss.

Another round of ringing begins, but my hands are wet so I don't answer. Blotting my face with a damp paper towel, I hear Mateo's attempt to reach me again. I toss the paper towel in the trash and squeeze past the long line that has formed, finally pulling my phone out and bringing it directly to my ear as I answer the call.

"Cat!" my uncle screams. "Jesus Christ! The house...the house is on fire."

The chill in my body returns and people's faces blur. Confusion and disbelief fill my brain as I utter a single word. "Gram?"

"Oh my God, Cat. The house...everything is gone...there's nothing left—"

My hands start to shake and my lips quiver. "Gram?" I yell louder. "Where's Gram? Is she okay?"

I can barely detect Johnny's muffled voice as he cries into the phone, telling me she's at the hospital.

"Please tell me she's okay. She has to be okay!"

My body is shoved in every direction as I push my way through the crowd, rushing to get outside when my phone signals another incoming call.

"Hold on!" I bellow into the phone and connect Mateo's call.

"Baby! I'm so sor—"

Wailing frantically, I cut him off. "I have to go! The...the house is on f-f-fire. I need to get home." My voice cracks at the thought of my grandmother suffering in any way.

"What?" he asks, yelling into the phone with confusion overshadowing his voice. "Whose house?"

"Mine! Gram's at the hospital."

"Fuuuuck!"

"I need to get home. I need to be there with Gram!"

I push the double doors open and step into the humid air as I search for a taxi. Frantically, I call out, asking if anyone knows where I can grab a taxi, but no one replies to the hysterical woman screaming.

"Okay. I'll be there as soon as I ca—"

A muffled conversation interrupts his thought. "Hold on," he says. Moments later, Mateo's panicked voice returns to my ear. "I'm coming to get you. Wait for me by the main entrance." His words barely register over the thundering of my pounding chest. I find the spot he's referring to and order my feet to carry me there.

Lively throngs of people, filled with elation from the concert, pass by and squeal, unaffected by my current state of devastation and shock as I wait for Mateo. Bowing my head, I pray as tears drip onto the concrete. The words I once whispered upon learning of my mother's accident creep to the forefront of my brain. Once again, uttering the same words, I make promises to God. *Please don't take her. You can have anything you want. I'll be good. I'll go to church. I'll do more charity work. Anything.*

Several horns blare as a black car comes into view, recklessly weaving through the busy traffic until finally stopping mere feet away from me.

The rear door swings open and Mateo jumps out, ordering me to get in quickly.

Uncontrollable sobs wrack my body when his arms reach around to hold me and I bury my face in his chest. He comforts me and consoles me as water continues to pour from my eyes. My fingers grip his T-shirt tightly and I can feel the heat from his body emanating through the thin, damp material.

"She's gonna be okay," he sighs quietly before showering

my head with soft kisses. "She still owes me a pot of sauce and lasagna."

A sad smile emerges on my lips at the memory of Gram's bargain with Mateo.

I pull back to look at him. "Thank you for coming to get me."

"He didn't have a choice," a voice states.

My eyes flash to the front of the vehicle where my father sits alongside the driver and then dart questioningly to Mateo.

"Why are you— What are you doing here?" I stammer, my gaze meeting his.

"Whether you want me or not, I'm still your dad," he replies before adding. "And I'm going to do everything in my power to get you home to Violet."

With a quivering chin and an aching throat, I offer a silent nod of gratitude.

"Do you need anything at the hotel?" Mateo asks.

I shake my head, knowing I've got my license and credit card in my small clutch. "I just need to get home."

"We'll have you there just as fast as we can," my father promises with a sympathetic smile.

"Hey, we're here," Mateo whispers quietly, rousing me from my slumber with small circles to my back.

"Where are we?" I ask, minimally lifting my head from his chest. My eyes flutter open and I peel my body away from his where I'd fallen asleep.

"We're home." Mateo says, rising and excusing himself to use the bathroom.

I look out the small window and find a lit hangar welcoming us.

My hands reach up and scrub the stiff skin on my face,

stained with salty tears. I grab my phone to call my uncle, looking for an update on Gram. Our quick conversation as I boarded the chartered plane did little to ease my fear and anxiety about my beloved grandmother.

"How are you doing?"

My eyes flash upward, finding the eyes of my father. His expression of worry is combined with one of agitation.

"I'm okay."

Just as he begins to speak, he slams his lips shut.

Silently, I implore him to continue.

"Let me know if you need anything. Anything at all. I'm here for you."

I inhale quietly, swallowing my pride while finding the strength to utter the next words. "Thank you for getting me home so fast. You didn't have to do—"

He interrupts me, searing me with serious eyes. "Cat, you're my daughter. Regardless of what you think, I love you."

I look away, slightly overwhelmed by the emotion bubbling in my belly.

"They're opening the door. You ready?" Mateo asks.

"There's a car waiting out front for you," my father announces.

The emotion rises and bursts when his words register. Unable to contain myself, I throw my arms around the burly man and squeeze hard, thanking him.

I think I've shocked both of us.

A simple kiss is placed on my head before he tells me to go.

Mateo leads me through the airport and out to the waiting town car. Thankfully, the airport is quiet and desolate at this hour.

"What a fucking night," Mateo sighs, pulling me close as we sit together in the back seat. "Can we go back twenty-four hours?"

"I should've stayed home. I knew Gram was getting

worse by the minute."

"Cat, this isn't your fault."

I blow the air from my lungs sorrowfully. "I know, but Gram needs me."

Quiet moments slip by as we travel along Interstate 95 toward Stamford Hospital and Johnny updates me about his mother.

"I'm sorry about the song," Mateo mumbles, breaking the silence surrounding us.

"I know," I utter. "I saw your face."

"I had no idea she was going to do that. She whispered in my ear and said I would be done in the industry if I didn't sing with her." He shakes his head angrily, his lips tightening as he spits, "She's a manipulative bitch."

"Yeah, I know. I lived with her." I agree with his assessment of the pop star.

"I can't even imagine how bad it was for you."

"It was awful," I toss sardonically. "But you know what? I don't care. I don't care about any of it. Chloe could have every song I've ever written. She can claim them all as her own. She could win Grammys for them...I don't care...as long as I get to keep Gram." I look up to the heavens and hope God is still listening.

"No way! That bitch is going down," Mateo counters crossly. "She. Is. Going. Down."

"Mateo, she's not important. Chloe is nothing to me, but you and Gram...you guys are everything to me."

Arriving at the hospital, we step out, speak to the nurses at triage and are quickly directed to an area where I find my uncle sitting on a plastic chair leaning on his elbows with his head bent.

"Johnny," I sigh.

When he drags his head up, I can see the agony on his face. His eyes are puffy and red-rimmed.

"Cat," he breathes, pulling me into a massive hug. "I'm so

sorry. This is my fault."

I stand on the tips of my toes, reaching up to comfort him with long strokes along his back and shush him when his tall body shudders with emotion.

"This isn't your fault. I'm sure it was an accident," I squeak, trying to remain strong for his sake.

"I should've been there. I shouldn't have left her alone," he cries into my hair.

"Then I should've stayed home, too," I counter.

Johnny sniffs and softly exhales, pulling away as I feel the presence of another person standing beside us. My eyes spring open in surprise and wonder when I see my best friend standing there with two cups of coffee nestled in a cardboard tray. Her usually bright green eyes are smeared with mascara.

"Mack!" I screech. "What are you doing here?"

I watch her eyes cut to my uncle's in a plea for help.

Johnny closes in, removing the tray from her tight grip as he sets it down on the chair. Inhaling sharply and straightening his stance, my uncle reaches out slowly. My eyes follow the movement of his hand as it slips into Mackenzie's. He laces their fingers and smiles at her before turning his attention back to me. "She's with me."

My mouth drops open and she chuckles quietly, mumbling coyly, "Surprise."

Blinking rapidly, I try to process this unexpected revelation. "W-what?" I stammer, darting my eyes back and forth between my uncle and my best friend. "Are you serious?"

"Actually, we are."

"You're the new flavor of the month?" I chide, the hurtful accusation causing her eyes to drop.

"Cut it out, Cat! Mackenzie and I have been together for months." He squeezes her hand reassuringly as he looks at her once again. "She's my...she's mine...and I'm hers."

My head feels as though it's going to explode and my knees wobble. "I need to sit down."

Mateo cradles me under his arm and guides me to the seat where Mackenzie's huge Marc Jacobs handbag sits. I look at it and shake my head in disbelief.

Johnny sits to my left and takes my hand while Mateo sits to my right and drapes his arms over my shoulder, each offering comfort in some way.

"What a crazy night." I scoff, replaying the entire day in my head.

"Mr. Ryan?" a voice asks as it draws closer. "I'm Dr. Finley."

All four of us rise to greet the young, handsome physician who stops just a few feet away. After a subtle side glance to Mackenzie who seems unfazed, I suppress a small smile, knowing if my best friend weren't suddenly dating my uncle, she'd be throwing herself at this man.

"Your mother is resting and doing very well. Aside from her sprained wrist, she's going to be just fine. We're giving her oxygen and we're monitoring her levels."

I sag in relief as Johnny thanks the doctor and asks when we can see her.

"She's sleeping now, but I'll have one of the nurses let you know as soon as she wakes up."

I shoot my hand forward after my uncle does, offering my own gesture of gratitude. The young doctor's hand lingers in mine for a moment too long and I smile awkwardly as Mateo puts a possessive arm around me. "Thanks again."

"I don't know if you believe in angels, but thank God the home health aide worker showed up when she did. She saved your grandmother's life. This could've ended very differently."

Dr. Finley finally releases the hold on my hand and nods before turning away.

I turn and find comfort in Mateo's arms. "Thank God she's going to be okay."

Johnny and Mackenzie step back to sit together as Mateo and I remain standing.

"That guy's lucky he left when he did," he hisses in my ear.

I pull back and look up with a questioning look on my face.

"Don't think I didn't notice the way he was looking at you and how he wouldn't let your hand go. I was ready to knock him out."

"*Ay, Dios mio.*" I chuckle, my use of the Spanish expression emerging pitifully. Dropping my gaze, I laugh at him and snake my arms around his waist. "Now you know how I feel about you."

Mateo cups my face and kisses my lips. "You are the sun, the moon and the stars. Everything bright in my world."

I feel his phone vibrate in his back pocket so I remove it, wondering who could possibly be calling at this late hour.

"Here," I grit, whispering after spotting Chloe's name.

Mateo takes the phone, grimaces and then powers it off.

"Thank you." A smile shines on my face until my phone rings. Mack hands me the phone, and my forehead wrinkles with question when I notice the unknown number. "I don't know this number."

Mateo looks over my shoulder. "It's fucking Chloe. Don't answer it."

"Chloe? How does she have my number?"

His reply is swift. "I used her phone a few times to call you, remember?"

I don't remember right away, but then vague recollections surface of the time his battery died or the time his phone fell in the pool.

I nod solemnly, pushing Chloe to the dark abyss where she belongs.

Finding as much comfort as possible on the hard, plastic chair, Mateo and I sit with my uncle and his girlfriend, waiting for the opportunity to visit with Gram.

"Why did you leave her alone?" I ask, turning to my uncle.

He sighs. "Diane called out sick so I called Sarah who said she could come, but that she would be late. I didn't think it was that big of a deal since Gram would be sleeping."

"How long were you gone?"

"Two hours at the most."

"Where'd you go for two hours?" I ask genuinely.

My uncle and my best friend share a look of guilt and shame.

"Mackenzie came home to surprise me and..."

Realization registers.

"So this is *your* fault!" I lean forward to face Mackenzie whose eyes are round and weary. My vain attempt to keep a straight face fails and I burst out laughing. "You two had a booty call and the house caught fire!?"

"Cat, I'm sorry," she answers quickly. "I didn't know...we didn't know—"

I hold my hand up and halt her words. "Mack, I'm just kidding." I chuckle. "This is no one's fault."

Sarah comes into view as she rounds the corner with tears in her eyes. "I'm so sorry, you guys! I should've been there with Violet."

I rise and hug her, assuring her that everything is fine.

"I think she was trying to cook. I don't really know."

I shush her and try to quell her emotions.

"All that work you just had done to the house. I can't believe it."

I cast a glance at Mateo.

"We can rebuild the house. That's the least of our worries," he affirms. "I'm just glad you were there to get Violet out in time."

Sarah chuckles. "Not without a fight. For a tiny thing, she's strong and feisty when she wants to be."

We share a light moment at my grandmother's expense.

When my phone rings again, I answer it quickly. It's the least I could do after what my father has done for me.

"Hi," I answer.

The quick conversation to find out about Gram ends

when Darcy's voice screeches in the background, demanding that Mateo return to Florida immediately. Her threats and promises to end his budding career mimic those of her daughter's.

"I'll call you tomorrow," my father says before he quickly disconnects the call.

"Violet is awake," a nurse announces as my uncle and I share a glance, wondering who is going to go first.

"You should both go," Mackenzie suggests.

"Yeah, you should," Mateo agrees.

I nod and give Mateo a quick peck on the cheek. "Te amo."

Following the wait for Mackenzie to let go of my uncle's embrace, I turn to her. "Hey, don't flirt with my man." I smile and wink.

"Don't worry, Cat. I've got one of my own. And he's a keeper, too."

Chapter Nineteen

AFTER LEAVING THE HOSPITAL AND GOING BY
the house to survey the damage, we checked into a
DoubleTree Hotel and didn't get to bed until nearly five
o'clock in the morning. I roll over and stretch my body,
tossing my leg over Mateo's hip as my hand slides around to
find his hard stomach. His hand moves to cover mine and he
exhales with a quiet groan.

"I'm sorry I woke you," I apologize quickly and start to
pull my hand away.

"I just fell asleep a little while ago." His throat is raspy
and low.

"Why?" I ask, snuggling closer and pressing my cheek to
his warm bare back.

"I was reading and thinking."

"About?"

"I'm done with Chloe. I'm leaving the tour for good."

Using my hand, I encourage him to shift his body so he
is flat on his back.

"Mateo," I breathe quietly. "Please don't do that on my
account. This is your dream."

Rolling me quickly onto my back, Mateo stares down at
me, caresses my face with his fingertips and shakes his head.

"No, baby. *You* are my dream. As long as I have you, I don't want anything else."

My eyes blur with moisture. "I don't want you to resent me."

"That's impossible."

My hand cups his jaw and my thumb slides across his bottom lip. "I'll stand by whatever decision you make."

"I've already decided. I choose *you*."

I bring his mouth to mine. "I love you," I mumble against his lips.

One simple kiss initiates a wave of passion, drowning each of us with emotion as he spreads my legs with a quick swipe of his and drives into me.

Hurried, frenzied thrusts pound my core as my nails rake down his back. Needing more to push me over the edge, I wrap my legs around Mateo's ass and cross my ankles, matching his every move while encouraging him with my words.

A flurry of garbled Spanish utterances flies from his lips when I scream through my orgasm, and he feels my core tighten around his massive erection.

Slowing the propulsion, my lover savors the moment until he can bear it no longer. With determination and purpose, Mateo surges forward toward his own orgasm, grunting animalistically as he spills his thick, hot seed in me.

I welcome the feel of his body on mine as he works to regulate his breathing.

"Have I ever told you how much I love fucking you?" he asks, pulling back with a wicked grin on his face.

I return his playful expression. "You may have mentioned it a few times."

A knock on the door startles us.

"Housekeeping."

Mateo asks them to return in a few hours.

I lie in his arms while he strokes my hair. I am completely

sated and utterly blissful, momentarily forgetting the reason we are in this hotel room until he interrupts my mental tranquility.

"I can't believe how fast everything burned. That fire spread like wildfire."

"Everything is gone." My body sags as images of red and white lights flashing combined with the odor of charred wood infiltrate my mind. Although I wanted to get closer to fully comprehend the damage, the fire marshal ordered us to remain at bay.

"I can rebuild it."

I smile sadly and thank him. "I'm not just talking about the house."

"What do you mean?"

"Everything inside is gone. Pictures, journals, my piano. My mother's belongings. Everything."

I sit up and gasp. "My uncle's computer."

"What about it?"

"He had everything for the lawsuit on there. He scanned pages of my journals as evidence. Now that *and* my journals are gone." I scrub my palms around my face and growl. "How am I supposed to prove my case without any evidence?"

"Shit"" Mateo exclaims, fully understanding my predicament. "We'll figure something out. She will not get away with this. I will make sure of it."

"Honestly, I shouldn't care. It's not important," I say, remembering my promise to God. "I'm just so happy Gram is alive and escaped virtually unscathed."

"Speaking of...we should probably get going..." Mateo sings, implying we need to shower and get to the hospital soon before we ensue round two because his erection is tenting against the soft cotton sheet.

"You're right. Let's go." I grin, hop out of bed and run to the bathroom.

An Uber brings us to get Mateo's car before we head to

the hospital. After a quick stop at Target to purchase some new clothes, toiletries and phone chargers since ours were left back at the hotel in Florida, we stop at the florist and pick up a bouquet of flowers for Gram.

"I guess all that stuff is gone, too."

"Randy said he would ship it home for us."

I tilt my head. "He did? When did you talk to him?"

"He called me last night when you were in with Gram."

I nod. "What did he say?" I ask even though I'm sure I already know. "Did he want to know when you'll be back on tour?"

Mateo chuckles quietly. "Actually, he told me not to worry about it. He told me to take care of you."

"*My* father said that? Are you sure it was him you were talking to?" I lift a brow and crack a smile.

"I know. That's what I thought, too."

"Knock, knock," I say, tapping the room and entering my grandmother's room on the sixth floor of the hospital. "How's my sweet little ol' grandmother?"

Gram's eyes sparkle with delight at my appearance. "Beth, you know I hate when you call me that!"

I flash my eyes to my uncle then to Mackenzie who offers a tight smile.

Swallowing the desire to correct her, I move in closer and offer a kiss on her cheek. Simply grateful that she is alive, I don't care what name she uses or who she thinks I am anymore.

"Gram," I caress her soft hand. "You gave us quite a scare."

"I just wanted to make dinner for my family."

I smile. "I know, Gram. When you get out of here, we can go to Mackenzie's apartment and cook." I toss my best friend a snarky grin, knowing how OCD she is. Or at least how she used to be. I have a quick, relatively recent flashback of her clothes strewn all over her apartment and now I understand why.

We visit with Gram and assure her things will be fine.

"We'll be right back."

My uncle and I step out of Gram's room to engage in a quiet conversation about moving her into an assisted living housing community where she'll be monitored by a home health aide like Sarah twenty-four hours a day. All meals will be prepared and delivered so there won't be the need for her to cook.

"I'm going to grab some coffee. Want anything?" Johnny asks, walking backward toward the elevator.

"No thanks!"

"Good afternoon," Dr. Finley greets me when he stops by to check on his patient.

"Hi."

"How's your grandmother today?"

"She's as good as expected, right?" I say.

"She's quite a lady," he says kindly. "And quite a flirt."

I return the bright smile and nod in agreement. "Yes, she is. She's been using her charm to marry me off for years."

Dr. Finley's light eyes crinkle with amusement. "No takers yet?"

"She's taken."

I turn to see Mateo glaring at the physician. "She's definitely taken." Mateo puts a possessive hand on my shoulder and pulls me back against his chest. "Thanks for asking though." His voice reveals a dark undertone.

Clearing his throat quietly but appearing otherwise unfazed by Mateo's demeanor, the doctor says he's likely going to discharge Gram tomorrow.

"Tomorrow?" I ask, thinking how that impacts our timeline and changes everything, forcing us to move faster to find her a place to live.

"Is that a problem?" he inquires, tilting his head inquisitively.

"Uh...no. It's just...you know our house kinda burned to the ground." I laugh humorlessly.

"I'll figure it out," Mateo interjects.

Dr. Finley pulls a card out his wallet, scribbles on it and hands it to me. My eyes scan the small card and I flip it over to read the name and number he's written.

"My brother is the manager of some rental properties. Give him a call and let him know I sent you."

Mateo snatches the card out of my hand and shoves it into his pocket. "Like I said, 'I'll figure it out.'"

"Take care. Let me know if you or your grandmother need anything. You have my number."

I watch Dr. Finley walk away and my face reddens with humiliation as I turn to Mateo.

"What the hell is wrong with you?" I ask through clenched teeth.

"You. Are. Mine," he grits, equally frustrated.

"No shit! I've always been yours and I always will be. You didn't have to behave like a Neanderthal."

"I'm a jealous man. You already know this."

"I do know it, but there's no reason for your jealousy." I exhale and run my fingers through my hair and readjust my low bun. "How do you think I've felt these past few months while you were on tour? I know how girls can be! I know they threw themselves at you and hell, my own father probably arranged for girls to go to your hotel room." I scoff. "Did you see me acting like a lunatic?"

I am hauled down the hall into a small alcove and pushed up against the wall. Mateo launches an assault on my mouth with his as he rolls his hips into my belly.

"You are mine."

"I know," I murmur through his kisses. "And you're mine, too."

"I don't care if a thousand girls were parading naked in front of me, I would never touch them. I only see you. I will fight any man who tries to make a move on you or take you away from me. Remember what happened between me and your uncle?"

"Yeah, but that was different."

"He tried to keep you away from me and I kicked his ass."

As if life's paths were set on a specific journey, Johnny walks past with coffee. "Whoa, whoa, whoa. Hold on a second! You did not kick my ass! If you ask me, I gave it back just as good as I took it."

Mateo pulls back and cracks a huge smile, shushing my uncle who is now laughing as well.

"By the way, even if you weren't here, there is no way in hell I was letting that playboy doctor anywhere near my niece."

"I am a grown-up, you know!" I chime in, reminding the two most important men in my life of my presence.

Back in Gram's room, we find Mackenzie sitting quietly with her laptop open.

"Someone's blowing up your phone," she says, looking at Mateo and pointing her chin in the direction of where his phone is charging.

I see the frustration on Mateo's face as he responds to several text messages.

"What's wrong?" I ask after he releases a torrent of Spanish curses.

"She's demanding I return tonight."

"Or what?" I challenge.

"I have an idea," Mackenzie suggests.

"You are a genius!" I say, drawing the curtain back to reveal an unoccupied hospital bed.

"And there it goes," Mateo says, tapping the screen to post the image on his social media platforms associated with Matt Cruz and Chloe Creed. "It'll buy me a little more time to figure out how to get out of the tour altogether."

"Chloe won't have a choice but to play the part of a supportive girlfriend when her fans see you laid up in a hospital bed due to extreme exhaustion."

"Ten, nine, eight, sev—"

"Hello?" Mateo says, answering Chloe's call. "No, *you* listen. You will give me the time I need or your fans will find out what a bitch you really are. We both know just as fast as they build you up, they'll tear you down. Don't fuck with me."

Gram exclaims, "Bravo" and claps her hands. "I like this guy. He needs to meet my granddaughter."

Deciding where to stay over the next several weeks is our priority. Mateo and I leave the hospital and search for a two-bedroom apartment while we decide what to do with the house.

By the end of the night, sleep beckons me, and I drift away into a deep slumber.

Mateo's whispered voice wakes me and my eyes scan the hotel room. I smile when I spot his reflection in the bathroom mirror where he's standing with a towel around his waist and a razor running over his stubble.

"Morning," I call.

Mateo's eyes meet mine in the mirror and my anxiety spikes when I hear him whisper a hushed goodbye.

After splashing water on his face, he grabs the hand towel and dries his skin, making his way over to sit next to me.

"Good morning, beautiful." He offers a chaste kiss on my lips and I narrow my eyes.

"Who were you talking to?"

The darting of his eyes and the deep swallow don't escape my notice. "Mateo!"

"I think I found a place for us to stay...temporarily."

"Okay," I sing-song, "but you didn't answer my question."

"I was talking to your father and he offered for us to stay there since they won't be back for another three weeks."

My back stiffens and I sit straight up. "There?"

Mateo swallows nervously. "His house in Greenwich."

"No way! Are you insane?! I'm not going there!"

Mateo's damp hands reach out and grab my shoulders. "Hold on a minute."

I force my head back against the padded headboard, close my eyes and exhale.

"Do you trust me?" he asks.

I drag my eyes open and find his gorgeous hazel eyes filled with promise and hope. "You know I do."

"Good. Now please listen to me."

"Oh, Cat I don't know," Mackenzie says, worry etched on her face framed by her red hair.

My uncle looks at Mateo. "Only if you're a thousand percent sure."

"I am," Mateo replies confidently. "Believe me, I wouldn't be doing this if there were another way."

Johnny looks at me and I nod, showing my support for Mateo.

"Okay then."

Mackenzie and I hug tightly before she and Johnny leave for the train station. "You have a lot of explaining to do," I whisper in her ear. "And for the record, I'm totally grossed out by you and my uncle."

Deep laughter materializes from Mack's belly as she embraces me again. "I love him and he loves me."

"He's old!" I yell.

"I'm standing right here, Cat!" Johnny waves his hand in

my face. "Am I invisible?"

"Sorry! It's going to take some getting used to. And just so you know, you both lied to me!"

"We didn't lie. We...skirted the truth," my uncle rebuts with a grin.

"I specifically asked you when you were going to introduce us!

"That's right. But you didn't need an 'introduction.' You already knew her," he says with a wide smile.

"Spoken like a true attorney!"

"And you," I growl, turning to face Mack with a pointed finger. "You said he had a lot going on."

"Trying to start a law firm, taking care of his mom and you...you're a pain in his ass sometimes," Mackenzie laughs.

"I'm coming for a visit soon," I shout as Mackenzie walks down the hall with...her man.

"Not if I'm already there," Johnny calls as they step into the elevator.

"Can you believe them?"

"Stranger things have happened," Mateo argues playfully.

We receive Gram's discharge papers and safely load her into the front seat of Mateo's car.

"Oooh," she says, running her small hand across the leather dash. "This is nice. It's very sexy."

Mateo looks in the rearview mirror and catches me rolling my eyes.

After a stop at Trina's and her gushing over my grandmother, we leave with bags full of clothing to last several months rather than just few weeks.

"I'll be back to work as soon as I can."

I return the hug and exit her shop, trying desperately to suppress the anxiety growing in me as Mateo points the car toward I-95 South.

"Mr. Creed said to make you as comfortable as possible. He said *whatever* you need," Patricia offers with a warm smile and a wink as we enter the impeccable and quiet house.

My father's house is nearly twelve-thousand square feet with seven bedrooms and eight bathrooms not including the addition Mateo did for the music studio.

Patricia ushers us to the far side of the house to where the guestrooms are.

"Who lives here?" Gram asks, shuffling into the large room adjacent to the room Mateo and I will share. "Donald Trump?"

I laugh. "No, Gram. I think he used to live down the street though."

"Where does he live now?"

"The White House."

"It smells filthy rich in here. Go get me one of my Yankee candles."

Mateo chuckles lightly. "Sorry, no candles allowed. You'll have to put up with the stench of the rich and famous for a few weeks."

Later that evening, after we've eaten a good home-cooked meal and Gram is settled in bed, Patricia calls Mateo's attention.

"Señor Mateo, perhaps you can fix the floor over there." She points to the hardwood by the door that leads to the music studio. "Sometimes it squeaks and so do the stairs."

"Sure, I'll see what I can do."

"Good night, Patricia. Thank you for dinner." I say as she turns and walks down the long hallway.

I follow Mateo as he leads me to Chloe's music studio and the home offices of Creed Records.

My eyes scan the room and take everything in. Memories come rushing back in as I recall standing in the booth with my headphones on.

"Do you miss it?" Mateo asks from his lowered position.

I shake my head. "No."

He walks to another part of the room and bends down once again.

"It was never about making music for others to enjoy. It was for me. I remember standing in the booth, looking out through the clear glass, and feeling trapped."

"Patricia needs to dust down there," Mateo says, clapping his hands together before telling me to follow him.

A solid door bears Darcy's name and title as Vice President of Creed Records. I roll my eyes, wondering how narcissistic she must be to have a label on the door in her own home. I walk in and look around the beautifully decorated space while Mateo moves about quickly.

If only these walls could talk I think to myself.

Walking over to her computer, I tap the space bar out of curiosity. Nothing. I don't know what I was expecting since she hasn't been here in months.

I step away and look at the mahogany bookcases which line the entire wall. Picture frames of Chloe grace every shelf as do her numerous accolades. One picture on the top shelf catches my eye and I stand on the tips of my toes to reach it.

Mateo's voice startles me, pulling me from the memory of the occasion. "Is that you?"

I nod. "Yeah, Chloe and I were in a talent show. I was so fed up by that point that I purposely screwed up my song, allowing Chloe to take first place. I look thrilled, don't I?" I laugh quietly, placing the picture back on the shelf.

"All set?" I ask, turning to face him as I wrap my hands around his waist.

"One more room."

I nod and follow him.

I lie awake naked in Mateo's arms, feeling utterly

worn out. I may need days to recuperate from having been stretched and splayed every which way while Mateo reached new heights of pleasure from my body.

"I can't move," I groan.

"Well you better get up and dressed soon."

"Why?" I whine in protest.

"Your father is on his way back."

"What?" I shriek. "You said they wouldn't be back for three weeks."

"*They*, as in Chloe and Darcy, won't, but your dad has some business to take care of."

"Mateo!"

"Cat, I know you don't trust your father and you have every reason not to, but I think he's changed. I think he wants to do what's right."

"Bullshit!" I yell, stomping out of bed and slamming the bathroom door shut.

The mental conversation in my head reminds me that while I may not trust my father, I do trust Mateo.

I finish my shower and step into the room. "Stop!" I demand when Mateo snaps a picture of me wrapped in a towel. "You know I hate when you take pictures when I'm not ready."

"They're candids. I have hundreds of pictures of you on my phone."

My eyes spring open and I respond sarcastically. "Yeah, I know!"

"When your father gets here, I want you to listen to what he has to say."

My blood boils and I clench my teeth. "You're lucky I love you so much."

"Trust me."

I refuse Patricia's help to clean up the kitchen after Gram's breakfast. "I made the mess, I'll clean it."

"That's my girl, strong-willed as ever."

I stiffen at my father's voice, praying quickly Gram doesn't remember him otherwise the few measly pans in the sink will be hurled in his direction along with some choice words.

"Sarah is here to pick you up, Gram. We need to get you dressed."

I walk past my father and usher my grandmother back to her suite.

"Who is that nice man?" she asks.

I lie quickly. "He's Mateo's friend."

I dress Gram warmly as a chill set in overnight.

"Thanks, Sarah. I'll call you in a little bit," I say, as I close the car door and watch them leave.

Returning to the house, I see my father and Mateo sitting in the living room, reviewing documents.

"What is that?" I ask, taking a seat beside Mateo.

"My contract with Creed Records and the agreement I signed when I went on tour with Chloe."

"There's a stiff penalty for breach of contract if he leaves," my father adds.

"You're the President of the company. Amend it and let him out!"

"It's not that simple, Cat."

"May I have a word alone with my daughter?"

Mateo glances at me and I nod after a moment of hesitation. While I'm grateful for the flight home from Florida and the roof over my head, I know what this man is capable of.

"I'll be in the other room. Call me if you need me."

"She won't need to." My father smiles warmly.

"Cat, I've been a terrible father. I was selfish and stupid. I abandoned my only child for...I don't even know what.

For the chance to make something of myself in the music industry? For the chance to have a star who bears my name? For the chance to find love with a woman who will never be your mother? I don't know what I was thinking. All those things weren't worth losing you. You trusted me and I let you down. You needed me to believe you and I didn't. You needed me to choose you and I chose them. I'm so sorry."

I cast my eyes downward and wipe the lone tear that falls.

"I know Chloe didn't write that song." He shakes his head. "She doesn't have the caliber of talent that you have. And I know *Darcy* didn't write that song. The only person she loves that much is herself."

My chin quivers at his words of validation.

An internal debate rages in me about whether I should provide an explicit account of what it was like for me to live with Darcy and Chloe after losing my mother or how I felt when I was left unnecessarily at Norwich Academy. But my lips remain still.

What's done is done.

"Mateo told me about the lawsuit and he also told me how you lost everything in the fire. Let me help you prove your case."

I look up with tears in my eyes. "Why would you do that?"

"Because you're my daughter. My flesh and blood." My father moves to sit next to me. "I believe you. Let me help you."

"How?" I cry. "How are you going to help me prove Chloe stole that song?"

"We already have a plan."

A particular ringtone interrupts our conversation and my father tells me to remain quiet when he answers.

"Hey, doll. How's Chloe?"

I cringe at the sound of her name and my father offers a reassuring hand on my shoulder.

He listens as Darcy drones on, screeching loudly into the phone. I can hear the vile names she uses when referring to Mateo.

"Oh, don't worry about a thing. I promise those two will get what they deserve. Trust me," he draws out slowly.

He smiles devilishly, continuing to listen to her narrative about poor Chloe's career.

"Like I said," he hisses like a slithering snake, "my daughter and her boyfriend will get exactly what they deserve." He exhales. "Maybe even more," he adds with a cunning smile.

"What are you doing?" I ask when he sets his phone down. "She'll kill you. That bitch is crazy!"

"I'm doing what I should've done years ago. I'm choosing you."

I search his face for any trace of malice or deceit and find none. My eyes move higher to his graying temples. "What about the tumor?"

The smile fades from his face, and he looks down before inhaling quietly. He releases the air through rounded lips. "It's a little bigger than last time. That's why I came home. I need to see the oncologist...and my attorney."

"I can go to the doctor with you if you want," I blurt.

My words shock not only my father but myself as well.

"I mean," I stammer. "I—um—"

He chuckles. "I think you have enough to worry about. I'll be fine."

My father leans forward hesitantly then kisses my forehead. "See you later."

Mateo and I spend the day with my uncle meeting with the fire marshal who determines the cause of the fire to be accidental; while the insurance adjuster assesses the damage to the house and writes it off as a total loss.

When I survey the rubble that remains, I break down in tears. My uncle, commiserating with my pain at the sight of his former home, is quick to comfort me until he is called away by the adjuster for a moment.

"We can rebuild," Mateo says, taking me in his arms.

"I want to start over somewhere else. Anywhere else."

He smiles. "Can you do me a favor please? Just pick somewhere warm because I'm going wherever you go and my Latino blood doesn't like the cold." He shivers as a cold breeze blows.

"I love you." I mumble, burying my chilly nose into his jacket.

"Te quiero más, mi amor."

We arrive back at the house after picking Gram up from Sarah's house where we thanked her profusely but declined the generous offer to keep my grandmother overnight.

My father's thick fingers fly to his lips when we enter the house. I whisper to Gram to be quiet which only makes her ask why she has to be quiet in her own damn house.

"No one's here. I have the television on," my father argues into his phone as he motions with his chin and tosses a pleading look for us to move along into the other room.

"Sorry," I mouth.

Mateo and I lie in bed that night following a conversation with my father about the tour.

"You might need to post a few more pictures of you "resting" to keep Chloe happy," he'd suggested ruefully.

Mateo searched Google for a romantic bathtub image and captioned it with, "Nothing like a hot bubble bath with C."

Fans went ballistic, "liking, retweeting and sharing" and Chloe had no choice but to share in their joyous comments.

"You're playing with fire," Chloe had threatened shortly after the image went viral, taking a jab at the current state of our situation. "And you're going to get burned."

"Clever. Is that all you've got?" he taunted her. "Hey there's this great song called you should record as your own. It's called Girl on Fire."

Chloe flew into a rage and hung up on him after she told him to fuck off.

"You might want to stop provoking her," I said. "We don't want this thing to backfire."

Mateo laughed at my failed attempt at some humor.

The next day while Gram naps, Mateo and I wander down into the recording studio and I sit at the beautiful piano. My fingers tap the keys lightly while my other hand joins to form a chord. I hum a melody, losing myself in the lyrics running in circles around my brain before connecting with my heart.

"What song is that?"

"The one I wrote about you."

"Once in a lifetime?"

My lips tighten into a hard, sad smile and I nod.

"You should record it."

"Why?" I ask, my fingers freezing on the white keys. "I don't want to share it with anyone but you."

"Then record it just for me."

"I'll think about it."

A few days later, eight to be exact, my fingers still once again on the keys when Mateo abruptly orders me to stop.

"What?" I ask.

"I think they're here."

My eyes widen. "Chloe and Darcy?"

The floor leading to the lower level creaks followed by raised voices.

"Come on," Mateo says, pulling me from the studio into an equipment storage closet.

My heart pounds in my chest and I pray no one can hear it.

Hurried footsteps bound down as the hardwood creaks

on each rung.

"How could you be so reckless?" Darcy screeches. "You're going to fuck everything up!"

"Mom, I didn't mean to get pregnant. I'm having an abortion anyway so chill out. Nothing is going to ruin my career. Not this baby, not Ronan and certainly not that lowlife Matt."

I hold Mateo close when I feel him shudder. I want to look into his eyes and tell him how wrong she is. He is the best man I know.

"What are you looking for?" Chloe screams as glass shatters against the floor. "Mom! Stop! Oh my god, you're acting like a mental case." Then she chuckles darkly. "You look exactly the way Cat did all those years ago."

"Shut the fuck up! Do not bring that up ever again! Randy said she has proof that you stole her songs and she plans on filing a lawsuit."

"Oh, for the love of God, she doesn't have shit. She's a fucking crazy person. And besides, if she still had her journal, it probably burned in the fire."

"And what about this new one? What about that one, Chloe? You think you're so goddamned smart. You blatantly stole this one right from underneath her nose, wiped your ass with it and smeared it in her face. Her uncle is an attorney, you know."

"You think Cat has it in her to go after me? She's weak and pathetic like her father. I'm sure her uncle is too."

Mateo's anger is bursting at the seams and I reach up to smooth over the hardened planes of his face, silently begging him to remain strong and still for a few minutes more.

"I think you've gone too far this time."

"Jesus Christ! What are you looking for?" Chloe asks again as the sound of doors opening and slamming shut filters in.

"Once in a lifetime."

"Yeah, what about it? It's my song now."

"I knew it sounded familiar when you showed me that paper in Nashville."

Nashville ? I think silently, wondering about the last morning I was there and Chloe came looking for tampons.

"So?"

"I read something just like that in one of Beth's journals. I think they wrote that song together."

My heart breaks at the mention of my mother's name and it aches simply knowing this viper has read my mother's precious and private words.

"I have to confront her," Mateo whispers through gritted teeth.

"Not yet, please," I implore, taking his hand in mine and kissing his knuckles.

"Where the fuck is it? Randall!!" Darcy screams at the top of her lungs.

"You're losing your shit, Mom. What's the big deal?"

"You have no idea what the ramifications will be if word gets out that you stole someone else's song. Your career will be over. All of this will be over."

"I stole my crazy stepsister's songs. I didn't fucking kill her mother."

The sound of a hard slap crackles through the room. "You shut the fuck up before I shut you up for good! Do you hear me?" Darcy bellows, her voice reaching an unearthly pitch.

"Mom!"

"I didn't mean to kill her. She wasn't supposed to die."

"I'm sorry. I won't ever say a word again, okay?" Chloe promises as she consoles her sobbing mother with shushes.

"Do you have any idea what it was like for me? Knowing the man I was married to was having an affair with his ex-wife?"

"You did the right thing though. She would've ruined everything."

Unable to contain himself a second longer, Mateo pushes through the door and stomps into the room with me hot on his trail.

"You fucking bitch!"

Darcy and Chloe jump at the sound of his angry voice.

"Matt!" Chloe shrieks.

"Oh my God! What are you doing here?" Darcy asks, wiping the tears from her eyes.

"He's probably coming to steal from us. He is Puerto Rican."

Anger rises from my toes and surges fast and furious as I step out from behind Mateo and cock my arm back, punching Chloe right in the center of her face. "For the last time, his name is MATEO!" She stumbles back into the rolling leather chair and hits her head on the desk.

"What the hell! Mom, help me!" she barks.

"Get up!" I order as my hands ball into tight fists. "Get up so I can show you just how crazy I am!"

"Cat, calm down," Darcy mutters quietly, raising her hands defensively as if attempting to tame the beast in me. "Please don't hurt Chloe, she's pregnant."

"You," I turn fierce eyes on her. "You killed my mother?! How could you?"

She shakes her head frantically. "No, Cat. I didn't hurt your mother. I would never have hurt her. It was an accident."

"You're a liar. I just heard you! Admit it. And then admit what you and Chloe did to me when I was young. How you tortured me, emotionally abused me then lied about me. Say it!" I reach for the heavy trophy on the bookcase and turn it upside down, preparing to use it as a weapon. "SAY IT!"

"Okay, okay," she sighs dejectedly. "I'm sorry. We're sorry. I was horrible to you. We both were. You didn't deserve it. None of it."

Tears stream from my face as Darcy apologizes profusely for the specific acts of abuse I faced while living in her care.

She went on to reveal how she conspired with Chloe to steal my songs and record them.

"We were wrong. So, so wrong. You didn't deserve that, Cat. You didn't deserve it."

I drop the trophy and sag in Mateo's arms.

"It's over, baby. It's over," Mateo repeats in my ear as my father enters the room.

"We've got it. We've got it all recorded."

Chapter Twenty

A MEETING WAS HELD A MONTH LATER BETWEEN my attorney, Jonathan Ryan, and the Creeds' attorney to reach an out of court settlement. My uncle offered a figure he deemed acceptable for lost wages, earnings and royalties for all songs that Chloe stole and recorded. Added to the list against Darcy and Chloe was also a one-time lump sum payment for the mental duress I suffered because of them. Last on the list was probably the most important item to me, the release of Mateo from his contract with Creeds Records.

"And then David says, 'I'm sorry John, but my client, Randall Creed, President of Creed Records, has instructed me to prepare a counter offer based on our facts.'"

"So? What was it?" I ask, bouncing with excitement as my uncle stalls with the final figures.

"Read it for yourself."

I look at my uncle, my mother's younger brother— the one man who has loved me unconditionally from birth, the one man who championed for me during my trials and tribulations, the one man who filled a void in my life left by the absence of my father— and I smile as the emotion threatens to rise. "Thank you. Thank you for believing in me when I didn't believe in myself," I say, even before I look at the figure contained in the business-sized envelope that slides across the table.

"I love you, kid."

Using my fingertips, I mop up the moisture spilling from my blue eyes before glancing at Mateo and shoving the rectangular package in his direction. My voice cracks. "You open it."

Those hazel eyes I love so much sparkle as he shakes his head, forfeiting the opportunity. "No, baby. This is all you. Go for it."

I inhale a deep breath and tear through the adhesive seam. I release the breath and pull the thick paper from its hiding place.

"No. Fucking. Way."

My face pales at the figure and I feel light-headed.

"There has to be some mistake," I cry.

Johnny smiles. "Apparently people all over the world love those songs Chloe sings. Who knew your words would strike a chord with people from Canada to Australia and so many other countries you'd never expect like Guinea and Thailand."

I cover my mouth with my hand as tears again fill my eyes. "What am I going to do with all this money?" I ask no one in particular.

"Oh, I don't know. Maybe you could give your uncle a loan to start his own law firm," Johnny says with a huge smile on his face.

He rises and leans in for a quick kiss to my cheek. "Listen, I've gotta run. I have a hot date with a sexy red head."

I slap his arm playfully. "It's still kinda gross about you and Mack."

"The money will be transferred electronically. I suggest you contact a financial advisor first thing in the morning."

"I will," I reply, nodding my head seriously.

"Mateo." My uncle extends his outstretched palm and the two men shake hands vigorously.

"I love you," I call out as my uncle walks toward the entrance of the diner. "But you're still old!"

I see his shoulders shake until he's out of sight.

"What do we do now?" I ask, shifting my body to look at my love.

"Anything we want," he replies before closing his lips over mine.

"I need a vacation. Somewhere hot and tropical." I say, looking out as light snow falls.

Mateo grins and presses a button on the old table top jukebox, stopping at Alicia Key's song *No One* . "I have the perfect place."

Epilogue

Six months later...

"THANK YOU FOR THE BOX OF MOM'S THINGS, too. I can't wait to read her journals."

"I know you'll find some good stuff in there," my father assures me as he hugs me.

"I promise to call you the week we get back," I reply to his suggestion to get together for dinner but cringe slightly, not yet feeling entirely comfortable with my father's affection. "Make sure you eat plenty of food before chemo."

Extending his huge hand, my father nods. "Mateo, have a safe trip. Take good care of our girl. She shouldn't be in the sun too long."

"I've packed lots of mosquito repellant and plenty of sunscreen."

"I wouldn't let anything happen to her."

We pull out of the driveway and continue along the Interstate bound for LaGuardia International Airport.

"Your grandmother looked good today, don't you think?"

I search my bag for a piece of hard candy, nodding in agreement. "Yeah, but I feel bad for leaving her behind."

"Baby, she's in the best care."

Whoever thinks money doesn't talk is sadly mistaken

because after Gram's initial application was placed on the waiting list, her second application, accompanied by a hefty donation for a new music room and additional funding to bring in weekly entertainment for the residents, was accepted and we moved her in two days later.

I reply to a text message from Mackenzie who insists on a double date with the four of us. "Ugh, still gross," I mumble, placing my hand on my stomach when a round of nausea flutters in my belly.

"What's the matter?" Mateo asks as he parks the car in the long-term parking lot.

"My stomach feels weird. I think the coffee creamer was bad or it could be that my best friend is hot and heavy with my uncle."

He shakes his head. "Must be the latter because I drank the same stuff and I feel fine." Opening the door, he steps out then pops his head back in through the door frame and waggles his eyebrows. "Or maybe all my hard work has paid off and I finally got you pregnant."

My eyes round with shock, my lips stunned shut. I open the door and step out into the cold winter air. "Have you been trying to get me pregnant all along?"

"How else am I supposed to keep you?" He grins and closes the trunk after removing our luggage.

"You could just ask."

The shuttle to transport us to the terminal arrives and we climb on board.

"What do you think Chloe is going to do about the baby?" I ask, happy to hear she didn't go through with her plan to terminate her pregnancy.

"Honestly? I don't know and I don't care," he replies, tapping out a quick response to Iza.

I exhale sadly at his comment.

"I'm sorry," he says. "I can't stand Chloe and the last thing I want to do is talk about her when I'm deliriously happy that after six months we're *finally* going on vacation and I get to have you all to myself for two weeks."

"How's Iza?" I ask, motioning to his phone when it dings again.

"Excited. Nervous. Happy."

"She's going to be great. Caleb is too."

I ignore the quiet growling emerging from Mateo's chest.

"He's good. He's going to do really well at MC Music."

"He better do *really* well and keep his eyes off of you or he's out. It's half my label so I get to say who's in or out," he counters sharply, displaying his jealous side.

"And since I'm the other half of MC Music, I say he stays. Besides, I think he has eyes for Iza now."

The shuttle stops at JetBlue and we proceed to check our bags and go through security to board our nonstop flight to San Juan.

"What do you think that guy did?" I whisper to Mateo, after seeing a prisoner being escorted through the airport most likely for an extradition.

"Has to be pretty serious I would imagine."

Mateo pays for my beverage, his muscle car magazine and two bags of M & M's.

He asks what's wrong when he notices I've suddenly become quiet.

"Just thinking about Darcy." *As she was led away in court.*

A hard puff of air releases forcefully from Mateo's lungs. "She's where she deserves to be."

"I know, but it's still sad to think she's going to spend the next ten to fifteen years in prison."

The case against Darcy Creed was swift since she pleaded guilty to 3rd degree murder which meant that she never intended to kill my mother. She cried on the stand and told her tale about her "crime of passion" when she'd learned of my father's infidelity with his ex-wife. I didn't believe her story, but the jury did. If Darcy had had money to her name, her attorney could have gotten her off on an even lesser charge, but my father made sure she was left penniless.

"Baby, are you going soft on me?" Mateo jokes as we move forward in line surrounded by other people going on vacation while others are returning to their homeland. I think of Mateo, who like so many children, was tossed back and forth between Puerto Rico and New York.

I laugh. "The day you go soft is the day I go soft."

"Cat, don't tempt me in public."

Mateo's need and raw desire to have me anywhere and anytime drives me wild. I am an active participant— his willing accomplice— who accepts his love freely and unconditionally at any given moment...except when we're sitting in church or singing with the choir.

"I always wanted to be a Boy Scout when I was a kid."

I choke on a sip of ginger ale. "You did? Why?"

"I liked the uniform and the idea of belonging to a club."

"Really?" I gasp, remembering how my childhood was stamped with the word *music* and music alone. "I didn't have time for anything when I was a kid."

"Our blue-eyed babies are going to do it all. Music, dance, sports, theater, robotics...whatever they want."

I hold my phone up to allow the flight attendant to scan my boarding pass and follow Mateo down the corridor.

"That's right...whatever *they* want."

"You know what *I* want?" Mateo leans down to whisper in my ear and sends a shiver down my spine while my eyes sweep upward, silently asking for the answer. "To join the Mile-High club." My eyes spring open. "Really?"

"I don't think I can wait three hours to have you again." His eyes fill with unadulterated lust and mischief as his lips meet mine.

I moan quietly and consider his offer, but quickly change my mind when we are seated in the very first row on the commercial flight.

"So much for the Mile-High club," I sigh.

"Someday when MC Music is the biggest label in the industry, we're going to have our own private plane and then..."

I extend my hand to Mateo. "Deal."

He slips his hand into mine and curls my fingers, placing a swift kiss on my knuckles. "Sealed with a kiss."

I awake from my nap to find Mateo scrolling through pictures on his phone.

"Hey," he says, kissing my forehead when I return from a quick trip to the bathroom. "Look at this."

He angles his phone so we both can look at the multitude of images of my face, my piano and my journal.

"What is that?" I ask, wiping the sleep from my eyes.

"Pages from your journal. I had taken them a long time ago because I was going to put them to music for you," he says quietly.

"I would love that."

"And look at this...even if Chloe and Darcy hadn't admitted to stealing your words, I had proof on my phone the whole time." Mateo swipes his finger and shows me the picture of me asleep with a pen and a piece of paper in my hand. He pinches his fingers together and zooms in on the image.

The words "Once in a Lifetime" are scribbled across the top of the hotel notepad.

I take the phone and stare at it for a long while before I hand it back to him.

A sad smile spreads across my face at the memory of having my private thoughts exposed to the world. Even after Mateo and I recorded the song together, I haven't decided if I want to release it.

It's ours and ours alone.

We spend ten days exploring the beautiful island of Puerto Rico. Mateo gives me a personal tour of the place of his birth, including all the typical tourist locations in San Juan, Arecibo and El Yunque, the spectacular rain forest with its amazing waterfall. We also enjoy some of the hidden gems only known to locals.

"Close your eyes," Mateo orders gently, guiding me to sit on a jutting boulder as the sky turns dark and bright stars blanket us. "Listen."

I wrap my arms around my bent knees and do as he's commanded. I close my eyes, feeling the warmth of the night air that covers my skin and listen to the natural symphony coming from all directions. I open my eyes. "What is that?"

"Coquis. Thousands of them."

"What are they doing?" I scan the area around me looking for the source.

"You won't see them. The coqui is a tiny tree frog native to the island. The males 'sing' to attract a female."

"Wow! So it's like a booty call?" I smile.

Mateo laughs. "Maybe."

"The first part of their song is "CO" and it wards off other males and the second "KEE" attracts the ladies."

"Oh, my God! You are such a tree frog. I'm going to call you Coqui from now on!" I grin, pulling his face close and kiss his lips. "Will you sing for me like the coqui does?"

"I'll do whatever you want. I'll sing whatever you want. I'll build whatever you want. I'll go wherever you want."

"You're giving me lots of power over you," I point out.

"You don't get it. You own me," Mateo says, dropping to his knees.

He looks down, inhales quietly and swallows hard before meeting my eyes as his lips part.

The most beautiful words spill from his lips as he sings about our love.

I want to travel through this life with you beside me as my wife,

   *Our story has just begun, our love's been through hell and fire,
but we won,*

   *I see my soul in your perfect blue eyes
   Eyes which never lie
   I'll spend forever tasting your lips. Your skin I'll always caress
      so please baby, say yes,
   I promise to be faithful, loving, and true to only you
   I'd be the happiest man for the rest of my life,
   If you say yes to becoming my wife.*

Through blurry eyes and hot tears, I stare at the man I'm going to marry. The man who will father my children. The man who will no doubt love me unconditionally until his last breath. The man who will be my husband.

My left hand is slowly raised and a diamond ring glistens in the moonlight, lingering at the tip of my fourth finger as he waits patiently for my answer.

"Yes. God, yes!"

He slides the ring in place where it will remain forever, and I wrap my arms around his neck.

"I love you so much!" I cry into his shoulder.

Mateo pulls back and looks at me before devouring my mouth with his. With ragged breaths and a gentle caress to my tear-stained face, he declares his love in his native tongue.

"Te amaré por siempre. Tu eres mi amor, mi corazón y mi vida."

I will always love you. You are my love, my heart, my life.

"I hope there's room for one more in your heart."

His forehead wrinkles for a brief moment when I pull his hand from my face and place it on my abdomen.

"What?! No fu —" His mouth opens and his hazel eyes fill with disbelief and wonder until comprehension settles in.

I smile and nod, covering his mouth to prevent the curse word from escaping. "Yes."

My body is swooped up and swung around like a ragdoll.

"And you better choose your words carefully, Daddy. Little ears will be listening."

About the Author

L.M. Carr, author of the Giving Trilogy, the Stones Duet, and two sexy stand-alone novels, is a wife, a mom, an educator, a reader and a writer who lives in central Connecticut with her family. When she's not sitting at her computer writing, she loves to get lost in a good book or spend time with family and friends.

After self-publishing the trilogy in 2015, a suspenseful romance tale about Mia Delaney and the sexy, arrogant single father Adam Lawson, L.M. penned the Stones Duet in 2016. This spin-off from the trilogy chronicles the story of Army veteran Shane Davis. Left jaded and cynical after his time in the military, Shane moves to Boston and meets a girl who changes his perception on the world around him.

In February 2017, From A Distance was released. An intricate and sexy romance about a motorcycle drag racer and his quest to hide secrets from a woman while the truth unravels before his eyes.

Looking to expand beyond Contemporary Romance, L.M. is working on a new romantic comedy.

L.M. Carr is a lover of "Happily Ever Afters" because the world is filled with enough sadness. Reading is an escape in which anything is possible. But like in reality, stories sometimes take you on a journey through Hell before you can reach Heaven.

Connect with her online!

www.authorlmcarr.com

52840253R00265